HIGH PRAISE FOR NATASHA LESTER

THE RIVIERA HOUSE

"Vivid, nuanced, and deeply moving. A superlative work of historical fiction."   — Christine Wells, author of *Sisters of the Resistance*

"Delectable and daring."
          — Bryn Turnbull, author of *The Woman Before Wallis*

"A memorable and compelling read!"
          — Kristen Beck, author of *Courage, My Love*

"Art lovers and fashionistas alike will be glued to this emotional page-turner."   — Kaia Alderson, author of *Sisters in Arms*

THE PARIS SECRET

"Don't move until you've finished this extraordinary book."
          —*Marie Claire*

"Meticulous attention to period details, impeccable plotting, and rich characterization will delight fans of Kate Morton or anyone in need of a gorgeously wrought...tale of love, loss, courage, and compassion."
          —*Booklist*, starred review

"Natasha Lester's latest historical novel is a drop-dead gorgeous winner!"   —Literary Soiree

THE PARIS SEAMSTRESS

"This rich, memorable novel unfolds beautifully from start to finish."
                            —*Publishers Weekly*, starred review

"A fantastically engrossing story. I love it."
                            —Kelly Rimmer, *USA Today* bestselling
                            author of *The Things We Cannot Say*

"Inspiring and so beautifully written. This was such a well-researched historical fiction that weaved romance, intrigue, and human emotions to create a story that will stay with you long after you've finished reading."
                            —The Nerd Daily

"Masterful...*The Paris Seamstress* is a lush and evocative story."
                            —Literary Treats

THE
RIVIERA
HOUSE

ALSO BY
NATASHA LESTER

The Paris Seamstress
The Paris Orphan
The Paris Secret

THE
RIVIERA
HOUSE

NATASHA LESTER

FOREVER

New York Boston

Forever
Hachette Book Group
1290 Avenue of the Americas, New York, NY 10104
read-forever.com
twitter.com/readforeverpub

First Forever Edition: August 2021

Forever is an imprint of Grand Central Publishing. The Forever name and logo are trademarks of Hachette Book Group, Inc.

The publisher is not responsible for websites (or their content) that are not owned by the publisher.

The Hachette Speakers Bureau provides a wide range of authors for speaking events. To find out more, go to www.hachettespeakersbureau.com or call (866) 376-6591.

Library of Congress Cataloging-in-Publication Data
Names: Lester, Natasha, 1973– author.
Title: The riviera house / Natasha Lester.
Description: First Hachette Book Group US Edition. | New York : Forever, 2021. |
Identifiers: LCCN 2021010625 | ISBN 9781538717318 (trade paperback) | ISBN
    9781538717301 (ebook)
Subjects: GSAFD: Historical fiction.
Classification: LCC PR9619.4.L48 R59 2021 | DDC 823/.92—dc23
LC record available at https://lccn.loc.gov/2021010625

ISBNs: 978-1-5387-1731-8 (trade paperback); 978-1-5387-1730-1 (ebook)

Printed in the United States of America

CW

10 9 8 7 6 5 4 3 2

To my father, who won't be able to read this book,
and who also may not be here when it is published.
You deserve peace and rest now. I hope it comes soon. All my love.

PART ONE
PARIS, 1939–1941

ONE

I'm going to be late," Éliane said despairingly to Yolande who, at age five, cared not a bit about Éliane's obligations. In fact, it was obvious from Yolande's clenched fists that a tantrum was bearing down upon all the Duforts and unless Éliane could find something other than a stale knob of bread for breakfast, Yolande would erupt and Éliane would miss her morning lecture at art school.

"We're all hungry," Angélique, the next oldest after Éliane, snapped at Yolande.

Éliane stared around at the grim and silent faces of her sisters. Twelve-year-old Jacqueline's beseeching eyes were fixed on Éliane, willing her to calm both Yolande's histrionics and Angélique's temper. Ginette, eight, was yawning, having been woken by the fracas of raised voices.

She *was* going to be late. But it wasn't her sisters' fault that their parents threw every available franc, including all of Éliane's pay, into their moribund brasserie and thus there was no food in the house. She whirled around and, despite the almost physical pain she felt at even contemplating it, she gathered all of her sable paintbrushes, threw them into a bag and said in a firm but loving voice to Yolande, "I promise you'll have a croissant for breakfast tomorrow. But only if you get dressed for school and let Angélique do your hair."

Yolande jumped up from her teary puddle on the floor, her blonde hair bouncing like her revived spirits as she threw herself at Éliane. "*Merci,*" she whispered, head buried in Éliane's skirt.

"I love you," Éliane said, stroking her sister's hair. Then, while Angélique was occupied with helping Ginette find her shoes, she spoke in Yolande's ear, "Angélique is scared. It's her first year of looking after you. Help her. Then she'll see that she doesn't have to worry about you so much."

And to Angélique, as she kissed her goodbye, Éliane explained, "Yolande just wants to be loved. Hug her. Then she'll behave."

It had only been six months since Angélique's fifteenth birthday. Her present had been to take over from Éliane the so-called privilege of getting the children ready for school, of bringing them home at the end of the day, collecting leftovers from the brasserie for dinner, feeding everyone and putting them to bed. Yolande and Angélique were each still chafing against the absence of Éliane, who now spent those hours at work.

Luckily Ginette and Jacqueline needed only a hug and a kiss and Éliane was able to leave, clattering around and around the whorling spiral of stairs from their third-floor apartment to the Galerie Véro-Dodat—a formerly resplendent Belle Époque *passage couvert*—below. It was lined with once-grand but now mostly empty mahogany shop façades, separated by chipped marble columns and still-gleeful cherubs—despite the fact that most were missing at least a toe, if not an entire leg. The dank odor of stale coffee emanating from her parents' brasserie settled around the globes of the old gas lamps, causing any patrons foolish enough to venture into the *galerie* to flee with their tastebuds unsullied.

Once out on the street, she continued on to the Musée du Louvre where she would study and work, unshackled from her sisters. The journey made her feel both the lightness of relief and the heaviness of loss as all the hugs and kisses and tiny affections were now Angélique's. Éliane hoped her sister treasured those affections the way she ought to.

At the Aile de Flore—the wing of the Louvre that stretched along the river—Éliane ran straight up to the École du Louvre. She took her seat in the lecture theater, looking over the rows of students for her brother Luc, but while Luc's soul was devoted to art, his body worshipped at the cafés of Montparnasse and he was absent again.

Monsieur Bellamy began to speak about Italian Renaissance painters and Éliane concentrated on long-haired and voluptuous women, on cherubs with all of their body parts intact, and on a chiaroscuro of religious chastisements. At lunchtime she left the building, never able to attend afternoon classes as her family needed the money she made from her work. Before she entered the museum proper and sat in her seat at the front desk, ready to direct patrons to the *Venus de Milo* and the *Mona Lisa*, she went to see Monsieur Jaujard, the Director of the Musées Nationaux. He had allowed her to continue at the École despite the fact that she could neither pay for her tuition nor spend a full day there.

"Monsieur," she asked politely, "do you know where I can sell my paintbrushes?" She pulled the items out of her bag, refusing to look at the last scraps of her childish dream of being a painter. "They're good quality, sable, and might suit a new student perhaps?"

Monsieur Jaujard studied her treasures, kindly avoiding looking at her face, which she knew was reddened with both the shame of asking for another favor, and from the loss.

"Leave them with me. I know a young man who might give you a good price."

"Thank you," she said, voice low, making herself give over the items by thinking of Yolande's face tomorrow when she had croissants for breakfast instead of stale bread.

Soon before the Louvre closed, Monsieur Jaujard appeared with an envelope, which he handed to Éliane. "For you."

She opened it and discovered at least twice what she had hoped to get. Now it was Monsieur's cheeks that flushed as she thanked him profusely, then left the museum, knowing she needed to spend the money that afternoon or it would be poured down the necks of her father and his friends at the brasserie.

Outside, the streets were quiet; the pall of Hitler's unknown ambitions casting a shadow over Paris. Éliane slipped into La Samaritaine and found two cheap but adequate *soutien-gorges* for Jacqueline, who had needed a bra for several months but, even if their mother had noticed her daughter's maturity in the fog of her tiredness from working eighteen hours a day at the brasserie, there had been no money to do anything about it. Once Éliane had paid for the undergarments, there was enough left to buy croissants too.

She was smiling as she walked home, knowing her bags held both goods and happiness for her sisters, until someone carrying two gas masks stepped onto the sidewalk in front of her. She looked away. But on the other side of the street was another Parisian laden with similarly disquieting objects.

Hitler could not really be coming for France. He had taken enough of Europe already. Still, she stopped walking and stared at her shopping bags. A bra would soothe Jacqueline's growing embarrassment over her rapidly curving body; a gas mask might save her life.

"Éliane!"

An arm slung itself around her shoulders and then, beside her on the path was her brother, Luc. One year older and as blond as she, he was grinning in a way that always made her smile.

"Do you remember my friend Xavier?" Luc began, lighting a cigarette and speaking around it, his arm still draped over her shoulders so she had to hold her own hand up to shield the flame from the wind. "He was at school with me for a couple of years before his family took him back to England?"

Éliane vaguely recalled a dark-haired boy, French-born but who'd mostly lived in England, being underfoot in the apartment several afternoons each week after school, many years before. He'd been a couple of years older than Luc, but Luc had decided that this Xavier was going to be the next Picasso and had coerced Xavier into giving him painting lessons. Never mind that Luc was supposed to be helping Éliane look after the children; he'd spend the time until dinner painting, and would whisk away the evidence before their mother came upstairs to tuck them into bed, at which time Xavier would be gone. He'd been a secret, like Éliane's own wish to be a painter—something that was spoken of only in the absence of parents on the top step outside the apartment at night, coffee in hand.

"I ran into him today," Luc said. "In Montparnasse. He was there to see Matisse. Matisse!"

"Matisse?" Éliane repeated, laughing now at her brother's enthusiasm. "Then he must have changed a lot since I last saw him. He used to wear those awful English short trousers—"

"They don't fit me anymore." A voice broke in from behind.

Luc laughed as if Éliane had said something hilarious and Éliane turned to see a dark-haired *homme* with oil-paint stains on his fingers. He was wearing a suit rather than short trousers, his shirtsleeves were rolled up, a jacket slung over his shoulder like a grown-up man.

"You're Xavier?" she said disbelievingly.

He nodded. "And you must be Éliane. Although I don't think I've ever seen you without at least one sister in your arms."

"Angélique looks after everyone now." As she spoke, she was, for almost the first time in her life, acutely aware of how simple her dress was. She'd made it from a remnant of fabric thinking it mimicked a Lanvin day dress she'd seen in a catalog, but now it felt like a child's attempt at playing dress-up.

Xavier, for all the paint on his hand, looked at least five years older than her, even though she knew he was only twenty-three to her twenty.

All at once, every church bell in Paris began to chime and Éliane snapped to attention. "I'm late," she said for the second time that day. "Give that to Jacqueline." She thrust her parcel at Luc. "I'll have to go straight to the brasserie, otherwise—"

She stopped herself from saying it but her hand strayed to her cheek nonetheless.

"Go," Luc said.

But he and Xavier walked almost as fast as she did and it meant they saw what happened: her father roaring, even though it was only five minutes past six, "Where were you?"

"Buying Jacqueline a bra, since nobody else will," she shot back.

Her father hit her, a stinging blow.

Out of the corner of her eye, she saw Xavier put a hand on the brasserie's door. She only let herself breathe out when Luc pushed him away and up the stairs to the apartment, where Xavier would see that much of their furniture was gone—sold off to pay Papa's debts—beyond the necessities of beds, a table, a sofa, and six chairs.

Her mother, who had come out of the kitchen at the sound of the blow, caught Éliane's eye and offered a sympathetic shrug.

If only Éliane could afford the luxury of a headache.

* * *

Éliane folded napkins until there was somebody to wait on. Customers were scarce and, as two tables were occupied by her father's friends—who were there for the heavily discounted wine—Éliane knew it would be a long time—or likely never—before she was permitted to be a full-time student at the École du Louvre.

Close to eight-thirty, she saw Angélique in the *passage* beckoning to her. She slipped out. "What is it?"

"Yolande can't find her doll. The one she likes to sleep with."

Éliane closed her eyes and tried to think. There weren't many places to hide anything in their sparse apartment.

"And my gloves are missing too," Angélique added quietly. "The ones you gave me for my birthday."

They both looked toward the kitchen where their father was cooking dinners.

Then Éliane's eyes locked with her sister's. "Maybe he hasn't sold them yet," she said. "Maybe I can find them."

"Yolande won't sleep without her doll."

Her usually feisty sister spoke resignedly and Éliane drew her into her arms, kissing her forehead, understanding how much effort it was taking for Angélique to think of Yolande's doll rather than her own precious gloves. "Give Yolande something of mine to sleep with," Éliane said, knowing that a sleepless Yolande would fray everyone's tempers. "And you can have my gloves."

Angélique squeezed her fiercely and, for the millionth time in her twenty years, Éliane wished she could gather up all of her sisters and run away. Surely she could do better than a bankrupt father and a worn-out mother? She frowned as she watched Angélique climb the stairs. Perhaps it was time to give up art school altogether and work at the Louvre in the mornings too.

The minutes ambled on. At ten o'clock, the bell tinkled and Éliane, who had been hoping to close up, turned to the door with a pasted-on smile.

Xavier stood there. "I was hoping I could get a glass of wine," he said, the accent of his mother tongue hardly marred at all by his time in England.

"Luc's not here," she replied, knowing her brother would be in Montparnasse, drinking wine too, and pretending that by visiting the cafés frequented by the artists of the School of Paris, he was producing artistic works himself. She'd expected Xavier would be with him.

"I've been in Montparnasse for two hours listening to Luc talk about muses with an artists' model. I was looking for somewhere less noisy."

"Well," she gestured to the sweep of empty chairs, "you've found the quietest restaurant in Paris."

He laughed. "It's probably not the best slogan to get customers in the door, but it's just what I want."

Éliane's smile was real now. She showed him to a table and poured some wine.

Xavier glanced at the kitchen, where her father's tipsy voice rang with a lewd song. "Can you sit down?"

She nodded.

Xavier passed the wine to her. "It's for you."

"Thank you," she said, sipping and feeling the dragging tiredness in her feet disappear. "Are you in Paris for a holiday?" she asked, suddenly eager to know more about this man who bought her wine and asked her to sit. "It seems a strange time to come." Beside them lay a newspaper; its headline shouted the disquieting news that the Soviet Union had signed a nonaggression pact with the Nazis. Éliane elbowed it away.

"It's because the times are so strange that I'm here." Xavier leaned back in his chair and she couldn't help but wonder why he was visiting her, his friend's sister, who hadn't had time to touch up her lipstick all day, who wore only a cotton frock and probably a red cheek from her father's earlier violence.

"I can't remember whether you know that my father owns an art gallery here," he continued. "He has one in London and New York too."

Éliane smiled wryly. "Back then, I was probably too busy yelling at small children while you were telling Luc about that."

Xavier smiled again and she found herself unable to look away from his eyes, which were dark brown, of a shade she wasn't sure existed in a tube of paint, and might be too difficult even to mix. It was like morning sunlight dancing on bronze.

"I don't remember much about your family, but I remember that you never yelled," he said.

Éliane stood up and pulled another glass down from the shelf. Despite the fact that her plan had been to sweep the floor and go to bed, she wasn't tired now. "I'll be back in a minute," she said.

She put her head through the kitchen door and spoke to her mother. "I'll lock up. There's one last customer. But he doesn't want any food."

Her father grunted, pulled off his apron and strode out, not waiting for her mother, who kissed Éliane's cheeks before she left. Then Éliane returned to Xavier with a bottle of wine, poured him a glass and heard her sigh of relief echo through the now-empty restaurant.

"Sorry," she said. "I'm not used to being here and doing nothing."

Xavier sipped his wine, studying her as if she were a portrait worthy of contemplation. "Do you still take care of your sisters? Luc said you're studying at the École with him. And working at the Louvre, as well as working here. But I think I remember that you used to paint. Like Luc."

Éliane gave a short laugh. "Not like Luc, no," was all she said.

Xavier waited. Éliane swallowed wine, twirled the glass around and studied the old rings of spilled Bordeaux on the table.

"I used to paint," she said carefully. "But canvases are expensive. And you need time to practice. I only take art history classes now. In the mornings. Just until my shift starts at the Louvre."

"Do you still have any of your work?" Xavier tilted his head down, trying to lift her eyes from the table and back to his face.

She let them drift upward. "I had to paint my canvases over in white and sell them," she said simply, finding herself studying him now.

The dark hair and the dark eyes and the blue shirt and the well-built physique all made him handsome but the thing that made him almost impossibly attractive was his manner. If his father owned art galleries around the world and Xavier met with artists like Matisse, then he had money and power and certainly his bearing and clothing suggested the confidence and self-assurance of someone who knew their place in the world. But rather than telling her stories about celebrated artists, he was asking her about her own art.

It was so heady—his kindness, the warmth and genuine interest glimmering in his eyes—that she pushed her wineglass away, not needing any further intoxication. "You started to tell me about your father's gallery," she prompted, wanting to know more about him too.

"I've just finished a law degree," Xavier replied. "It was my compromise with my father: I'd go to Oxford, and he'd let me have what he calls my final fling with oil and canvas. A year in France to learn the gallery business from him, and to paint in my spare time"—he grinned ruefully at the palette of blues on his right hand—"and then I'll stay in Paris to take over the gallery's European interests, and my father will take care of America and England. With Hitler so unpredictable, we need to be here to make sure everything is secure in case…" He paused.

"Do you think there'll be war?" she asked somberly.

"I don't know."

Éliane leaned forward, into the conversation. It was a topic her parents seemed wholly uninterested in, that Luc laughed off, and that she didn't want to frighten her sisters with.

"I hope Hitler thinks he's done enough," Xavier said. "He has Austria, he has Czechoslovakia; he now has an alliance with Russia. And he's either expelled every artist from Germany and his newly claimed lands who's Jewish, or who doesn't paint exactly what he wants, or he's made sure they'll never work again. He's not just seizing nations; he's destroying their art and culture too."

"I hadn't thought about that," Éliane said slowly. "How something like war might affect art. Which is silly, because all I have to do is look at history to see it isn't only people who suffer when countries fight."

"Everything suffers when power and money are put in front of avaricious men. And I'm starting to think there are more avaricious men than there are decent ones." Xavier sipped his wine and shook his head. "Sorry. I didn't mean to come here and talk about melancholy things. I came because…"

He looked at her with those eyes, as startling as the chiaroscuro of a Rembrandt painting, then blinked, and she somehow felt as if he had scratched her heart with his eyelashes. "I wanted to make you smile," he said, not looking away, unabashed by the regard for her that his words implied. "Like you smiled at your brother this afternoon on the street. You have a beautiful smile."

She couldn't help it. Not just her mouth, but her entire face was suddenly recast into a beam of happiness, which Xavier returned. She didn't say, even though she wanted to, *Your smile is beautiful too.*

TWO

On her way to work, Éliane saw more and more people buying gas masks and torches. Then, as she sat at the desk at the Louvre, her mind bounced between newspaper headlines claiming that Belgium and the Netherlands had mobilized troops to defend themselves against Hitler's likely ambitions, and Xavier. She'd seen him every night over the past week, always after ten o'clock when the brasserie was closing and they could have a glass of wine together and talk.

She'd told him things she'd never spoken aloud to anyone, disloyal things about her family—and about Luc. That her brother's perpetual absence from the École du Louvre, where he was supposed to be studying and was thus excused by her parents from having to work, sometimes made her so angry—or perhaps envious—that no such option was open to her. Had she the time to sit in a Montparnasse café all day and all night, she would produce something more than wine-headaches and gossip.

"Not that I have any illusions about my ability as a painter," she'd said, eyes fixed to her glass rather than Xavier's face, which was etched with a compassion that made her eyes want to fill up. "Having no time to spend with paints and canvases means that what little talent I might have had would never develop into anything. But to write about and study art all day long, rather than just at the École in the mornings would—"

She broke off, cheeks reddening as she realized she'd been saying everything that was in her heart even though she hardly knew the man opposite her. Except that he left Luc and Montparnasse each night to come and sit with her.

"Would what?" he had asked, voice soft. "Give you something fine in a day marked from dawn to midnight with work and family responsibilities?"

She felt as if she were betraying her whole family, including her sisters who were not to blame, when she said, looking at him at last, "Yes."

"I'm sorry," he'd said.

One tear escaped at the futility of her wish. Xavier had watched it fall, hands tightening into fists, brow tautening into a frown, as if he too wished for her to have that impossible future.

A museum patron, asking for directions, drew her back into the Louvre and once she'd sent him into the sculpture gallery, her restless eye landed on the Uccello painting *The Battle of San Romano*. A wild black horse reared for attack in the foreground, the red spears of lances foreshadowing what would happen.

She shivered. Art did not always soothe; it sometimes spoke too clairvoyant a truth.

"Mademoiselle Dufort." Before her stood the tall and dignified Monsieur Jaujard, face as grave as a Renaissance portrait.

"We're closing the museum tomorrow for three days for essential repair work," he said. "I need as many people to help as possible. Will you come? And your brother?"

"*Bien sûr*," Éliane replied. "And I have another friend who is a painter and who owns a gallery."

"Please ask him to come too."

Before she could ask any more, Monsieur Jaujard moved over to one of the *bénévoles* in the gallery and had a similarly short conversation.

Éliane sat down in her chair. The Louvre would be closed for three days. It was unheard of.

The ferocious tangle of horses in the painting beyond quivered, as if ready to charge through the foyer. A group of people entering the museum spoke in strong voices about the *Boche*, and Hitler.

It would be impossible to fortify the museum properly in just three days. What, then, did Monsieur Jaujard intend to do?

* * *

When Éliane, Xavier, and Luc arrived at the Louvre the next day, it was to find at least two hundred people—students, Louvre employees, the women who ordinarily worked at the Grands Magasins du Louvre, men from the department store La Samaritaine—gathered there.

"We are moving the artworks to keep them safe. One well-aimed bomb and..." Monsieur Jaujard didn't finish his sentence before a shudder crested through the crowd. "But it's not just bombs that frighten me."

His voice echoed solemnly through the museum. "Adolf Hitler is waging a war against civilization. At a rally in Munich, he spat as he said that he would *lead an unrelenting war of extermination against the last elements which have displaced our Art.* He has shown, in Germany and Austria and Czechoslovakia, that he will destroy all paintings he thinks degenerate— all of our great Impressionists and Cubists. He's shown that he will steal for himself anything that meets his supremely narrow definition of 'Art'— our Rubens, our Titians, our *Mona Lisa.* I pray that he will never enter the Louvre. But if he does, he will find little of value left here to destroy."

Éliane looked up at Xavier as everyone around them cheered. She couldn't cheer. Not because she didn't agree with Monsieur Jaujard. But because she had never imagined things were so desperate. Irreplaceable paintings were never moved unless catastrophe was foreseen. Now she truly understood the intent of the German–Soviet nonaggression pact: the Nazis were coming for France.

They were coming for Angélique and Jacqueline and Ginette and Yolande. For this museum and all of its art, for that great intangible treasure that could make one weep or turn away or suddenly grasp the concept of wonder. Éliane had seen it happen, had borne witness to the altered visage of a Louvre patron when an artwork reached out and stroked its hand down the back of a neck and the viewer shivered, astonished—and was never the same again.

Would any of them ever be the same after this?

It began. The men carried wood, cotton batting, sandbags, cylinders—every conceivable packing and protective material—into the main gallery. Monsieur Jaujard supervised the removal of the Louvre's stained-glass windows. Some of the students from the École removed paintings from the walls. Xavier was asked to help code crates to keep their contents secret—*MN* for Musées Nationaux, followed by letters denoting which department the artwork belonged to, and then a work's individual number. Secretaries rattled out, in quadruplicate, lists to match numbers with paintings. The sound of nails being hammered into crates thudded insistently on.

Luc, who had a painter's sensibility and could therefore be trusted with such delicate work, was to remove the largest paintings from their frames, roll them carefully around cardboard tubes and insert them into cylinders.

Monsieur Jaujard gave Éliane a list of artworks and sheets of colored disks. "You are to place the yellow disks on the crates holding most of the works. The green dots are for the major pieces. Two red dots for those we could never imagine losing. And three red dots for the one painting in all the world that must be saved," he finished.

"*La Joconde.*"

"*Oui.*"

After she had affixed dots to cases containing the French crown jewels, Egyptian antiquities thousands of years old and an oak column with the massive *Wedding Feast at Cana* rolled inside, Éliane was one of the few people present when the *Mona Lisa* was taken off the wall. She saw it tucked into a red velvet–lined poplar crate, onto which she placed three red disks. She was also present when Monsieur Jaujard wrote a note to Pierre Schommer who would be receiving this unusual cargo at the Château de Chambord, designated temporary triage center for centuries of priceless art.

La Joconde's crate, unlike the others, bore only the letters *MN*. In Monsieur Jaujard's letter, he asked Schommer, on receipt, to add the letters *LPO* in red to complete the code. Only the crate marked thus would contain the real *Mona Lisa*.

I will remember that, Éliane told herself. One day, it might be important.

At nightfall, she watched as the *Mona Lisa* escaped with the first convoy of trucks. She felt Luc slip in beside her, watching too. "I can't go and serve wine to father's friends now," she said, even though she knew her father would punish her for missing her shift at the brasserie.

"No," Luc agreed, uncharacteristically serious. "You can't."

As they walked back inside, they surveyed the near-empty palace. White rectangles of unfaded paint now adorned the walls rather than baroque artworks, plinths stood purposeless and the grand galleries echoed with shouts as if it were a railway station rather than a place of contemplation and beauty. She tried to picture a world without Paris as its soul; tried to imagine Paris without the *Palais du Louvre* at its center; the museum without works of art in her heart. It was impossible.

She thought she saw Luc blink, as did she, but then he walked off into the dust that glistened in the air like tears.

Near dawn, the *Winged Victory of Samothrace*, almost six meters tall and made of one hundred and eighteen pieces of marble, was moved from her home atop the Daru staircase. She shone that morning, alabaster wings extended, a goddess reminding them that battles could be won and that humans didn't just wage war; they made things of magnificence too.

Ropes attached to a wooden frame surrounding the statue were hoisted, pulleys turned inch by inch, and *Victory* rose into the air. She was set down upon a ramp built over the staircase and, once aboard, thirty tons of statue descended.

Some people turned their heads away and covered their eyes. Éliane barely breathed. Xavier stood beside her and, for the whole time—long and slow and endless—it took to move *Victory* down fifty-three steps, she could feel his heart racing. The gasps of the crowd magnified every teeter, every totter.

Victory could not fall.

Something touched her hand. Xavier's fingers intertwined with hers. She held on.

Just three more steps. Two. The very last step.

Finally, the statue was safe at the bottom of the staircase. She had not broken into a thousand pieces.

The collective sigh of those gathered to watch was the sweetest sound, like a hymn, picked up by the stone walls of the empty room, singing on and on.

"I want to believe it's a promise," Éliane said to Xavier, nodding at the exultant goddess. "That war won't come, and nobody will die."

"I want that too." He hadn't let go of her hand.

But, around them, it looked as if the war had already begun: sand-bags were piled up against the statues too large to move, pieces of wood lay strewn about like the debris of an explosion and people marched past with grim faces.

And she suddenly knew, the same way she could sense when Yolande was sick—waking in the middle of the night to feel her little sister's forehead—that the promise she wished for would be broken. War *was* coming. It was only a question of when. And whether any of them would, afterward, be able to watch *Victory* re-ascend the staircase intact and alive and victorious.

* * *

Monsieur Jaujard told those who had been there all night to take a break. Luc vanished to visit his latest *amour* and Xavier and Éliane left the museum together, hands still joined.

They walked through the Jardins des Tuileries, across the Place de la Concorde and then into the Jardins des Champs-Élysées. To their left, the Seine threaded between buildings and somewhere a broom scratched against cobblestones. Sun poured down like a blessing, the chestnut trees lifted their arms exultantly to the sky and birds serenaded, accompanied by the gentle percussion of the fountains. Even the flowers danced in time. It was the kind of autumn day that was almost too beautiful— nature showing that she could make the grandest artwork of all—and it emboldened Éliane to ask something she'd wanted to but had worried would be too intimate. But her skin touching Xavier's, his body beside hers rather than across a table, and his eyes resting always on her face told her so much that was private and personal—and made her feel there were perhaps some pieces of Xavier that were meant only for her.

"Will you show me your paintings?" she asked. "That's if you're not tired of art after last night."

"I'll never be tired of art." His grip on her hand tightened.

Soon they reached the Rue La Boétie and Xavier pushed open the door of a gallery named Laurent's.

"There you are," cried a man who looked like an older version of Xavier: tall, dark hair threaded with gray, distinguished.

"This is Éliane Dufort," Xavier said, introducing her. "And my father, Pierre Laurent."

"At last," the man said, shaking her hand warmly. "I understand you appreciate art. Would you like to take a look?"

He gestured to the walls on which were hung a vivid and sensual display of semi-naked women reclining on sofas or in chairs, surrounded by vibrant wallpaper, vases blooming with flowers, rainbow patterned fabric. After the strange night of emptying a museum, seeing so much color and light was like ingesting life.

"Matisse's *Odalisques*," she said, walking toward them.

"A woman who knows her artists," Pierre said approvingly.

And then he melted away, like turpentine into paint, allowing Xavier and Éliane to wind their way through reds and blues and vivid emerald greens.

"It's the color of your eyes," Xavier said to her of that last hue, glistening silkily in a pair of painted trousers. "Not always," he amended. "Not when you're working at the restaurant. But, right now, they are."

"Because I'm with you." The truth was too hard to contain.

Xavier's own eyes shone now, gold leaf on black. The colors of the paintings seemed to leap out of the frames and sparkle in the air between them, the reds glowing in her cheeks, flushing her neck.

Xavier's hand found hers again. "My paintings are upstairs. If you still want to see them."

She nodded, her eyes tracing the movement of his lips as he spoke, his eyes traveling over her cheekbones and down to her mouth too.

He led her upstairs where, amongst the artworks, she saw a light-filled corner by the windows set up with paint tubes, an easel, rags streaked with pigment, a palette alive with ideas. Xavier pointed to the canvases stacked against the wall and she flipped through them, startled: Luc had said Xavier was good, but that was an understatement. And knowing how much she yearned for the joy of painting, Xavier hadn't once boasted of his skills, had hardly mentioned his own work. Standing there, with Xavier's art beneath her hand, she felt her heart ache over the depth of understanding his reticence implied and then blossom because of the same thing. He *knew* her. And he cared.

She realized she'd said not a word about his paintings and that her own reticence right now might not be so easy to read. "I especially love this one," she said, stopping at a canvas that was even more powerful than the rest.

"Édouard de Rothschild bought that one. I'm delivering it to him tomorrow."

"Rothschild," Éliane repeated, awestruck. The various Rothschilds, including Édouard, owned some of the most important private art collections in the country.

"Sometimes…" Xavier hesitated and she lifted her eyes to his, letting him know that she wanted to hear whatever he had to say. "Sometimes," he continued, "surrounded by the scale of talent on the walls downstairs it seems painfully obvious that I'm merely gifted rather than a virtuoso. That I should concentrate on the buying and selling of virtuosity instead of reaching for the impossible. But then I sell a piece to someone like Rothschild and I wonder if…If maybe I shouldn't be practical. If I can somehow make a life as a painter. It's hard to stop."

"It is," Éliane said. "But I think it's even harder to regret something…" *You've given up in order to feed your family.* The words sounded too much like self-pity, so she didn't say them. "Don't stop," she said instead, reaching out her hand to touch the palette, to run her finger over the shiny pools of dried color.

Another hand joined hers, not touching the paint but her skin, the back of her hand, her wrist. Xavier stepped in very close to her, so close she could hear that his breath was faster than it should be.

"Éliane." He said her name as if it were precious—as if she were precious.

He lifted his hand from hers and rested it on her face, his thumb running over her cheekbone so softly: a sable brush painting warmth onto her skin. Each movement forward seemed to take an eternity; every next moment was further away than she wanted it to be.

And then it happened. A kiss she felt in her fingertips, her toes, the ends of her hair. A kiss so beautiful that a tear fell from her eye.

Xavier swept away the tear, moving his lips to kiss the place where it had lain. She turned her head, wanting his mouth back on hers and their bodies stepped into the embrace too, her hands on his back, his cupping her face, joined like the golden, shimmering couple who knew of nothing beyond the other in Klimt's extraordinary *Kiss*.

Then, from down the stairs came Xavier's father's voice, calling, "Hitler invaded Poland."

* * *

Éliane burst through the door of the apartment to find her mother sitting at the table, face covered with her hands, weeping. She stared. Her mother never wept, not even when she burnt the skin off her forearm on the ovens at the brasserie.

Luc was there too. And their father. Luc picked up the letter from the middle of the table and passed it to Éliane. Her brother and her father had been called for military service.

Angélique spoke in a shaking voice. "On the radio, they said if Germany doesn't withdraw from Poland by five o'clock tomorrow, France will declare war. And Britain too."

"You'll need to use your money to buy everything now," their father said, glaring at Éliane. "And nor will our maestro be able to finally earn anything from his artistic talent." The sarcasm in the last word had Luc glowering at his father, arm raised.

Éliane propelled her brother out of the apartment and down the stairs. They sat at the bottom beneath the mahogany portal, which bore the words *33 Escalier*. Broken glass from the paneled mirrors on either side reflected a shattered world and a cherub leaned drunkenly above them as if it might fall from its perch at any moment. Éliane passed her brother a cigarette and lit one for herself.

"Military service," Luc said bitterly. "So much for my dream of being a painter to rival Picasso."

Why then, Éliane didn't say, *over this last year, didn't you paint more, work harder? Why were the cafés of Montparnasse more appealing than your art?*

He gave her a rueful grin. "If I'd known..."

Éliane stared at the empty shops, at the fine threads of smoke writhing into the morning, at the decaying brasserie two doors down. "I'll have to give up art school, won't I? I'll work at the Louvre and the brasserie and do nothing else."

Luc nodded. "Mother won't be able to run the brasserie by herself."

That night in bed, Yolande clung to Éliane. Ginette, Jacqueline, and Angélique did too. Their father and their brother were going tomorrow to fight a war and Éliane would be the one left behind to keep her family safe. She sang a lullaby to her sisters, *"Au Clair de la Lune,"* Yolande's favorite. When Angélique turned dark eyes toward her, Éliane smiled as if to say, *Everything will be all right.*

Soon, they all slept. Except Éliane.

* * *

Luc disappeared early the next morning and returned just before it was time to report for duty. He pulled an envelope out of his pocket. "Xavier introduced me to Rothschild. I sold him a painting."

Out of the envelope spilled more francs than Éliane had ever seen. Her father was the first to seize the money. He kissed it, then kissed his son on the forehead, wrapping an arm around his shoulder. Angélique whooped, the younger girls crowded around, looking up at Luc as if he were a king, and their mother sank into a chair and stared at both the money and her son in utter disbelief.

"You sold a painting to Rothschild?" Éliane said, then laughed. They had money. And Luc had a wealthy patron. A dream had risen out of the ashes of yesterday.

"I said you were a maestro." Their father ruffled Luc's hair, none of yesterday's sarcasm apparent now.

"I bought you all something," Luc said, presenting his sisters with wrapped packages, which they squealed over, and out of which tumbled gifts more appropriate for his artists' models: jewelry, silk stockings, copies of Paris *Vogue*.

"You can look after the money," Luc said to Éliane. "That's your present." He grinned and Éliane felt a twinge that he hadn't bought her something too. But the twinge was gone almost immediately—having custody of the money was the most practical gift of all.

"Which painting was it, maestro?" she asked teasingly.

"It's of me, with one of my artists' models. I called it *The Lovers*," he said wryly. "I suppose it's a painting of love."

A painting of love. The words made her remember the feel of Xavier's lips on hers just yesterday. So much had happened since then. What would happen to her and Xavier now that France was at war? They had hardly begun, and now...

Éliane tried to recall the painting her brother had described, wanting to keep thinking of love, not war. There were many pictures of models at his studio in Montparnasse but they were usually reclined on sofas and wearing very little, which she didn't think was to Rothschild's taste. "I can't remember it," she said. "I wish I could see it."

"The only way to do that is to find a way in to the Rothschild mansion."

"I'm proud of you," she told him. "I always knew you'd be famous."

"You'll have to bow and scrape before me when I return victorious, having routed the Germans and made my name as a painter," Luc said, laughing.

She laughed too. "Look after yourself. And..." She hesitated, wondering for a fraction of a second if she meant it. "Look after father."

"He can look after himself," Luc said. And then he was gone.

That night, as Éliane's mother took over her husband's duties at the brasserie, Éliane's mind was not on waitressing. Her eyes darted to the door at every tinkle of the bell.

Finally, earlier than usual, Xavier arrived. War had doused the appetites of Parisians and the restaurant was empty. Éliane felt her whole face smile as she took in the dark hair, dark eyes, late-evening stubble; the divineness that was Xavier. Before she even spoke to him, she was kissing him, for a long, long time.

Eventually, she rested her forehead against his. "I forgot to say hello," she said, abashed at her eagerness.

He smiled. "We should always say hello like this. In fact," he murmured against her lips, "I didn't say hello either. So now I should." And he kissed her again, searchingly, fiercely.

"Thank you for taking Luc to see Rothschild," she said to him once she'd drawn back a little, only enough to be able to speak, her body still held tight against his. "He would never have bought one of Luc's paintings without your recommendation."

"Without Luc, I would never have met you," Xavier said. "So I owed him something." One of his hands moved to stroke a curl that had escaped its pins. "Did you know that I love your hair?"

They made themselves sit at a table, on opposite sides, the distance between their bodies a gap that required constant breaching: her foot touching his leg, him lighting a Gauloise for her, their fingers grazing as softly as a fine-tipped brush tracing a line on canvas and Éliane wondered how it was that a canvas did not shiver the way she did.

* * *

For many months thereafter, it was a strangely beautiful time. There wasn't really a war. The Nazis stayed away. The French called it the *drôle de guerre,* mocking Hitler. Nothing changed except for the nightly blackout, the absence of Luc, and of their father, and the tumult of feelings Éliane had for Xavier.

She continued to work, even though the Louvre was now a museum with little in the way of art—just some sculptures too big to move and only about ten percent of the paintings remaining. Monsieur Jaujard kept Éliane on as he knew she needed the money. She helped him with the job of liaising with the various châteaux—the depots across France that now held the Louvre artworks.

One evening in winter, after leaving the Louvre, she approached the apartment with trepidation, knowing she needed to check on her sisters before she started at the brasserie. Their father was home on a fortnight's furlough and it had ignited all tempers. But she could hear nothing as she climbed the staircase. Even without their father's presence, on a normal evening at six o'clock, Angélique would be shouting at Yolande or Yolande would be cackling over some mischief she'd wreaked on Angélique. There was only blissful silence.

Éliane couldn't believe what she saw when she opened the door. Angélique composedly stirring something in a pot, Ginette working on mathematics at the table, Jacqueline gathering up plates and cutlery for dinner—and Xavier sitting on the floor with Yolande in his lap, reading a book to her.

The sound of the door closing made everyone turn and stare guiltily at Éliane. No one spoke.

Then Xavier stood up, sliding Yolande from his lap. His tie and suit jacket were slung over the back of one of the chairs. He wore trousers and a shirt that had probably once been pressed and clean but were now wrinkled. His shirtsleeves were rolled up to the middle of his forearms and his antique silver watch looked, in the shabby apartment, like a thieved trinket in a raven's nest.

"I'd meant to be gone by the time you came home," he said, glancing ruefully at his watch. His expression exactly matched Angélique's: that of a person who'd done something wrong and knew they'd been caught.

Éliane turned to Angélique, speechless. Why was Xavier sitting in her apartment reading her sister a story when he should have been at work?

Angélique put down the spoon and placed her hands on her hips. "I went to the gallery and asked him to come," she said.

"You did what?" Éliane's eyes flicked from Xavier to her sister.

Éliane had never asked for one single thing from Xavier. And she loved that he had never offered her money, which she would not accept. He occasionally bought small things for her sisters: a kite for Yolande, a book for Ginette, a fresh apple for Jacqueline, a paste hair-clip for Angélique. But to give her money would be pity and charity both and it would make them unequal. It would make her weak. She had so little that she could be proud of but she was proud of the way she cared for her sisters.

"I went to the Louvre," Angélique said quickly. "But the museum isn't open so I couldn't get in. And I…" She paused, remorse coloring her cheeks red. "I caused the problem, so I had to fix it." Here Angélique glanced at Yolande protectively, affectionately, and Éliane's heart squeezed.

"What happened?" she asked, relenting a little and moving closer to Xavier.

Angélique shrugged. "I said something to Father that I shouldn't have."

"Did he hit you?"

Xavier reached for Éliane's hand.

As far as Éliane knew, she and her mother were the only ones who suffered the physical blows of her father's temper. If he started on Angélique, there was no way Éliane could continue to work while he was here. Then they would have no money at all.

"No. But he threw all the food he'd brought upstairs for our dinner on the floor. Yolande was hungry. We were all hungry," Angélique added, drawing Yolande into her side. "So I went to see Xavier to ask for some food."

Éliane tried to let go of Xavier's hand but he wouldn't let her. In fact, he slid his arm around her waist as if he meant to keep her close to him, always.

"But he didn't just give me food." Angélique's voice was defiant now, as if she expected Éliane to scold her. "He came here and looked after everyone while I cleaned up the mess."

"Oh, Angélique" Éliane said. There was too much anger in her family already. She would not contribute to it. She crossed over to her sister and hugged her. "Thank you," she said, "for fixing everything."

And Angélique began to cry. Éliane stroked her hair and shushed her while Xavier ladled soup into bowls and placed them in front of Yolande, Ginette, and Jacqueline, leaving a spare bowl out for Angélique.

"You should eat," Éliane said to her sister. "And..." She pulled a little of the money Luc had given her out of the envelope and told Angélique to buy all of the children some ice cream after dinner. Angélique stared at her as if she were mad. But maybe one ice cream every six months would give Yolande something lovely to think about whenever food was short. Éliane had Xavier, but Yolande had nothing: no doll to cuddle, just a careworn mother and a five-year-old's understanding of the world.

"I need to go downstairs," she said to her sisters. "I'm already late. Sleep tight."

She left the apartment with Xavier. He stopped on the landing and turned to her, eyes dark with a mix of different emotions: concern, anger, and a tenderness so exquisite it was all she wanted to see.

He touched her temple, threading his fingers through her hair.

She flinched as she waited for him to say something she'd hoped he would never say: *let me help you.*

Instead he said, "I love you, Ellie."

God, she was going to cry. But she didn't want to give him her tears. She reached out for him, felt the heat flare between her body and his before she kissed him more deeply than ever and he stepped her backward against the wall so they could be as close together as it was possible to be.

After a long moment he drew away, face flushed, eyes glittering so brilliantly she could almost see the blue and the gold and the green and the red—all the colors—flaring in the brown. "I can't keep kissing you, Éliane," he whispered. "It's too good." Then he asked, a little hesitantly, "Does that mean you love me too?"

She laughed and couldn't stop herself from kissing him again before she answered. "Do you even need to ask? Of course I do. More than anything."

His smile, that she'd once thought beautiful, was now sublime.

"I love you, Xavier."

"There are so many things I want right now, Ellie," he said. "But the thing I want most of all is to walk you out of this apartment and make sure you never come back."

She stiffened and closed her eyes. The offer of help she dreaded was coming.

But he lifted her chin and kissed her eyelids until she opened them. "I know you can't," he said gently. "That's part of why I love you. You're the most unselfish person I've ever met. But tonight," his voice was firm, "I'm walking you into the brasserie and staying until there's at least one other customer there because you're late and I know what happens when you're late. It's only one small thing out of all the millions of things I want to do. So please let me."

Now she *was* crying: over the memory of Yolande cuddling into him, her cheek pressed against his chest in a way she'd never sat with her father; over the fact that Xavier somehow loved her; over him trying to do what he could but not doing more than that because he respected her.

"Thank you," she said.

"I would do anything for you, Éliane."

And she believed that he would.

THREE

Then came May 1940. The Germans pounced on Belgium and threatened France from the north. A prayer vigil was held at the Notre-Dame, and Sainte Geneviève's relics were carried through the streets. Éliane stood with her sisters, holding Yolande on her hip, and watched the coffer of holy bones pass by. It was so small; a Panzer would crush it like an ant beneath its armored tracks. *Don't*, she told herself as Yolande's hands squeezed tight around her neck. *Don't think about what else might be crushed by the Germans.*

The government promised that, despite some reverses, it would remain in Paris and stand firm. Xavier looked worried, and told her every day that he loved her and she told him the same.

But then the Nazis crossed into France.

Somehow in Paris the theaters and nightclubs played on but the streets filled with refugees streaming in from the north of France where the cities of Arras and Amiens had fallen. The British army ran home, leaving the French people to defend themselves. The boom of cannons became unceasing, the threat of planes was always overhead, the war right on their doorstep. But there were no French soldiers in the city. Just civilians—and not many of them, as most Parisians had begun to flee. First the wealthy had driven away in their cars in late May, but now even families like Éliane's were leaving. Éliane had no idea where her father and Luc were: with the floundering French army in the north? Or had they been taken prisoner like so many others?

Some of her questions were answered that night when she was walking home along the *passage*. A hand on her arm dragged her into the void beneath the stairs.

"Luc!" she cried. "What are you doing here?"

Then she saw his face. Hard-set. All trace of her carefree brother gone.

"I'm a deserter," he said bitterly. "The French government doesn't deserve any more bodies. But you all have to leave. Go south. The Nazis will be in Paris within days."

Éliane shook her head. "I have to stay," she said. "Someone has to work. I'll need to send money to everyone."

"I knew you'd say that. Which is why I didn't tell you first that Father has been taken prisoner, along with tens of thousands of men. I wanted you to choose to stay, not stay because you thought you had to."

Éliane's hand lifted to touch the cheek her father had liked to hit. She spared one thought for him—that his suffering would not be too great—and then she thought of Angélique and Ginette and Jacqueline and Yolande and their mother instead. "There's no other choice," she said. "The others will leave in the morning."

"And I'm going to have one more night in Montparnasse." The grim set of Luc's face was more like someone taking what pleasure he could while it still existed, rather than someone who would treasure it.

And she knew then that *she* wanted something to treasure.

She didn't go to the brasserie. She went to Xavier's gallery and whispered in his ear.

"Are you sure?" he murmured.

"Yes."

Not long after, she stood beside him in a hotel room: a Left Bank aging beauty with white voile curtains billowing charmingly at the window.

"I love you," Xavier said to her, fingertips sketching her cheekbone.

"I love you too," she said, almost helplessly, because it was impossible to put into words the disturbance in her body and in her mind and in the air whenever she was with him.

Xavier withdrew a package from his pocket and held it out to her. "They use ten thousand jasmine flowers from Grasse and twenty-eight dozen *roses de mai* in every bottle."

Éliane slipped the wrapping off to find a square glass bottle filled with an amber-colored liquid, bearing the word *Joy*. She unstoppered it and the scent was almost as heady as inhaling Xavier.

"And they only make fifty bottles a year," he continued. "So almost nobody else will ever smell the same as you. Which means I'll always be able to find you."

She stepped in closer to him.

"No matter what happens," he finished.

She put the perfume down.

Then she half-turned and he half-spun her around, moving her long blonde hair to one side, and undoing one button on her dress, stroking the skin that had been revealed at the base of her neck. The next button parted from the fabric: more of her skin for him to explore. How would it be possible to survive this act? Her body was already alight and he hadn't even kissed her.

"Xavier," she whispered and he kissed her once, so lightly she almost missed it, on top of her shoulder.

There was one more button. He turned his attention to it, then to the new skin beneath. She was going to die.

In the quickest of movements, she pulled her dress over her head and let it fall to the floor.

So much skin revealed now, so much for him to discover, first with his fingers and then with his lips. Parts of her body she hadn't even known were erotic were transformed into realms of hedonistic pleasure: her elbow, her earlobe, her hip bone, the small of her back. She hardly realized she was lying on the bed beside him; all she could think was how much she loved him, the way he was intent on her, on making certain she enjoyed this, her first time with a man. He would be the only person she would ever do this with. Until the end of time, his was the only body she would know, the only body she would ever want to know.

He looked up at her and smiled and that was almost enough to send her hurtling into whatever it was she could feel blazing, not far away. She touched his face, exerting just enough pressure to draw him upward so that his lips, for the first time since they'd entered the room, met hers.

And then there was nothing at all beyond Xavier and Éliane and their sudden and searing nakedness and the ache of something that was both inexpressible and hardly enough, something so towering she was almost afraid.

She fell asleep afterward and when she awoke, her breath caught at seeing Xavier, everything the same—darkest brown hair and eyes, the smudge of black on his cheeks and chin from stubble, the curve of his lips—but something different too, an intensity of expression more concentrated than ever.

He placed a box on the pillow. "For you."

"You can't keep giving me things, Xavier," she said gently but firmly.

"I've given you two things," he said. "The perfume and this. Do you know how hard it's been not to give you more, these last few months? How hard it's been not to give you everything? This is yours, if you want it."

The way he said those last words—*if you want it*—made her untie the ribbon, peel back the paper and open the lid. A quick flash of blue, a rounded cabochon with a white star caught inside it, two square-cut diamonds on either side, a band of white gold.

"It's a star sapphire," Xavier said as he set the ring free from the box. "This one has twelve rays, making it even more rare and more beautiful. But not as beautiful as you." He smiled as he slipped it onto the ring finger of her left hand. "Will you marry me? Please?"

It was that final word, the quiver of vulnerability within it—as if this handsome, bewitching, confident man worried that she might refuse him—that made her fall so far in love with him that there was no end to her fall.

She kissed him, breathing her answer—*Yes, of course*—into his mouth and then it was happening all over again. Kisses. Bodies. Hands. Mouths. She imagined the second time would be a disappointment, that nothing could match the first. But it surpassed it in every way.

When she woke next it was after midnight and Xavier was sitting on the window ledge, the curtains rustling like spirits around him. The way he was looking at her, so intently, as if he were memorizing her, had her smiling and stepping out of the bed and over to him. Beyond them lay the spires of the city, the moon, the artistes speaking furiously of both art and war in the cafés below.

Xavier's hands reached for her hips and drew her closer to him. "I'm...I don't know how to say this." He closed his eyes and her heart shuddered. He looked as if everything inside him hurt.

"What is it?" she asked, touching her lips to his to banish forever anything that could make him feel like that.

He opened his eyes. They were blacker than any night had ever been. And then he said, "I'm leaving. For England. My..." He ran a furious hand through his hair. "My father's closing the gallery here." His voice was incredulous.

Éliane felt herself take a small step back.

"I only found out today." His awful, unbelievable words continued. "We have to leave tomorrow. The Germans are coming, Ellie. They'll be here soon, despite what the radio says, despite what the French government says. Everyone who can is leaving Paris. I wish I could take you with me. But…" He faltered, as if trying to make himself believe his next words. "We can still have everything we want. It may just take a little longer."

Ellie. Nobody in the world called her that, except him. She had, until then, loved the sound of it in his mouth.

Her head shook from side to side, dislodging what she thought she'd heard and trying to re-form the words into something that didn't make her heart hurl itself against her chest, like childish fists thumping out her incomprehension.

"You're leaving?" she said, her words the tiniest and thinnest of whispers.

"There's one last ship from Bordeaux. I have to make sure my father gets to England safely—"

"But…" Éliane broke in, then stepped further away from him, stumbling a little, unbalanced by pain and the sudden rush of understanding. "You knew you were leaving before you came here tonight. You *knew*. And you didn't say anything."

He reached out a hand for her but she was beyond his reach. "If I don't get my father out now, he'll be trapped—"

Éliane's laugh was a knife tearing through the night. "Trapped? *Quelle horreur.* Like the French people who have no London home to run to."

Hot tears scalded her eyes. "How dare you? How dare you tell me now, after everything we just did." She tore the ring off her finger so ferociously that it cut her skin. "How dare you not tell me this first," she finished, voice small.

"I couldn't," he whispered. "I didn't want to ruin tonight. I didn't want to ruin everything."

Tonight was more than ruined now; it was ash.

Perhaps if he'd looked away, stared at the floor, not met her eyes. Then she could have hated him outright. But he kept his gaze upon her, steadfast, so that she could see love shining like starlight in the pools of his eyes. That hurt her more than anything. He loved her, but he was leaving her.

And he hadn't loved her enough to tell her first. He'd put his body before her heart.

She had never sworn before, nothing more than a *zut* or a *mon Dieu,* had certainly never called anyone a bastard, but the word came flying out. *"Tu es un salaud!* And a coward!" She threw the ring at him.

It hit his shoulder, falling to the floor and clattering against the wood.

Éliane pulled her dress over her head. Then she stormed out, vowing that she would not cry, not ever, not for him; he did not deserve it.

* * *

It was almost dawn when she returned to find Luc, her mother, and all her sisters gathered around the table waiting for her. She knew that Luc had told them they had to leave. Nobody asked her why she looked so pale or where she'd been. And as Yolande said, "Éliane must come with us," Éliane took all of her heart from Xavier and gave it to her sisters.

They were more precious than any *Winged Victory* or *Mona Lisa* and if those artworks had to be sent away, then so too did her sisters.

"I'll send you money enough to buy lots of ice cream," she said, giving her mother the envelope of Luc's money, which she'd somehow known to save.

"How will we know what to do if you're not there?" Angélique said, her lip trembling like Yolande's.

Éliane pulled them both into her arms. "You'll know because I've taught you everything." She made herself smile and Angélique bless her, smiled back, pretending she saw the humor. And Yolande was persuaded to believe that they were about to set off on an adventure.

The Duforts didn't have a car, so the train was the only option.

They waited for days at the station, unable to get a place on the over-full carriages. Days of crouching down—Yolande wailing in Éliane's arms—when hundreds of Luftwaffe planes roared over and bombed the industrial arrondissements of Paris. The sound was like thunder in their heads. Éliane could feel her arms and legs shaking and she knew that, despite the protestations of the government, the Nazis were almost in Paris. Her sisters could not be here when they arrived.

Black smoke crested above them, annihilating the sun. Amid the howls and screams all around them, Éliane heard a woman cry that she'd heard the Germans were butchering children, castrating men, raping women. *No*, she wanted to shout. *No*. This could not be happening.

A sudden boom cracked through the sky. Everyone screamed, cowering, not knowing what might fall down upon them next. Angélique, Ginette, and Jacqueline added their sobs to Yolande's, holding on to Éliane, almost pulling her over.

Éliane's eyes met her mother's. "You have to go now," she said, gesturing to the throng of people walking south.

Her mother nodded. Éliane kissed her cheeks.

Then she kissed Angélique's; her blonde hair covered with a scarf, blue eyes wide. Jacqueline, dark-haired, clutching her mother's hand. Ginette, her reddish curls bouncing hopefully on her shoulders. Finally, little blonde cherubic Yolande. Éliane almost couldn't let Yolande go, almost couldn't watch as Yolande, crying for Éliane, was dragged away by their mother, almost couldn't stand still with a smile frozen on her face, almost ran after them and told them to stay.

When she could no longer see her family, Éliane sat on the floor of the station and sobbed.

At the apartment, Luc was waiting for her.

"What will we do?" she said dully, the apartment too quiet without her four sisters romping through it.

"For now," he said, "we wait. But soon, if we have to, we fight."

* * *

The only way to get the truth was to tune in to Radio Stuttgart. It told Éliane that Pétain, France's Vice-Premier and so-called Hero of Verdun, had lied: the French government had not stood firm. They had run away to the spa town of Vichy and declared Paris an open city, leaving it undefended. Leaving Éliane and the others who had stayed in the French capital to the mercy of the German army.

What would happen? Éliane tried not to think about what the woman at the station had screamed about the Nazis. She found the sharpest knife of all from the brasserie and Luc did the same, even though she knew the knives wouldn't even scratch a Panzer, and would be no defense at all against a gun.

Then she and Luc stood at the open window of the apartment, watching. There was no one outside: more than half the population had left, train stations were closed, hospitals evacuated, shops shuttered over, newsstands stood empty and streets waited desolately for patronage besides that of abandoned dogs.

"How is it possible?" she murmured to her brother. It was summer in Paris; she should be sitting in a café in the sunshine drinking coffee and breathing in cigarette smoke, dizzy from the scent of roses blooming extravagantly in the Jardins du Palais Royal. Instead, all she could smell in the reek of burnt-out incendiaries and the ash of government papers set alight before the ministers escaped was subjugation. Paris lay hidden beneath a shroud of charred sky, all light fled along with the leaders.

"I don't know," Luc replied in a similarly desolate voice.

She wiped her face and her hand came away black with soot as if she'd also transformed from bright watercolor to charcoal. Behind her, the radio bellowed that the Germans would soon arrive in Paris. There would be no violence—unless the French people started it. Then the Germans would have to retaliate.

Éliane and Luc stared at the knives in their hands, which looked like toys now.

"All Parisians are to remain inside for forty-eight hours!" the radio announcer ordered.

Not long after, motorbike engines reverberated through the stillness. In the windows of several apartments on the opposite side of the street were people standing like Luc and Éliane, rigid with fear. Fragments of German language began to assault the air outside and gray streamed over the many-colored canvas that had once been Paris. Loudspeakers boomed: "You have been betrayed by your government! Any aggressive act toward the German army will result in death!"

And thus the war had somehow ended, not with stubborn fighting and implacable will but with everyone running away.

Éliane wanted to shut her eyes and make it all stop. But as her lids half-closed, she saw Xavier in the white-curtained window telling her he was leaving. For just a few seconds, she was glad that he had. He was Anglo-French. The English and the Germans were at war still. The half-Britishness of his blood might have meant repercussions for him and his father if he'd stayed. But the way he'd told her he was leaving— and his appalling timing—were betrayals that hurt like nothing she had ever known.

"Xavier's gone," she told Luc, trying to say it flatly, without inflection, as if it didn't matter. But her voice was husky with all the tears she was refusing to cry.

Luc slipped his hand into hers and squeezed it. She held on tightly; he was the only person she had left.

After the prescribed forty-eight hours had passed, Éliane told Luc she was going outside. "Monsieur Jaujard might expect me at work. I don't know—do you think everyone is just going to go back to work as if today is a normal day?"

"I don't know. I can't go out because I'm technically still a deserter. Unless the war has somehow ended and the radio forgot to tell us."

"Until there are no Germans in Paris, the war hasn't ended," Éliane said firmly.

She picked up her purse and crept down the stairs, through the *passage* and onto the pavement. Red and black swastikas hung grotesquely on every building. Panzers prowled along the Rue de Rivoli. Already, there were signposts in German that directed the conquerors to their various new headquarters in all the luxury hotels. If the Nazis were erecting signposts that signaled an intent to stay.

She had thought she couldn't possibly feel any more despairing. She had been wrong.

"Mademoiselle," a man said in German-accented French, and Éliane shrank against the wall at the sight of a soldier in German uniform.

"After you," he said, indicating that she should continue on her way.

She scurried on.

At the Louvre, she let herself slowly into her chair and sat with her forehead resting on her hand.

A touch on her shoulder roused her. "Your family?" Monsieur asked.

"They left," she said.

"Good."

"Is the *Mona Lisa* still safe?"

"Yes. She's been moved to Loc-Dieu, an abbey. It was once called *Locus Diaboli*—the place of the devil," Monsieur Jaujard said quietly.

Éliane shook her head. "I think perhaps the place of the devil is now Paris."

* * *

Not long after, the Armistice was signed. The war was, apparently, over. Éliane refused to believe it. But it made no matter; France was sliced into several pieces, one occupied—the zone where Éliane lived—and one supposedly free—the zone governed by Vichy where she hoped her mother and sisters had found safety. She waited desperately for a letter from them. None came. But they had enough money to last a few weeks. They would write when they needed more, she reasoned.

June passed into July. Theaters and shops reopened. Posters exhorting the abandoned people of Paris to put their trust in the Germans papered the city. Bikes and horse-drawn carts replaced cars on the streets. French radio and newspaper operators were closed down and German-approved ones took their place. The Germans looked to be settling in to the city forever.

And then.

Parisians started to return from the south. But not Yolande. Not Angélique or Ginette or Jacqueline. Not her mother.

Éliane checked the mailbox each day. It was always empty. *Write, Angélique,* she prayed each night. *Write to me and tell me where you are.*

The brasserie remained closed. Éliane stayed on at the Louvre. Now that it was just her and Luc, they had enough money for food. Éliane would have traded it all for news of her sisters. The hunger of wanting to know was insatiable, scratching always inside her.

Every day, the phantom sounds of her sisters' voices echoed in the apartment: Angélique cajoling Yolande to get dressed, Ginette reading Yolande a story, Jacqueline trying to sing *"Au Clair de la Lune"* for Yolande but Yolande saying, *I want Éliane instead.*

"I want you too, *chérie,*" Éliane whispered to the empty apartment.

One night she arrived home from the Louvre to find her brother dressed in black, bag in hand.

She stopped still in the doorway and stared at him.

He looked out the window rather than at her and swore.

I'm leaving, Xavier had said, wearing the same look on his face that Luc wore now: as if he knew he was about to break her heart.

But maybe Luc was leaving now because…"They're back?" she asked, hurrying inside, calling, "Yolande!"

Luc swore again.

The familiar lack of sound in the apartment—the absence of giggles and groans and tantrums—was deafening.

"It's been four months since they left," Luc said, speaking more gently than she'd ever heard him speak, even to his artists' models. "There's been no letter. They would need money by now. They would have had to write to ask you to send it. But they haven't." He paused. "You know what it means?"

Éliane shut her eyes. But she couldn't shut her mind. It put pictures alongside the words she'd read in the newspapers or heard on the radio about the roads out of Paris in June turning into rivers of people running south. A thick and suffocating crowd of desperation.

Éliane shook her head. But Luc had opened a breach in her hopefulness and allowed doubt to fall in.

The Germans had strafed the lines of civilians fleeing Paris, causing stampedes. Those not shot had been trampled. There had been too many people and not enough food. Bodies lined the roadsides like wheat stalks, the newspapers had said.

She put a hand to her mouth but the sob escaped anyway.

How could she have let Yolande believe she was setting out on an adventure? How could Éliane have stayed behind, in the relative safety of Paris, and let them go?

"They should have taken the children," she said brokenly. Yolande's eyes were surely more beautiful than any artwork. "They should have taken the children to the châteaux and the abbeys to keep them safe. Not the artworks."

She turned to the window and pressed her palms and forehead

against it, staring out at what had once been a city of art and of fierce sisterly affection and first love. Now that the scumble had been removed, it was showing up everything that had lain underneath and that she had known nothing about: Pétain's cowardice, the Nazis' deadly and unstoppable ambition, her sisters' deaths.

How did you mourn four girls lost before they'd reached adulthood?

She felt Luc step in beside her, saw the wet marks of her tears on the sill joined by ones she hadn't shed.

"You're going," she whispered.

He nodded. "I'm joining de Gaulle's Free French Forces. I'm not a painter anymore." He kissed her forehead and pulled her in close, embracing her hard but not for long enough.

Then he left to do what he'd said they must: to fight.

Before, it had just been words. But now it was something she must do too so that Angélique and Jacqueline and Ginette might forgive her. So that Yolande might forgive her.

"*Brûle en enfer*, Monsieur Adolf," she said to the empty apartment. "For what you did to my family, I will find a way to make you burn in hell."

FOUR

The Louvre was a place where the memory of lost artworks lingered in the white oblongs of unbleached paint that adorned the walls. And Éliane's apartment held similarly poignant souvenirs: Yolande's blonde hair tangled in a comb, Angélique's flower boxes in the window embrasure, wilting despite Éliane's lavish watering. The perfume Xavier had given her. Every night, she tried to resist unstoppering the bottle and smelling the scent, tried to close her heart against Xavier's words: *I'll always be able to find you. No matter what happens.*

But she didn't want to be found by someone from whom she was separated not just by a vast body of water, but by cowardice.

To escape the memories, she went to the Louvre early each day and stayed until past nightfall, keeping herself busy with telephone calls and paperwork about the museum's art collections, now housed in various châteaux. She didn't smile at anyone except Monsieur Jaujard and she spoke to the Germans on the streets only when necessary and always in French, even though she knew enough German to converse—languages and art went hand in hand. She had studied both Italian and German at the École, and Xavier's grandmother had been German and he had taught her more during the *drôle de guerre*, saying it might be important.

And so life dragged on, with Éliane watching and waiting for some kind of insurrection by the French that would evict the Nazis and send them running back to Germany. For an opportunity to make good on her promise to fight too.

But nothing happened. Resignation was everywhere and within everyone, as if Parisians thought this was how life would be from now on. That was almost the worst thing of all.

In late October, as she sat at her desk at the Louvre, the smack of running boots sounded on the marble floors. Suddenly, a German with a gun was standing in front of her, and more armed men were shouting at her and at Monsieur Jaujard.

She leapt out of her chair and backed away, into the filing cabinets. "What do you want?" she asked tremulously, eyes fixed on the guns.

No one answered; they simply prodded her out of the way, opening files and pulling out papers and eventually, she realized with disquietude, ransacking whatever documents they could find that pertained to the inventory Monsieur Jaujard had been ordered to compile—an inventory he had told Éliane to work on as slowly as she could—of the Louvre artworks hidden throughout France. At least, she thought, trying to find whatever consolation she could, neither she nor Monsieur Jaujard had written down the code on the *Mona Lisa*'s crate. At least there was no complete record to steal of the various locations of the paintings, other than in Monsieur's head; the Germans would have only scattered pieces of a complex mosaic.

Thankfully it was all over in less than ten minutes. The boots retreated. She sank into her chair, closing her eyes, wondering whether she could ever get used to the terrible proximity of so many guns. How could art provoke raids at gunpoint? And would the Nazis be back once they realized so much information was missing?

Monsieur Jaujard told her to go home, but returning to an empty apartment after that would be worse than staying. So he made her a coffee and they talked about art instead.

The very next day, a representative from the Einsatzstab Reichsleiter Rosenberg—or the ERR, a taskforce Éliane had heard spoken of by

Monsieur Jaujard with dread, its mission to "safeguard" artworks in Germany's conquered territories—visited the Louvre. Monsieur had wondered if the Nazis might define safeguarding in a manner different to how he would define it. Éliane had been unconcerned; the Louvre's artworks were already safe and would not require the Nazis' protection. But yesterday's raid made her wonder if she was naive to imagine the Germans would leave the Musées Nationaux treasures alone.

The ERR official strode into Monsieur Jaujard's office and shut the door. Éliane bent her head to reading the latest communiqué from one of the Germans' many bureaus but her eyes continued to stray to the closed door behind which a Nazi, whose job was to take artworks into custody, sat.

The door opened at last. Monsieur Jaujard indicated Éliane. "Mademoiselle Dufort would be happy to help." Then, to Éliane, he said, "Some artworks are being taken to the Musée Jeu de Paume. We have been permitted to make an inventory. You will help the gallery's caretaker, Madame Valland, with the inventory."

Happy? She would not be happy to help the Germans compile yet another catalog of artworks. But there was something Monsieur was trying to tell her with his expressionless face.

Then Monsieur Jaujard said to the ERR representative, "Mademoiselle Dufort does not speak German."

Éliane slid the letter written in German that she had been reading under a pile of paper.

She followed the Nazi outside, past the Arc de Triomphe du Carrousel, still majestic despite the fact that there had been no triumph. Then into the Jardins des Tuileries, past *Diana the Huntress,* poised, ready, hand reaching back to take out an arrow. If only Diana wasn't frozen in sculpture. Éliane almost felt her mouth turn up into a smile at the ridiculousness of looking for help from a statue. But she kept the smile inside her, rather than on her face, holding on to that one rare moment of humor in a world she'd thought had stolen all light away.

Finally they marched along the Grande Allée where naked elm trees sketched charcoal against the sky. At the Jeu de Paume, which housed the Musée des Écoles étrangères contemporaines, they halted. Outside the museum stood a line of soldiers with guns on their shoulders demanding that her chaperone show his papers and explain who Éliane was.

Éliane no longer felt any urge to smile. Why would a museum be guarded by armed men?

What she found inside made her gape. The Jeu de Paume had been closed since the Germans arrived in Paris but now it was busier than Les Halles on market day. Boxes and crates and cartons containing artworks sat in exquisite and precarious piles on the floor. Men hurried here and there, studying paintings, shouting. A pair of curvaceously rococo eighteenth-century sculptures stood disconsolately and utterly out of place in a museum that had once been devoted to contemporary and foreign artwork.

As she turned around to take it all in, Éliane bumped into a tall man who was wearing the queerest uniform she'd ever seen: a swastika lurked on the jacket alongside a Red Cross insignia. The man stiffened, face half hidden by his cap, expression made harder to read by the one glass eye staring dispassionately at her. "Mademoiselle!" he roared.

"Colonel von Behr." The soldier who had brought Éliane saluted and began to speak in German, explaining that Monsieur Jaujard had sent Éliane to help with the French inventory.

Colonel von Behr was, Éliane knew, the head of the ERR. At the word "inventory," he withdrew his attention from Éliane and turned it toward a woman whose dark-rimmed glasses overshadowed her face. She was unobtrusively sorting through a crate of artwork and writing in a notebook.

Von Behr strode over to the woman and closed her notebook with a snap. "There will be no inventory. *Désolé*," he added with a wholly unapologetic smile.

"Send her back," von Behr said to the man who had accompanied Éliane. "Only Madame Valland may stay." He gestured to the bespectacled woman who, Éliane knew from her work at the Louvre, had been the well-respected curator at the Jeu de Paume before the Occupation. "Somebody who knows the building must be its caretaker."

Éliane's eyes skittered around the room. So many paintings. Where had they come from? Not the Louvre depots of Chambord and Loc-Dieu and Valençay; none of these paintings belonged to the Louvre.

And then she saw it. An oil rendering of a man with a celestial globe, his face alight from both the sun spilling in through the window and the beauty of his own thoughts. It was Vermeer's *Astronomer*. Owned, Éliane knew, by Édouard de Rothschild. But here it was, leaning against a wall. A German boot clattered past, knocking it awry.

"Oh no," she said, reaching in past the fear of so many Nazis gathered in one room and stretching out a hand to save the painting before it was ruined. "This mustn't be left on the floor."

"Must it not?" von Behr inquired coolly.

A younger man wearing dark Nazi jacket and trousers, tie fastened to strangling above well-polished buttons, his blond hair a mockery of sunshine and his eyes an indeterminate shade between blue and green looked up from his paper and pen. He asked, shyly, in French, "You know paintings, Mademoiselle?"

Éliane nodded.

The blond man spoke diffidently to von Behr, the flush on his cheeks deepening with each sentence. "We have no library to help us verify the artworks. There are so many to catalog. It will take too much time— and he is coming soon. Anyone who knows paintings will be a great help." By the end of this speech, the young man's cheeks were blood-red and he stared at the floor.

Colonel von Behr's finger drew Éliane's chin upward. "Do you speak German?" he asked her in German.

Éliane stared dumbly at him.

"If my nephew wants you, you can stay," he continued in French. "You can assist Madame Valland. She tells me the museum is too large to run without help. And you will be of use to my nephew." This last was said with a smile. The whole of it was spoken with insolence.

Éliane tried not to shiver; she knew he would feel it. But she was unsuccessful.

The expression in von Behr's one seeing eye altered from bored amusement to cold steel. "As I have told Madame Valland, you are never to speak about your work. No one from the Louvre is permitted inside. No one without an Ausweis is allowed to enter. You saw the guards outside."

He withdrew his finger, and Éliane's chin dropped subserviently down, meeting Madame Valland's eyes on the way. There, Éliane found only blankness.

"Thank you for my assistant," Madame Valland said to von Behr, smiling. "You are very kind."

Éliane stared at Madame Valland who was French and who should never smile at a German.

Von Behr withdrew and Madame Valland spoke to the man von Behr had called his nephew. "I see there is a new delivery, Monsieur König. Perhaps—"

König broke in, not rudely like his uncle, but with firmness. "Your notebook, please. You heard my uncle. There is to be no inventory."

Madame Valland passed over the book.

"Please arrange an Ausweis for Mademoiselle…" König looked questioningly at Éliane.

"Éliane Dufort."

"For Mademoiselle Dufort. Familiarize her with the museum. That is all."

Once König left, the smile collapsed from Madame Valland's face and Éliane took the opportunity to ask, "Why do I need an Ausweis for an art gallery?"

"You'll need to show your permit to the guards when you enter and leave each day. But questions are dangerous things. Ask no more, and you can't get into trouble." Madame Valland beckoned for Éliane to follow her. She gave the impression of a mouse, something small and insignificant and easily overlooked—even though she was taller than Éliane and about twenty years older too—in her nondescript black skirt suit, round glasses, brown hair scraped back into a bun. "All you need to know is that the Germans cannot empty their own wastepaper baskets. Or change the lightbulbs. We will do that for them. For now, you may tidy the ground floor galleries. Remove all the discarded packing materials. König, and others like him, will do the rest."

The rest of what?

Éliane didn't ask. Instead she completed a form for her Ausweis and began to tidy. The five small galleries at the rear of the museum were empty of people, so she started there.

She spun in a slow circle, taking in the quantity of artworks around her, and recalled a conversation she'd had the previous day with Monsieur Jaujard. He'd looked so serious and so sad that Éliane had asked him what was wrong and he'd said, "A new order has been issued demanding the safeguarding of Jewish-owned artworks, which have been declared goods without owners. The order states that the Jews are *hors de tous droits*. That they are…" His voice had lowered, becoming so quiet that Éliane had to step close to hear him as he forced terrible words from his mouth. "Like cattle. They are outside all law, including the Hague Convention. Thus their property is no one's. Which means it can be confiscated by the Germans."

Like cattle.

Outside all law.

Hors de tous droits. Without rights.

How must it feel, Éliane had wondered, to have such things said of you simply because of the God you chose to worship?

Now, Éliane's heart thudded against her chest as she reached a tentative hand toward *The Astronomer.* Édouard de Rothschild was Jewish. But nobody would take Édouard de Rothschild's paintings from him, surely? He was a wealthy and important man, with an unrivaled collection of art.

Perhaps this painting was a fake.

Éliane crouched down to study it, a painting she knew well from her studies but had never had the luck to be so close to. She saw at once how the browns and blacks had been used expertly to evoke the mysticism of the knowledge seeker at the center of the picture: a man who might accidentally see too much in his celestial globe and thus have his head removed.

Was she, now, seeing too much? Footsteps sounded some distance away. Éliane's heart beat faster still.

She turned the painting over. Stamped on its back, obliterating the Rothschild family crest, was a swastika.

* * *

The intrusion of more boots, many boots. She replaced *The Astronomer* carefully in the crate beside a dozen other works of world renown. It appeared that Édouard de Rothschild's entire art collection had been brought to the Jeu de Paume, a gallery now run by Nazis with guns. She hadn't imagined, when Monsieur Jaujard told her about the "safeguarding" of Jewish goods, that he'd meant paintings like these. Was that why Monsieur had wanted an inventory made? So that someone might know what other kinds of violence were being enacted in this new kind of Kristallnacht?

Éliane gathered up armloads of paper as German voices filled her ears. *Do you speak German?* von Behr had asked her. Her muteness had implied that she didn't. And Monsieur Jaujard had told them she didn't, even though he knew she could. *Listen*, she told herself.

"Fräulein. Please take this," the man called König said to her in French, interrupting her thoughts. He placed a painting in her arms that was covered with a sheet. "It belongs in the room upstairs, right at the end."

Éliane walked upstairs to the very last gallery. She set down the painting in her arms beside a Salvador Dalí, then removed the sheet and saw that she'd been carrying a Picasso: a woman on a beach, naked, neoclassical in style, the woman's face joyful and bathed in sunshine. Éliane's gaze swept the room taking in more modernist paintings: a Matisse, a Van Gogh, a Braque.

Footsteps sounded from behind again. Éliane's outer body froze but everything inside moved twice as fast: her heart, her blood, her breath.

Luckily it was Madame Valland. "This room is for what they call 'degenerate' art," she said somberly. "The Führer does not like anything modernist, or failing to meet a dozen other criteria that are nothing to do with art and everything to do with one man's corrupt scruples. I have named it the Salle des Martyrs."

The Room of the Martyrs.

Madame Valland disappeared and it was as if the walls of the gallery had spoken—or the women in the paintings, or the artists behind the paintings—telling Éliane that nothing was as it seemed, and that she would have to discover for herself how to find answers when questions were not permitted. She remembered her vow—*brûle en enfer*—and that she had wanted the Nazis to burn in hell for what they had done to her family. Perhaps here in this strange museum she would find a way to make that happen.

* * *

The next day, she walked to work past rows of Nazi uniforms standing to attention outside the Hôtel de Crillon and the Hôtel de la Marine. Above her, the Luxor Obelisk in the center of the Place de la Concorde stabbed at the sky as if it were trying to pierce through the gunmetal and find the promise of blue, a promise she sought too. But all that fell down was rain, a sleety and persistent drizzle muddying the paths in the Tuileries and soaking through Éliane's shoe leather. The long black boots of the Luftwaffe guard, set against the Jeu de Paume, were like tar dripped onto a Monet painting.

Éliane tried not to look at any of it. She hung her head down and reminded herself of three things: she did not understand German; she was there for her sisters; she must see everything and say nothing and, in so doing, work out why the Nazis had taken so many immensely valuable artworks to the Jeu de Paume. What she would do with that knowledge once she had it was uncertain but, as gaining it would be difficult enough, it was all she could think of right now.

The guards tarried over her Ausweis but it didn't unnerve her like it had yesterday: she wore her purpose like a shield. König arrived just after Éliane and he said to the guard, politely, "She can enter. We have work to do."

Éliane followed him into the museum.

"You slept well, Mademoiselle?" König inquired.

Éliane nodded, then saw the slight flush on König's cheeks. Talking to her made him blush. She swallowed down the taste of bile in her mouth.

Despite her intention to be unsurprised and outwardly calm, it was difficult not to be overawed by the contents of the museum. Sumptuous rugs—owned by one of the Rothschilds—decorated the floors; portly upholstered Louis XV chairs sat in pairs opposite sets of sleeker Directoire armchairs—the Rothschilds' again. Sèvres vases, Meissen and Dresden lace figurines, oriental Celadon jars, brilliantly polished silverware and patiently ticking gilded clocks adorned eighteenth-century chiffoniers. Verdant Aubusson tapestries hung from walls in pastoral shades of green and stained-glass windows leaned drunkenly and irreligiously against pillars.

In each gallery Éliane traversed, she saw the same thing: walls invisible beneath the excess of artwork. It seemed as if the entire stock of the Seligmann, the Wildenstein, and the Bernheim-Jeune galleries—galleries neighboring Xavier's father's—was now here. So many masterpieces come together in an exhibition that would be difficult for an established museum to pull off. But Éliane felt no frisson of excitement at being able to reach out and touch any of them. She felt only that same brackish dread in her stomach, heard that same recurring question blazoning in her head: why were the paintings there?

She felt someone step in beside her.

"*Incroyable*," Madame Valland murmured, but not as if she were awestruck. Rather, Éliane heard a note of despair in her voice, almost hidden, like the skulls Dutch painters concealed within a still life—the warning amid the majesty. And Éliane saw on her face something other than meekness and obsequiousness: a stark unease lurked behind her glasses.

At the same moment, von Behr strode into the room and Éliane knew that he could not be allowed to see Madame Valland's stupor. So she turned and pretended to trip on a nearby table leg. A sharp tinkling of glass sounded an alert as the profusion of crystal vases atop the table shuddered. Madame Valland wrenched her eyes away from a Rembrandt.

"Fool!" Von Behr's hand flicking out to strike Éliane's cheek was like that of her father's. She accepted the slap without flinching.

"Find someone less clumsy," he barked to Madame.

"Ah, but then I would waste time training them," Madame Valland said, bestowing her servile smile upon von Behr. "I'll teach her to mind her feet instead."

Von Behr ran his eyes over Éliane's face and down her body. "I suppose we're unlikely to find anyone quite as young and decorative." He left the room and Éliane gathered she'd been saved, for now. And that Madame Valland's smile had helped.

"*Merci*," she whispered.

"And thank you too," Madame Valland replied, voice low. Then, louder, "Straighten the vases, Mademoiselle Dufort."

Von Behr reappeared with a group of men in white coats, who whispered their astonishment over the gathered objects to one another in German.

"I want everything cataloged and organized," von Behr shouted. "And quickly. We have important guests arriving soon who want to see an exhibition, not a mess. König," he barked, and the younger man stepped forward. "You're in charge. Ilse!"

A blonde German woman with a simpering smile and a dictation pad stepped forward. "My office," von Behr said to her, charm smoothing his vowels now. "We have work to do."

"But Uncle—" König put out a hand to stop von Behr's departure. "We need a reference library. So many of the works are French and none of us are experts in French art."

"There is no reference library," von Behr snapped. "Use your brains. I thought you were all art historians."

König's cheeks burned from his uncle's scolding and he stepped back quickly into line. As he did so, he caught Éliane watching and, thankfully, rather than seeing her curiosity for what it was, he flushed more elaborately still and ducked his head to stare at the floor.

As soon as von Behr and his secretary left the room, Éliane, still straightening vases, listened carefully to the vigorous spread of complaints. Von Behr knew as much about art as a peasant. The only work he was doing in his office with his secretary was physical. There were too many works to catalog properly. Did von Behr wish to tell the

Reichsmarschall that a painting was by Boucher when it was, in fact, by Courbet?

Only a fool would mistake a Boucher for a Courbet, Éliane thought. Courbet would as likely paint a sprawlingly naked Callisto on the verge of being ravaged by Jupiter as he would paint a drudge tidying a museum. Was she the only person in the room who knew anything about French art? That might be an advantage in her search for answers.

But another question was now begging to be added to the thousands she already had. The men had mentioned the Reichsmarschall. There was only one Reichsmarschall: Hermann Göring, Hitler's deputy. Why would such an important Nazi visit this relatively minor museum when he must have so many more important things to do?

Explanations were elusive that day and all throughout winter as truck-loads of artworks arrived daily. Works by Monet, Sisley, Degas, Frago-nard, Velásquez, Titian, Rubens, Boucher, van Gogh, Renoir, Gaugin. So much art that it was almost vulgar, as if Athena herself, goddess of the arts, were romping through the galleries, indulging in an aesthetic orgy. The white-coated art historians, like surgeons sizing up limbs, attended to this waiting room of lost souls, trying, and often failing, to organize them into schools or years or some such category, to decide which paint-ings were amoral and thus consigned to the Room of the Martyrs. Éliane stored everything away in her mind, not knowing what use the informa-tion might be but unable to simply do nothing.

However, the brutal winter soon curbed Éliane's ambitions to do anything other than survive. Food rationing was put in place but, in order to get ration coupons, one had to queue at the Mairie. The first time she did so, Éliane waited for five hours in a long line of people, progressed only a little and eventually gave up. From then on she paid one of her neighbor's children to queue for her, like so many Parisiennes were forced to do.

It wasn't just ration coupons that had to be queued for—it was the food itself. Almost all her money had vanished by the time she'd paid the same child to line up and buy food for her and as the cost of everything, even bread, spiraled.

There had been a glut of peaches and grapes throughout fall—so much so that she had never wanted to see a peach again. But, by winter, she measured the days by what her neighbor's child was able to procure. Always a knob of bread and some *café nationale*—a mix of ground chickpeas and acorns that served as coffee.

Some days, "A potato," he would say, handing it over and she would smile. Potato, bread, and coffee was filling enough, she had learned.

But the next day: "A rutabaga," he said, and she had to force herself not to grumble.

She boiled the rutabaga that night, staring hard at it, wishing it might transfigure into an egg. She hadn't seen an egg for almost a fortnight and the mere thought of an omelet made her mouth water. But the rutabaga remained the color of a bruise and its watery, limp taste had her going to bed early; experience had taught her that sleep could sometimes quash the hunger pains.

Once a week at most, the boy might appear with a piece of meat so small it would fit into the palm of her hand; those were the best days of all. On those nights, she made dinner last for almost an hour, cutting off tiny piece after tiny piece, letting it sit on her tongue, before chewing slowly. But then the meat would be gone and she would be sitting alone in her apartment. Without the distraction of the viands, winter pressed itself more forcefully in through the shuttered windows, making her shiver. There was no coal available anywhere.

She retrieved one of the old art books she'd hidden from her father in a cavity behind the mirror on her bedroom wall and ran her hand over the cover in apology. She didn't open the pages and look inside, merely ripped the book in half, put it in the grate and set fire to it. Then she bathed hurriedly and readied herself for bed. By the time she slid under the covers, wearing her coat, scarf, gloves, and a knitted balaclava over her head, the fire had died.

Her hands were as red as the devil and throbbed from chilblains. Her stomach roared in protest. Rain smacked against the window. A Nazi shouted *"Achtung!"* on the street outside. Éliane shut her eyes and tried to think about something nice, but couldn't.

The next morning she dragged herself out of bed, shivering, hands looking even more raw than yesterday. The glut now was lemons and she cut one into eighths like an orange, pulled off the peel, closed her eyes and shoved it into her mouth, making herself chew and swallow. She had a sip of water, then ate the next piece of lemon, and then the next until she had finished.

Before she left for work, she watered the turnips, carrots, and potatoes she was growing in planter boxes near the window. She didn't have the space to grow as much as she wanted but, in just a few days, she thought they might be ready to harvest and then she would be able to add perhaps half a carrot to her daily diet. Or even use one of each vegetable to make a broth; it would have to last the week, to be sure, but imagine having a warm entrée of soup before her potato-and-bread main course.

She realized she had closed her eyes, as if she were dreaming of the most grandiose pleasures. Her laugh rang strangely through the empty apartment. She left then, hating the silence that replied to her. The stink of the rabbits her neighbors kept and killed for food hung rankly in the stairwell.

She hardly cared about artworks at all now.

FIVE

At the museum, where she had never expected to find anything to ease her desolation, Madame Valland took two potatoes out of her bag and handed them to Éliane. "For you."

"I can't," Éliane protested even though she wanted nothing more than to eat each potato raw right then and there.

"The Louvre gardens have been given over to vegetables," Madame Valland said, putting the food onto the desk in front of Éliane. "If you stop each night in the Cour Carrée, there will be a basket waiting for you."

She was going to cry over potatoes. Where once tears had been saved for death and heartbreak, now they fell for food, and for friendship. "Thank you, Madame," Éliane whispered.

Two eggs appeared beside the potatoes. "I have family in the country who send me food. I can't eat it all."

Éliane stretched out a finger to touch the eggshell, to make sure it was real and then she almost did the same to Madame Valland. Was she real?

Instead, she shrugged off her coat—her mother's old fur, which had been bought secondhand twenty years ago at the Puces. The slurry falling from the sky that morning had made it deadweight and dripping. "I'd be better off wearing an animal," she said, somehow finding another laugh bubbling from within at the idea of striding around Paris with a bear on her back.

Madame Valland's eyes twinkled behind her glasses. "That's the spirit you need."

And Éliane understood that Madame was an ally. In this strange world where everything surprised her—the unnerving rat-a-tat of German boots, the sudden roar of a tour bus full of German soldiers pointing at the sights of a city they now thought of as theirs—and in this strange museum where she had once made a vow, only to forget it in the face of hunger, an ally was the most precious thing of all.

She looked across at Madame Valland, who was tucking her bag into a drawer with an altogether different smile on her face than the one she showed to von Behr. The light in her eyes was spiritual, as if she had, not God, but some other, greater purpose. As if she had made a vow to herself and had kept it.

"Madame," Éliane began, not at all sure what she was about to ask.

"Call me Rose," Madame said.

Before Éliane could say anything more, König appeared. "Excuse me," he said, eyes on Éliane. "There's to be an exhibition tomorrow. It's very important that everything goes well. We'll need you," he indicated Éliane with a shy half-smile, "to serve champagne to the guests."

"She will be pleased to help." Rose's deferential smile had returned and the transformation from a woman who had inspired something in Éliane moments ago to an inconsequential and subservient creature was astonishing. Indeed, König didn't even wait for Rose to finish speaking before he left.

After he'd gone, Éliane said to Rose, "I don't know if I can serve them champagne."

"Of course you can," Rose said briskly. "Imagine the conversations you'll overhear. I need to check on the heaters." She slipped out.

Éliane took some time to get started with her own work that day. Her conversation with Rose turned over and over in her mind. Rose had said vegetables would be waiting for Éliane at the Cour Carrée.

That meant Rose had been speaking to Monsieur Jaujard. Éliane had
been forbidden to talk to her former boss and, she assumed, Rose had
too. Rose was very good at behaving in a way that meant most people
overlooked her; indeed, Éliane's first impressions of her had been that
she was a biddable maiden aunt whose sole purpose in life was to be
obliging to everyone. But why would someone who wanted to oblige the
Germans imply that eavesdropping on those same Germans would be a
reward for Éliane tomorrow, a reward that would assuage her guilt over
serving them champagne?

More questions. But of a different nature now. Had Rose also cried
over the hostages in the galleries, imprisoned not just in oil and watercolor, but in a frame of Nazi guns and greed?

* * *

The next day, the day of the exhibition, Éliane paid careful attention
to her face and her hair, coloring her lips a deep red and brushing on
a thick coat of mascara that brightened her eyes to Paris green, a color
whose lucent beauty hid its true danger. She arranged the loose curls of
her blonde hair around her shoulders, and selected a navy dress that was
gathered at the shoulders to emphasize the yoked sleeves and the softly
draped bodice. It belted at the waist, highlighting her figure, before the
skirt flared gently out.

At the museum, von Behr prowled up and down the entry foyer, cap
pulled low to hide his false eye. "Champagne," he called to her when he
saw her. "Now!"

Éliane tried out a smile of her own.

He stopped his stalking. "König!" he called. And his nephew came
running, dressed in his official blue-gray Luftwaffe regalia, trousers bal-
looning over high-shine black boots. He skidded to a stop when he saw
Éliane.

Von Behr laughed. "Doesn't our little fräulein scrub up well?"

König nodded keenly, before catching himself amid a too-obvious fervor.

Von Behr laughed again. "Your job today, Mademoiselle, is to make sure our guests never run out of champagne."

"*Certainement*, Monsieur," Éliane replied courteously, understanding that her smile and her makeup and her dress and her obedience had pleased von Behr, and made her job of finding out answers to questions—who was the mysterious exhibition for, what would happen to the artworks afterward, why were the works being exhibited?—much easier by ensuring she spent the day in the galleries rather than the office. The sensation of hunger vanished in the face of her determination to put the day to good use.

The purr of a car pulling up outside had both von Behr and König standing stiffly to attention. Éliane took up a bottle and waited with it at the bottom of the stairs. The doors of the museum opened.

First to enter was none other than Reichsmarschall Göring, second-in-command to Adolf Hitler, and head of the Luftwaffe, whose planes had perhaps killed her family. Today he wasn't wearing one of the brilliantly white uniforms he was usually photographed in. In fact, he looked like a vagrant, sporting an ankle-length beige coat that buttoned over his girth, and a crumpled hat on his head.

Éliane was so distracted by the scruffiness of the man who was second-in-charge of the nation that had vanquished her country that she didn't immediately notice the person who had walked through the doors with Göring, standing beside him in a place reserved for an important adviser. It meant that he had warning before their eyes met—but she didn't. When she finally saw his face, nearly all of the self-control that had kept her countenance impassively arranged vanished and she almost dropped the bottle of champagne on the ground—an act that would surely get her fired.

And for a minute she wanted that. Wanted to be told to leave so she could walk out the doors and forget that Xavier, a man she had loved, was chaperoning the Reichsmarschall of Germany into a Parisian museum.

Her hands gripped the bottle just in time.

"Are you going to pour that or strangle it?" Xavier asked coolly, in German.

Göring laughed.

Her shock saved her. She continued to stare, rather than reply, and dimly heard von Behr say contemptuously to Xavier, "She doesn't speak German."

And now she was done for. Xavier would reveal her subterfuge and von Behr would fire her. Or…

You are never to speak about your work. You saw the guards outside, von Behr had said to her three months ago, back when he had thought she couldn't understand the language in which most of the museum's operations were conducted. She looked at von Behr's wolfish face and knew he would do nothing so kind as merely firing her.

She wanted to shiver. She wanted to recoil. Instead, she met Xavier's gaze and used the memory of Yolande to make sure she didn't look away.

After only a moment, his eyes left her face and he spoke in careless French. "We're all thirsty."

Never had it been so hard to tilt a bottle, to pour liquor cleanly into a glass, to judge the upward rush of foam so it didn't overflow. Never had it been so hard to breathe. *Just a minute more and you can escape*, she told herself. Thirty seconds. Fifteen. She was done.

But then König—shy, blundering König—caught hold of her hand. "You've hurt yourself, Mademoiselle?" he questioned.

There was nothing she wanted less than to have her chilblains, the marks of her suffering, pointed out to these men. Her first thought was to hide her fingers behind the champagne bottle rather than tell a Nazi she was burning her art books to keep herself warm. But the same fire that had allowed her to look Xavier in the face just now until he had been the one to turn away made her say to König, innocently, "I hope it isn't contagious."

König immediately released her hand and Éliane felt another of those strange and surprising smiles begin to creep over her face at the success of her mischief.

"You can make love to her later." Xavier's mocking voice broke in, erasing all the humor from the moment and making Éliane's cheeks burn as furiously as König's, with both rage and mortification.

She knew she needed to leave the room and compose herself. She indicated the empty bottle to von Behr. "I'll fetch some more," she said.

He nodded, before turning to his guests and clapping Xavier on the back as they spoke.

Éliane went straight to the bathroom, sat on the lid of the toilet, and covered her face with her hands, trying to believe it wasn't Xavier out there. When had he returned from London? And—a question that made her head throb, and her heart too—why was he laughing with Nazis?

The bathroom door squeaked. Someone came in, pushed open the doors of the other two stalls. Éliane could see a pair of black men's shoes stop outside her locked cubicle door. Then Xavier's voice: "Éliane."

Not Ellie.

"What are you doing?" he asked.

Her voice was low and black-edged with fear. "What a person normally does in the bathroom." *Crying*, she didn't say.

"If they find out you speak German, they will kill you."

They will kill you. It was worse than she'd thought. What *was* she doing? Putting on lipstick and smiling at a Nazi and thinking that would get her some answers. But, really, how was any of this her business?

She swallowed. "Then my life is in your hands."

She unlocked the stall door, pushed it open and walked past without looking at him. "We'll see how much value you place upon it."

* * *

Xavier returned to the main gallery soon after Éliane, who had recovered only minimal self-command.

"What a collection," she heard Xavier say. "Shall we?"

He led Göring over to a painting and spoke about its provenance, the artist's use of grisaille in the underpainting, as if he were Göring's artistic adviser, a job for which he was certainly qualified. As she listened to him speak, she couldn't help but study him, trying to be sure this was really Xavier, not a man who merely looked and sounded like him.

He wore an impeccable dark suit. She'd always thought he looked devastatingly handsome in a suit and today was no exception. In fact, over the last nine months, he'd become more charismatic than ever, wearing a careless smile and an easy confidence that caught the eye and held it, fixed on him.

Göring stepped forward to see more closely the techniques Xavier was speaking of. The Reichsmarschall was not a man of the world right now, but a man stunned, like a child visiting a toy shop for the first time. His eyes stroked figures on canvas, traversed the curves of bodies laid bare on wood. His pace was slow and careful. He paid special attention to the Fêtes Galantes—lewd and nude depictions of eighteenth-century garden romps—and to Boucher's *Venus*. Éliane saw Venus flinch in a way that an oil-painted figure could not possibly do and she knew she'd been wrong. Göring wasn't like a child in a toy store but a man in a brothel. What did that make Xavier?

She had to close her eyes against the thought. It was too much. She had made love to Xavier. She had *loved* Xavier. She wanted to be sick.

Everything suffers when power and money are put in front of avaricious men. And I'm starting to think there are more avaricious men than there are decent ones, Xavier had once said to her. Perhaps what he was doing paid very well. Perhaps the heartless man who'd told her he was leaving right after he slept with her for the first time was the real Xavier.

And so many Parisiennes were working for the Nazis as if they were just ordinary human beings, which the Vichy government insisted they were. As if Occupation was the way life would be, always. As if the restaurant owner who did not provide a menu written in German, or the salesman who turned his back on anyone in a Nazi uniform, were the aberrations and everyone else was normal. As if what Éliane felt about the Germans was both foolish and atypical. But it wasn't. *She* wasn't. And Xavier was not worth her heartbreak.

She opened her eyes and turned her attention to the painless and uncomplicated act of serving refreshments. No other guests arrived. The fuss and ceremony were for Göring alone. But she still didn't know why.

Göring was close to Vermeer's *Astronomer* now. The moment Xavier said the word *Vermeer,* desire passed in the plainest of languages over Göring's face.

"I've always wanted a Vermeer," Göring said to Xavier. "I narrowly missed out on one in Austria."

"I believe that one now belongs to the Führer," Xavier said.

Göring's response was a curt nod. He splayed his legs, one hand resting atop his cane, and studied the painting. As he did so, he slipped a hand into his pocket and something tinkled within, like coins. He withdrew both his hand and the items, moving them around his palm as if they soothed him. Éliane stepped forward with the bottle of champagne and saw that the musical notes came from a dozen emeralds rolling through Göring's fingers like the most extravagant worry beads and that the jewels and the Vermeer, far from soothing him, thrilled him.

Éliane's curiosity had brought her close enough that she knew she had to stifle the gasp that was, right now, escaping her. Fortunately Xavier, at the same time, began pointing out the objects in the painting: the strange diagram of circles on the wall, the astrolabe of worlds unknown, the open book on the table.

When his spiel ended, she waited, certain there would be more. But it seemed as if, along with his scruples, he had lost both his fine mind and his artistic sensibility for he had not once mentioned the astronomer's hands. They were the most important part of the painting. The Xavier of old would never have overlooked the *elan vital* of the work.

She did not know the man in front of her at all.

"I want it," Göring said to Xavier.

I want it. The painting was Édouard de Rothschild's. There was no possible way for Göring to acquire it. What was going on?

Éliane's eyes swept away from the painting, passing over Madame Valland. Her own confusion was expressed on the older woman's face. But that would only be possible if Madame understood German too, which she supposedly did not.

Xavier and the Reichsmarschall moved along the gallery to another painting, one Éliane did not know. It was a magnificent work and she felt her heart open to it immediately, had to still her feet to prevent herself from walking toward it.

It was a painting of a couple embracing and it somehow held within it the history of every famous artistic kiss—Klimt's, Rodin's, Hayez's—but this one surpassed them all, borrowing from their brilliance and making a masterpiece. The couple were framed by a window embrasure, the night sky an oceanic blue above them, punctuated by a white circle of moon. The female figure's hand was on the man's cheek. Her face was rapture captured in oil. The male figure's face was almost obscured by the woman leaning in toward him, but for the single exquisite tear of lovesickness that could be glimpsed in the corner of his eye.

Éliane wanted to fall into that painting. And then she saw, in the corner, the artist's name: Luc Dufort. She stared in astonishment.

It must be the piece he sold to Édouard de Rothschild. Why had she ever doubted her brother's talent? He had made something extraordinary. And she wished she knew where he was hiding, wished she could write to him and tell him that she was sorry.

"Is this one important?" Göring asked Xavier.

Xavier shook his head emphatically. "A minor work by a minor artist. Modernist. Degenerate."

How could she have ever loved such a man?

"Take it to the room upstairs," von Behr ordered her.

But stupefaction had slowed Éliane's reactions and she didn't move.

"*Allez-y!*" von Behr snapped. "Unless you want another one?" He lifted his hand.

Éliane raised a protective arm to her cheek, hating herself for her weakness. Xavier said to von Behr, smiling, "Save your energy for Chez Marguerite."

Chez Marguerite was a brothel. These men were going from a gallery in which they had been salivating over paintings they had no right to possess to a brothel where they would do the same to women. Éliane took the painting off the wall, knowing she had to leave the room before she cried.

* * *

On her way home from the museum, Éliane stopped at the courtyard of the Louvre and found the basket Rose said would be waiting for her. She rummaged through it and found not only more potatoes, but leeks and a turnip too. And right at the bottom nestled a tub of cold cream. Éliane pulled it out slowly.

She knew almost all Parisians used the murky gray market that sat outside both the legitimate and impossible way of doing things with ration coupons, and the bribery and corruption of the black market, a place where only Germans and collaborators profited, and which she would never support. The gray market was a Parisian going to the country every weekend to buy the vegetables and meat that were more plentiful there and bringing them back and distributing them to those who had no relatives in the country from whom they could get food. The gray market was Monsieur Jaujard—for who else could have done it—slipping a tub of unobtainable cold cream into a basket under the cover of potatoes.

But how had Rose already conveyed to Monsieur Jaujard that Éliane's hands were sore and she needed cold cream? And where had he found it? No matter. It was a lovely end to a terrible day.

Her hands were so painful that she slipped off her gloves, opened the tub and slathered them in cream right then and there. Then she walked on to her apartment, trying to relocate her spirits, trying to let the kindness make up for everything else.

She hadn't quite managed it when she entered the *galerie*, climbed up three flights and found a surprise waiting for her that nearly made her tip backward down the stairs. Sitting on the top step was a young woman with blonde hair covered by a scarf, and blue eyes no longer wide.

"Angélique?" she whispered, terrified that she was being visited by ghosts.

"Éliane!" the ghost-woman cried, flinging herself at her sister.

Éliane's arms closed around her. Angélique was warm and real but much too thin. "I thought you were all…" She couldn't say it. "Are the others inside?"

Éliane started to move away, to open the door, to feast her heart upon Yolande and Ginette and Jacqueline and her mother but Angélique wouldn't let her go. Instead, Angélique sobbed the same way Éliane had done when she had thought she was all alone in Paris.

"They aren't…" Angélique hiccuped. "They…"

Éliane's joy splintered. But she didn't let Angélique see. Instead, she led her into the apartment, sat her down, made her a cup of coffee and sat beside her.

"The Stukas flew over," Angélique said bleakly. "I lost Ginette in the panic. And the others…" She buried her face in Éliane's shoulder. "Afterward, I had to close Yolande's eyes."

It was almost too much. Almost too hard to hold back her own sorrow and concentrate on giving Angélique the comfort she needed. Éliane stared fixedly at the ceiling, ignored the ache in her throat and held her sister.

"It took so long to get back here," Angélique said at last. "I…I took all the money from *Maman* but she'd lost some of it and there wasn't much left. I had to work whenever I could for food and to earn enough for the train." She looked down at her blistered hands and Éliane thanked God for those blisters, which had come from working in a field perhaps, or in a house sweeping floors, rather than from the kind of work Xavier and Göring had joked about today.

"I tried to send a letter," Angélique continued. "But they said most mail from the Free Zone wasn't reaching the Occupied Zone."

Éliane took her sister's face in her hands and spoke softly to her. "You are so brave. And you're home now. I can look after you."

Angélique's face crumpled in a way that reminded Éliane, bittersweetly, of Yolande.

Later, Éliane told her sister that she'd been moved to the Jeu de Paume. She didn't mention the paintings crowded inside, or Xavier. She'd been warned by von Behr not to say anything to anyone and she didn't want to put her sister at risk. Nor had she the courage to tell

Angélique that the man who had once brought food and comfort to their apartment was now a friend of the Germans.

"You're working for the Nazis." Angélique's voice was bleak, accusatory.

Éliane flinched.

She stood up and walked to the window, not wanting to become angry with her sister, who didn't understand this new life in Paris.

Below, on the street, Éliane saw the café opposite that now boasted a German menu. A warm fire blazed inside and German patrons wearing bayonet gray ate large, hot, steaming meals. The café owner and his daughter looked healthy and robust. Their hands were unblemished by the cold. The patronage of Nazis ensured they suffered no deprivation. They were doing what they'd been told to do by the Vichy government.

Just like Éliane had told herself she must continue to do her job so that she had food to eat. So that she could do something for the kidnapped artworks. But what had she done? Eavesdropped on a few conversations. What good was that? Was she, perhaps, as bad as Xavier?

The Astronomer should still be hanging in the Rothschild mansion. A Reichsmarschall should not run his acquisitive eyes over a painting that had stood proudly unmolested in French hands for decades.

Strangely, Yolande's voice sounded ghostlike in her ear: *Éliane must come too.* But Éliane had stayed. And if she didn't make something of that, then she would fail her sisters again, as she had in June.

She remembered how she had felt that afternoon when she had seen Luc's painting of the couple: replenished. In a city of people who were cold and hungry, that was no small thing. The world, and the people of Paris, had need of their art.

"Why are you working for the Nazis?" Angélique's voice was insistent. "Why?"

Why. That was what had been driving Éliane until now. Trying to understand why the paintings were being gathered, for what purpose.

But what if she thought instead about how much she already knew? Who owned the paintings. Which paintings were in the Jeu de Paume. What if she wrote it down: the name of every stolen painting, every thieved sculpture so that sometime in the future, the world would know what the Nazis had done.

They will kill you, Xavier had said.

Earlier that week, seven anthropologists from the Museum of Man who had printed and distributed an underground newspaper urging resistance against the Nazis had been shot. What would the Nazis do to Éliane if she did write down what she knew?

They will kill you. The words repeated in her head but, this time, she didn't shiver. She was hardly alive now.

"No, Angélique," she said resolutely. "I'm working *against* the Nazis."

SIX

The next morning, as the exhibition continued, Éliane waited for an opportunity to take her first step. She was required to pour champagne again and she did so while von Behr gestured to at least twenty chests lined along one wall. When she saw them, Éliane couldn't help the exclamation that escaped her. They contained jewelry even more astonishing than the French crown jewels. Diamonds and rubies and emeralds and gold and pearl.

"They were acquired from the Rothschilds," König said. "We know how fond you are of such treasures, Reichsmarschall."

Indeed, Göring was lavishly adorned that day, with stacks of precious gems ringing his fingers, a jeweled baton swinging carelessly in his hand. He wore a spectacularly bright white uniform on which an embroidered eagle, its wings outspread and ready to pounce, soared over the breast pocket.

"Perhaps you can look at those last," Xavier said to Göring. "It's not my area of expertise. I have a meeting with a dealer this afternoon that I can't miss."

Éliane waited for Göring to upbraid Xavier for putting a dealer ahead of the Reichsmarschall, for speaking with such arrogance. She saw von Behr bristle but the Reichsmarschall nodded.

"We'll begin with the paintings," Göring said, motioning Xavier forward.

And Éliane realized that Xavier had changed utterly. He had the same dark hair, the same brown eyes flecked with gold. But, over almost a year, he'd become someone who had the true measure of the Nazis' second-in-command; Xavier's lack of deference, his self-importance, and obvious knowledge of art made the Reichsmarschall respect him.

At noon the men left the gallery for lunch. Éliane judged from von Behr's laughter, Göring's lusty bellows, and Xavier's self-satisfied smile that they wouldn't return for some time. So she made herself take her first step toward doing something. She slipped away to von Behr's office on the pretext of collecting the dirty glasses.

It was impossible not to be afraid, not to hear her own heart trying to alert the museum staff to what she was doing. She tiptoed in and almost screamed when she saw another figure at von Behr's desk.

Rose. Her eyes were damp.

Éliane walked over to the desk, eyes fixed on the paper Rose was staring at. She forgot her heartbeat, forgot that von Behr might return, forgot everything except the need to see what the paper said.

She read it once. Then she read it again. When she looked at Rose, her own eyes were wet too.

She had her answers now.

Typed in black on white was a set of orders pertaining to all the so-called goods without owners now imprisoned in the gallery, goods that belonged to Jewish families: the Rothschilds, the Seligmanns, the Wildensteins and many more. The orders had been signed by the Reichsmarschall.

The artworks would not be returned to their rightful owners. Instead, they would henceforth be divided into five categories. Category one: artworks for the Führer, who would have first choice from the spoils. Category two: artworks for Göring, who could take what was left after the Führer had satisfied himself.

Éliane's mind grappled with the fact that Göring had, with a stroke of his pen, taken complete control of the Jeu de Paume. It had been bad enough when Éliane had thought the paintings were being placed under German "protection" at the museum but now she understood the artworks had not come to the museum to be protected. They had come to be exhibited to Göring and then taken away by the Nazi elite. The Ausweis, the armed guards, the secrecy all made sense now. The Jeu de Paume was not a storage facility, but a transit facility. The Nazis were thieves, plundering art on a scale so immense it was almost breathtaking.

Éliane laid a hand on Rose's shoulder.

What would happen if anyone found them in von Behr's office with this incendiary in their hands?

The clock struck the half hour.

"We need to go," Éliane said as the world outside returned with a sudden punch of color and noise.

"Turn right when you reach the corridor," Rose said firmly. "I'll turn left. Then we won't be seen near this office together."

Éliane followed Rose's instructions, which had been given quickly, as if she'd thought such things through, as if she had, in fact, been carrying out some sort of what—surveillance? Surely it was ridiculous to imagine Rose spying on the Nazis?

Or maybe it wasn't ridiculous at all.

* * *

Soon after Göring and the others returned from lunch, shouts were heard outside, the doors of the museum were flung open and Monsieur Jaujard, accompanied by Count Wolff-Metternich, appeared, both walking determinedly forward. Éliane remembered that Monsieur had thought the Count, who was the head of the Kunstschutz—the German art protection unit—was on the French people's side even though he was working for the Germans. He had decreed that the artworks owned by the Musées Nationaux—which included all the Louvre artworks— could stay safely in the depots they had been moved to. *Thank goodness*, she thought. *He will stop the exhibition. He will stop Göring.*

"I would like to accompany you on your tour of the museum," Metternich said to Göring. "The Kunstschutz is responsible for the safety of works taken into protective custody." Monsieur Jaujard stood gravefaced by his side, eyes flicking just once to Éliane, a desperate plea written there.

Göring smiled at Xavier. "Another organization to deal with." He turned on Metternich. "I am in charge here. And I have with me the people I need. My guards can escort you out."

The emphasis on the word "escort" made it perfectly clear that force would be used if needed.

Silence, thick as impasto, coated the gallery.

All the evils had well and truly escaped Pandora's jar and had gathered in this museum, closing the lid tightly on hope.

And Éliane understood that she and Rose were truly alone in the Jeu de Paume with criminals who would silence anyone who might protest, criminals who were stealing artworks from French citizens because it was easier to do than stealing artworks owned by the French state: that level of theft would be much harder to conceal. The smart thing to do would be to convince herself that none of this was her business. But Monsieur Jaujard's glance had told her this *was* her business.

She circled the gallery as the art historians began to remove the paintings from the walls and pack them into crates. Into one crate went a Goya, a Rembrandt, and Vermeer's *Astronomer*. *Twenty pieces*, she told herself firmly. Even if she could remember just twenty artworks then, later, those twenty paintings could perhaps be recovered. But if the paintings were leaving—where were they going?

The rubbish bins were out by the loading dock. She picked up an empty champagne box and hurried out.

On the dock, she saw crates being numbered: *H1, H2, H3* and so on. And *G1, G2*... After reading the note on von Behr's desk she knew the letters meant: H for Hitler and G for Göring. But where would Hitler and Göring have the artworks sent? That was another piece of information she needed to uncover.

The first truckload of crates pulled away. There was only one *Astronomer* in the world. And it had vanished.

Éliane realized Rose was on the loading dock too, smiling her *Mona Lisa* smile: a smile that hid nothing because she had nothing to hide; or a smile that hid much more than anyone suspected. Éliane knew it wouldn't be good for both of them to be out there. She caught Rose's eye and she thought Rose gave her a quick nod so she went back inside and stood, hand resting on an eighteenth-century sculpture.

"Mademoiselle Dufort!"

She turned her start of surprise into an eager smile for von Behr. "Yes, Monsieur," she said politely.

"Our art adviser," he indicated Xavier, who was laughing with Göring on the other side of the gallery, "tells me these belong with the degenerate works. Take them upstairs." Von Behr gestured to a stack of modernist paintings that had been singled out like lepers.

"Certainly," she replied, glad for any job that put her in such close contact with the paintings.

Eight times she went up and down the stairs with a painting in hand, storing its title and the artist's name in her mind. On the ninth occasion, as she was committing the details of a Monet to memory, she heard a sound outside: Madame Valland's voice, loud. "Where has that girl got herself to?"

Rose appeared and whispered, "They want us to tidy the gallery. Von Behr was wondering why you were taking so long." Then she nodded at a painting that hung on one of the walls. "She looks like you," Rose said.

Éliane glanced up and saw that Rose had pointed to Luc's painting of the embracing couple set against a blazing moon and a sky that made her believe that blue was the true color of love and passion, like the hottest part of a flame, and that everyone had, for centuries, been wrong in believing red to be the hue of hearts and ardor.

The loud rap of a shoe sounded on the wooden floor. Éliane, lost in contemplation, assumed it was Rose moving to the exit.

"Her hair isn't quite like mine," she said to Rose.

She gasped when a man's voice replied derisively, "No, your hair is unpaintable," as if nobody in the world would ever want to capture museum-drudge Éliane's hair in oil on canvas.

Xavier fixed on her the eyes of the unmoved. "Be careful, Mademoiselle. You have taken a long time up here."

She blanched. He had given her two warnings now. She understood the subtext: there would not be a third.

Still, the hurt of having been so thoroughly used made her lift her chin, fixing her own eyes on Xavier now. "Just go downstairs and tell them," she said stoutly, even though she could feel her heart trembling with the fear she refused to show. "Tell them I speak German. It could hardly hurt me more."

She hadn't meant to say that last sentence; hadn't meant to admit that his running away to England on the same night he'd made love to her, and her shocking discovery of his traitorous relationship with the Nazis meant anything at all to her.

He smiled, a cold and contemptuous twist of the mouth that would have perfectly suited von Behr. "Holding on to that knowledge is more useful than giving it away," he said. "It will ensure your compliance—at least until the work Göring requires is done and we don't need you or your compliance anymore."

He left then, which meant she was saved from hurling the nearest painting at him in the same way she'd thrown the engagement ring he'd given her.

She stood very still for a long moment, repeating one word in her mind: *don't*. Don't seethe at Xavier. Don't think about him at all. Don't waste your anger and your fury and your passion on him. Let it burn into something useful instead: the resolution to not give up. Not until every one of the thousands of paintings now in this museum, stolen by Hitler and Göring, was restituted to its rightful owner.

All she needed was help. And she was almost sure she knew someone who was on her side.

* * *

Éliane lurked in the Tuileries until she saw Rose exit the museum. Then she followed her along the Grande Allée, through the Jardins and across to the Louvre, where Rose hurried into the courtyard and entered the private apartment of Monsieur Jaujard.

Éliane waited only a moment before she knocked on Monsieur Jaujard's door.

It opened.

Rose smiled at her. "I was hoping you'd come."

Behind her, at a table, sat Monsieur Jaujard. And Luc. Her brother was involved too. Luc raised his glass at her and she felt her whole self beam.

And Éliane knew there was no going back from this moment, whatever it was; that the minute she stepped inside, she would be caught up in something larger than herself, something substantial, something that would both scar her heart and mend her heart, something with joie de vivre and with grace. Something like art.

Or, she thought as the door closed and Luc lowered his glass and her smile dropped and she remembered that she and Rose were custodians of a secret the Nazis would kill to have kept: something that might be the end of them all.

PART TWO
SAINT-JEAN-CAP-FERRAT, FRANCE, 2015

SEVEN

Euphoric sunshine beamed down upon Remy from an equally rhapsodic sky, as if the elements were demanding that she step into line and appear similarly joyful—sorrow and the French Riviera were obviously incompatible. Remy frowned. This was why she shouldn't get up early, and almost never did anymore, except that last night had been so bad she hadn't even managed to fall asleep as she usually did at first light.

She climbed out of bed, intending to draw the curtains on the unrelenting dazzle. When she reached the window, she saw a man sitting downstairs on her terrace, in her sun lounger, reading a book. He must have sensed the movement at the window because he looked up, shock erasing the repose that his body had worn as easily as vintage Levi's. He leapt up, strode across the terrace and disappeared down the stairs that led to the sea below.

Remy tugged the curtains closed. One thing she'd counted on was that here, in a house accessed only by a private road that served just two residences, she'd be truly alone. *Don't come back, whoever you are*, she thought.

She lay back down on the bed, begging sleep to claim her but it continued to ignore her so she rose again, slipped an antique cream peignoir over her liquid satin 1930s slip and dragged herself downstairs. She made coffee and rummaged around for the key to the terrace doors, which she hadn't opened since she'd arrived in Saint-Jean-Cap-Ferrat yesterday.

Once on the terrace, she felt her body instinctively stretch into the sun and her limbs almost soften. She turned her head from side to side, easing out the kinks, eyes sweeping over a formal parterre garden of topiary-edged ponds ornamented by urns and delineated by gravel paths. A series of water cascades rose up to the Temple of Love atop the hill, a copy—one of the gardeners had told her when she'd first visited, nearly two years ago—of the Petit Trianon at Versailles. In front of her, the Mediterranean frolicked resplendently, waves flickering up to kiss the sky, carefree in a way she could no longer be.

She turned her back on it all and dropped into the sun lounger. There was a small box of books beside it, as if the man she'd seen earlier had planned to spend a lot of time lying there, reading. She flicked desultorily through the books, many of which bore the distinct orange and white covers of Penguin Classics. Scuffed pages and penciled prices on the inside indicated they'd been purchased secondhand, perhaps from the book market in nearby Nice. It was an eclectic mix—*A Spy in the House of Love* by Anaïs Nin, *In Cold Blood* by Truman Capote, and Angela Carter's *The Bloody Chamber*. Remy picked up the last and began to read until she could feel the sun burning her face. Then she stood and faced the water again. She would go for a swim. Cleanse herself. That was why she'd come, wasn't it?

In the internal patio of the house, a mosaic-tiled double-story void lined with caramel-toned Verona marble columns, suitcases and boxes overflowed discordantly. From them, she extracted a strapless, powder blue, 1950s Catalina bathing suit. White trim ran across the bust and a flourish of white bow sat on one hip. She hid herself under a Mexican sombrero, also from the fifties, as well as a pair of cat eye sunglasses that were retro rather than true vintage. Sunscreen, a towel, a water bottle, *The Bloody Chamber* and she was ready.

She descended the steps, realizing halfway down that people were gathered on the far side of the cove. Her neighbors perhaps, although that was a loose term considering her gardens stretched on for a good two hundred meters before meeting their property. The cove and the road were the only things they shared.

She didn't look across, so there was no need to wave or be drawn into conversation, just dragged a sun lounger out of the little storage shed, dropped her things onto it and dived into the water. She gasped at the sudden cold, but also the forgotten feel of the ocean all over her, something she'd once been so used to. She plunged downward, shutting out the thoughts that always intruded—the reasons why she'd stopped swimming in the sea in Australia—stroking out until she was tired. Then she returned to the shore and collapsed onto her lounger, lying still, eyes closed, not reading and not thinking, while her body recovered from the exercise.

When at last she opened her eyes, she gasped again, but in fright. Right beside her was a child, a girl, perhaps five years old. The girl smiled and all Remy could do was stare until the tears started up, too fast to hide.

A man approached, calling out, "What are you up to, Molly?" Then, to Remy, "Sorry if she's bothering you."

He came close enough to see Remy's face and he stared. At the same moment, the child registered that Remy's response was not normal. The girl began to cry, properly, the way Remy wished she could. She jumped up, grabbed her bag and hurried back to the house.

What had she become? A woman who could not smile at children, but who made them cry instead.

* * *

Once safely on the terrace at the house, she sank into the sun lounger to catch her breath. The goal of her three-month sojourn in France was to forget, to recover, to reassemble herself into a human kind of being. So far, she'd failed miserably. She pulled out her phone and sent a text to her best friend Antoinette, who responded immediately and without sympathy, which was typical.

What do you expect? You've been in France for less than a week. Moving on from what you've been through takes years. Forgive yourself for today and forget about it. Go to the beach tomorrow. Small steps. xx

Remy put her phone down, knowing only Antoinette would be thoughtful enough to say small steps instead of baby steps. Which meant that the least she could do for Antoinette was to try the beach again tomorrow. She couldn't do any worse than she had today, so that at least was a comfort.

She pulled Angela Carter's book out of her bag and, as she did so, realized that the box of books had gone. She felt a twinge of disappointment. The eclectic mix had appealed to her. Perhaps the man, whoever he was, would realize one was missing and would come back to collect it. She would, in return, be gracious enough to let him use her lounger each morning provided he was gone by ten and that he left the box behind.

She found herself smiling, suddenly and shockingly. Some reflexes of the body never disappeared. But it was ridiculous that she couldn't even manage to get through a swim at the beach without crying and now, here she was, imagining herself bargaining for books with a stranger.

The day passed in macabre tales of wolves and murdering husbands and one with an ending so grim she had to put the book down and wipe her eyes over the fate of the Snow Child. The damp of tears was an altogether familiar thing but she didn't, for once, hate herself for it. She let that reflex of the body take her over just like her smile had and she cried herself empty, which made her realize that although she thought she'd been empty before, she hadn't been. So much grief, and the terrible anger too, was still inside her.

It was hard to move after such a bloodletting, but the doorbell sounded. Remy stepped cautiously toward the door, opening it to find a man standing there.

"I'm your neighbor," the man said in an American accent, gesturing to the house further along the private road.

Remy blushed a brilliant red. It was the man who'd seen her crying on the beach that morning.

"I wanted to apologize for Molly, my daughter. She's a curious kid and can sometimes be kind of annoying."

"She wasn't," Remy said. She could almost hear Antoinette's voice in her ear, telling her to explain for once, that putting the words into the universe might actually make her believe it had happened. That people would be less embarrassed by knowing than by accidentally discovering later, after they'd put their foot in it. The words came out, almost as if Antoinette were sticking her hands down Remy's throat and dragging them out. "I'm a bit overemotional. My husband and daughter died almost two years ago and your daughter is about the same age as mine. Seeing her made me... sad," she finished.

"Jesus Christ," the man said, looking stricken. "My wife died about a year ago. So I know how you feel."

No, you don't, Remy wanted to shout. I lost a husband and a child.

Then she felt shame sweep over her. It wasn't a bloody competition. Since when had she become so callous?

But of course she knew exactly when. It was in Sydney at half past four on the first of November 2013, when she'd answered the phone, expecting it to be a call about work, when instead it was a call that only happened to pretend people on television screens. A car accident. Catastrophic. The police officer's story, later: *Your husband was driving a little too fast and so was the other car and while it wasn't his fault, perhaps if everyone had been driving at the speed limit...* Then a pause, which was the worst thing of all.

Her husband was picking up their daughter because Remy's meeting had run late; she'd called him at the last minute and asked him to do the school run. He'd said he could, but he had a meeting straight after and it would all be a bit of a rush. That was why he was speeding: because Remy was stuck in a meeting.

Remy hadn't been there when her daughter died.

There was no forgiveness she could ever offer herself for that.

"Daddy!"

Remy blinked. The speeding cars drove away. Her daughter's face remained omnipresent.

Molly, the girl from the beach, appeared and Remy steeled herself.

"I told you to stay home," the man said.

"But I missed you," the girl said endearingly.

She pushed past her father, letting herself into the internal patio, having seen behind Remy what could only be described as a candy store for any little girl brought up on princess stories. "Look, Daddy!" she cried. "Dress-ups!"

"They're not really dress-ups," Remy said. "I sell vintage clothing," she explained to the man.

"Look!" Molly said again, and Remy winced as a three thousand dollar Givenchy gown from the 1960s was pulled over the head of a five-year-old.

The man smiled at his daughter. "I'm Matt, by the way. Matt Henry-Jones."

"Remy. Remy Lang. I think..."

She started to explain about the special nature of the clothes as Molly tossed the Givenchy onto the floor and picked up a very delicate 1920s dress with a tulle overlay. Her probing fingers stabbed straight through the tulle, leaving a hole Remy knew couldn't be easily mended.

"Oops," Matt said. "Girls and dresses, you know." He shrugged as if he expected camaraderie.

"I think it might be best," Remy said, trying not to be witchy, but needing to protect clothes that had lasted for decades and that were now being massacred, "if you don't touch anything else." She smiled beseech-ingly at the girl, who pouted.

"Just one more maybe," Matt said and Remy shuddered as the girl, who seemed to have an unerring sense for what was most valuable, zeroed in on a precious, museum-quality Vionnet.

"That one's worth about ten thousand dollars," Remy said firmly and Matt at last responded with parent-like behavior.

"Maybe leave it, sweetie," he said as Remy shepherded Molly to the door. The girl tried to duck and dodge back to the clothes with all the litheness of a professional football player.

Matt reached out an arm for his daughter. "I came over because my folks own the house next door. We're having a party tonight. They'd love you to come."

"I can't," she said automatically.

"Or won't?" Matt asked gently, as if perhaps he did know what kind of excuses one used to ensure life remained within one's control. "You don't have far to walk if you decide you want to go home."

The girl was making another attempt to get to the clothes. "All right," Remy said, in order to get Molly out of the house with only one irreparable gown in her wake. "What time?"

"From eight o'clock. Come on, you rascal." Matt finally caught his daughter around the waist. "Let's go back to the beach."

* * *

One small thing at a time, Remy told herself at eight o'clock that night. For now, all she had to do was find something to wear.

There were at least a dozen sets of beach pajamas in one of the boxes in the patio and she rifled around until she found a 1920s cream silk pongee set with an abundance of embroidered flowers blooming around the bottom of the trouser legs and the collar. They were sturdy enough, despite their age, and she slipped them on, wondering as she always did, about the person who'd owned them. She'd bought them at an estate sale in New York from a woman who'd had a scandalous past as a show-girl and then as one of the first female obstetricians in Manhattan, and who had then married a banker and set up a clinic devoted to women's health. Her daughters and granddaughters now ran the clinic and Remy wondered what it would be like to leave such a legacy. But also how a person could be born, like her daughter Emily, only to then slip away with so little fanfaronade, her only legacy the empty space in Remy's heart.

Remy felt her corset of guilt tighten. How dare she even think about going to a party and enjoying herself when Emily couldn't? At the same moment, her phone vibrated with a message from Antoinette.

I hope I timed this right. Don't feel guilty. Emily won't come back if you refuse to have fun. She won't come back if you don't smile or chat with people or listen to music. But if you don't do all of those things then we lose you, too. And I don't want to lose you as well. xx

Only Antoinette could write a message like that.

I love you, Remy replied. *Thank you.*

She walked down the steps to the beach and across the pebbles to where people had spilled out, like colorful umbrellas, down to the water. Fairy lights sparkled on the cliff, and on the shore an assortment of antique lounge chairs and sofas and low tables and vases of flowers had been set out. A tangible conviviality and joy flowed from everyone, reaching out a tentative finger toward Remy and she wondered what it would be like to take hold of it.

"Remy?"

She turned around to see Matt smiling at her. "My daughter's asleep, so you don't have to worry," he said.

Remy blushed and wished he hadn't mentioned it. "I'm really sorry for making her cry. Great party," she added, hoping to move the conversation on. "Your parents own the house?" She gestured to the clifftop upon which perched a Mediterranean-style villa, more modern than Remy's antique delight.

"They bought it not so long ago and now they plan to spend every summer here. This is kind of a housewarming, and kind of a family reunion. Everyone under the one roof for the first time in years. We all live in New York—my brother and my sister too—but we have to come to France to spend time together. Here's my mom. And Dad. Come say hello."

Remy was led over to a couple who stood hand in hand, the woman wearing an elegant black jumpsuit and the man in linen shorts and a white shirt, correspondingly refined.

"This is Judy and Alistair," Matt said, introducing his parents. "And my sister, Lauren." Matt beckoned a woman over. "Her husband Tom's over there." Matt pointed to a man waving his arms wildly, in the midst of an extravagant story. "This is Remy. Who I told you about."

Another man stepped in to join the group and Remy recognized him from her sun lounger. "This is my brother Adam," Matt continued.

Judy and Alistair greeted Remy with enthusiasm and kisses on the cheek, as did Lauren. Adam barely moved his head in a nod of greeting and Remy suddenly recognized that casual aloofness. She'd met him before, in her Sydney-life, when she'd been the Head of Fashion at IMG, organizing fashion weeks in Australia and throughout the Asia-Pacific region. She'd seen him at New York Fashion Week too; he was a photographer and had once been, she thought, good, but he'd become lazy or careless in the last few years and his work no longer interested her. She'd seen him again earlier this year when, in her new incarnation as a vintage fashion curator, she'd supplied outfits for a shoot for *Vogue* in New York, where she'd been staying with Antoinette. Adam had been the photographer.

"You're such a romantic figure," Judy said, smiling. "At first I wondered if your part of the beach was beautifully preserved in a decade different to ours; you looked like a forties or fifties film star this morning. Lauren and I made up quite a story about you, didn't we?" She nodded at her daughter, who laughed. "Alistair said we're always hoping for people to be more interesting than they are. I hope you don't mind that we were discussing you."

Remy was about to explain, through her blushes, why she was wearing decades-old clothes when Matt interrupted. "I meant to say something before Remy got here so you wouldn't put your foot in it, Mom. Remy's husband and daughter died a couple of years back. She's upset, not romantic."

And there it was. The truth scattered around them like broken glass.

Remy couldn't breathe. *Why did I come, Antoinette? Why?*

The silence was catastrophic.

"Oh my dear…" Judy tried to apologize. Lauren did too.

But the world had stopped turning and Remy stood frozen and exposed upon it.

Then she caught Adam's eye. Surprisingly, he didn't look away or rush to add more sorrys to the pile already placed before her. He just kept his gaze on her and offered her the here-and-now of one person. One moment in time separate from all the other moments of past and future hurts that had happened or were yet to happen. Somehow, it steadied her.

She could breathe again. She made herself speak and her voice didn't waver all that much when she said, wryly, "Yes, I'm the widow. But I don't come with a warning sign, so you can't be expected to know."

She saw Judy's face relax a little. And Remy relaxed too as the sense in her words stopped her from hating herself. She *didn't* come with a warning sign. This would happen, often. She had to get used to it.

Then the little girl—Molly—approached, not looking in the least as if she'd been asleep. Around her neck was a locket—or half a locket. Remy recognized it as one that had been in her house that afternoon, an antique silver locket that, when whole, had been something she'd planned to feature in her next lookbook.

"I thought you were in bed, darling," Judy said to her granddaughter. The locket flashed in the fairy lights and Judy bent down to inspect it. "Whatever do you have there?"

The girl grinned. "My treasure," she announced.

"I don't think that's yours," Judy admonished. "Did you find it on the beach?"

Matt glanced down at his daughter's purloined jewelry. With sudden comprehension, he looked at Remy. "Is it yours? Shit."

"Daddy," scolded the girl and Matt laughed.

Judy didn't. She bobbed down to her granddaughter's height. "Molly, we never take things from other people without asking. It's broken now. Remy will be very upset. Please say sorry."

"Sorry," the little girl muttered, looking annoyed rather than contrite.

"That looks kind of expensive," Adam said.

Judy unhooked the locket from her granddaughter's neck. "It's an antique. Please tell me she hasn't ruined a family heirloom."

"Nothing like that," Remy said, then realized she was going to have to explain as Judy was genuinely contrite and clearly uncertain if Remy was telling a white lie in order to be polite. "I run a business called *Remy's Closet* where I sell vintage clothing and jewelry. I buy it, sell it, keep it, and loan it out to magazines for fashion shoots. I bought the locket from an estate sale." She shrugged, for Judy's sake. "Old things break."

"But how much did it cost?" Judy asked, while Lauren took out her phone and began scrolling. "I think it must have been expensive."

"Is this you?" Lauren asked excitedly, passing over a phone opened to Instagram: *Remy's Closet*. "It *is* you. Holy cow, you have one hundred and fifty thousand followers. You're like a celebrity."

"We've met," Adam said flatly, as if this was bad news.

"We have," Remy agreed.

"You two know each other?" Judy asked.

Remy shook her head emphatically. "No. Like I said, magazines sometimes use pieces from my collection for shoots. Celebrities use them for the Oscars and parties. Occasionally, I run into photographers."

"But how do you sell the clothes?" Lauren asked. "And which celebrities have worn them to the Oscars? We need to sit down with drinks and hear all about this."

Remy couldn't help laughing, locket almost forgotten, as Lauren, who was clearly expert at organization, summoned up cocktails, three cozy chairs and herded her mother and Remy into them while they plied her with questions. She explained her background and that she bought from estate sales and markets and magazine wardrobes, from all the contacts she'd made over many years of working in fashion, and had an extensive mailing list of subscribers who received a newsletter from her every quarter with pieces for sale, supplemented by shots on Instagram where she sold the less important pieces.

"I'm here to shoot my next lookbook," she explained, "except that my photographer had to have her appendix out and has canceled the shoot. I'm either going to have to take the shots myself—which I can do as I have the equipment, but it's so much harder—or find someone else."

"Adam can do it!" Lauren cried.

"Yes," agreed Judy.

"Oh no," objected Remy. "I can't afford Adam Henry-Jones."

"We owe you," Judy insisted. "For Molly having broken that locket. It's our way of repaying you."

"Absolutely no need," Remy said. Adam Henry-Jones did not have the right style for her lookbook, and nor, she suspected, would he wish to have his skills offered about so freely.

"Then you must come for lunch on Saturday," Judy said and Remy could see that Judy was the type of person who wanted to feed everyone out of their misery, to pile homemade pasta and blankets and kittens upon them until they felt better.

"It's palazzo day on Saturday, so I was planning to go to Nice." Remy shook her head and amended her words. "I mean it's market day."

"Palazzo day?" Lauren queried.

Remy managed to laugh at herself. "I call it that because the market in Nice in summer is full of vintage palazzo pajamas. Seventies, Pucci; it's the psychedelic rainbow cornucopia."

"Can we come too?" Lauren asked eagerly, almost bouncing out of her seat.

"We wouldn't want to be in the way but it sounds as if you're more familiar with the markets, and with Nice, than we are," Judy added. "I want to learn my way into life here, rather than only being familiar with the beach. We'll all go. Alistair," she called out to her husband. "Adam and Matt, come here a minute."

The men wandered over and Judy told them her plans.

"We're having a family summer," Judy added to Remy. "Where we try to do as much as possible together. I hope you won't think it's a nuisance to have all of us come along."

Judy's manner and smile could alter the most firmly held views and Remy's plans to be mostly alone over the summer were melting like ice cream in the sun. It was only one morning. She could manage that, surely, with a few galvanizing texts from Antoinette.

"But what about Molly," Matt said to Remy. "Won't that be…awkward."

She pretended to misunderstand. "I don't mind about the locket."

"But—" he started.

Adam interrupted. "Isn't there a book market in Nice?"

"There is," Remy said.

"Good. I need some new reading material." Unexpectedly, Adam smiled at her and she found her own mouth smiling too.

"Me too," she said. "I just finished *The Bloody Chamber* and I need something less gruesome to follow it up."

Matt interjected. "The house." He indicated the pale pink palace on the clifftop. "Is it yours or do you rent it?"

"It's a relative's," Remy said, not wanting to explain.

She sat for an hour or so after that, content to listen to Judy and Lauren and the other people who drifted over to join them. She answered Judy and Lauren's questions about where she was from, telling them she'd been born in London, raised in Sydney and had spent the last year in New York, staying with her friend Antoinette. "I couldn't stay in Sydney with everything familiar around me after…" *They died.* It was the part she could never say.

"You are truly a cosmopolitan woman," Judy said, letting Remy's sentence fade away.

"With the best wardrobe," Lauren added.

"Come over and look through it any time," Remy said, surprising herself.

So many surprises in one night. And she realized that New York, too, had become familiar in a way that hadn't necessarily been useful: it had become the place where she'd escaped to mourn, so that's what she'd done. She'd come to this corner of France to mourn still, and to work, and hadn't anticipated the effect of strangeness: strange people, strange ocean, strange sky. And so she had, unexpectedly and for a couple of hours, enjoyed the beauty of a summer night by the sea in one of the loveliest places in the world. But it was tiring, and her dawn catnaps had not fortified her sufficiently for so much conversation. She excused herself and walked across the pebbles to her steps, coming upon a lone figure skimming stones.

"Sorry for using your terrace," the figure—Adam—said as she drew near. "I thought the house was empty."

"You were escaping," she said, guessing that perhaps a summer with family where the instruction was to do everything together might be wearing for those who took family for granted and had never had it stolen from them.

"Looking for solitude," he corrected.

Which was something Remy understood.

"You can use the terrace in the morning," she said. "I don't get up very early, so there'll be plenty of solitude for you."

She continued up the stairs, not waiting to hear him demur or accept because she didn't care one way or the other what his answer was, but glad to find that something like kindness still existed beneath her carapace of hurt and anger and the desperate, clinging sadness.

EIGHT

R emy woke the next day surprised to discover it was seven in the morning and she'd been asleep since midnight. She lay there for a moment, letting the unfamiliar sensation of a good night's sleep, a wakening without exhaustion, settle over her. Was this what moving on was like? Tidal shifts, occurring each day, unnoticed by most but sweeping to those perched on the shore of each alteration.

She stretched, stood up and did what she always used to do at home in Sydney first thing in the morning—moved to the window and peered out at the weather. Another perfect Mediterranean summer's day. Below, she saw a man wearing black board shorts, and with a curlicue of tattoo inscribed onto his upper arm, reading in the sun lounger. So, Adam *had* come. He must really be desperate for solitude.

She went to the bathroom, had a shower, put on her swimsuit and by the time she was downstairs making coffee, Adam had gone. She stepped onto the terrace and found herself breathing in the day as if she expected it to be a gift, a thing of joy. Her stomach curled tight with remonstrance or maybe it was just the ordinary spasm that accompanied the unfamiliar, a kind of nervousness about a day where new and unexpected things might continue to catch her unawares.

She sipped the coffee. Her stomach relented. A book waited for her on the sun lounger. *Frankenstein*. She sat down, opened it and began to read.

Some time later, the burn of the sun on her skin roused her and she realized an hour had passed. She stood and walked up the cracked white steps that were flanked by two once-bright urns—their colorful paintings fading in the sun—to the lookout on the edge of the cliff. The balustrade curved out grandly in front of her, outlining a view over the limitless water and the coastline sweeping around to Monaco. Sunshine poured down upon her shoulders and on the lush green of the hedges between the balustrades. An abundance of soft pink roses reached up worshipfully to the sky.

Below, Adam and Molly and a dog were playing in the water a way out from the shore. Adam threw the girl up and out so she landed with an enormous splash, no more than an arm's length from him, and then he picked her up and did it again. Molly's shrieks of laughter were the only sound in the hot, still silence.

A movement caught Remy's eye: Matt hurtling down the steps carved into the cliff face, calling out to his brother. Adam turned his back on Matt for just a millisecond, as if gathering himself. Then he put Molly on his shoulders and walked back through the water to the shore, where he deposited the girl beside her father.

Judging by Matt's sharply pointing finger and Adam's folded arms, a strained exchange took place between the brothers. Finally, Matt grabbed his daughter's hand and dragged her up the steps, Molly pulling away and gesticulating at the water until Matt picked her up and carried her. Adam directed the dog to follow Molly, then strode back into the water and swam around the point and away.

Remy shook her head. Even happy families were clearly unhappy. And it wasn't her place to spy.

She returned to her grand pink villa. It had been built in Italian Renaissance style, she'd been told by the gardener, and the soft pink of the walls was offset with white trim on the balconies and the arched window alcoves, and the marble columns that held up the first-floor terrace. It *was* magnificent, she conceded as she passed into the patio's double-story void, a square that one had to pass through to reach any of the rooms, which all opened out along the sides of the oblong. It would be the perfect place to photograph her vintage treasures, the kind of backdrop one might marvel at in *Vogue*.

Remy began to sort through the mess Molly had created yesterday, moving boxes to the *grand salon*. Treating it as a stockroom was probably a terrible way of using the stunning room, which had painted antique wood paneling on the walls. Deliciously plump cherubs frolicked in a chariot flying across the sky-painted ceilings and two fireplaces adorned with delicately draped women holding up the marble mantelpieces sat on either side of the room. At the far end, light spilled in through the curved windows, through which was a view of the endless sea.

She sat down and once she had a shortlist of pieces for her lookbook, she emailed a couple of photographers she knew, neither of whom was available at such short notice. She'd have to take the photos herself. It was what she'd done for her first two lookbooks—using a tripod and remote control—in the early days of this business that nobody understood and thought was a peculiar hobby. But her subscriber numbers had grown incredibly fast, and her customers all loved beautiful things, so she'd taken the plunge the last couple of seasons and had the book shot professionally. After that, her followers had tripled and her stock had sold out. And she'd been so busy that she'd been able to keep her mind occupied with things besides endless mental replays of life with her daughter and her husband.

She went outside to investigate the gardens properly, to see how she might style some of the shots. She nodded to the two gardeners who came in once a week to keep things in order, then crossed through the parterres and past the lookout. Towering palms and avocado and orange trees rose above her until she passed through a Spanish-style portico and found a shaded haven of bright orange bird-of-paradise flowers, and the redolent fragrance of jasmine. The air was cooler there and she felt it gentle away the sweat on her skin. She reached up her hand to stroke the vivid pink skin of a pomegranate about to burst with ripeness, breathed in the summer-sweet scent of honeysuckle, heard the soft drowsy buzz of a curious dragonfly.

She needed something dramatic to suit the sharp points of the Strelitzia: perhaps the daybreak-blue, off-the-shoulder Tina Leser jumpsuit. And she had the perfect Hanae Mori piece to shoot against the wooden pavilion of the next garden, which had a distinctly Japanese flavor. Something romantic in the Temple of Love, she mused. And then it came. The shocking and familiar wave of shame, a shame that twisted quickly into fury at herself.

She had spent almost an entire day without thinking of Emily. Or Toby.

She turned and marched back toward the house where, in the tidy spill of roses from the parterres, a weed caught her attention. She bent to yank it, furiously, from the ground. See how easy it was to remove things from a landscape? One pull and a plant now gone. One morning in the fresh air and her daughter and husband vanished from the shrine she had erected in her mind.

She pulled out another weed, then another. She was still on her knees in the dirt in her swimsuit when she heard a woman's voice call her name.

Lauren, with Adam in tow, approached, waving gaily and calling "Hi."

Remy stood up, brushing dirt off her legs, realizing she must look like a child with grubby knees, long blonde hair pulled into an untidy ponytail and no sense to garden in the correct attire. Lauren began to effuse over Remy's swimsuit, a golden yellow Cole of California two-piece Swoon Suit that had been designed during the Second World War from acetate satin.

"I have another one inside if you want to take a look," Remy heard herself say, anger at herself softening in the face of Lauren's delight. "It doesn't have the laces at the sides but it's a really similar style."

"I'd love to!" Lauren said, beaming and following Remy back to the terrace. "But don't let me get distracted from why I'm here. Mom and I and Adam"—here Lauren glanced sideways at her brother—"insist on you using Adam as your photographer. We looked at your Instagram account and saw that you'd sold a locket like the one Molly broke for two thousand dollars and we just about died. And before you say anything polite, know that you'll be doing us a *huge* favor."

Lauren indicated Adam. "He's so bored he's going to chew his own arm off if he doesn't have something to do. He's incapable of relaxing. We've decided to break Mom's rule of no one working for the month so we can repay you."

They were inside now, in the *grand salon*. "Holy cow," Lauren said, stepping over to the pile of vintage swimsuits.

"I have a feeling that a couple of days of your time would be worth more than my locket," Remy said to Adam. "I can do it myself."

Adam shrugged. "Then you'd be taking a step backward. When Lauren told me I had to do this, she made sure to wave your old pics in my face. You did a good enough job on your first couple of shoots, which I can tell you did yourself, but the last ones, where you obviously used photographers, were way better. Why go backward when, here I am, having my services offered about so freely?"

He stared pointedly at his sister, who made a face at him, and something in the way he smiled in response made Remy sense that he was teasing Lauren rather than complaining.

"I'm the bossy middle child who interferes in everything," Lauren explained, laying a careful hand on ruffles and ties and polka dots. "Whereas Adam is the aloof older sibling who hates to be interfered with, and Matt is the younger brother who's as spoiled as they come and whose messes Adam and I are forever cleaning up. Is this it?" She held up a white swimsuit with a floral print, eyeballs practically spilling out of her head, and Remy knew she'd fallen in love. It was one of the things she enjoyed most about what she did: matching a vintage treasure to a new owner who would cherish it as much as the first or second owner had, giving the piece a new life.

"Try it on," Remy said. "Just go through there."

Lauren disappeared into the next room with the bathing suit and Remy said to Adam, "I'll tell your sister I have someone else to take the photos. Really."

"How much could you have sold the locket for?" he asked, arms folded, the black edge of the tattoo peeking out from beneath the shirt he'd added to his board shorts. He, like Lauren and Remy, was barefoot.

"It doesn't matter," she said.

"Then it sounds like a couple of days of my time will definitely be as much as the locket."

Before Remy could protest again, Lauren appeared in her swimsuit. "I am never taking this off," she said, twirling.

"You look like Rita Hayworth," Remy said. It was true. With Lauren's reddish-brown hair, curved figure, and creamy skin, she did, in her forties swimsuit, look like a golden-age movie star.

"Wait till Tom sees me in this." Lauren grinned.

Adam mock-groaned. "If you two walk around the house any more loved-up I'll have to break all my promises and leave. You see," he said to Remy, "letting me escape for a couple of days to shoot some clothes is doing me a favor."

Remy actually found herself laughing. "Okay. But you're not paying for the swimsuit," she said to Lauren.

Lauren won that argument too. She left the house triumphant, having got her way, plus a new swimsuit into the bargain, leaving Adam to get a quick brief from Remy about the shoot.

She led him through some of the rooms in the house: the tapestry room, a too-grand bedroom that Remy didn't use, the *petit salon* with its curved banquettes, and he looked around with a critical eye.

"I like each image to be its own story," she said, bringing up some pictures on her phone as she spoke. "A lot of vintage fashion sellers use white backgrounds or dress models, but for my lookbook I like people to see that the dress is a possibility. The house will be a fabulous backdrop, especially for the evening gowns, and I thought I could do some of the swimwear and daywear pieces outside. I don't use models; I model myself. Not because I think I'm beautiful or anything like that"—she had once modeled, years ago; it was how she'd got her start in fashion but the minute you told people that, they critiqued you, looking for all the flaws and imperfections that a model shouldn't have—"but when I've used dress models or hired models, the pieces don't sell as well. It's *Remy's Closet*, so people want to see me in the clothes. It's really normal for vintage sellers to model their own stuff," she added, as if she were presenting a case and she frowned inwardly at herself for feeling like she had to justify herself to Adam Henry-Jones who'd worked with the most beautiful women in the world.

"I get it," he said. "Like I said, I did a bit of research. Some of your competition have Instagram pages that look like shit; I don't know how they sell anything. And most professional models wouldn't have the right look for this. You need something more timeless, and you," he eyed her critically, "have that nonspecific look that works for this. Do you want to start on Saturday after we get back from Nice?"

"Okay," she said, and then added, because she had to be sure, "I really want the clothes and the background to tell a story together. It's not just about taking overly sophisticated, cutting-edge shots."

"Don't worry, I won't inflict my style on you," he said, turning to leave.

She hadn't meant to be so unbelievably rude. "Sorry," she said.

"That's not what I meant. I just meant that some of your older work was very…" She hesitated. "Poetic. I like that quality."

"Louise Dahl-Wolfe. Steichen. Hoyningen-Heune. That's what you're after."

"That's it exactly," she said, surprised.

"See, I still have some of my soul left." He crossed the terrace and took the steps down to the beach.

What a puzzle he was. Definitely aloof, as his sister had said. But his sister clearly adored him and he, her. He was aware of his flaws but also astute enough to mention Dahl-Wolfe first, which she wasn't sure many other male photographers would have done. Unable to relax, Lauren had said. But Remy had seen him completely relaxed that morning in her sun lounger.

She turned into the *grande salle* and began to excavate more boxes. She had plenty of work to do before Saturday afternoon, which was just how she liked it.

* * *

The unexpected sound of a car arriving two nights later roused Remy from her reverie of silk velvet and polished cotton. She opened the front door warily and was engulfed in a set of arms.

"Antoinette!" she exclaimed. "What are you doing here?"

"Well," Antoinette said, stepping inside with an enormous suitcase, "when you told me you were doing a shoot with Adam Henry-Jones, I couldn't resist inviting myself along. You absolutely cannot do your own makeup and hair, although I know you're more than capable. I want you to look every bit the professional you are, so you need an entourage. That's me."

Remy laughed.

Antoinette hugged her tighter. "I haven't heard you do that since forever," she said. "Being here is good for you."

"But aren't you supposed to be in Byron Bay?"

Antoinette usually made an annual pilgrimage to Byron Bay to be detoxified, keeping up the ritual even after her move to New York from Sydney two years ago. "I am. But I took the plane to France instead."

"I have no green smoothies," Remy said, leading her friend into the *grand salon*. "And too much coffee."

"Best kind of wellness retreat then." Antoinette grinned.

"It's so good to see you." Remy was very aware that her eyes were leaking.

"You too."

Remy and Antoinette had met as teenagers when they were both doing occasional modeling work. Antoinette's Italian parents owned a hair salon and, as all models were expected to have above-average skills in applying their own makeup and organizing their own hair, Antoinette had been the one to teach Remy. They'd attended university together and had both worked their way up the ranks at IMG, Antoinette as the Marketing Manager, then Head of Fashion in New York, and Remy as Head of Fashion for Asia-Pacific. Antoinette had been Remy's bridesmaid and Emily's godmother. Which meant that Antoinette had mourned too, Remy suddenly realized, when Emily and Toby had died.

"I'm sorry," she said, shamefaced now. "I never asked you how you were."

Antoinette's eyes filled with tears now. "That would have been an act of empathy beyond a saint," she said, slinging an arm around her friend's shoulders. "I miss Emily's cards," she said and Remy remembered how Emily had liked to make surprises for Antoinette, little cards that she would ask Remy to take to work and hide somewhere, in a place where Antoinette would stumble across them during the day. In return,

Antoinette had, every time she visited, hidden something for Emily: a fairy wand, an unusual shell, a book.

"Well," Remy said, after they'd both been silent and struggling for composure for too long, "I'm sure I could write you a card. Then you might actually be able to read what it said."

Antoinette gave a half-laugh, half-sob. "Look at you, trying to make me feel better. Maybe a week in France has done more than you think."

"It's definitely made me see," Remy said as she opened a bottle of wine and poured out two glasses, "that I've thought a lot about myself over the last couple of years and hardly ever about anyone else. It's actually nice to think of someone else for a change. In the way I always used to think of Emily first: choosing a restaurant that had kid-friendly food, timing my meetings in New York so I'd be able to call her before she went to bed. I still can't walk into a restaurant—not that I've been to one for ages—without first wondering about their kids' menu. Then I catch myself and realize I won't ever have to think about that again and I remember all the times I sighed over having to go to a place that served pizza and pasta when all I wanted was a Thai curry. I hate myself forever having begrudged her a pizza. I hate myself a lot," Remy concluded.

"Anger and bargaining," Antoinette concluded. "The third stage of grief. You've got depression, loneliness, and reflection to look forward to next."

"Grief really is the gift that keeps on giving," Remy said, swallowing her wine and then she and Antoinette burst out laughing.

The night continued in a similar vein outside on the terrace overlooking the sea, with the silvery cascade of water flowing down from the Temple of Love above, its delicate splash like music in the night; the perfume of roses soaring on the breeze; the Henry-Joneses' house lit up beside them. Remy and Antoinette reminisced and cried and laughed and eventually went to bed, where Remy lay down, expecting wakefulness. But she felt lighter, as if the anger had lifted somewhat. She hoped that depression wouldn't be waiting for her in the morning.

* * *

Antoinette was there to wake her in the morning instead, with coffee and complaints. "There's no food," she scolded. "We'll drive into town and get some."

Remy rubbed her eyes. "Oh God, it's Saturday. We're going to Nice with the Henry-Joneses. We can get some food at the markets."

"Ooooh, you're quite the best of friends with them."

Remy sat up and walked toward the window, looking out at a glorious day, but she felt heavy again, as if the previous night's shift had been only temporary. The sun lounger was empty and she imagined that Antoinette's habit of waking early and contorting her body into yoga poses would have frightened Adam away.

"Is Adam as gorgeous as everyone says? I've somehow never met him. And is he single? Instead of detoxifying and cleansing, I could easily be tempted to get a little dirty with him." Antoinette grinned and Remy found a smile.

"That's better," Antoinette said. "What time are we going in to Nice?"

"I said we'd leave at nine."

The doorbell sounded.

"You know it's nine now, right?" Antoinette said.

"Shit!" Remy whirled away from the window. "This is why people dealing with anger and bargaining shouldn't make plans."

"Shower," Antoinette ordered. "I'll entertain them for fifteen minutes."

Remy did as she was told, showering and tossing on a home-sewn 1950s fit-and-flare sundress in navy polished cotton with a checkered sash around the waist, which someone had made with love from a McCall's pattern. She whisked her hair back into a hasty ponytail, found large sunglasses to cover the effects of last night's wine and skittered down the stairs sixteen minutes later.

"Sorry," she apologized and was immediately swept into Judy's arms.

"Not at all," Judy said, kissing her cheeks. "We were having a lovely time talking to Antoinette."

Behind everyone's back, Antoinette cocked her head at an unseeing Adam and pretended to fan herself from the heat.

Remy pressed her lips together to keep back her smile, then caught sight of an ostentatious array of flowers.

"From Molly and me," Matt said, pointing to the flowers. "To apologize for the jewelry. If my brother can donate his photography services, the least I can do is buy a few flowers."

Remy feigned appreciation for the flowers, which were a haphazard assortment of succulents and calla lilies and strange gray flowers, pointy and modern and as out of place in the house as faux-distressed denim.

"How many cars will we need?" Lauren began to organize everyone and it was decided that Remy's car and one of the Henry-Joneses' cars would be enough, with Antoinette then adding hers to the mix as nine people in two small French cars would be decidedly squashy.

"I thought you might want squashy if you're sitting next to Adam," Remy whispered to her friend and Antoinette smiled and said, "I'm not planning to share my car with anyone other than him."

Judy, Alistair, Molly, and Tom piled into one car, Lauren somehow managed to squeeze past Antoinette and into Antoinette's car, which left Remy with Matt.

They set off along the road into the town center, winding along the water's edge, and then along the highway to Nice. Remy, for want of something to say, asked him whether he and his family had come to Saint-Jean-Cap-Ferrat for a special occasion and Matt looked suddenly serious.

"It's complicated," he began, voice heavy with some kind of oversized emotional baggage. "But I feel like I can tell you. Like *you* might understand."

Remy kept her eyes fixed to the road, angry with Matt for thinking death—which she imagined he was referring to—could be a bonding mechanism. "No need to explain," she hurried to say. "We can talk about something else."

He shook his head. "I'd like to talk about it. It's about Molly. She's . . ."

"You really don't have to tell me," Remy said. "Maybe instead we could—"

"I need to start telling people about it," Matt insisted, "especially now that Molly's getting older and can understand what's going on. Molly isn't . . ." His sigh was dramatic, but genuine. "My wife and I tried to have a baby for years," he said flatly. "Turned out I was the problem, so the doctors suggested we use a sperm donor. But Sally, my wife, didn't want a random stranger fathering her child."

No. Remy felt her insides twist. She thought she knew what Matt was going to say and that the news wasn't necessarily his alone to impart.

"Adam agreed to be our donor," Matt went on. "He agreed knowing it meant nothing, that it was just a transfer of DNA which, let's face it, he wasn't about to put to good use."

Remy flinched. That a baby could be thought of as a piece of DNA. That Matt could speak of his brother like that. "I don't need to—" She tried again.

But Matt pressed on. "Just like always, Adam didn't hold up his side of the deal. He was meant to be a distant uncle. But he started visiting us each week, playing with Molly, calling to ask about her, offering to babysit if we wanted to go out. Eventually Sally told him to stay away or she'd get a restraining order. Adam'll say that Sally was crazy; you've really got to be suffering pretty bad to earn his compassion. Sally wasn't crazy; Adam was. He was the one trying to steal all Molly's love away. So, after that, we didn't see Adam for a couple of years."

It was impossible not to interrupt. Matt's story made Adam seem like a nice guy trying to get to know his daughter. And then to be threatened with a restraining order. God, how that would hurt. "You know that love isn't finite," she said as gently as she could. "If Molly loved Adam, it wouldn't mean she had less love for you."

"Well, I guess we'll find out soon enough." Matt's voice was hard with sarcasm. "Mom and Dad said we all had to be a family again. So they've forced us to come here for a month. Which is completely against Sally's wishes but my parents seem to have forgotten they ought to respect the dead."

Remy tried again. "Kids can love so much…" She stopped, dangerously close to tears. Emily had been full of love for everyone. She'd never been reserved or shy but bursting with questions, eager to find the beautiful kernel inside everyone that made them easy to love.

"You sound like him. Has he already told you—"

"God no." Remy was emphatic. "I've hardly spoken three words to him."

"I don't agree with you. Love *is* finite. Mine's been used up on Sally. Don't you feel like that too? That you'll never love anyone again?"

"I don't know," Remy whispered, because she did feel like that, all the time. But she didn't want to bolster Matt's terrible theory. Nor did she want to admit that her feelings for her husband were not so pure as Matt's for his wife. The anger and resentment and blame—he was speeding with their child in the car, for God's sake—had made him into someone she couldn't love. So how could she have used up all her love on someone she told herself she didn't love? It made no sense. Nothing did.

NINE

Remy leapt from the car as soon as they arrived in Nice, desperate to get away from the thoughts Matt had made press upon her.

"You look like a great cloud of misery on this beautiful day," Antoinette said by way of greeting.

Remy managed a wan smile. "Thanks for being brutally honest," she said. "But I need a reprieve for the next hour or so, okay?"

"Only for an hour though."

"Grab a coffee if you want." Adam, who'd climbed out of Antoinette's car, spoke unexpectedly. "I know where the markets are. And it'll take Mom twice as long to walk there as it should because she'll want to exclaim over everything on the way."

"Thanks," Remy said gratefully. An espresso and ten minutes with Antoinette were just what she needed.

"He's very swoony," Antoinette said as they ordered coffee. "He has zero interest in me and we'd drive each other to distraction—I talk too much and he too little—but he's lovely to look at so I'm prepared to forgive him for his lack of interest in me."

"Are you serious?" Remy asked as their espressos arrived. "You normally charm the pants off everyone."

"I assure you his pants will be staying on. Except in my dreams."

Remy burst out laughing. "Second time in two days," she said in wonder. "I should be well and truly onto depression in about ten minutes. What will I have to look forward to after that?"

"Testing."

"What the hell is that?"

Antoinette shrugged. "I have no idea. I'll look it up once we get through depression. For now, let's go shopping."

They quickly caught up to the Henry-Joneses. Remy led the way to the Cours Saleya, where red and white striped awnings hung over market stalls. The flower sellers were lined up behind a profusion of blossoms and the dress sellers a little further down were blooming with florets of a different kind.

Everyone's pace slowed as they joined the throng of contentment that was market day. The cafés lining the Cours Saleya hummed with conversation, and the smell of coffee and pastries billowed mouth-wateringly through the air.

"I should have bought your flowers here," Matt said, frowning. "I thought you said it was just clothes?"

"It's everything," Remy said, feeling a sudden burst of happiness that she was going picking, as she liked to call it, searching through mountains of junk to find the one or two pieces that made it all worthwhile.

Judy was completely distracted by the flowers, Alistair with helping his wife carry the armful of blooms she'd purchased, Tom—Lauren's husband—was staring at the rows of vendors with a pained expression on his face, Antoinette was preventing Molly from snapping the heads off an arrangement of roses, Matt was trying to tell the flower-seller in loud and drawn-out English that one broken flower wasn't a big deal, Lauren was wincing, and Adam had vanished.

"A fabulous family outing," Lauren said. "Show me how to find a pair of palazzo pajamas to make it all worthwhile, please?"

"Over here," Remy said, pointing to stacks of clothes.

They began to rifle through, Remy keeping a watchful eye on Lauren's sorting lest she miss anything worthwhile. They both saw it at the same time. A rainbow of brilliant color, swirling over the fabric in a way only Emilio Pucci could do.

Remy held it aloft. It wasn't quite the palazzo pajamas she'd spoken of but it was a one-piece romper and Remy knew it would look stunning on Lauren.

Lauren squealed as if she were Molly's age. "Oh my Gawd! Will it fit?"

Remy examined the suit. "It's a vintage size ten, which is about your size. And it has the genuine Pucci tag and signature on the fabric. There's a little bit of bleed here—" Remy pointed to where the bright purple had bled into the white, "but we always expect some imperfections in a vintage piece. Hardly any underarm discoloration, which is another thing to look out for. And it's not too pricey."

"Should I get it? But don't you want it?" Lauren's face was like that of a child told to give her last piece of candy to someone less fortunate.

"The pieces I'm doing for my next lookbook are more twenties to forties. This won't work with them. But I bet it will work on you."

Pucci playsuit purchased, Lauren was happy to rummage by herself, showing off her newly acquired vintage-clothing hunting skills to Judy. So Remy walked along Place Pierre Gautier to the town square where the old book market was located, wondering if she could find a few Penguin Classics to give to Adam as a thank-you gift for doing the photos, when she bumped into him, bearing a box of books.

"I thought I'd see if there were any less gruesome Penguin Classics," she said. "But it looks like you've beaten me to it."

He pulled a book out of the box and held it up. Bram Stoker's *Dracula*.

She laughed.

"I don't know what else is in there," he said. He looked relaxed, just as he'd been on the sun lounger that first morning, as if browsing by himself through the book market had been the restorative espresso he'd needed. "But I saw *Dracula* and figured the rest would be okay."

He shifted the box to his other arm. "Do you want to get out of here and get started? Or has Lauren got you stuck here for the day?"

"No, she's doing very well by herself. I'll just grab Antoinette; she's doing my hair and makeup, which I know makes it sound like amateurs' day out, but she's actually good."

He shrugged. "I don't suppose there's any chance of making a . . ."

"Quick getaway?" she finished. "I think I've reached my limits of sociability for today, so yes." She stopped. "That makes me sound like a total bitch. Your family are lovely. It's not them."

"I know what you mean. See you at the car."

* * *

Back at Cap-Ferrat, while Antoinette busied herself in the dressing room with her array of tools, Adam beckoned Remy over to look through some sheaves of paper.

"I printed these out last night," he said, looking around for somewhere to spread out the images amongst the abundance of rococo chairs with carved fruitwood frames and elegant velvet upholstery, and the gaming tables that looked so spindly a piece of paper might prove their undoing.

He settled for the mantelpiece above one of the fireplaces. "I thought we could replicate some of these iconic shots. It might be fun, and it's something I could never do for *Vogue* or *Vanity Fair*. I like the idea of using something from the past to show off the past. Like this one." He pointed to a Louise Dahl-Wolfe image of a model before a fireplace, back to the camera, wearing a gorgeous silk and lace nightgown. "And this one. Steichen's *Perfection in Black*."

"I love that," Remy breathed, studying the stunning image of a woman in a long black evening dress standing beside the open lid of a grand piano, the lid's curve perfectly matching the line of the woman's hip.

"I know it's a bit shadowy but…"

"No, let's do some in black and white. I can always accompany the main images with a standard color shot of the clothes on a dress form so people can see the details. I feel like doing these in color would ruin them."

Adam smiled at her and Remy felt, for the first time in almost two years, a camaraderie with someone she hadn't known since forever like Antoinette.

"I was hoping you'd say that," he said. "I know it's all about the clothes but sometimes—" He stopped, the hint of an old frustration in his voice.

"You must get tired of having to do what everyone else wants," Remy said.

Adam shrugged. "It's all about the house style, not my style. I knew that when I got into fashion photography. I wanted the money and the certainty over artistic pleasures and penury."

"But what do you want now?" Remy asked. "We don't always want the same things, fifteen years on."

"I'm ready!" Antoinette called, interrupting them.

It was probably just as well as Remy was certainly prying. And she already knew too much about Adam, after what Matt had told her. Now, standing in a room with him, seeing the effort he'd put into something he'd practically been forced into doing, Remy couldn't help but think about Molly laughing as Adam threw her into the water. As she did, guilt turned her stomach over in its old, familiar way. But this time, it wasn't guilt over Emily.

It was because Adam had no idea that she knew. And she understood enough about him—he was not so much aloof as quiet and private—to know he would hate that she did. And that he would hate it even more if she pretended not to know.

"We'll just be a sec," Remy said and Antoinette, bless her, left the room.

"Adam," Remy said, using his name for the first time ever and she could hear how her tone had shifted from the lightness of sympathetic curiosity, how her head had dropped from looking up at him to staring at the table. "I feel as if I have a piece of you that I'm not meant to have, a piece you wouldn't want me to have. Matt told me about Molly this morning," she blundered on, when she probably should have stopped to think more carefully about how to say it. "He told me that you're her biological father. I don't know why he did and I don't know why he thinks that a child's love has a limit…"

She trailed off. She'd sensed the stiffening of Adam's body as she'd started to speak. Now she could feel his fury dropping suddenly over him like a winter wool cloak, banishing every other emotion from the room.

Adam swore, then stopped himself. "I'm sorry he told you," he said shortly.

She dared to look back up at him and wished she hadn't. She saw something she recognized too well: the ferocious hurt of a person who knows this particular pain is never-ending and who can't believe they'll have to endure it for the rest of their life. As much as she wanted to, she didn't look away from his heartbreak, just like he hadn't turned away from hers that first night on the beach after Matt had announced to everyone that she was a childless widow.

"I'm sorry too," she said quietly. "But only because you've known me for five minutes and it must hurt to have something so personal given away so freely." She touched his arm, the only gesture of compassion she could offer. "I understand if you'd prefer not to do this anymore."

Across Adam's face now spread a look of bitterest revelation. "That's why he told you," he said slowly.

"What?"

Adam shook his head. "Nothing. Let's just do it. Anything that keeps me away from my brother right now is a good thing."

So Remy left Adam alone and went to get herself made up by Antoinette while Adam set up the cameras and soft boxes and reflective panels and everything else needed to make sure the light and shadows and highlights were just right.

They began with the Louise Dahl-Wolfe shot by the fireplace, of Remy in a blush-colored 1940s silk and lace nightgown, her back to the camera. It didn't require much of her but the next shot, the piano shot, did. She changed into a black liquid satin 1930s evening gown that hugged every curve on her body before flaring out at her ankles. Its sheen matched the gloss of the piano exactly. And her pose needed to mimic the piano lid exactly too, one hand placed on the instrument, hip curved gently to one side, head turned to her bent arm. Thankfully, all the unused modeling skills she'd once possessed came back to her like breathing.

Adam adjusted the reflectors, wanting less light, not more, snapped, checked the image and said, "You've done this before."

"I modeled a long time ago," Remy said. "It's how Antoinette and I met. And I know I look nothing like I did twenty years ago but, like I said, the buyers prefer to see me in the clothes."

Adam held the camera up and began to shoot. "I think women are usually more beautiful from their mid-thirties onwards. They know more, have felt more, and you can see it in their faces. Young faces are mostly really blank."

"You know," Antoinette said as she approached Remy to tidy an errant curl, "you're nowhere near as much of an asshole as I'd heard."

"Antoinette!" Remy said, horrified.

But Adam actually laughed for the first time ever. "I can be an asshole if you want. I've had plenty of practice. Usually when I have the editor and the stylist and the fashion director and the market team and the producer all leaning over my shoulder, telling me how to do my job. And since I don't have an assistant today, I'm about to ask you to move the reflector closer. But I'll say please so I'll just be an ass this time."

Antoinette laughed and Remy smiled. This was actually fun and she was glad she'd acquiesced to Adam doing the shoot. He'd been respectful and, rather than moving her this way and that as photographers were wont to do, he simply asked her to do what she felt most comfortable doing and only gave a small amount of direction when the light or some other technical aspect wasn't working.

The final shot for the day was of Remy in a stunningly draped Vionnet gown, its back looping down like a cape to leave all the skin from her neck to the top of her sacrum bare. Adam wanted to shoot it outside, at the top of the steps leading to the cliff, with dark blue sky behind her so all that was visible was the white balustrade, blue and white urns, white dress and blue sky. He shot a few test pics, frowned, and beckoned Antoinette over. Antoinette peered at the camera and said, "Yes, she'll probably want to see it."

"What is it?" she called and Adam gestured for her to take a look.

It was ordinary, in any fashion shoot, but especially in a vintage fashion shoot, for the model not to wear underwear. It ruined lines of dresses, it appeared as rogue straps, it cast a shadow; it did all manner of things nobody wanted to see in an editorial spread in a magazine, or in a dream shot atop Cap-Ferrat. Remy wasn't wearing anything under the dress and, as she stepped over to Adam's camera, she could see that the light had made the fabric slightly transparent and the outline of her naked body, back to the camera, was just visible.

"It's a beautiful shot," Antoinette said.

And it was. Adam had captured a Remy she didn't know existed, body outlined beneath the gown, poised on the edge of the world, ready to leap off and venture forth into the blue and the sun and the promise of everything that was backdropped theatrically and bewitchingly before her. Her profiled face, tilted slightly upward, looked yearning, as if there were something just out of shot that was worth leaping over the edge of the cliff for.

It was Remy of another time, not this grief-soaked time; a promise of Remy that she wasn't sure she wanted kept—because how could she? How could she leap anywhere when she wanted to be beneath the ground, atop her daughter's coffin, arms around it, whispering, *It's all right, Mummy's here. Mummy's finally here.*

"Dammit," she said as the tears spilled over too quickly for her to stop them, ruining her face, ruining the day, ruining everything. That was the only promise she was certain of: that ruin lay everywhere, not a venturesome, wide open future.

"It's not the photo," she said quickly, not wanting Adam to think that, after he'd worked for free all day, she hated his work. "Well, it is the photo but not the way you think. It's just so…" Her voice trailed off. "Hard," she finished bleakly.

There it was, said aloud. She wasn't all right and she didn't know, despite everyone's assurances to the contrary, that she ever would be. And now, on top of everything, she understood that out of the chaos would emerge a different Remy to the one she thought she'd be. A Remy without Emily, without Toby.

"Let's call it a day," Antoinette said decisively.

"Sure," Adam said.

Antoinette ushered Remy into the house and poured her a wine.

Remy sipped but it tasted like nothing so she pushed it away. "I think a wine after every meltdown isn't the best idea."

"I'll make some food," Antoinette said, her Italian heritage making her turn to the one thing her family had made her believe would always bring comfort.

"No," Remy said. "You're going to Ventimiglia tonight. You don't need to cook for me."

Antoinette was supposed to be catching up with some of her hundreds of cousins in a town near the Italian border.

"I'm not going," Antoinette said.

"You are," Remy said, and even she could hear the fire in her voice. "I'm not a baby and I don't need a sitter. I just needed to cry."

The sound of a clearing throat made both Remy and Antoinette turn. "I'm packed up," Adam said, cameras and gear slung over his shoulder. "What time do you want to start tomorrow?"

Remy liked the way he didn't assume that one breakdown meant she would be incapable of working the next day.

"I don't think—" Antoinette began, but Remy interrupted. "Whatever time suits you best for light," she said.

"If we can start shooting around eight? Otherwise the light gets too harsh."

"Eight is fine," Remy said. "See you then."

Adam departed and Antoinette shook her head and gave Remy a hug. "I take the hint. I'm smothering. I'll go to Ventimiglia. I just want to take all the hurts away, you know? But I guess no hurts would mean not living at all."

* * *

In the silence of the house, Remy paced, then picked at some salad. She knew Antoinette would scold her for not eating but she wasn't hungry. She kept seeing herself in the photo, seeing a future-Remy whose first thought upon waking might not be Emily. It was like looking into a kaleidoscope where, with one turn of the hand, she would be broken up into pieces and then reassembled differently.

It was like looking down at her left ring finger and seeing that it was all tanned now, that there was no longer a white band tattooed into the skin where her wedding ring had once sat because she'd locked the ring in a drawer so she wouldn't always think about Toby trying to hold down the cloth and the food and the wineglasses on an especially windy day when he'd tried to organize both a dinner and a proposal by the sea. She wouldn't have to remember the way he'd eventually laughed and said, as everything blew away, "Well, if what I'm about to say doesn't make this day memorable, that certainly will." Wouldn't have to remember how much she'd loved him for not letting gale-force winds get in the way of asking her to marry him.

But even without the ring, she remembered.

She went outside and stood on the clifftop. Below, she saw a figure cutting through the water, then a head emerging, hands wiping water from a face: Adam. He pushed his hair off his brow, picked up a towel and gave himself a desultory drying off before another figure appeared. Matt.

Remy waited, braced, for Adam to shout at his brother, to swear at him for letting Remy, a virtual stranger, know his secret. But he didn't speak: Matt did, and Adam simply nodded in reply. The one-sided conversation continued for a few minutes, Matt doing most of the talking, and Adam occasionally uttering a word or two. It was clear to Remy that Adam was not going to confront his brother; he was going to let it all sit inside him and she saw in that a noble strength, a grace that his brother did not possess and nor, perhaps, did Remy.

Then Matt climbed back up the stairs to the Henry-Joneses' house and Remy saw Adam's shoulders drop inches downwards, the tension leaving with his sibling. He tilted his head back as if relieved and saw her standing on the clifftop. Rather than pretend she hadn't seen what had happened, she gave a quick wave.

Adam crossed the cove and took the steps up to her house.

TEN

I forgot my box of books," he said and Remy remembered the carton from the markets.

"Come in." She led the way inside where the stillness of the house wrapped itself around them.

"Where's Antoinette?"

"She's spending the night with her cousins. Do you want a coffee?" Remy asked, surprising herself with the invitation. "I can't sleep so coffee seems the logical medicament."

Adam laughed. "Why not?" he said. "I'm not feeling especially sleepy after swimming for an hour."

"You didn't say anything to your brother," she said, back to him, as she ground coffee beans.

"My mom doesn't deserve for us to have yet another fight."

What Adam had said to her that morning—*That's what he wanted*—replayed in her mind, along with Matt saying, *If my brother can donate his photography services, the least I can do is buy a few flowers*, as if there were some kind of competition. Not, Remy knew, for her, but for any moment of ascendancy and she also knew that, far from the impression given out by Matt, Adam was not the aggressor in their relationship. What Adam had not wanted to say to her was that Matt had been trying to sabotage the shoot, knowing either that Remy would pull out from embarrassment or that she would tell Adam she knew the whole story and then he would pull out.

"What was it like," she asked as the grinder stopped whirring, "to be threatened with a restraining order?"

In the stark silence that followed, she thought it likely that Adam would stalk off. "I was trying to understand," she explained, "what it would be like to know your child was there, alive, but you couldn't see her. I think it would be impossible." Emily wasn't there so Remy couldn't see her. But what if Emily were still alive and Remy still couldn't see her? She turned around and passed Adam his coffee.

He wrapped his hands around the cup. "It's like someone has kicked you in the balls," he said sharply. "And then the guts. And then the head. And then done it all over again, every damn minute of every damn day, but harder each time in case you ever start to not feel it. Which you never do."

"That's a very apt description," she said softly. "Apart from the balls, which I obviously don't have."

Adam gave a half-smile. "Maybe of a different kind, you do. Starting up a business after what happened to you must take grit."

"My friends called it stupidity." She hesitated, not intending to say any more but his confession had loosened something in her.

She led the way outside and dropped into a chair. "You can take the lounger," she said. Then, her own disclosure. "I quit IMG straight after it happened. They told me they wouldn't accept my resignation; that I needed time to think. Antoinette kept telling me the same. But I knew I could never go back there."

She stopped herself from saying anything more, shifted a little away from Adam and toward the certain and inexorable sea. She could feel him waiting for her to continue, liked that he hadn't pushed her by asking why, had just offered her a space she could place her words into if she chose.

So she did, going back in time to before, a place she wished she could inhabit every day. "After I had Emily, I went back to work when she was six months old," she said, speaking to the ocean. "It always made me furious how so many women gave six years of their life to a law degree, say, and then worked as a lawyer for maybe only another six years and then became pregnant and gave it all up—all that intelligence and all that time leading to a life of playgrounds and strollers. Toby was a lawyer and I had my dream job; neither of us was going to give it up. Then, at the funeral, Toby's sister said to me, *You must regret all those years you let someone else look after Emily.*"

She heard Adam's sharp intake of breath at the savagery of that particular cruelty.

Remy's voice was low and husky with all the tears she was trying so desperately hard not to shed. "My mind added up all the hours Emily had spent with the nanny and I..." She paused. There was no other way to say it. "I freaked out, right there in the church with everyone watching. I sat on the floor and I couldn't stand up; I don't even know how I got out of the church. I think someone carried me, took me home. I lay on my bed and cried through the entire wake thinking, *So many hours. So many more hours I could have had with her.* I wanted those hours back so badly—I still do. I wanted to undo everything. My life, myself. I think that was the day the kicks really started..."

Her voice trailed off into the night, her strange, sad confidence like the decades-old light of a long-dead star finally reaching earth. It was too much truth, too much Remy. Adam would surely stand up and walk away.

But instead he said, "Family can be both the best thing and the worst thing."

From the way he spoke, she guessed that, waiting to be heard now, was a strange, sad confidence of his own. So she offered him the same silence to place his words into.

Eventually he said, "My mom thought, right from the start, that the whole thing with Matt would end in tears. But how do you say no to your brother when he asks you to give him a child?"

Adam closed his eyes for a moment. Traces of shadow sat beneath the sockets, the only sign of the personal cost of his own grit—grit that got him through every day in a house with his daughter in arm's reach and a brother who wanted to keep her from him.

"Matt married young," he continued, opening his eyes. "He met Sally in his first year of college and they married the day after graduation. She'd had a brain tumor in her teens so, even though we all thought they were way too young to get married, what could we say? Matt loves to take on the weak and oppressed and save them. He and Sally tried for years to have kids, thinking she couldn't because of the treatments she'd had for her tumor, only to find out it was Matt who was infertile. He told me I was the only one who could help them; that a child was the only thing he and Sally wanted. So I agreed. I found out later that they suspected Sally's cancer had come back. They knew there was a possibility they were bringing a child into the world who would lose its mother. I was furious with them but how can you be furious with a dying woman? It was all so fucked up."

Adam rubbed the deep furrow the conversation had etched onto his brow. Lining his voice, Remy could hear the kind of shattering she found inside the most perfect vintage gowns; the destruction of years evident only if turned inside out.

"Then Molly was born. And she was so beautiful." Another silence followed, the kind of silence in which Remy could feel the ghost-damp of unshed tears. "About eighteen months later, Sally and Matt told me to stay away or they'd get a restraining order. It was the worst damn day of my life."

The cry of a seabird echoed above them.

When the bird quieted, she spoke. "Do you . . ." She hesitated, not sure she should say it but the moon was temporarily hidden and it seemed as if things could be said into this kind of darkness, as if the words would spill over the edge of the cliff and be carried away by the water, rather than churning only in the confines of one's mind. "Do you play it over and over, not changing it because you know you can't, but hating yourself for every minute of that day that you somehow caused?"

"Yes."

There was nothing more to say after that, no confidences greater than those they had shared. She understood now that in recent years he'd worked relentlessly against anything truly beautiful, shooting technically perfect but lifeless images, because in anything truly beautiful there was the shadow of Molly—and of the kind of love he wasn't allowed to have. And she also understood that it was a gift to be shown another's heart in the way Adam had shown Remy his: to see that it was broken and bleeding but exquisite still.

A shiver of breeze tiptoed over the terrace.

"What about your family?" Adam asked, standing up and they both walked, going nowhere in particular, not toward the sea but over the parterres and amongst the roses. "Don't they worry about you, over here by yourself?"

"They do," Remy said, pausing. "I'm adopted," she added. "Which doesn't mean my parents love me any less. It just means..." She considered what she was trying to say. "I think, for my mum, being given someone else's child has always troubled her, deep down. Maybe the child could be taken away because it's not really hers. I'm probably conducting poor psychoanalysis," she hurried to add. "I know my mum loves me. But she takes to heart the phrase: if you love something, set it free. She told me to come here. That I shouldn't come back until..."

Until you can face life, her mother had said to her on the phone that night from Sydney, while Remy was curled up in bed, sobbing, having woken from a nightmare about Emily alone in the back of the ambulance. Remy had screamed at her mother that life wasn't something you squared up to in a boxing ring. It was the relentless every day, a hidden tick inside you that had to be endured. That phone call was not one of Remy's finest moments.

"Until?" Adam asked gently.

She stopped in front of a magnificent rosebush, its petals tumbling into the pond so it looked as if she could step in and bathe in flowers. "Until I can face life." The words fell out.

"Does anyone ever do that?" he mused.

It was a terrible question for a beautiful night. "It's a good thing Antoinette isn't here," Remy said, trying to lighten the mood. "She'd be throwing us off the cliff by now."

Adam smiled. "She seems like the kind of person who says it like it is."

"Which is often good. Occasionally annoying."

"I'll bet."

In the moonlight, she caught sight of her watch and realized it was midnight. "We should get your books. I'm sure they'll be better company than me."

"Less inquisitive perhaps," he teased.

She led the way back to the house and into the *petit salon*, where beautiful antiques mingled with disrepair and her vintage treasures sprawled lasciviously over the delicate Louis XIV chairs. The box sat on the gold-upholstered sofa fitted into the curved alcove beside the fireplace. A painted panel had been inlaid on the wall behind, a fête galante, in which curvaceous young women frolicked with young men. Opposite, several Picasso nudes adorned the wall. All around was life and lust and happiness.

"How'd you come by the house?" he asked as he picked up the box.

"It's actually kind of an inheritance I came with when I was adopted. A month or so after Emily and Toby's funeral, when I hadn't really managed to get out of bed, my mum told me that, when she'd adopted me, I'd come with the deeds to this house—and also the instruction that I was only to be given it in my time of greatest need. She said she'd forgotten all about it; hadn't even understood it thirty-six years ago when she took me home. But that now she did. She sent me here after the funeral."

Adam whistled. "What an inheritance."

Remy moved a pile of dresses off the banquette and sat down. "It's where *Remy's Closet* started. I was in the worst and most self-pitying phase back then and I was sitting in one of the bedrooms—crying, of course—when I saw one of my fifties sundresses in the brightest red in the closet. It was so joyful that I hated it. I snapped a pic of it, shared it on my private Instagram account, begging one of my friends to take it off my hands. Someone bought it within about five minutes and I spent that afternoon purging every beautiful thing from my life via Instagram."

She smiled. "I can't believe I'm telling you about both my rampant self-pity and my rampant Instagramming while self-pitying."

He laughed. "Hey, I'm a photographer; I'll never knock anyone for Instagramming."

She laughed too. "Then I had to mail everything. And for some reason, I defaulted back to my IMG days of making everything perfect: I bought beautiful vintage cards from the markets and gorgeous wrapping paper and made each parcel something you'd want to unwrap and I realized I hadn't thought about Toby or Emily for a couple of hours. It was the first time that had happened. I also realized that I needed to not think about them sometimes or I would actually lose my mind. So *Remy's Closet* started. It's been . . . a savior, I guess."

The words that had been coming freely became tangled now and she stood and pretended to inspect one of the beautiful vases on the mantelpiece. "I hadn't even thought at that stage about what I'd do. I had . . . I had Toby's life insurance money. But how do you bring yourself to spend money you've been given in exchange for a life?" Her hand closed over the mantel, knuckles bloodless.

She'd done it again. Brought misery back into the conversation.

She was glad he didn't pursue it. Glad he gave her a moment to find something else to say. "Anyway," she said, taking the conversation back to where they'd started, "finding out more about the house is on the very long list of things I intend to do once I can face life again." She gave him a wry smile to let him know she was okay. "What did you get in the box?"

He set it down on the wooden gaming table and pulled out a few orange and white covers. "Here's one for those guys." He held up *Lolita* and pointed to the painted men tearing clothes off simpering maidens. "And here's one called *Dead in the Morning*. That should work with our current selection."

Remy laughed. "Did you ask for weirdest box in the shop?"

"I must have that kind of face."

Remy extracted a couple of books about art and one called *Modern Masters of Photography*. "Or maybe you have that kind of face?"

"Yep, that's me."

"So modest," Remy teased as she withdrew another book. "Wow. Look at that," she said when she saw the title.

Le Catalogue Goering, it read, followed by the subtitle: *L'histoire insensée de la plus grande collection d'art jamais volée*. The unbelievable story of the greatest of all art thefts.

"I've heard about this," Adam said, opening the book and flicking through it. "Göring, as in one of Hitler's cronies, stole a ton of paintings from France during the war and he cataloged all of them. This was published not long ago. Look," he pointed to a painting. "A Vermeer. Monet. Renoir."

Remy leaned over his shoulder but he was taller than her and she couldn't see properly. He moved to the sofa and sat down and she perched beside him while he turned over more pages.

"*An odious hunting trophy, the fruit of the villainous plundering of jewels of European art,*" he read, translating from the French introduction.

"You've obviously learned a bit of French while working in Europe."

The book fell open suddenly, as if an ill wind had blown in, forcing the pages to turn and creating a portal into a future Remy could never have imagined might exist. Her eyes fell on the new page and she froze. She took the book from Adam. "Why would that be in Göring's Catalogue?"

ELEVEN

Wat is it?" Adam asked. "You look sort of…"

Remy stood up and switched on every light in the room. She pushed the box of books on the gaming table to one side and lay the catalogue down. Then she braced both hands on the table and bent over it, staring at one of the paintings. Impossible. And her already overwrought mind could not deal with any more impossibilities. She slammed the book shut with a noise so loud they both jumped and the book fell with a crash to the floor.

"Too much murder and mayhem for this time of night," Adam said wryly as he bent to pick up the book.

"How about cassis?" Remy said. "I have a bottle hidden away in the kitchen from the last time I was here. I'm sure," she consulted her watch, "one in the morning is a good time for cassis."

"Okay. So long as you're all right."

"I'm fine," she said, aiming for bright but achieving brittle.

She marched into the kitchen, found the cassis, poured out two glasses and soon they found themselves outside again, cassis in hand, talking about fashion shoots and models and meaningless and hilarious things, laughing in the way that only happens after midnight and liquor.

Which was most likely why it happened.

Remy set down her glass and Adam set down his. She had meant to begin another story about the shoot where she'd first met Adam but they were standing so close together and her words caught somehow in her throat as the moon glided out and scattered light around them and Adam leaned down and kissed her.

It took perhaps two seconds before Remy recovered. She placed her hands on his chest and pushed him away. "What are you doing?" she demanded. "*What* are you doing?"

The moon scudded away. Darkness fell. She couldn't see Adam's face, could feel only the acute stiffening of his body and the flash of, not anger, but hurt, perhaps. Which was rich because if anyone out there was hurt, it was Remy.

"Goodnight," she said.

She stalked inside, shut the door, and snapped off the lights. Then she dropped onto her bed and lay staring at the ceiling for every minute of every hour until dawn.

* * *

Closing her eyes didn't help. The entire night continued to play over in microscopic and horrific detail: the unexpected glimpse into Adam's psyche; her own confessions. The catalog. The painting she'd seen in its pages.

It had all started there.

Then the cassis. The type of conversation that a man and a woman might have after midnight with *apéros* in hand. The humor, the pleasure of talking about things that didn't matter and feeling a meeting of minds. The imperceptible move of two bodies closer.

Remy squeezed her eyes tighter to blur the image. She hadn't even realized what was happening. It was like her mouth had kissed Adam back while Remy wasn't paying attention.

She understood why Adam had kissed her. It was the logical

progression. She also understood, in part, why she'd reacted the way she had. But there was something more in it that she couldn't face, yet.

It was still dark when she threw on her swimsuit and went down to the shore and did what Adam had done the night before, stepping into the water and swimming until she was exhausted. Then she returned to the house, thinking to go to bed and finally sleep but the cassis bottle and glasses and coffee cups of the night before were strewn everywhere and she definitely didn't want to have to explain that to Antoinette.

She found a pair of beach pajamas, a pale pink set with an ultra-high waist, flared legs, a halter neck, and scooped-out back. They were hand-made, painstakingly so, as if they might have been a bride's gift to herself for a seaside honeymoon decades ago. Then, even though it was only seven in the morning, Remy set to work to clean and scour and put the *petit salon* to rights, frowning at Adam's box of books still on the gaming table.

She'd almost finished when the sound of a knock on the front door startled her. She opened it to find Adam there, unshaven, clearly not having slept either.

"I'm sorry," he said. "Really sorry. That was a dumb thing to do. I don't know why I did it. Other than, as someone once said, I'm an ass-hole and I do stupid things way too often."

Remy offered him a small smile. He frowned, obviously having expected her to push him away again, or yell.

"It's not your fault," she said. "You don't need to apologize. But thank you for doing it. Last night we were two people sharing confidences, wine, the early hours of a morning. It was completely normal that one person might kiss the other in those circumstances. I can see that now. But it made me realize…" She rested her hand on the doorframe, knowing she was about to share yet another confidence and unsure why she kept giving these pieces of herself to the man in front of her.

Somehow, she found her voice and plowed on. "It made me see that

I'm not normal. I'd fooled myself, for that hour or so while we were talking outside, into thinking I was. That I could have a drink and a laugh and behave as a functional human being. When you kissed me, I realized that the idea of kissing anyone was repulsive to me. Which is clearly not normal and also—" She hesitated. "It was unkind of me to make you feel as if what you'd done was in any way repulsive. I'm sure most women wouldn't think so. You could be, I don't know—" She cast a round for a suitably impressive comparison. "Chris Hemsworth, and I'd still be repulsed by the idea of kissing."

Adam was listening to her intently and she knew he understood. But there was more she needed to say and if she didn't give him the rest then she wasn't being honest like he had been with her. *Then Molly was born,* Adam had said last night. *And she was so beautiful.*

It was the most revealing of all the small intimacies they'd shared. It told Remy that he was a man capable of the most deep and intense love and that he had, through iron will, suppressed and concealed that love so that nobody, except now her and perhaps his mother, understood. But she found she couldn't look at him while she told him the rest.

She stared at her bare feet, at her toenails that matched the pink of her trousers.

"A part of me enjoyed the kiss," she said and she felt his attention fix on her, felt his surprise and also his relief that he hadn't so utterly misread a situation and taken advantage of a grieving widow, which was how he must have seen it.

"I hated that part most of all," she said quietly. "So I lashed out at you. I hated that I craved comfort when nothing can ever comfort my daughter who is locked in a box in the ground. I was mad at myself," she said, looking up at him at last, "not at you."

"Remy," he said. Then, "I don't even know what to say. Thank you. You could have just let me think I was an asshole." He stopped and a glimmer of a smile appeared on his face and she realized how much she liked it when he smiled, how clear his eyes became, how unguarded he suddenly was. "But maybe not a total asshole if you enjoyed it a bit."

Remy felt her own mouth smile in response. "Now you *are* being an asshole," she said.

"But at least I made you smile."

"Come in and get your books," she said, laughing. "And actually take them this time. I'm not your library."

"I bet you do have a library in here somewhere," he said as he followed her through the columned Italian patio, then the magnificent *grand salon* and into the *petit salon*.

"I do. It's full of dust. I need to move here for a year and put everything in order. But it's too much like planning ahead and I'm hopeless at that right now."

Le Catalogue Goering lay on the table beside the box. Adam picked it up. "What was in here?" he asked. "This started it all."

"It did," she agreed. "First I need food. I've had nothing but coffee and cassis and my stomach is demanding something more. Then I'll be able to explain."

"Eggs," Adam said. "We need eggs. Didn't Antoinette bring some back from the markets yesterday?"

Remy followed Adam into the kitchen where he proceeded to open the fridge, take out the eggs and various other things, chop and whisk, locate a frying pan and then begin to cook.

"What?" he asked when he realized she was staring.

"Nothing," she stammered. "I'll pick some oranges and make juice."

She walked across the terrace to the orange trees and stood for a minute, not seeing oranges but seeing Toby, the way he'd always ordered takeout if she had a late meeting and wouldn't be home in time to cook, the way he had no idea where the frying pan was or how to even crack an egg. She hadn't given it a second thought—Toby was hopeless in the kitchen, was the joke they all shared, although Remy had often done it with gritted teeth, especially during Fashion Week when she didn't even have time to pour cereal into a bowl.

She returned to the house, juiced the oranges and then they both went outside, plates in hand, frowning at the sun that had risen ferociously hot, making the terrace feel oppressive already.

"What about that thing up there?" Adam asked, pointing to the white structure at the top of the water cascade.

"The Temple of Love?" she said. "Can you be trusted in a Temple of Love?"

He laughed. "Is that really what it's called?"

"Yep," she said. "But you're right; it's shady. It'll be the best place. So long as you're on your best behavior."

"I promise," he said, suddenly serious.

"I'm joking," she said.

"I know. But..."

"Too soon?"

"Maybe. Let's go eat."

So they took their breakfast—which was fast becoming brunch—up to the temple. As they walked, they talked about the photographers whose works had inspired them the day before—Dahl-Wolfe, Steichen, Hoyningen-Heune—and Remy knew that Adam, someone she'd known for just a few days, was now a mate, like Antoinette but also different. He didn't push her ruthlessly like Antoinette, but he did make her shift. They both made her laugh, but Adam also made her think. A new friend, a new affinity, unexpected, something she hadn't known she needed.

They laid their plates on the table in the pavilion. The ocean glittered one hundred and eighty degrees around them. They could hear it purr, could see the Monet-esque beauty of all the different gardens, could feel the delicious warmth of the shade and none of the harshness of the sun.

"This is amazing," Adam said. "I don't know how you don't just pack up and move here." Then he looked at the other thing she'd brought with her. "You brought the book."

"I did."

Remy opened *The Göring Catalogue* to the page that was engraved on the inside of her skull. "This painting." She pointed to one of the black-and-white images in the book.

It showed a couple, nothing but a couple—no setting, no backdrop—just their embrace, their entangled and inseparable gaze, a gaze that held in it everything that was worth living for and also, somehow, everything that hurt: love, and loss.

"It's on the wall of my bedroom in Sydney. It always has been. It came with me, like this house, when I was put up for adoption. But how do I have in my possession a painting that Hermann Göring stole seventy years ago from someone in France?"

PART THREE
PARIS, 1941–1943

TWELVE

We'll start tomorrow," Rose said, as calmly as if she were talking about taking up knitting.

Luc, always more prone to excitability, raised his glass and toasted, far too loudly for a clandestine meeting. "To tomorrow!"

But Monsieur Jaujard didn't admonish him. He smiled, and so did Éliane and it was a real, unrestrained beam, one that filled her whole face and shone from her eyes as well. In response, she saw Rose's mouth lift upward and the eyes hidden away behind the glasses sparkled too. Because, after six months of these meetings, where they had talked through every idea and plan and suggestion, every threat and problem and danger, they were finally going to start doing whatever they could to hold the Nazis to account.

It had been so hard for all of them over that six months to watch as more and more art collections owned by Jewish families were taken to the Jeu de Paume: thousands of paintings and tapestries and stained-glass windows and statues. Rose and Éliane had eyed the stacks of Rembrandts, Van Dycks, Velásquezes, and Van Goghs with terror. But, while they couldn't stop what had already been done, they could, they had decided, document everything so that, at a glorious time in the future when there were no more Nazis, artworks could be saved and reunited with their owners.

"Everyone knows what their priority is," Monsieur Jaujard said, bringing solemnity back to the meeting.

Éliane nodded. She was to persuade König to let her help him catalog the artworks—she knew art and most of the German art historians at the Jeu de Paume didn't, unless a piece was Germanic or by one of the Dutch masters. If she helped with the cataloging, she would be able to record, in a notebook she and Rose were to hide behind a painting of the Führer in their office, the names of the artworks that came into the Jeu de Paume and who they had been stolen from.

Rose nodded too. She was to find out where the artworks were being sent. They had seen codes written onto crates and they understood the codes represented the places where Göring and Hitler were storing the pieces but they had no idea—yet—what the codes meant.

Luc didn't nod, but swallowed wine and tilted his glass at Monsieur Jaujard, who was to be the diplomat and the organizer: keeping the Nazis' hands off the Musées Nationaux treasures and acting as the bridge between the women and Luc. Luc would, in turn, spend his time moving between Paris and the countryside, taking messages from Monsieur Jaujard to the fledgling Resistance groups, both men working to somehow inform the Allies of the whereabouts of all the paintings, so that, should the Allies ever stir themselves to help France, the country's entire cultural heritage wouldn't be destroyed.

Four people doing what they could for art.

It was almost curfew when they left Monsieur's apartment, Rose giving Éliane a quick hug before she hurried away. Luc and Éliane walked back to the Galerie Véro-Dodat together, Éliane hoping that Angélique would not still be awake. That was the hardest thing of all; lying to her sister. Pretending that she waitressed once a week to earn a little extra money, thus accounting for her late nights. Pretending that Luc could only find odd jobs in the countryside, which meant he moved around a lot and wasn't often in Paris.

An empty bus drove past them, and then another, driving in the direction of the Marais. Two more followed just thirty seconds later. Éliane frowned. She noticed Luc staring after the busses too.

"Isn't that a little strange?" she asked him.

"Yes," he said. "Let's get home."

They hurried on. The sounds Éliane could hear—the roar of another bus, shouted German words, the crash of a bin knocked over—scraped away her earlier optimism like a palette knife scoring through yellow, leaving behind a thick layer of black. The decrepitude of the *passage*, when they finally turned into it, was almost soothing, reassuring her that everything was still the same. "Perhaps we're just on edge because we know it all begins tomorrow," she said to Luc when they reached the top of the stairs.

He nodded, but the moment they were inside, he opened a bottle of wine that he'd taken from the cellar in the brasserie and began to drink it quickly. For one terrible moment, he looked like a younger version of their father, like a man determined to ruin himself as the world ruined itself around him.

"I saw your painting," she blurted, wanting to give him something more than the present, a memory of the Luc he had once been and could be again after all of this was over. "The one you sold to Rothschild. It's in the Jeu de Paume. It's magnificent." She'd meant to tell him back when she'd first seen the painting but Luc was in Paris so little and she'd been so caught up in what he and Rose and Monsieur Jaujard were doing that she'd forgotten to mention it.

But it didn't make him smile as she hoped it would.

"The couple embracing in front of that magnificent sky, and the moon; it's all so well done. But I like the figures best," she went on.

Luc refilled his glass, not acknowledging her words, focused only on the wine. Perhaps, rather than inspiring him, what she'd said had reminded him of all he had lost.

"I'm sorry," she said.

"I'll see you in a week," he replied, dismissing her, and she knew he would stay at the table until dawn before returning to the countryside.

But it was Luc who woke her the next morning, his cheeks reddened and his breath audible, as if he'd been running. He pressed a finger to his lips, indicating Angélique. Éliane slipped out of the bed, closed the door to the room and followed Luc over to the window.

"The busses," he said quickly. "I came back to tell you because I heard from a friend of mine..."

"What?" she asked, not knowing how those busses, strange though they'd been, could make her brother look so grim.

"The Nazis took hundreds of Jewish men from the Marais last night, Éliane. They put them on the busses and drove away."

"Where to?"

"Nobody knows."

The Nazis were stealing paintings and sending them away. The Nazis were stealing people and sending them away too. But she knew the people weren't being taken to Germany to adorn drawing rooms. What would happen to them?

"Do you still want to do this?" Luc asked, a curious light in his eye as if this unexpected step taken by the Nazis had quickened something within him, was the spark he'd once used to find in artists' models and absinthe.

What would happen to *them*? The question asked itself again in Éliane's head but, this time, "them" was not a group of unknown people; it was herself and Luc and Rose and Monsieur Jaujard. If König let her help him and then realized she was recording the information about the paintings in a secret notebook, would he put her on a bus to a secret destination too?

She suppressed the thought. First, convince König to let her help him. She would think about the rest of it later.

"I still want to do this," she said.

"Be careful," was all Luc said to her before he left.

* * *

Éliane dressed with care, choosing the plain cotton dress she'd worn the night Xavier had first come to the brasserie to see her. She quashed that memory, doing up the buttons, glad that the dress still fitted her well enough despite the fact that she'd lost a little weight over the months of rationing, glad that it made her look young and naive, as if she could never be smart enough or brave enough or cunning enough to spy on a Nazi.

"You look pretty," Angélique said when Éliane emerged from the bathroom. "I always liked that dress on you."

Éliane kissed her sister's cheek and shared a cup of *café nationale* with her, neither grimacing at the watery taste they were too used to now.

"I feel like today is going to be a meat day," Angélique said as she gathered up her string bag to do her day's work.

Angélique, despite being only seventeen, had turned out to be expert at getting to the front of food queues and obtaining more than stale bread and rutabaga, making Éliane suspect that her neighbors had been taking some of the food she had paid them to buy for her. Another subtle example of collaboration with the enemy; it was everywhere, a stray dog on every street.

"But what kind of meat?" Éliane said, teasing. "Fox? Wolf? Elephant?"

Angélique laughed, still one of the best sounds in the world after the long months of her absence, a sound Éliane tried to provoke as much as possible.

"I think even beef would be easier to get in Paris than elephant," Angélique said. "And that's saying something. How about I bring you home a whole wild boar?"

Now Éliane laughed; she had once, as a small child, been sick in the brasserie's kitchen at the sight of a side of boar hung up to bleed out. "Angélique, if you can find a wild boar, I will happily butcher it for you." She smiled at her sister as they turned their separate ways: Éliane going to earn the money; Angélique to spend it however she could so that they had enough to eat.

The sun seemed to be of the same mind as Éliane and her sister. It shone like midsummer, warming the air so that Éliane tipped her head back, soaking it in, this one small and wonderful thing stoking the hope she had carried inside her since last night: that she and the others would make a difference. That she and the others would hurt the Nazis, just as the Nazis had hurt them. Such a priceless thing, hope. Éliane had learned over the last few months that it stood, with love, beyond the concept of value—and that she had to tend it whenever she could.

It was with regret that she brought her head down, erased her smile and made herself ingenuous, artless, a young woman in awe of her conquerors, walking to work to serve them.

She was halfway through the Jardins des Tuileries when she saw Rose step in front of her.

Éliane turned immediately and walked over to one of the more protected benches beside the path. She and Rose never met up to walk to work together. They had agreed not to appear friendly, to be a boss and a worker, to do nothing that might make the Nazis think they were close. If Rose was in the Tuileries, it was because she needed to talk to Éliane right now and Éliane knew it would be best to do that out of plain sight.

The women sat down. Rose passed her a newspaper.

French Prisoners Killed as Retribution for the Shooting of a Loyal German Soldier, said the headline.

Éliane knew that a Parisian had shot a German soldier on the Métro several days ago in a small and very public act of resistance. But what the newspaper told her now was that the Nazis had decided to kill dozens more Frenchmen to right the balance and deter others from any similar act of resistance. Who would resist if they knew their actions cost the lives of so many others?

Éliane shivered even though the sun still blazed down.

"What the newspaper doesn't say is that the men were guillotined," Rose said quietly. "Their heads left to rot in the sun."

There was nothing else Éliane could do than close her eyes.

"Do you still want to do this?" Rose's words were the same as her brother's the night before.

Did she? Éliane thought now. What if she slipped up, said something at the Jeu de Paume that gave her away and then von Behr arrested not just Éliane but Rose too?

Éliane sliced off the thought.

When she opened her eyes, she saw not just the gardens in front of her but the things that were gone. The statues melted down for munitions. The absence of art in a city where it had once been everywhere. She remembered that small white oblong on the wall of the Louvre, all that remained of the *Mona Lisa* in France's capital. The feeling that swept over her then was a little like hunger, but not for food. It was the famishment of her soul.

It would not be possible, she knew then, to live for years and years without the *Winged Victory* flying over the grand staircase at the Louvre. It would not be possible to live in a world emptied of everything but murderers. Civilization was more than a mass of people; it was also the beautiful things that came from minds and hands and that touched hearts. Her heart, and everyone else's, needed to be touched often if any of them were to survive. And there was only one way to make that happen.

Save the art.

"I have to," she said to Rose, who took off her glasses and blinked and Éliane saw, for the first time, the wretchedness that this woman kept hidden while doling out eggs to Éliane and doing what she could to protect her. Rose was art too.

Now, it was Éliane who blinked.

* * *

Éliane and Rose's plan was to create some mischief of their own in the place where devilry was the natural order of the day. Led by von Behr, debauchery had become common practice at the Jeu de Paume and infighting and rumor and innuendo circulated like oxygen through the museum.

Rose made her way to the main gallery where she was to send one of the secretaries, who was having an affair with an art historian—even though the historian's wife worked at the museum too—to one of the little-used galleries in time to see her lover engaged in behavior worthy of a Boucher painting with a different secretary.

Éliane waited until she heard loud shouting and wailing and, hoping it meant Rose had succeeded, made her way into the main gallery, which everyone had left to investigate the commotion. She took advantage of the fuss to turn to König, who was ignorant of the noise and frowning over a painting.

She ran her hands down her skirt as if she were nervous, gave him a tentative smile and gestured at the painting. "It's by Berthe Morisot," she said.

The relief on König's face was immediate. He glanced around, realized there were very few people in the gallery with them, and that his uncle was nowhere to be seen, and handed her a notebook, a timorous smile on his face now too. "Please," he said. "Fill out any details you can."

It couldn't be that easy, Éliane thought as she scanned the page quickly. *Remember the names of the paintings and their owners*, she told herself, for it was all listed there. It would be impossible to recall so many, but if she let herself be overwhelmed, she wouldn't remember any at all.

"He's coming tomorrow! Keep it in your trousers!" Von Behr's bellowing voice, returning from the fracas, made both König and Éliane jump and there was no time for her to hand the notebook back to König without his uncle seeing.

It wasn't that easy. Of course it wasn't.

Éliane swallowed, as did König beside her. She turned frightened eyes on him, not having to act this time, but having no idea whether König would have the courage to stand up to his uncle or whether he would sacrifice Éliane instead.

"What are you doing?" von Behr asked Éliane, charm dripping mendaciously from every word.

Éliane kept her pleading eyes fixed on König, whose head swiveled between her and his uncle. When he finally stilled his head, it was turned in his uncle's direction, not Éliane's.

"She's helping me."

Never had it been harder not to exhale her stupendous relief all through the gallery.

"Are you not smart enough to do it yourself?" von Behr inquired of his nephew, his tone, if anything, even more charming and also more terrifying. Éliane was sure König would back down and that her one attempt at spying was over.

She tried not to think of busses, or of guillotines.

But König stepped closer to her, and further away from his uncle.

"It's physically impossible to do it without an art reference library," König replied quietly, but with a determination that reflected his serious desire to perform his duties in an exemplary fashion.

Yes, he might have stood up for Éliane but he still thought that cataloging stolen art was an imperative and important job, not an act of wickedness. But Éliane did not let that thought show on her face.

"Mademoiselle Dufort was helping me," König repeated. "Helping me to get the Reichsmarschall's catalogue updated in time for his visit tomorrow."

König was smarter than she'd thought. Bringing Göring, von Behr's boss, into the conversation might sway his uncle. Her racing mind also turned over what König had said. *The Reichsmarschall's catalogue.* Did that mean there was a master list somewhere detailing everything Göring was stealing? If only she could find it.

Von Behr took the notebook from her. "No French staff are to write anything down." To König, he added: "For you, she can stay. But charm her with champagne in a bedroom instead."

Éliane's eyes flickered from König to von Behr. She wasn't entirely sure, but it seemed that von Behr hadn't thrown her out because he thought his nephew was interested in her—and he wanted to encourage such interests in a man like König, who was certainly not a red-blooded and swaggering male like his uncle. Where she had thought to use König's blushes to convince him to show her his notebook, von Behr was suggesting something more, something she would never do—something she hadn't even considered as a consequence.

Von Behr left, everyone around them fell back to work and König said to Éliane, "Mademoiselle. May I call you Éliane?"

Another of those diffident smiles crept across his pale face. His eyes were of too light a blue to hold in them any deep emotion and he didn't wait for her to acquiesce before he spoke again. "Mademoiselle... Éliane...I would like to invite you to dinner this evening."

The word *never* almost fell from her mouth and she only just swallowed it. The timing of his question was not a coincidence. Either standing up to his uncle had made him feel brave enough to ask her for more, or he thought she was indebted to him for his actions. No ordinary French girl—which she was supposed to be—would say no to dinner with a German official unless she wanted to mark herself out as a Nazi-hater.

Besides, her countrymen were being guillotined. Her sisters had died. All Éliane had to do was eat a bowl of food—which many starving Parisians would say was no hardship at all. If she couldn't push aside her disgust for the sake of the thousands of paintings kidnapped by the Germans, then she didn't deserve the reward of her country liberated at some time in the future.

She molded her face into a smile. "Perhaps a drink," she said, knowing the only way to play this would be to rely on the fact that König had gentlemanly manners and she had so far played the innocent.

"A drink would be more than I'd hoped for," König said earnestly, hand pressed to heart like a caricature of a lovesick man.

At least König would provide her with plenty of unintentional humor and thus she could do it, Éliane told herself, and she also told Rose the same thing later that day in the bathroom.

"Over a drink, I have a better chance of convincing him to let me help with cataloging the paintings," she said.

"You're probably right," Rose said reluctantly. "I wish I could go with you."

"You'd look as out of place in the kind of bar König is likely to take me to as von Behr would in a nunnery," Éliane said gently.

It made Rose laugh, and her frown relax. "Be—" she began.

Éliane interrupted. "You can't tell me to be careful every day. Not if you won't let me tell you the same. I know you were in von Behr's office while he was shouting at everyone in the gallery. Did you find anything?"

Rose shook her head, lit a cigarette and leaned against the wall, looking almost young, as if spying and furtive bathroom conversations were more her style than scraping back her hair and pretending to be a mouse. "The logbooks recording every shipment of artwork out of the gallery are kept in plain sight on the loading dock. But the code words they use for the final destinations make the logbooks useless. Until I find out what the codes are…"

"We have only half the information we need," Éliane finished.

"If you can digest König and champagne, then I can find a code book," Rose said, stubbing out her cigarette. "The Germans write everything down. Somewhere, they'll have written down the codes. I'll stay late tonight after you leave with König. I don't want to say that his interest in you is useful but…" She gave a wry smile. "I just did."

Then Rose passed Éliane the packet of Gauloises. "Take these. You'll need them more than I will tonight."

With that she left the bathroom. Éliane smiled at both the gift and the words. If only there were a thousand Roses in Paris right now, all the Königs and von Behrs wouldn't stand a chance.

THIRTEEN

That evening, König met Éliane at the museum's exit. He slipped his arm through hers, a gesture so forward it rendered him momentarily speechless, which was fine with her.

They walked through the gardens and into a city where Éliane's searching eyes saw flashes of spirit. Written in the dust on a vélo-taxi were the words *Vive de Gaulle*. A Parisian man in a café stretched his legs out onto the sidewalk so König was forced to step around him.

"I've been informed by Göring's art adviser that this is an excellent place for a drink," König said as he turned in at La Grenouille, a bustling bar where, thankfully, intimate conversations of any kind would be discouraged by the noise.

"Göring's art adviser?" Éliane repeated. She'd seen Xavier a handful of times in the museum over the past six months and still wasn't sure exactly what he was doing there, but this description seemed to fit.

"Yes. Monsieur Laurent. The man who accompanies the Reichsmarschall to the Jeu de Paume. He met with von Behr this afternoon to ensure all was ready for tomorrow's exhibition and I…" König blushed in his usual way and tried to cover it by lighting a cigarette. "I asked him if he could recommend somewhere I could take you. He knows Paris well and he is also," König smiled a little self-consciously, "more of a man of the world than I am. Cigarette?"

There were many cruel things packed into those two sentences.

Xavier had suggested König bring her here. He might as well be pimping her out. She wished it hurt less and angered her more.

König clicked his fingers for the waiter, who scurried deferentially over. "Champagne," he ordered.

Éliane leaned awkwardly toward König as if she were truly interested in him. She needed to gain his trust, and quickly. She had never had to work at cultivating someone's belief in her before: Yolande and her sisters had given it unwaveringly and, with Xavier, it had simply existed, right from the start. Which it certainly didn't now.

Éliane picked up her champagne glass and drowned the memory. "Where are you from?" she asked.

"I grew up in Berlin," he answered. "I was a pianist at the conservatoire, before..."

Before Germany invaded Europe. She wondered what euphemism he might use, but he left the sentence unfinished.

"Do you still play?" she asked.

He nodded. "Herr von Behr has a piano at his apartment. I use it some evenings when we gather there. It is..."

Another unfinished sentence. "It is," she prompted.

"My consolation," he replied. "Cigarette?" he asked her again and, this time, she nodded slowly. It was impossible to think that a man like König would need consolation.

He leaned over to light the cigarette for her, watching her mouth. She dropped her hand to the ashtray. "It's so busy at the museum," she said nonchalantly.

"Two hundred important collections to catalog and sort, as well as countless other works from less significant collections." König sighed. "The richness of the artworks is extraordinary. The French people are lucky the Germans are safeguarding them."

"We are so lucky," she repeated. "Do you think the Rothschilds appreciate their good fortune?" She kept her eyes wide, her voice soft, letting the sarcasm fizz only inside her.

He laughed heartily. "The Jews appreciate nothing. We signed an armistice with the French government, not the Jewish people, which means their artworks aren't protected by the Hague Convention. So it's up to us to redistribute them to those who are more worthy."

Before Éliane could digest that piece of reasoning, a voice interrupted. "I see you're enjoying yourselves."

The voice was cooler than she remembered it, and certainly sardonic, mocking both her and König. It was Xavier, and the contrast between him and König was both striking and infuriating.

Xavier was tall and confident and absolutely at home in occupied Paris amongst the Nazis.

König was puny and stuttering and looking up eagerly, like a child seeking a father's approval. "We—we took your advice."

"But not with the champagne." Xavier raised a contemptuous eyebrow at the bottle in the ice bucket. "I'm sure she deserves something finer, doesn't she?" His tone clearly suggested she deserved nothing of the sort.

If it wasn't for the fact that two hundred collections of artworks were at stake, she probably would have picked up the bottle and tipped the contents of it over Xavier's head. As it was, she said as flatly as she could, "Given that I haven't tasted champagne for more than a year, this is quite satisfactory."

"Not for me," he said. He turned toward the bar before Éliane could tell him that neither his advice nor his presence were wanted.

She had perhaps three of four minutes to get what she needed from König before Xavier returned. She focused only on that. "I hope I was helpful this morning with your notes?"

"You were such a help!" König cried. "We haven't enough people who can identify artworks painted after the mid-nineteenth century."

"Remember, Monsieur, that I know French art very well. Today I saw a Degas, a Toulouse-Lautrec, and a Rodin sculpture." She stopped there, not wanting to ask. He had to believe everything was his idea. "Perhaps I could talk to my uncle again."

"He listens to you."

König smiled at the flattery, was still smiling when Xavier sat between them and poured champagne into three fresh glasses, despite the fact that neither Éliane nor König had finished their first.

"Here's to tomorrow's exhibition," he said to König, raising his glass. "I trust everything is ready for the Reichsmarschall?"

The glass in König's upraised hand wobbled a little as if he were somewhat afraid of Xavier. Éliane wanted to close her eyes. What could Xavier have done to make people fear him? Something worse than what the Nazis did?

She would not be able to swallow champagne. She took out the cigarettes Rose had given her. König held out a lighter to her. When he realized Xavier had done the same, König withdrew. Which meant letting Xavier light her cigarette for her, a cigarette she now doubted she'd be able to smoke.

She had to look at him and it was almost shocking. That his eyes were exactly the same as they had always been, a lustrous, indescribable brown. She hid her own unsteady hand in her lap.

"Everything is ready for the Reichsmarschall," König said to Xavier. "I hope he'll be pleased with what we've gathered for him." He added, somewhat wistfully, "Herr Göring is anxious for a Vermeer. The Führer took *The Astronomer*, of course. It's the second time Herr Göring has lost a Vermeer to the Führer. I wish I could procure one for him."

I believe that one now belongs to the Führer, Éliane remembered Xavier saying to Göring six months ago, and she also remembered Göring's abrupt acknowledgment. The Reichsmarschall had lost something he wanted, to the only man in the world with more power than him. She made herself nod sympathetically, attention fixed on König, ignoring Xavier.

As König sipped champagne, the words began to flow more easily than they did in the museum with his uncle around. Éliane began to understand that both her presence and Xavier's presence made him boastful, as if he needed to prove his importance and power to each of them. "Herr Göring hopes to build the most splendid collection of art in all the world to display in his manor, Carinhall," he said expansively. "It will be his legacy. But the Führer is also building a grand collection for his Führermuseum. I believe Herr Göring to have the better taste but not the money—"

He stopped and Éliane knew he had recollected himself. But he had told her enough. That Göring and Hitler were engaged in a feud over art. Could she and Rose somehow fuel Göring's resentment that his art collection was always to be limited by Hitler's needs?

There was a loud crash of glasses, followed by a burst of laughter. Xavier said something that was impossible to hear. He frowned. "I wish there was somewhere a little quieter to talk about business."

König nodded his agreement. "Herr Göring said the same thing last night. My uncle likes to enjoy the Paris evenings, as does the Reichsmarschall, but sometimes their enjoyment interferes with the conversations that need to be had."

The quietest restaurant in Paris. The idea leapt with catlike suddenness into Éliane's head. It was possible Luc would kill her. But it was also possible that this would be the best thing she could do for France. If König and von Behr and the Reichsmarschall could relax with wine and discuss their abhorrent business in a place where she and Luc might overhear them, then how much more progress might they make?

"I know a very quiet place, Monsieur," Éliane said, taking out another cigarette and leaning across to König to allow him to light it for her.

This time, when he watched her inhale, she didn't drop her hand to the ashtray. "My brother has been hoping to reopen our family's brasserie. I used to waitress there and would be happy to do so again for customers like you and the Reichsmarschall. I think the Reichsmarschall would be very pleased if you were to find him the quiet restaurant he wishes for."

"That's a wonderful idea!" König cried. And then, "Don't you think?" he asked Xavier, still unable to make a decision for himself.

She cursed herself for not having waited until Xavier had gone to make the suggestion. Xavier would be certain to squash her idea like an insect underfoot. He knew she had no love for the Nazis.

"The Reichsmarschall has very high standards," Xavier said to Éliane, pouring himself another champagne.

"I think my standards will be high enough for those who choose to come," she said coldly.

"Then I'll let the Reichsmarschall know," Xavier said crisply. "A month should be enough time to put things in order."

* * *

When Luc was next in Paris, Éliane told him about her impulsively conceived plan. "We have to somehow convince Angélique to help with the waitressing but without telling her why," Éliane said. "She can't find out what we're doing." She remembered the men guillotined by the Nazis and her whole body shuddered.

"I know what to do," Luc said, right before Angélique opened the door, the basket in her arms only half-full with food

She crossed to her brother, smiling. "You're back. For how long this time?"

"Longer than usual," Luc said. "In fact, I'll be working in Paris now, not in the countryside."

Angélique kissed his cheeks. "Good. I hope that means you've got a job that pays you enough that you'll actually have some money left for food?" She said it half-teasingly and half-seriously, never having understood why they were always having to send him some of Éliane's precious money. "Couldn't he just eat a few of the grapes he's picking," she would grumble to Éliane. "He's surrounded by food, unlike us."

But of course Éliane couldn't say that Luc was really running back and forth from Resistance groups to Monsieur Jaujard. And all she could do now was brace herself while she told Angélique they had to reopen the brasserie.

Angélique laughed. "Why? Aren't there already enough restaurants in Paris for the Germans to fill their ample stomachs?"

"It's been requested," Éliane said, knowing she would have to mention Xavier very soon.

Angélique picked up a pile of clothes she'd washed earlier that day and began to fold them. "By who? Who even knows we own the brasserie?"

Éliane's eyes met Luc's. "Xavier has requested it," Éliane said.

"Xavier?" The hankies in Angélique's hands fell to the ground.

"Yes, Xavier," Luc said impatiently, taking the burden from Éliane and unpacking it more ruthlessly than she would have. "He's working with the Germans. They want somewhere quiet to discuss their illdeeds. He wants to offer them the brasserie so he can elevate himself even more in their opinion. In exchange, he doesn't tell Colonel von Behr that Éliane can speak German. Xavier's seen her at the gallery, Angélique."

Angélique stared at her brother and then at her sister. "He can't be…"

"He is," Éliane said, drawing Angélique into her arms.

Angélique held on the same way Yolande had used to whenever Éliane tried to leave the apartment in the mornings. "You never said," Angélique whispered.

"I couldn't." Éliane knew that a tear was leaking from her eye. She lifted a hand to stroke Angelique's hair, bringing it momentarily to her cheek to erase the evidence of her own distress.

"I didn't know that was why you kept working at the museum," Angélique said, stepping back and studying Éliane's face. "I didn't know that Xavier—" Her voice choked on the name and she shook her head, still trying to understand. "That Xavier had threatened you. Can't we refuse? I don't know if I can work there without…" She frowned, fury taking over from incredulity. "Without tipping a pot of *boeuf bourguignon* on his head."

"Angélique." Luc sounded as merciless as their father. "We can't refuse. What do you think they'll do to us if we refuse? Grow up. Xavier isn't who you thought he was. Who is, these days? We all do what we must to survive. And we must open the brasserie."

Luc was so relentless and so good at creating a story to cover up both his and Éliane's real intentions that Éliane was momentarily afraid. This was what Luc must be like when he left the apartment and caught a train to the countryside and sat around fires with other angry young men, all vowing to overthrow the Germans.

"Luc will cook," Éliane said quietly, wishing she could take away the hurt and anger filling her sister's eyes. "He used to occasionally help Papa, so he knows enough. You and I can serve. We don't have a choice."

Luc left then, banging the door behind him. Éliane wished she could follow and thank him for doing what had to be done, but Angélique was still so young and Éliane was the only mother she had.

She picked up the washing and pointed to a patch on one of her slips, wanting to move Angélique's attention onto something ordinary. "It's so thin. I worry it will tear right through each time I wear it."

Angélique took it from her sister, inspected it, blinked away tears and said, "You should replace it. But where would we even find one now? And how could we afford it?"

"There's so much we can't afford right now, Angélique."

Angélique ran her finger over the worn patch on the slip. "Including saying no to a man like Xavier."

"Yes."

* * *

Over the next two weekends, Éliane scraped fat out of the brasserie ovens and washed and ironed tablecloths while Luc employed a kitchen hand and studied their father's old recipe books, marking out the dishes he knew he could manage. Angélique used paint Luc had found to touch up the walls, polished the glasses and cutlery and told Luc she could easily bake the bread and cakes. Then, at almost midnight on Sunday, the siblings stood in the middle of the brasserie surrounded by tables decorated with white cloths, candles, and vases.

"I'll go to the markets at dawn to replenish the kitchen," Luc said. "I can get a restaurant permit allowing us extra—so we'll all have food to eat at last. There's enough wine in the cellar. I need a week to make up the stocks and sauces and to prepare the menu. We'll open next Tuesday at six o'clock."

"Giving me exactly half an hour to walk home from the gallery, change my clothes and come downstairs before the first of the monsters arrive," Éliane said.

"You can open half an hour later." Xavier's voice came from the doorway.

She whirled around, as did Luc, their eyes catching, and Éliane could see that he was scared too. If she were ten years younger, she would reach out for her brother's hand, but instead she accepted Xavier's cool gaze as her deserved punishment for not minding her tongue.

"They won't be here until seven," Xavier said crisply. "So you needn't open until half past six. That should give you enough time to right yourself."

He cast a withering eye over her face, which was red with exertion, damp with sweat, and probably filthy too. She smelled of grime and grease. Whereas Xavier was clean and his suit was pressed and he smelled like the cologne he had always worn.

And she realized suddenly that he would be in the brasserie with her most nights—with his German *amis*, sitting at a table where he and Éliane had once kissed. And she would have to pour his wine and take away his dirty plate and smile the whole time.

"I don't think there is enough time in all the world for things to be put right," she said quietly.

Luc stepped in front of her lest she say any more.

Éliane had forgotten her sister, who spoke now. "I can't believe you," Angélique said to Xavier.

He'd been about to leave but he turned back and stepped much closer to them all. "Never say anything like that. It's better for everyone if nobody knows…"

He was so near that if Éliane put out her hand, she could stroke the jaw she'd once been unable to stop touching. He was so near that when his eyes, made black by the dim lighting, met her gaze and the lamps flickered gold across his face she saw, for just a moment, the Xavier of 1939: a man who'd made her insides swirl into the most intense and perfect flame.

After only the slightest hesitation, Xavier said, "It would be better for everyone if nobody knows that Éliane and I once believed we loved one another."

His eyes were now a diabolical shade she couldn't name, turning her insides to ash. "None of us knows you," she blazed. "Not anymore. So you needn't worry."

Unperturbed, Xavier strolled away down the *passage*, perfectly at ease in the world of Nazi-occupied Paris.

FOURTEEN

The night before the brasserie was due to reopen, while Angélique was stuck in the kitchen preparing the pastries, Luc and Éliane slipped away to Monsieur Jaujard's apartment for their first meeting in a month.

Éliane had some good news to share. "König worked up the courage to ask his uncle if I could help with the cataloging and von Behr agreed. But only before exhibitions when they're busiest of all. Still, it's better than nothing. I'll write everything down in our hidden notebook as soon as I can and then Rose and I will alternate taking the notebook home and recording the information properly."

The shift in the mood of everyone at the table was a tangible thing, as if a wash of gold had been brushed suddenly over the gloom.

"Will it be safe to do that?" Monsieur Jaujard asked, concern etched into his forehead as he poured red wine out for all of them.

"The guards don't search our purses," Rose said.

"And safe is a relative term now," Luc observed. "Éliane simply being in the museum isn't safe. If we spent all our time worrying about what's safe—"

"If I'm writing in the notebook, Rose keeps watch. And I do the same for her." Éliane cut off her brother, who had downed the wine in one swallow. "More important is something König said to me when I went out with him. He told me that Hitler has twice beaten Göring to a Vermeer painting. Can we do anything with that..."

Her voice trailed off. In her lowly position, there was nothing she could really do to stir Göring's jealousies. But nor could she just give up.

"What if," she continued, thinking aloud, "we put some of the paintings meant for Hitler into Göring's crates and the Führer found out that Göring had his paintings?"

Rose was the first to nod. "We could do that. A small thing, but..."

"Enough small things can become infuriating," Luc finished. "If Göring loses his influence with Hitler, this might all stop. The Jeu de Paume is there because of Göring. If he's no longer a force, then it could be closed down."

"Then we might not lose the collections they haven't yet found," Monsieur Jaujard added. "Like the Schloss collection."

The Schloss collection, gathered by another Jewish family, was world renowned. It was comprised of exactly the kind of paintings the Germans most wanted: centuries-old Dutch and Flemish masters. Fifty million francs' worth of art.

The Nazis had been searching for it but nobody, not even Monsieur Jaujard, knew where it had been hidden. The Schloss family had been ingenious and that had infuriated both von Behr and Göring.

"Imagine if we were able to keep it safe by stopping Göring," Rose said and suddenly it seemed possible that they might. On every face was a smile now.

"On nights like this," Rose continued, squeezing Éliane's hand, "when winter hasn't yet come and we're not frozen down to our bones, and everyone around me is friend not foe, I feel like dreams aren't that far away from coming true."

Indeed, Éliane could almost see, like a fresco on the far wall, just out of reach, a time when art would be for everyone again, not just for those with power. And again it was Rose who gave her strength even though

Rose lived alone and didn't have a brother and sister to comfort her. Rose had once been the curator of the Jeu de Paume and now she was its caretaker. She had lost so much and yet, here she was, trying to make everyone else feel better.

"Nobody's dreams will come true if we just sit here and talk about them," Luc said, returning them all to reality. "We need to leave here tonight with more action planned than Éliane writing the names of paintings into a notebook. We still don't have the codes for the locations they're taking the paintings to. And I don't know how I'm going to manage liaising with the Resistance now that Éliane's turned me into a chef."

"It will be worth it," she said to her brother, refusing to acknowledge that her stroke of apparent genius might prove to be another waste of time.

"It had better be," Luc grumbled before Monsieur Jaujard interjected.

"We do have another action planned," Monsieur said stoutly. "England has people in France who are working against the Nazis. One of them is, amongst other things, liaising with the Allies about the art. Let me talk to him. He might be the key to making sure Hitler finds out that Göring has a painting meant for him—if you both think that might be possible to arrange."

Both Rose and Éliane nodded vigorously, and in unison.

* * *

At half past six the following evening, Éliane arrived at the brasserie with her face freshly made up, hair waved and pinned back, one blonde curl curving across her brow, her old uniform on, hands having thankfully recovered over summer. The mirror told her she looked polished and presentable and she hoped it would be enough for König to tell her something useful now they were out of the frenzy of the museum and in a place where food and champagne might loosen his tongue.

In the kitchen, the smell of braised beef, garlic and onion, and potatoes baked in duck fat filled her nostrils and she almost felt nauseous with hunger, having eaten nothing besides a peach all day.

"Quick," Luc said, pointing to a plate piled high with all of the things she could smell. "Eat before we open. You look like you might pass out."

Éliane didn't even bother to sit. She found a fork and began to work her way through the meal with the diligence of an art restorer saving a masterpiece. She hadn't eaten so well since June 1940, over a year ago. After five minutes, nothing was left on her plate.

Angélique laughed at her. "I did the same thing half an hour ago. Tell me why I ever thought opening the brasserie was a bad idea?"

The bell on the front door tinkled, announcing the arrival of their first patrons. Éliane placed a smile onto her face, kissed her sister's cheek, and said, "That's the spirit."

The party entering the brasserie included Xavier, the Reichsmarschall, König, an art dealer or two, von Behr and his mistress, singer Arletty, the Chambruns, and several other German-loving Parisians. Éliane showed them to the best table, by the window.

"We'll have some Bordeaux. One that's at least ten years old," Xavier said to her as he sat.

Éliane withdrew to rummage through what her father had not drunk of the wine cellar and found a bottle that met Xavier's requirements.

"König," von Behr said as she stood by his side to fill his glass, "look at your Mademoiselle. You should take her out for an evening."

Éliane passed out menus, wishing to turn their attention to the food but von Behr appeared to be fortified with either wine or malevolence.

"Show her Paris," von Behr continued, grinning, unconcerned that his nephew was so scarlet his hair had taken on a pinkish glow, "enhanced with German *éclat*."

"He already has taken me out," Éliane said, hoping to surprise von Behr into silence. "But now I'll be here every night to serve you, so I won't be able to experience any more of your *éclat*." Fortunately, the men around her were as illiterate in tone as they were in art and her sarcasm passed by unnoticed.

"You already have!" Von Behr slapped his nephew on the back. "I didn't think you had it in you. Now I know why you want Mademoiselle Dufort to work so closely with you. But we can't let waitressing cool your blood." He raised his glass into the air as if struck by inspiration. "We'll have a party! That will allow our *fräulein* to have an evening off—if we aren't here, we won't need to be served."

"We have a special braised beef brisket tonight," Éliane said. "Can I get that for everyone?" She saw her sister glare fiercely at Xavier as she walked past to greet more guests, more Germans who'd likely seen Göring's uniform glowing spectacularly white in the window, like an advertisement.

Von Behr was not deterred by brisket. "Somewhere special," he continued. "A way to celebrate Germany and our Führer and our many victories. A *grand maison*. Not in Paris; we'll have a weekend party. Where would you recommend?" He turned to Xavier.

"Beef briskets all around, please," Xavier said to Éliane. As she gathered the menus, Göring said something to Xavier that made her press a hand firmly onto the table in order that she might keep her balance.

"When we were discussing Carinhall," the Reichsmarschall said in his heavy, slurred voice, "you mentioned that you have a house on the French Riviera. Whereabouts?"

"At Cap-Ferrat." Xavier didn't elaborate but he didn't need to, not for Éliane.

It was suddenly 1940 again and Éliane and Xavier were in bed together on that one night they'd shared and he was describing the house to her: the soft pink of the walls; the pleasure garden with fountains that danced in perfect time to music; the sun-filled drawing room looking out to the sea beyond; the *petit salon*, which he preferred to the *grand salon*—it had gold sofas built into the alcoves in a sweeping curve made for lovers, where they would sit together. The house where they would go for their honeymoon, he'd said, so that Éliane could see the sea for the first time, and they would make love in every room.

"That will do for a weekend party," Göring said.

In the kitchen, Éliane poured herself a healthy slug from the nearest bottle—most likely cooking port, but she didn't care.

"What is it?" Luc asked.

"Nothing," Éliane replied. "They're all having brisket."

She piled a bounty of slices of thick, soft white bread into a basket and carried it to the table of Nazis. Von Behr tapped her hand. "It's settled. A party by the Mediterranean. You'll accompany König."

"There'll be women enough at the party without needing this one." Xavier took control of the conversation and dealt with Éliane in his usual contemptuous way. "Besides, the house is being extensively renovated and won't be available for some time. So we can move on to more important business. At the museum tomorrow," he said to Göring, "we'll finalize the exchange. Our friend Rochlitz," he nodded at the art dealer across the table, "will leave with a dozen of the modernist works from the upstairs room. In exchange, you'll receive the Titian you want."

The Reichsmarschall forked brisket into his mouth. "We will do more exchanges. It's a good way to rid ourselves of the *impressionnistes sauvages* and expand my collection in the process."

Éliane's mind worked furiously fast as she refilled glasses and the bread basket, and interpreted German, while pretending not to understand anything. If she had translated correctly, Xavier was planning to give a dozen impressionist works from the Salle des Martyrs to the dealer to secure a Titian for Göring.

She wished she'd spat in their food. If that exchange really happened, and if it continued to happen, it would mean so many paintings lost to the general art market. Finding a code book would only tell her and Rose the whereabouts of the works that had been sent to Göring's and

Hitler's depots. It would be no use in helping them track paintings taken and resold by a dealer.

She and Rose and Luc and Monsieur Jaujard had thought they were making a little headway. The fragile vision of the night before of a future restored of its artworks vanished.

"Mademoiselle!" Von Behr's voice, sharp, sliced into the canvas of her thoughts.

"*Désolée*, Monsieur," Éliane murmured, hoping no trace of her comprehension showed on her face.

"Perhaps she's thinking of König," Xavier said to von Behr, and von Behr stopped staring at her for long enough to laugh at the joke.

"We need more bread," von Behr ordered her. "And a smile for König." He laughed and elbowed Xavier and Xavier laughed too.

Éliane turned every furious emotion inside her into a sudden and brilliant smile. It had the effect of quieting the entire table, of making König blush so furiously red he could have powered the entire red-light district, and of making von Behr say, "Perhaps I shouldn't give her to König after all."

It took almost more discipline than she had not to shudder. Not von Behr. No.

* * *

The following day, Éliane dusted behind König and von Behr, who stood together in the largest of the upstairs galleries in the Jeu de Paume. A set of slow and heavy footsteps sounded on the stairs, accompanied by a lighter, faster pair. Into the gallery came Göring, the art dealer from last night, and Xavier. Göring filled all the space in the room as his eyes fondled the paintings.

"Is everything ready?" Xavier asked von Behr in a voice that indicated he expected only a "yes" in response.

König's head bobbed up and down like a nervous horse and he and von Behr ushered the Reichsmarschall into their offices while Xavier took the dealer to the Salle des Martyrs.

Not long after, Éliane saw the dealer descend and re-ascend the staircase twelve times, each with a painting in hand. While she tried to dust the banisters as laggardly as she could, it was almost impossible to make out all the pictures. She was certain she saw a Picasso go by—his style was easy to recognize—and definitely a Degas but, as for the others— they were lost, perhaps forever.

It was hard not to be despondent after that. But she consoled herself with the knowledge that, if it hadn't been for the conversation she'd heard in the brasserie, she would have had no idea what was happening. Reopening the brassiere had already proved to be a smart decision.

After the dealer left, in order to restore her spirits, she crept into the Salle des Martyrs, meaning to sit on the floor and allow herself just five minutes to look at something beautiful—Luc's painting. But, in the shuffling and sorting of artworks for the dealer, Luc's picture had been moved and it took her several minutes to find it, wedged right at the back of the room. She maneuvered it out, leaning it against a wall, shifting another painting aside as she did so, one which made her stop what she was doing and stare, agape. How could it be?

There was Luc's painting, the one she'd been looking for, propped against the wall where she'd just put it. But here in her hands was another almost exactly the same. This one showed a couple, nothing but a couple, just their embrace and their entangled and inseparable gaze, a gaze that held in it everything that was worth living for and also, somehow, everything that hurt.

It was undoubtedly the same couple from her brother's painting, *The Lovers*, but set against an absence of setting: no moon, no sky, no window embrasure to frame them. They didn't need a moon, Éliane thought, or a sky. They had all that within them and more: love, and also loss.

There was no question her brother must have painted this one too, even though it wasn't signed: the couple in each was too similar to have emerged from the oils of a different artist. And if the first painting she'd seen by her brother months ago had moved her; this one beside her now almost felled her. While the first might be named *The Lovers*, this one was *Love*. Tears brushed mercilessly against her eyes.

She lowered herself to the floor, standing both artworks side by side, studying the faces of the two lovers in each, her eyes returning again and again to the work that showed just the two figures embracing. Certainly the painting with the backdrop of moon and sky was excellent, but the one without was sublime. What she saw in the oils swirled onto the canvas was not two people but a love that existed out of time and out of place: endlessly, neverendingly. Forever after.

It was hard to believe that her heart could still hurt over Xavier, considering all the other hurts it had suffered, but right now it ached. It ached over the man she had thought he was, but who he had never been. It ached with the knowledge that what she had thought was love had been something else entirely. And her heart ached too because it was no longer whole: she had given so much of it to Xavier and now those pieces were lost or, worse still, kept in a locked box and brought out occasionally to be laughed over.

* * *

She found König in one of the galleries pulling at his collar, his hair not quite as slick as usual, as if he'd been worrying at it. She slipped in beside him. "I find the Reichsmarschall terrifying too," she said softly.

König let go of his collar and smoothed his hair. "He's happy with today's business, which is good for all of us." He pressed a smile upon her. "Do you have time to help with the cataloging? It would be nice to do some of it with you."

She wondered briefly if König ordinarily romanced women over paintings and the image of König serving a woman a Dutch master in place of dinner made her smile, which in turn made König smile all the more and then she almost laughed at the comedy of her thinking one thing and him thinking another. "Where shall we start?" she asked demurely.

"See here." He pointed to a sheet on which he'd begun to record details. "The headings are marked. It's important you use these as they correspond to the headings in Göring's Catalogue."

"What is that?" she asked, innocent eyes fixed on König's face.

König looked over his shoulder, but they were the only ones in the room. Still, he lowered his voice and whispered in her ear. "It's a book that is almost a work of art itself. I'm entrusted with it. It contains the details of every artwork that will eventually be hung at Carinhall after the Allies surrender. Photographs of the work, the artist's name, the medium and dimensions. I wish you could see it, see how well these paintings look out of the hands of the Jews and in the possession of someone who deserves them."

How she wished not to have heard the last part of that sentence. And how she wished she could see the catalog too. "I suppose it is secret," she said.

The sharp rap of boots sounded not far away. Éliane stepped away from König and over to one of the paintings. "I don't want your uncle to think I'm not working," she said as she diligently began to record details of stolen paintings.

"I will look after you, Mademoiselle," König said, very seriously, leaning in far too close to her. She wanted desperately, nauseously, to step away from whatever he was about to do.

She had never been more thankful for von Behr, who passed through the gallery just in time to prevent König from carrying out his intention.

"What a pretty tableau!" von Behr bellowed in French. "If this little infatuation is giving you the balls to seduce women while you work and finally become the kind of man who would choose a woman and whiskey over a piano concerto, then perhaps I'll leave her to you after all."

Éliane did what König and von Behr expected her to do, which was nothing. She stared at the floor, letting the red of anger color her cheeks like embarrassment, while König spluttered at his uncle. "I…we were…"

Von Behr laughed. "You were charming her. I don't blame you. Now I have similar work to do with Ilse." He left, still laughing, and König concentrated furiously on his paper while Éliane pretended to do the same.

But she wasn't thinking about artworks at all. She was thinking about what had just happened. Last night, she had been truly scared of von Behr. Now, she wondered if König might turn out to be the best way of protecting herself from his uncle. Which would mean getting close to König for two reasons: to find out more about Göring's Catalogue and also because she might need a shield. It was bad enough when she had wanted one thing only from him, but to need him for two reasons was frightening in its own way: how could she refuse his advances while still hoping to make use of him?

Thankfully Rose soon came to rescue her, saying to König, "I need Mademoiselle Dufort to return to her regular duties now. She will be happy to help you again tomorrow."

Éliane gestured to the papers in her arms. "Where shall I put these for you, Monsieur?" She gave him a smile, bashful but encouraging, and he hesitated for only a moment before he said, "In my office is a marble-topped chiffonier. If you could leave them on top, please."

"Certainly."

She knew exactly which chiffonier he meant as she and Rose had combed both his office and von Behr's for the code book—all the Germans left the museum between noon and two each day for lunch, which gave the women plenty of time to investigate every drawer, cupboard and cabinet. The chiffonier was merely decorative and had no storage within it—or so she and Rose had thought. But Éliane knew, because hundreds of desks and tables and sideboards had traveled through the Jeu de Paume over the months, how many of them had ingenious secret compartments or drawers that the historians marveled over.

What if the chiffonier did too?

She set the papers down. The office was silent. She was sure all the historians were in the galleries. Göring and Xavier had left. Von Behr had said he was working with his secretary, which was code for Do Not Disturb. She ran her hands over the chiffonier.

A door slammed, most likely out on the delivery dock, echoing through the museum. She froze, listened, waited. Silence again. At the very top, along the decorative cornice, she felt something move. The cornice was not simply an adornment; it was a drawer. She eased it open, wincing in anticipation of a betraying squeak of wood on wood but it was well oiled and thus well used.

She only had to open it halfway when she saw it. A maroon leather-bound book. Gold embossing stamped on the front read: *Le Catalogue Goering.*

She felt her body start, as if simply seeing the words could conjure up Göring's presence in the room behind her, catching her in this criminal act. And there was a smaller notebook beside it, unlabeled. Did she dare flip open the cover and see what it was? How much longer until König returned to his office?

She reached out a hand to touch it. A voice called in German, "Delivery!" Footsteps sounded, everywhere.

The cover opened. On the first page a careful hand had written: *Schloss Neuschwanstein, Bavaria: HANS.*

It was the code book. *HANS* was recorded in the logbooks as the destination for most of the shipments selected for Adolf Hitler.

So many of the things she and Rose needed were right there before her, things that were both sword and honey: treason or triumph depending on whose side you were on. The Nazis had shot the first Frenchman accused of treason almost a year ago. As 1941 marched onwards, they had promised to kill between fifty and one hundred French hostages in retaliation for any act of rebellion against the Germans, as well as murdering the perpetrator. If anyone found Éliane right now, she would die, as would almost another hundred Parisians.

A laugh. She almost dropped the book but saved it before it crashed to the floor and gave her away. It was Ilse's deep, Germanic giggle and it was coming from the hallway. Von Behr had finished his "work" and Éliane would be finished too if he caught her.

She slid the drawer in much less carefully than she had opened it. Its traitorous creak had her almost unable to hear anything beyond the sound of her heartbeat pounding in her ears, its pressure against her chest. Another squeak. The drawer was shut at last.

Now to get to the door and out into the hallway without anyone noticing.

Footsteps rapped just outside. Her eyes raked frantically over the room and saw only spindly antique furniture that would provide no protection whatsoever. There weren't even any drapes on the windows to shelter her. She stood, frozen, and so obviously guilty.

The steps continued on, past the office.

She almost couldn't help but exhale her relief, a sound that would give her away. She crept to the door, opening it a crack. Thank God! There was nobody in the hall. There wasn't time to wonder who might be about to turn into the hallway. The opportunity was there now and she had to take it and trust her guardian angel.

She passed through the door. The bathroom was only a few rooms down and she just reached the sanctuary of silence and cold tile before her heart exploded.

* * *

Éliane and Rose waited a few days after Éliane had seen the code book in the chiffonier in case it was a trap. Then Rose stole into König's office while he was at lunch and copied down the destinations and their corresponding codes. That night, she arrived at Éliane's apartment before curfew, after the Germans had finally left the brasserie and Éliane had finished waitressing, and after Angélique was asleep.

Éliane opened the door with the biggest smile she'd worn since 1939. She swung Rose around into an impromptu jig, whirling her into the apartment and hearing Rose laugh for the first time ever.

"You'll wake the neighbors," Luc complained from the table where he was sitting before a half-empty bottle of wine.

Éliane exaggeratedly straightened her face, which almost made Rose laugh again, and they both sat down at the table, smiles still lingering on their mouths.

"Let's start work," Rose said, passing one notebook to Luc, keeping one for herself and giving another to Éliane. "We need to record the exact destination each painting has been exiled to. I don't want our records to rely on code words in case anything happens—"

To us. They each turned away from the unspoken end of Rose's sentence.

Instead, the three of them worked until almost four in the morning, updating their notebooks with the names of the Nazi art depots: Schloss Neuschwanstein; Herrenchiemsee, a group of more palaces in Bavaria; the monastery of Buxheim. When they'd finished and they all sat bleary-eyed, Éliane said, "We're winning. Not the Germans. For the first time, I feel like it's true."

Even Luc smiled as he lifted his glass and finished the last of the wine. "We're winning," he repeated and Éliane could see that they all believed it.

FIFTEEN

Nothing dampened Éliane's spirits over the next month as she and Rose won more rounds. Monsieur Jaujard told them that his English contact would make sure Hitler knew Göring had taken one of his paintings if she and Rose could somehow slip a work promised to Hitler into the crates being sent to Göring.

Éliane and Rose looked at one another and said simultaneously, "The Fragonard."

It was settled. The Fragonard—*Girl with a Chinese Sculpture*— would be swapped if they could manage it. Göring had particularly admired it in one of the exhibitions and it made sense that he might try to take it for himself.

They waited until lunchtime when the Germans left the building. "I'll move the painting and you'll keep watch," Rose told Éliane.

"But—"

"I'm old and easily overlooked," Rose said firmly. "Even if someone does come back from lunch unexpectedly, they'll walk right past me. Whereas you're apt to be noticed. If we're using your physical advantages with König, then we'll use my physical disadvantages for everything else." She gave Éliane a mischievous smile and Éliane had no choice but to shake her head in mock exasperation.

"Fine," Éliane said. "But—"

"I'll be careful." The smile was gone now and, before Éliane's eyes,

Rose grew smaller, more hunched, no animation on her face. She hurried out to the loading dock where the crates were packed and marked with *H* for Hitler and *G* for Göring, alongside their coded destinations, ready for transport the following day.

Éliane picked up her mop and bucket and stood by the door, scrubbing a mark she'd been careful to leave with her shoes earlier. Her eyes weren't on the floor, but on the far entrance, watching for any Nazi who might return early and catch them doing something all the smiles in the world wouldn't save them from.

Click-click-click. Painting frame after painting frame knocked against the one behind it as Rose searched. As much as she wanted to, Éliane couldn't turn to see exactly what Rose was doing, had to use only her ears to try to understand how close Rose was to succeeding.

Twenty long minutes ticked past.

Then Éliane heard a little noise of triumph. She heard Rose creep over to Göring's crates, heard the sound of a lid removed and then immediately replaced, could almost feel Rose's exasperation when she realized the crate she'd opened was already full. Thud. Another lid. Then another. The clock moved relentlessly fast.

Silence on the dock now. What was happening? Then the faintest sound of wood sliding against wood as a painting was slipped into a crate.

Éliane's breath leveled. They would get it done.

But then she heard—thank goodness for the Nazis' boots—the noxious rap of feet. Her foot shot out and kicked her mop bucket over, sending water flowing across the gallery floor.

"*Mon Dieu!*" she cried, as if horrified by her clumsiness.

König rounded the corner and Éliane didn't have to try to look scared.

"You won't tell your uncle?" she said pleadingly. "I was looking at the art and I forgot the bucket..." She hung her head. "I'm sorry, Monsieur."

"I won't tell him but clean it up quickly." König glanced over his shoulder toward the museum entrance the same way Éliane wished she could look back over hers to see if Rose had hidden herself.

She needed König to be so thoroughly dazed and tongue-tied that he wouldn't think of going out to the loading dock at all. So she crossed over to him and planted a quick kiss on his cheek. "Thank you."

"Mademoiselle," he whispered, moving in closer.

The noise of people entering the museum interrupted them, rousing König, whose boots clicked over the floor in the opposite direction to Éliane and the loading dock.

Rose appeared almost immediately. "Get that mess cleaned up," she snapped at Éliane.

Then Rose gave her a small smile. She must have done it! The knowledge gave Éliane the strength to mop a thousand floors.

The next day, Monsieur Jaujard's British contact arranged for an anonymous letter to be sent to the Führer about the switched painting. They waited to see what would happen.

* * *

But nothing happened for months.

Despite that, their confidence grew into 1942. The valuable Schloss collection, the most important of the few Jewish collections still at large, remained elusive despite von Behr shouting about it almost weekly and paying informers to search for it. And successfully exchanging the Fragonard meant that Rose and Éliane tried other, more daring things. Most nights they slipped into König's office and took home the loose sheets that he was to transcribe into Göring's Catalogue. It meant they no longer had to rush to note down everything while they were at the museum. They could copy records out carefully at night in their apartments. Their notebooks were becoming comprehensive records of the Nazis' greed and the extensiveness of their thieving, and included much of the information needed to find and return the paintings to their owners—should the Occupation ever end.

There were losses, too: exchanges continued to take place from the Salle des Martyrs, and the fate of those works remained unknown. Other losses, of a different kind: in June 1942, all Jews in Occupied France were forced to wear a yellow star.

"They won't do to the Jewish people what they're doing to their artworks, will they?" Éliane asked Rose in the bathroom of the museum that day. "They won't send them away?"

"I don't know," was Rose's despondent answer.

They found out soon enough.

Perhaps in retaliation for the RAF raids that were taking place most nights now, perhaps for no reason other than to be sure everyone knew the Germans were the masters, oppression became a way of life. All too soon, Jews were no longer permitted in public places. Then they were rounded up by the Nazis in such large numbers that everyone looked over their shoulders now.

The Nazis were taking the art. They were taking the people. What would they take next, Éliane wondered.

Near the end of summer, the moment Éliane arrived at the museum, König hurried over and said, "Go upstairs to the cleaning closet."

"Why?" Éliane asked, even as she heard von Behr shouting for everyone to gather in the long gallery at the foot of the stairs.

"He's had an unpleasant telephone call from the Reichsmarschall. Go now," König said, almost gently.

Éliane didn't go to the closet. She waited at the top of the stairs where she could hear von Behr shout, "Which idiot among you is so illiterate he can't tell a G from an H!"

And she knew that Hitler's Fragonard had been discovered in Göring's crates. It was hard to breathe. They were playing with a voracious kind of fire. Who knew what von Behr would do after being berated by the Reichsmarschall? Who knew what Göring would do if he'd been chastised by the Führer?

"You!" von Behr shouted. "Out! Now!"

Éliane held on to the balustrade and watched as Rose Valland was escorted out of the Jeu de Paume.

Had von Behr seen Rose do something? Or was it just bad luck and she was a convenient outlet for von Behr's temper?

Letting Rose leave without making any kind of protest was one of the hardest things Éliane had ever done. But she knew she had to. Their plan had misfired. She'd lost Rose in the process. Rose wouldn't want to see Éliane marched out too.

There was nothing to do but appeal to König. She sat on the floor of her broom closet and wept.

König found her there. "Mademoiselle," he said, passing her a handkerchief.

"I cannot work without Madame Valland," Éliane said, letting fear enlarge her eyes and quiver her lips. "I don't know how the fire systems work. Your uncle will be furious if they fail."

König squatted beside her and lifted a hand to brush the hair from her brow. "So many things went wrong this morning. My uncle thought he'd found some artworks Herr Göring particularly desires, but the information was wrong. He had to tell the Reichsmarschall this, but Herr Göring was already fuming about a painting that had been incorrectly delivered to his care, which had displeased the Führer. Once everyone is calmer, I'm sure my uncle will allow Madame Valland to come back."

"I'm sorry for your uncle," Éliane lied. "And for you."

"Thank you." He smiled at her and suddenly filled more space in the closet, as if her words had enlarged not just his spirits, but his entire self. He stood, holding out a hand to her.

Éliane allowed him to lift her from the floor.

"I'll see what I can do about Madame Valland." Then he leaned over and kissed her lips.

Éliane froze.

* * *

On the way home, Éliane tried to make herself believe she had the stomach to endure more of König's kisses, if that was what it took to get Rose back into the museum. She tried to draw strength from the fact that the weather was still warm, that she would soon have dinner at the brasserie, that she and Angélique could find solace in whispered jokes about the Nazis each time they passed one another in the kitchen.

She'd almost worked a half-smile back onto her face when a boy bumped into her, set down his paste and began to affix a poster to the wall on the Rue de Rivoli. The words on the poster caught her eye and she stopped still, causing the pedestrian traffic to funnel around her, cursing. But she couldn't move; could only read the text—the substance of her nightmares—again and again.

A new law had been passed, the poster decreed. The relatives of anyone involved in anti-German activity would be imprisoned and punished too, no matter if they were innocent.

Before today, she had consoled herself with the thought that if she were caught smuggling the pages of Göring's Catalogue out of the museum, Luc would be able to continue with his part of the work unhindered. And Angélique who had done nothing, would be safe. But now she understood that if she were caught in any act of resistance, Luc and Angélique would be arrested too. Which meant Éliane had to try harder than ever to avoid any suspicion falling upon her.

* * *

Éliane spent more time on her hair and makeup than usual that night, wearing what was now her best dress—the navy silk-satin with the yoked sleeves, belted waist and flared skirt—as the rest were fraying and faded with wear. The long sleeves hid the thinness of her arms and the draped bodice highlighted the curves she still had, although the belt was drawn in at least an inch tighter than it had ever been.

"You look beautiful," Angélique said when Éliane emerged from the bathroom. Then she frowned. "You're not dressing up for the Nazis. Or for Xavier—"

"I never think about Xavier," Éliane snapped.

Angélique's face collapsed and she turned away. "We've run out of soap," she said shortly. "And there was none to buy. I'll have to wash the clothes with just water. I cut up one of Ginette's old skirts to patch yours; the seam had torn. We might as well burn some of the ration coupons for heat as I'll never find the things the ration coupons are meant for. And Luc said there was no money left over from the brasserie after he'd bought all the wine, half of which he drinks. So we have only your money to last us until Monday."

Éliane tugged on her sister's hand. How many other eighteen-year-old girls across the city were doing their entire family's washing, shopping, cooking, mending, queuing, and worrying so that the others could work? "I shouldn't have snapped. Today was just..." She shrugged. Everyone's days were hard. Hers was no harder than her sister's.

"Rose was fired," she tried to explain. "I need to convince König to persuade his uncle to let Rose come back."

Angélique melted into her arms. "Thank God. I thought maybe you actually liked them..."

"I hate them." Éliane drew back so her sister could see the truth blazing in her eyes. "But sometimes I have to do whatever I can to help others. Can you go along with it? For Rose?"

Angélique nodded. "I'll help too," she said decisively and it was only later that Éliane realized she should have asked her sister what she meant. She saw only that her sister had also spent more time on her makeup that night and she looked as pretty as any young woman in Paris.

The brasserie was popular now: after Göring's first visit, word had spread to the Nazis and it was full most nights. Which, Éliane thought as she and Angélique reached the *passage*, should mean there was at least a little money left over to buy soap on the gray market, or a small bolt of fabric to make a new skirt. Luc couldn't be drinking that much wine.

One of their neighbors pushed past on his way to the stairs. *"Putain!"*—whore—he spat at Éliane. Éliane said nothing. But the memory of König kissing her hung like a grotesque tapestry in her mind, and her heart whispered timorously: *Aren't you though?*

Von Behr, Xavier, König, and Göring entered the *passage* then. She and Angélique were late.

Éliane waited at the door, ready to show them to their usual table. More guests arrived and Éliane hurried back and forth from door to tables. Von Behr, who was drunker than usual, likely still furious from the afternoon and therefore more deadly, began clamoring for Bordeaux.

"Can you take him some," Éliane whispered to Angélique.

Éliane was explaining the menu to a German couple when she became aware of a commotion at von Behr's table. She looked up to see that he had threaded a repulsive arm around Angélique's waist.

Never had Éliane moved so fast. "Angélique I need you in the kitchen," she said, standing on von Behr's other side and smiling so hard she wondered if her face might crack.

"But I need amusement," von Behr said, hand tightening on Angélique hip. "I'd never noticed that this one is just as lovely as her sister."

Éliane's eyes met Angelique's. Angélique shook her head as if she could read Éliane's furious thoughts, but if von Behr didn't move his hand very quickly, nothing would stop Éliane from exploding.

"If you want amusement, don't waste your time on novices," Xavier said, looking accusingly at Éliane. "Novices so incompetent they can't even bring the champagne that was ordered." This last was said in a tone so withering—even though Xavier hadn't actually ordered any champagne—as if Éliane were the most useless thing in all the world.

"You shouldn't talk to her like that." All heads at the table turned to look at König, who had spoken. His voice was steady and he didn't blush.

"You shouldn't," König repeated, looking from his uncle to Xavier.

It took von Behr three or four blinks to recover before he let Angélique go and clapped his nephew on the back. "Well played, boy! A girl loves a knight to rescue her."

Éliane indicated with her head that Angélique should fetch the champagne. She heard herself exhale as her sister left the table.

Von Behr turned to her and she hoped he hadn't noticed her sigh of utter relief. "I hear you want me to allow your fellow Frenchwoman back into the museum. Are you so stupid that you don't know how a sprinkler system works?"

Keep smiling, Éliane told herself. She curved her lips upward and fixed her eyes on von Behr, needing him to never look at her sister or touch any part of Angélique's body again. Von Behr's hand found Éliane's hip this time.

Crash!

"Mon Dieu!" Angélique cried. She had returned with the champagne and had somehow dropped the bottle on the floor. She fled to get a cloth.

"Well, *she* is definitely incompetent," von Behr said to Xavier. "And as for you—" He fixed his attention back on Éliane, hand not leaving her hip. "Perhaps I will allow Madame Valland to return. But know this." His voice was a blade of gray, sharp against the silence. "If there is one more mistake, she will never come back. If I ever discover that any of the French workers in the museum had anything to do with today's error, you will discover just what expertise the guards at the museum have.

They won't care how stupid you are, nor how pretty you look when you smile. And for the rest of this week," he finished, settling back in his chair and lighting a cigar, "you can run all of Ilse's errands. She would prefer to remain with me and I like to protect all my mademoiselles."

He was threatening her with so many things that Éliane had to look at the floor and give in. "As you wish, Monsieur," she whispered.

Von Behr turned to König and conversation resumed. Éliane blindly took a champagne bottle that Xavier was passing to her, which he must have reached over to get from the ice bucket on the sideboard. She poured, but her hand shook and she couldn't make it stop and she knew von Behr would notice as the champagne dripped onto the table.

Then Xavier's elbow knocked her and she spilled even more. "You'll also need to fetch a cloth," he said exasperatedly, despite the fact that it had been his fault.

She escaped to the kitchen where she found Angélique crying, Luc drunkenly telling her to mop up her face, clearly incapable of working himself, and the two old men he'd employed to help him sweating under the strain of keeping up with the meals.

She wanted to throw something, preferably a bottle of champagne. Instead she said to Angélique "You can do the washing up and clear the tables. I'll do all the serving. But we need food, Luc. They're all too drunk and they're waiting for their meals. Put down the wine and cook something!"

Luc began to laugh. "How would I get through a night without a little helping hand?" he said.

She needed a cloth. She needed some air. She needed not to think about König defending her, not to think about von Behr's hands on her and on her sister.

She pushed open the side door, which led to the corner of the Rue du Bouloi and the Rue Croix-des-Petits-Champs. She slid down the wall and crouched there, like a vagrant, elbows on knees, hands over face.

She didn't hear the door open from the kitchen, nor a footstep, heard only a voice say, "You need to replace Angélique Von Behr doesn't like clumsy waitresses. You told me that your standards would be high. So far, they're not."

Éliane's hands fell away from her face and she knew Xavier could see her tears and her shame and her pain but she hadn't the strength to keep it from him.

"Send her home, Éliane," he finished, voice as cold and hard as the last shard of their love, gone forever now.

SIXTEEN

W hen the Germans finally left the brasserie, there was half an hour left until curfew. Éliane asked Angélique to clean up for her and then she almost ran to Monsieur Jaujard's apartment, not telling anyone what she was doing, fumbling with the key Monsieur had hidden in the courtyard.

She slipped into the apartment, waiting only until the door had closed and then she said in as quiet a voice as she could manage, given her agitation, "I need to get Angélique out of Paris."

She told him what had happened and finishing by saying, "Even if Angélique doesn't work at the brasserie, von Behr can still get to her. Maybe he wouldn't, maybe he's too busy with Ilse Putz, but I can't take the risk. Seeing his hands on her..."

She sat down at the table and tried to swallow the tears but she felt them leak onto her face.

Monsieur Jaujard sat down beside her, resting his elbows on the table, hands steepled together, a deep frown etched on his brow. He passed her a handkerchief. "I can find a position for her at one of the depots. At Montauban, with the *Mona Lisa*."

He gave Éliane a small smile and for the first time that night she felt something other than dread twisting in her stomach. Monsieur Jaujard, mustachioed, hair combed back, neatly dressed like any ordinary Frenchman, a man who had spent most of his life traversing the grand halls of the Louvre, was anything other than ordinary; he was a man who would add the care of Éliane's sister to his cares for France's entire cultural heritage.

But her relief vanished the next moment when he added, "The only trouble will be getting her an Ausweis."

An Ausweis. A special pass allowing someone to travel from the Occupied Zone to the Free Zone. An Ausweis had to carry a Nazi officer's signature and be approved by the German high command. Éliane knew how difficult it would be for Monsieur Jaujard to get hold of one. And if von Behr heard about it... She shivered.

"I'll see what I can do," he said gently. "Don't lose hope."

Éliane tried to blot the tears but more came. "Hope," she said bleakly. "Sometimes it's such a burden, isn't it? And at other times it's like the marrow of your soul."

Her soul entirely lacked hope that night as she walked home, making it back just before curfew, only to find Luc leaving the apartment. "Where are you going?" she asked.

"I have messages to deliver for Monsieur Jaujard," he said, ready to hurry away down the steps.

"I was just with Monsieur Jaujard."

Luc shrugged. "He knows you have enough to do. He's not going to bother you with messages he's already passed on to me." His foot was on the first step when he stopped. "Why were you at Jaujard's?"

"He's going to give Angélique a job at one of the Louvre depots. But he needs an Ausweis."

He gave a half-laugh. "I don't know how you're going to get one of those."

It was his drunken unconcern that did it. All the rage Éliane had quashed came out now and she hissed at her brother. "She's our sister, Luc. How can you bear the thought of von Behr groping her again? Or worse?" Her voice was too loud and she stopped herself from saying any more.

He held up a placating hand and donned his forgive-me smile. "You're right. Get her out of Paris. My mind's on other things and I'm sorry. I have to pass on these messages and it's already curfew..."

Éliane's anger retreated a little. Luc *was* doing everything he could to make sure von Behr left Paris forever by keeping the Resistance informed, the Resistance that might one day rise up against the Nazis. She kissed his cheek. "Go. See you in the morning."

And he went off into the shadows. Éliane pushed open the door to the apartment and jumped at the sight of her sister sitting in one of the chairs.

"Where does Luc go?" Angélique asked. "And you—I know you go out at night sometimes."

Éliane kept her face composed as she sat in a chair opposite Angélique, able to tell part of the truth for once. "I went to see Monsieur Jaujard to ask him to give you a job in the Free Zone, at one of the depots. You can't stay here."

Angélique crumpled into tears and Éliane knew she was crying for everything: their mother, their sisters, the lack of food, the lack of heat, the endless queuing for so little, the memory of von Behr's hands on her hips. She held her sister and let her cry, giving Angélique what was left of her strength. Then she tucked her into bed.

"Can you sing *'Au Clair de la Lune,'*" Angélique whispered and Éliane nodded, singing softly about a couple searching for a light, a couple who find love instead. How she wished the world were as simple as a children's lullaby.

Just before Angélique fell asleep, she mumbled wearily to Éliane, "Xavier knocked that bottle out of my hands—and he did it deliberately."

Éliane's laugh was short and sharp as she recalled the hostile, almost threatening way he'd told her to send Angélique home. "He almost knocked a bottle out of my hands too. No doubt he was hoping for it to land on von Behr who might have then locked us both up in prison somewhere."

"I don't know…" Angélique began and Éliane felt so sorry for her sister who still didn't understand that their lives were now peopled with monstrous creatures who had walked straight from the canvas of Hieronymous Boschs's *Hell* and into Paris.

She kissed Angélique goodnight and told her she loved her.

In the early hours of the morning, she heard Luc return. He tapped on her door, his face a study in gray. "They're rounding up Jewish people again," he said. "Putting them in busses and taking them away. It's worse than before. The streets are—" He stopped and Éliane could see that he was startlingly sober. "I saw a woman throw her child from the window so that it wouldn't be taken. Then she jumped out after it."

"No," Éliane whispered, squeezing her eyes tightly shut. Then they flew open. How dare she try to block out the horrors that others were living?

She held on tightly to Angélique then, knowing that if Monsieur Jaujard couldn't get her an Ausweis, Éliane would get one any way she could.

* * *

The following night at the brasserie, von Behr's first words to Éliane, before he had even ordered a drink, were, "Where's your *petite soeur?*"

"She had to look after an elderly relation who is unwell," Éliane said.

Only after the Ausweis had somehow been procured would she tell von Behr that the elderly relation lived in the countryside and would require care indefinitely. And that her name was Lisa. She almost smiled as she wondered what the *Mona Lisa* would think if she knew she was being referred to as an elderly relative. Those flashes of humor were lifesavers and this one helped her to smile now as König held out a small and tightly wrapped cluster of edelweiss.

"The Führer's favorite," he said. "I hoped the flowers would show you that I respect you. That, if you let me woo you, I think I could please you."

Éliane stared at the white stars in her hand, reminded of the painting of the couple in the Salle des Martyrs, the couple without sky, without stars. *Woo her.*

Her eyes unwittingly flicked up at Xavier, who had once wooed her too, so well that she had thought, when she'd made love to him in that white-curtained hotel room: *until the end of time, his was the only body she would know, the only body she would ever want to know.*

She blinked furiously and Xavier caught her.

"I suppose waitressing is out of the question when you have flowers to marvel over?" he said scornfully. "Our glasses are empty."

She was certainly not going to cry now. "Yes, you must be parched," she said, her tone matching his.

As she was the only one serving, the night passed in a blur of meals and wine and raucous laughter and innuendo. It was only after everyone had left and Éliane was again mopping floors that she realized there was a card in König's bouquet. She extracted it, thinking to throw it away, but it was thicker than she expected so she opened the envelope.

What was inside made her slide into a chair.

It was an Ausweis for Angélique.

Éliane stared at it for only a few seconds before instinct made her return the pass to its safe nest between the blooms of edelweiss.

She was almost certain there had been no card when König gave the flowers to her. Who had put it there? How would Monsieur Jaujard have managed to hide it in a bouquet König had bought for Éliane?

She did not mop or tidy with her ordinary carefulness. Her only thought was to get the Ausweis upstairs and into Angélique's hands.

Angélique's smile when she saw what Éliane held was so bright it almost overpowered the blackout. Then it fell. "What about you?" she asked Éliane.

"Don't worry about me."

"Somebody should," Angélique said, serious now. "I'm worried about Luc. He drinks too much. And he's not as strong as you."

"I'm not strong," Éliane said as she embraced her sister. Angélique's presence had made her strong. But now she was going away.

The door clicked open and Luc appeared.

"I'm taking Angélique to the station as soon as curfew ends," Éliane said to him. "I have the Ausweis."

"You have the Ausweis," Luc repeated, staring at Éliane in a way she did not understand, the play of expression on his face moving from scrutiny to apparent comprehension, at which point he laughed. "Of course."

Of course.

"You know who arranged it," Éliane said slowly. "Who was it?"

"I have no idea, little sister," he said, picking up a bottle of wine before he disappeared into his bedroom, closing the door behind him.

* * *

When she returned home from the station, having put Angélique on a train to the Louvre depot of Montauban, Luc was getting ready to go to the markets. There was a little wine left over in the bottle he'd opened the night before and Éliane poured it into a glass and drank it.

"Do you ever think," she asked her brother, "that instead of saving paintings, we should be saving people?"

Luc wrapped her in a conciliatory hug. "A country is much more than a collection of people, Éliane. We're saving the part of it that we can. You have to believe that others are saving the pieces they can save too."

"But what if…" Éliane sat at the table and all of her darkest fears came pouring out. "What if it's all for nothing? What if the Germans are here forever? Then nobody will need the notebooks Rose and I are keeping because there'll never be an end to this. Will people look at us later and say we put our efforts into the wrong things? That *The Astronomer* is not worth as much as a life?"

She expected Luc to protest that he had to get to the markets. She expected she would have to comfort herself from missing Angélique and from the terrible doubts that poured over her now like black rain.

But he walked over to the window, his blond hair catching the early morning sunlight, the blue of his eyes not dulled by wine and she realized that, while she lived with him and worked with him, she knew so little about him now. They had always used to steal moments together to talk: at cafés in Montparnasse, out on the top step, in the alcove under the stairs. He would tell her who he was in love with—a different woman every week—about a painting he'd finished that he hoped might sell, or about a painting that didn't sell. Only then, in the span of about thirty seconds, would she see another Luc: a disappointed Luc. Not the spoiled and loved brother who depended on the admiration of his siblings and the romances with his artists' models and the unwavering belief of Éliane, who had always said to him: *Next time. Your painting will sell at the next salon.*

He's not as strong as you, Angélique had said and Éliane had not, at the time, thought it was true. Luc was the older brother, the one who talked his way out of anything he didn't want to do and into everything he did. Luc was the laughing, unbeatable, energetic force while Éliane was the dull, conscientious, motherly creature who had used to care more about whether her sisters had enough to eat than about whether she might ever sit down with a canvas and paintbrush again.

When had she last heard Luc laugh? When had he last romanced a lovestruck woman? What had happened to the little studio in Montparnasse that he had once shared with a dozen similarly artistic young men? She had not once asked.

Her gaze shifted to the bottle Luc had drunk almost to its end the night before, on top of whatever he had drunk at the brasserie, and she could not believe she'd placed the weight of her fears onto him.

Before she could apologize, he said, very gently, "Paintings and people are each worth very different things. Every human has a different value depending on who's doing the valuing. You'd save me from anything, perhaps you'd even save König because your heart is too soft, but you would not save von Behr. I would save none of them, perhaps not even myself. It doesn't matter. Without art, we're not truly alive. Take away all the musical instruments and the songs and the sculptures and the books and the sketches and the paintings and it's like taking away food. Nobody would survive. So yes, it's worth it."

Éliane remembered the cavernous emptiness of the Louvre without its jewels, and the way her brother's painting in the Salle des Martyrs of the couple entwined had made her body ache and her heart long for the end of now, for a time in the future when those aches and longings could be assuaged.

She found a smile. "Thank you," she said. "And I'm sorry. You have enough to do without buoying up my spirits."

"You have the most difficult job of all," he said, turning to face her. It was the first time Éliane had heard him speak to her with admiration. "You spend all day and all night in the company of Germans you're trying to fool. You have no pause, except when you sleep and, if your dreams are like mine, then you have no rest at all. I might be a drunk who wasted his chance to be an artist, but I know courage when I see it."

He walked over and kissed her forehead, taking the wineglass from her. "A true artist feels everything, Éliane. A true artist doesn't run from the pain and into a glass of Bordeaux. That's how I know I'd never have been a true artist anyway. It might not be the legacy you imagined leaving but what if, one day, *The Astronomer* is back in France and a woman stands before it and it stirs something in her heart that she'd forgotten was there. That's a grander and more far-reaching legacy than most of us can ever dream of."

He hurried out before she could say, *I love you, Luc*, words he probably wouldn't want to hear anyway because what consolation were they in the face of the self-confrontations the war forced upon them: the loss of dreams, the struggle to find a purpose in the ash of Nazi oppression, the bleak and terrible present they were living through with only the idea of "one day" to drive them on.

* * *

That bleak and terrible present did not let up over the winter of 1942. One day, near the end of the year, the guards at the Jeu de Paume checked and rechecked Éliane's papers and then, for the first time ever, her bag too. Her bag was empty of anything except lipstick, a little money, and her ration book, but Rose's—

Her entire body became as still as unsculpted marble although she continued to stare unconcernedly ahead, waiting for the guard to finish. In Rose's bag were the pages they had taken the night before from Göring's Catalogue. Had she already arrived? Is that why they were checking Éliane's bag? No, that didn't make sense. To find the papers, they would have had to check Rose's bag in the first place, and there was no reason to check bags—they had never done so before. Why were they doing it now?

Her mind was a ferocious swirl, a Kandinsky painting run wild. Out of the corner of her eye, she saw Rose approaching. Rose would notice the guards' zeal, would turn and hide the papers somewhere—but where on such a wet and miserable day?—and then return with her unremarkable face and lackluster suit.

But she didn't. She kept walking forwards, was beside Éliane now, was handing over her bag and Éliane waited for the guards to point their guns at them both but they only barked, "Move!" at both women, who hurried inside.

Éliane didn't dare to look at Rose. Instead, she slunk away to the bathroom at the first opportunity, checking all the stalls and waiting for Rose to arrive.

It took too long, so long that Éliane began to think she must have dreamed Rose's arrival and the Nazis had caught her and everything would be exposed and she and Luc and Angélique and Monsieur would all be taken somewhere and—

The door opened. Rose! Éliane flew to her and hugged her so tightly that Rose gasped.

"You'll kill me before the Germans will," she chided macabrely.

"What's going on?" Éliane asked.

"The Allies invaded North Africa."

The Allies invaded North Africa.

Éliane opened a cubicle door and sat on the closed lid of the toilet. North Africa wasn't far away. An actual invasion. Maybe France was next. Her head whipped up and she met Rose's eyes but Rose shook her head.

"Not France yet," Rose said gently.

Éliane closed her eyes. Then she shook herself. Anything positive was worth storing in one's heart.

Surely they could all put flesh on the bones of their hopes now. The Germans had been in Paris for two and a half years. Surely 1943 wouldn't begin without the Allies coming to chase the Nazis away, finally and forever.

"We'll have to bring the pages of the catalog back to the museum on our bodies," Rose said, returning them to the reality of a guarded museum in which she and Éliane were spying and stealing and trying to ensure an artistic future survived until victory.

Éliane nodded. It was the only way. But…"How did you know they would check our purses today?"

"I was warned. We'd best get back to work." Rose hurried out of the bathroom because they'd been gone too long, especially on a day when the Germans were already jumpy. But who had warned Rose? Monsieur Jaujard? He must have greater access to the Allies than Éliane knew.

But Éliane's hopes were soon reduced back to a skeleton as, in retaliation for the North Africa landings, the Germans seized control of Vichy France and stamped their boots down harder on the whole country. Everything changed.

It was the little things at first. There were no chestnut sellers on the street that December. Paris in December had always smelled, to Éliane, of coal braziers and hot butter and nuts roasting, ready to be tipped into a paper cone to warm cold hands. But the chestnuts had disappeared, along with liberty as, again and again, the Germans placed the city under curfew, with no one allowed on the streets after six o'clock—except Nazis with guns and sticks who wanted someone to beat, someone to shoot.

With Angélique gone, the household tasks fell to Éliane. Her chilblains came back worse than ever, provoked not just by the cold but the endless washing of dishes at the brasserie and scrubbing her clothes and Luc's in freezing water. She took to wearing her gloves even while inside. Not long after that, another jar of cold cream appeared for her at Monsieur Jaujard's apartment.

"*Merci*, Monsieur," she thanked him fervently.

Monsieur shuffled awkwardly, glanced at Rose and began to talk of the Germans' latest crime—the theft of a valuable altarpiece that the Belgians had given to him to protect.

"No," Éliane said despairingly, a sentiment echoed by each of them.

They had been counting on the fact that even though Monsieur Jaujard had had to inform the Nazis about the châteaux and other depots where the Louvre treasures were stored, the Germans would leave the artworks owned by the French state alone. That the international furor likely to result from any Nazi thieving of *The Wedding at Cana*, for example, would be judged by the Germans to be best avoided. But if they had stolen an altarpiece owned by the Belgians—didn't that put the *Mona Lisa* at risk too?

That evening, as Éliane walked home, she passed signs warning of the danger to health from eating cats—which many Parisians were doing. Her coat was soaked from the winter-damp air and she felt it with dismay; even with half the fur having fallen out, it would never dry in time for her to wear it to bed that night. She debated about whether to line her clothes with newspaper for insulation or burn the paper for a short and furious burst of heat. Summer, with its warm weather and the possibility of the Allies invading France and saving all the people and all the paintings, couldn't come soon enough.

SEVENTEEN

S ummer eventually came, along with the capitulation of the German army at Tunisia and the clamoring rumor that the Allies would invade Europe by August. From then on, the Germans no longer shouted before they shot, and the murder of *résistants*, their families, and hostages became a daily occurrence. Still, Rose and Éliane continued to arrive each morning at the Jeu de Paume with papers from Göring's Catalogue stuffed in their bras or hidden in their girdles. If anything, the Nazis' cruelty made them more determined.

Éliane was on her way to the bathroom first thing one morning with those very papers, which she planned to remove in order to return them to König's office, when she saw Göring, König, Xavier, and von Behr engaged in a heated discussion. Göring's jeweled fingers flashed furiously, von Behr looked as browbeaten as he usually made everyone else feel, König was stammering and Xavier appeared, as always, unperturbed. She needed to hurry. It would not do to be called over to serve them champagne while she had their secrets hidden in her underclothes.

She scurried to the bathroom only to have the door open moments later. Rose snapped, in a way that let Éliane know something important had happened, "Hurry up! We need to stocktake the cleaning supplies."

After checking that König was still being lambasted by Göring, Éliane raced to his office, placed the papers quickly but carefully inside the chiffonier, then darted to the cleaning closet where Rose said in a whisper, "I heard von Behr on the telephone. The Schloss family has been arrested."

The Schloss family, who owned the one private Jewish collection that hadn't yet been discovered.

"Oh no," Éliane said, voice louder than it should be and she pressed her hand against her mouth.

"But it wasn't the Germans who arrested them," Rose went on. "It was the French government. And the Schlosses were given up by a French informant."

Éliane's stomach turned even as she pretended to sort through bottles of turpentine. There was always so much they didn't know. That some French people were as bad as the Germans. The Nazis were making it well known that they would offer money and prestige and protection to informants, and sometimes it felt as if more and more French people were turning toward the occupiers rather than away from them. What did the Resistance have to offer, when set against the here and now of German cash? Just hope and future, intangible and faraway things that would not feed families or buy tailor-made clothes or purchase power.

And another irreplaceable collection of art was on the brink of being found and thieved. "Why would the French government arrest the Schlosses?" Éliane asked.

"I don't know. All I know is that the Schloss family have been living in a villa on the Chemin des Moulins in Saint-Jean-Cap-Ferrat where they thought they'd be safe. Nobody yet knows the whereabouts of the collection. But von Behr is so confident jail will make the Schlosses talk, and he'll then somehow be able to take the collection from the Vichy government, that he's scheduled an exhibition of the works in a fortnight's time."

Éliane's hand curled despairingly around the handle of her mop. "I'll find out more from König at the brasserie tonight."

How many times would she have to let König kiss her in order to find out what they needed to know? She'd been so thankful that working every night at the brasserie gave her no time to go out with him, that their rendezvous were limited to cataloging sessions at the museum and that all she'd had to endure were very brief and occasional kisses on the rare moments she might find herself alone with him on the loading dock or some other secluded place, which, of course, she avoided. But the Schloss collection had somehow and somewhere been kept safe for three years. It couldn't be discovered by the Nazis, not now.

"I worry that von Behr will want to go down there," Rose said, eyes fixed on Éliane's face.

Éliane didn't think through the meaning of Rose's words because she was too busy steeling herself to touch her lips to a Nazi's once more. She only understood later, at the brasserie, what Rose had meant.

Von Behr was ebullient that night, ordering more and more champagne. As soon as Éliane had taken their orders, he said to Xavier, "The renovation of your house must be finished now? Some of us have business to attend to in Saint-Jean-Cap-Ferrat. Order him," von Behr said to Göring. "Order him to put on a party for us."

Xavier smiled in a way that suggested von Behr was being crass. "I don't need to be ordered. This weekend. My house is yours."

Von Behr turned to Éliane and trapped her with his one cruel eye. "You will escort my nephew to the party. For the entire weekend."

König choked on his wine. But he didn't object.

There was no way to say no. Certainly not if she wanted to keep up the ruse that she was a Parisienne willing to serve her German masters.

"Monsieur König has not asked me," she said, eyes down, hiding everything, like a woman in a Renaissance painting.

"I have, on his behalf."

Everyone at the table quieted, waiting for her to speak.

"I would be delighted," she said.

She withdrew to the kitchen and threw up in the sink. The weekend was two days away.

She spent the hours until closing time conjuring up and discarding excuses. If she didn't go, she had no doubt she'd lose her job at the museum. And, most importantly, it would raise von Behr's suspicions about not just her, but about everyone connected to her.

But she could not sleep with König, not even for an art collection.

She didn't come up with any kind of plan that night, or the following day. Rose watched her with solemn eyes.

The night before she was due to leave, Luc spoke to her coldly— the same tone he'd used with Angélique when he'd told her they were reopening the brasserie. And Éliane felt as Angélique must have felt then: as if she had no choice but to do what her brother wanted.

"If you don't go," he said, "you risk blowing not just your cover, but everyone's. They'll want to know why you're suddenly so unwilling to accommodate them. Believe me, one distasteful act can be quickly forgotten if you think about the greater good it does. Think about Angélique rather than König."

Luc was right. She would have to spend the weekend with Reichsmarschall Göring. With von Behr and Xavier. In König's bed. How much more would she have to endure for the promise of a future in which awe and wonder survived?

* * *

Ordinarily, Éliane would collapse into bed and be soundly asleep within seconds; the fatigue of more than fifteen hours spent in German company, pretending to be a different Éliane, sent her falling into painterly dreams where the voices of watercolor figures rumbled, occasionally speaking so loudly and sharply that she thought she should open her eyes and climb out of bed to make sure there wasn't really someone in the apartment talking to Luc. Dreams where König's lips swirled grotesquely, painted not with oils but with blood. Dreams where von Behr's glass eye fell out and rolled away and suddenly he could see everything and Éliane was the victim of his terrible awakening.

But, that night, Éliane sat at the table long after Luc had passed out in a drunken slumber, which she knew he did every night although she was rarely awake to witness it. He would still get up at dawn to go to the markets to buy produce and, in between all of that, he would take the information from Éliane and Rose and Monsieur Jaujard and pass it on to the Resistance and whoever in Britain cared. That was why he'd snarled at her. He was an artist who had given up his art for this and he did not want her to waste his sacrifice.

But hadn't they all given up their art? Their art was now survival and it meant doing things that made a heart ache in the same way that her heart had ached the first time she'd seen *The Raft of the Medusa*, men turned to cannibalism so desperate were they to live.

Time passed as she sat with a bottle of wine and too many thoughts and she was startled to find, at two in the morning, that she had finished the wine and the door to the apartment was opening. Her reflexes, dulled by alcohol, were slow to react and she hadn't even the corkscrew in hand when Xavier, of all people, stepped into the apartment.

"Éliane," he said, shock evident on his face. "Where's Luc?"

"He's asleep." Bewilderment made her answer without her usual hostility and then she recalled that Xavier was the enemy and he was in her apartment and he wanted Luc.

Xavier swore. "Can you wake him?"

"Can I wake him?" Her voice was meant to be loud and incredulous and defiant, implying that she would somehow bar the way to her brother's room, would defend Luc with her empty wineglass, but it came out small and scared and stunned.

Then, while she was staring at Xavier in stupefaction, she saw him actually reassemble himself: his posture change, his face harden, his aloofness drawing over him as suddenly as if he had pulled on a coat. "I'll wake him," he said stonily.

It was the sudden and purposeful shift in Xavier's demeanor that made her realize he'd opened the door and asked about Luc in a manner that suggested he was familiar with nightly visits to Éliane's apartment. His shock had been that *she* was the one sitting at the table, as if he'd expected to see someone else. It also made her see that the Xavier who'd walked into the apartment was a man she recognized from before the Occupation and he'd somehow transformed, like a person used to making such shifts, into the man she'd learned to despise.

As he strode past her, the complete absence of alcohol fumes following him had her sniffing the air. Unlike von Behr and Göring, on whom you could smell the alcohol and see its effects even if blindfolded—and Luc too—she could smell nothing on Xavier even though he'd been drinking with Nazis since seven o'clock. Yet he looked, right now, absolutely sober.

Éliane pictured the brasserie, where the same byplay happened night after night: Xavier ordering champagne and Bordeaux. But how many times did Éliane actually refill his glass? Once, perhaps twice at most.

She stood up.

In Luc's room, Xavier stood by the bed, saying Luc's name over and over but having no effect on the unconscious form. He swore again, feelingly. "I have something to give him but I need him to know what it is."

"If you tell him anything now," Éliane said slowly, as her mind reconsidered things she'd thought she'd witnessed over the last two years, "he won't remember it in the morning."

Xavier stared at the still-sleeping Luc. "You're right." He pointed to the kitchen table. "Sit down."

Éliane did so, hardly noticing his tone or lack of manners, so absorbed was she in the sudden removal of her own glass eye and its replacement with one that saw more clearly. But it wasn't until his next words that everything made sense.

Xavier pulled a parcel from his pocket. "In there," he said, "is a vial. In that vial is something you can put into König's drink tomorrow. It will seem as if he is very drunk for several minutes, and then he'll fall asleep. He won't wake until morning. At which time you'll have to take care of yourself."

England has people in France who are working against the Nazis. One of them is, amongst other things, liaising with the Allies about the art, Monsieur Jaujard had said. A true Nazi-lover would not bring her a vial to knock out König so she wouldn't have to sleep with him.

Xavier was quick, but Éliane, roused from incomprehension, was quicker. She was at the door and standing in front of it before he was.

"You're not working for the Germans," she said.

* * *

"Éliane," Xavier said, voice rough. "Move."

"No," she said.

He cursed for the third time that night, then turned his back on her. "I'm just helping you out of a situation I can see you don't want."

Xavier hadn't told the Germans she could speak their language. He'd knocked into the champagne bottle she was holding so von Behr wouldn't see her shaking hands—and that was the same night he'd made Angélique drop a different bottle so she could leave the room and get away from von Behr. He'd put the Germans, men from whom Luc and Éliane needed information, in the brasserie. He'd distracted von Behr with brothels when he'd been about to slap Éliane a second time. He'd made sure not to bring the Germans to the brasserie until seven so she had more time to rest. He'd renovated his house at Cap-Ferrat for an inordinately long time in order to avoid Éliane having to go to a party there. And now, suddenly, when the Schlosses—who'd been living at Saint-Jean-Cap-Ferrat just nearby—had been arrested and a collection of paintings was at risk, his house was available for a party.

He had done so many things that she had not seen and now she saw them all and it was like looking at the most painstaking and sublime artwork and she was left unable to breathe.

"You got the Ausweis for Angélique," she managed to say.

"Don't say that." He faced her now, brown eyes inked with fury—she had never seen him angry before—and she could feel it radiating from him even though he stood several paces away. "You don't know what will happen to you if anyone finds out you're involved—"

He cut himself off and she felt herself sag against the door.

This wasn't rage at her daring to study his life and draw a fantastic conclusion; this was a temper of fear. Fear that something might happen to her.

She had hated Xavier and the whole time he had been helping her.

"I need to sit down," she said. "Please don't go."

She sank into the nearest chair and she thought for a moment he would ignore her and storm out but the fight evaporated from him too and he sat opposite her.

"Never talk about the Ausweis," he said quietly.

One of his hands reached up to rub his forehead and she saw the façade he'd worn so carefully for almost three long years fall away, replaced by a face she knew but that had hardened—an obvious consequence of the work he was doing—and that looked so tired. How exhausting it must be to always be one thing—the opposite of everything he really was. How exhausting to go out each night and drink wine with men he most likely hated. How exhausting to have Éliane's loathing always sitting there in her eyes while he was trying to do much more than she was for her people.

"I'm sorry," she said. So inadequate. But nothing existed in the world that could express what she meant.

Xavier shrugged.

"You're the liaison Luc and Monsieur Jaujard deal with."

A slight nod. Then a long exhalation. "Madame Valland and Monsieur Jaujard wanted to tell you after the first meeting you went to. Luc and I didn't. I still wish you didn't know. If the Nazis find out what I'm doing, everyone who knows me will be arrested. I can't even begin to tell you what they do to those they arrest, Éliane. It's inexpressible."

Éliane tried to imagine one human doing inexpressible things to another. It made everything inside her ache.

She stood up and took another bottle of wine from Luc's store, opened it, filled two glasses and brought them to the table, passing one to Xavier. They each took a long swallow.

Éliane reached out for the vial. "Thank you for this. I don't know…" She faltered, sipped, and then started again. "I don't know if I would have been able to go through with it. Whether, at the last moment, I might have kicked König away and ruined everything. But you have to do so many worse things. *I* am the coward."

Xavier didn't reply. He closed his eyes as if he had a headache and was trying not to show it, as if his eyes were so tired that, should he blink too hard, he might fall asleep right there at the table. A silence stretched out that was impossible to fill because what was there to say?

"Nobody here is a coward, Ellie," he said softly, opening his eyes, and her heart squeezed.

Her hand tightened around her glass and she knew she couldn't look at him. What if she saw, not just the man she had loved, but a man she loved still, a man she loved in a way that was suddenly so agonizing she wasn't sure she could endure it? Right now, she felt as if her heart might burst open with the force of it, spilling a liquid red stained black with waste.

What had she thrown away? Something that could never be recovered, not now. She had abused him and hated him and he was a chevalier, lion-hearted. He had given his heart to France, which was the worthier recipient of such a gift.

"I'm working for the British War Ministry," he said at last. "They understood that, given my background and connections, we could use the artistic aspirations of the Nazis to insert me into their core, where I gather information." His voice was prosaic, recounting facts to this woman who had become his responsibility because of what she knew and what she had involved herself in.

"So you're not here just to protect the art?" she asked, trying to understand.

He shook his head. "No. That's evolved as another objective. A lesser objective. But it's all so tangled up now. The people I get my information from are involved in art theft on a scale almost incomprehensible. I try to manage both sets of interests. I give Madame Valland and Monsieur Jaujard what time I can."

He stood up then, swiftly, and Éliane knew she wouldn't make it to the door before him and also that he'd told her all he was able to. He stopped at the doorway though and said, "I'm driving to Saint-Jean-Cap-Ferrat now. I'll see you there tomorrow night. If you find out any-thing, try to tell me. It's best for all of us if we pass information along as soon as we can because none of us know how long…" He paused, then finished, quickly, as if the words were painful on his tongue, "How long we might have before we're discovered. It could be tomorrow night, or in three months' time, or next year. Be careful."

He had said that to her once before and she'd taken it as a warning and it was a warning again, but of a different kind. "And don't forget the vial," he added.

"Did you know…" She almost couldn't ask it, which really would make her a coward. She tried again. "When you told me you were leav-ing France back in 1940, was it because you'd been asked to do this?"

That vast and empty silence again, which was an answer in itself.

Then he said, "Yes. I didn't know what it would involve, back then. No one did."

The door closed and he was gone, the empty wineglass the only thing that attested to his presence, that and the scent of him still in the air—a smoky, woody amber like a fire extinguished but still lingering. And the knowledge, scratching open the falsehood she'd believed and revealing the sgraffito of truth beneath: Xavier had never been a coward.

She had thrown his ring at him and now she hated herself.

PART FOUR
SAINT-JEAN-CAP-FERRAT, FRANCE, 2015

EIGHTEEN

How do I have in my possession a painting that Hermann Göring stole seventy years ago from someone in France?

"That's not what I was expecting you to say," Adam said after he'd digested Remy's question.

"Why?" She said the word that had beaten a migraine into her head the night before. "Why would a painting I own, a painting I've always had in my bedroom, be in this catalog?"

Adam studied the image. "It's pretty small—maybe it just looks like yours?"

Remy shook her head emphatically. "I've seen this painting almost every day for my whole life. It's the same one."

Adam pulled the book closer. "*Le Traître*," he read. "I think that means *The Traitor*. That's kind of a weird name for a painting that looks like..."

"It's a couple embracing. Like they're in love," Remy said. "It's just them and there's nothing else in the painting—no setting or backdrop. It's really beautiful. Are you sure that's what it means?"

Instead of answering her question, he said, "Am I going nuts?" He pointed to the title of the next entry in the book, which was text only, without an accompanying photograph.

Remy leaned over, studied the word and said, "It looks like it says *bébé*. I understand enough French to know that means baby. Thank

God I'm too young to be Göring's love child or I'd be seriously freaking out right now. Was Göring trading in babies as well as art?"

"I doubt it." Adam frowned. "What are you going to do?"

Remy was quick to reply. "Nothing." It was definitely one too many things to deal with right now. "It was all a long time ago. Who knows why my painting's in there." She ate a mouthful of egg, then, even though it was delicious, pushed the plate away. "I need to go for a walk."

"Is that my cue to finish your eggs as well as mine and leave you alone?"

Remy smiled. "You know, you really ought to do something about that completely false reputation that follows you around. You're as much of an asshole as Antoinette is a retiring wallflower. You know she thinks you're hot. You should be kissing her."

He laughed. "Well, I'm going to totally shatter whatever is left of my false reputation by saying you need to eat your eggs. You'll feel worse if you don't eat. And my inner chef will suffer a huge crisis of confidence."

Now it was Remy's turn to laugh. "Crisis of confidence? Adam Henry-Jones?" She put a forkful of egg in her mouth, chewed, swallowed, sipped some juice and said, "Happy?"

"No. My inner chef will feel insulted unless you eat it all."

"Your inner chef is the asshole."

They were both laughing, so easily, so naturally, in a way Remy couldn't remember having laughed for the longest time when she heard footsteps and turned to see Lauren's head appear at the entrance to the temple.

"I knew you were here because I could smell your signature dish," Lauren said, coming across to kiss her brother's cheek.

"Your inner chef only has one dish?" Remy said teasingly to Adam.

"Yep. But it's a pretty good dish. Have you come to round me up?" he asked his sister. "I guess I'm in breach of the rules of our holiday."

"You are," Lauren said. "But so am I. Molly is being a pain—I love her but sometimes…" She rolled her eyes. "Matt is excusing her appalling behavior on the grounds of grief and Mom is trying to be patient but I can tell she's about to explode. And why are you looking so—dare I say it—relaxed? Earlier this morning I thought you were about to tip coffee over me."

Remy couldn't help a quick glance at Adam and he at her, both knowing why he'd been less than relaxed that morning before he'd come to apologize to Remy.

Lauren noticed their shared glance but thankfully continued talking. "I found Matt nosing around your darkroom. Your prints were ready so I brought them with me before he started shuffling through them. I knew that would make you explode and then between you exploding and Mom exploding, we'd be a mess." She handed Adam an envelope.

"Thanks," he said, not opening it.

"I only brought them here so I could look at them," Lauren said.

Adam shook his head with part-mock and part-real exasperation. "You're such a brat sometimes."

"What are they?" Remy asked.

"Shots from yesterday," he said. "I couldn't sleep last night so I developed some of them. Sometimes it's good to see them as prints rather than on a screen."

He pushed the envelope across to her.

Remy stared at it, on the one hand shy of seeing the pictures inside, but also eager to see whether Adam Henry-Jones had worked any magic with her clothes.

"For God's sake," Lauren said, reaching over, opening the envelope and pulling out the prints.

"Lauren!" Adam said.

"Someone needed to take charge," she said, smiling irrepressibly at Adam. "Wow. You really are a genius sometimes, big brother."

Remy's hand itched to take the prints but Lauren was engrossed in them. "I think *I'm* going to explode in a minute. Can I see?"

"Sorry. Of course you can." Lauren passed her the photos.

The first was of Remy, or of Remy's back. She was crouched in front of the fire, wearing a 1940s nightgown with a rose silk skirt and a lace bodice, hands on her knees, arms braced, staring at the flames in a way that suggested she was waiting for something longed for, as if at any moment the door behind her might open and she would jump up and run to whoever was coming inside. Her pose, or the way Adam had framed the shot, made it seem almost as if she were afraid to turn around and look at the door because to see nothing—or something other than what she'd hoped for—would break her heart.

She appeared to be so much a part of the story Adam had created that she shivered, wondering if time had somehow opened up and she had, at the exact moment he'd taken the shot, fallen into 1943, a time when, to hear a longed-for and unexpected door opening must have been the most marvelous thing of all.

Adam cleared his throat and she realized she'd been staring, transfixed, for a very long time. "Here," she said, passing it to him.

The next picture was the last one he'd taken. Remy's body silhouetted inside the white gown in a sensual and reverent way, as if the camera were paying homage to her. The sky was a brilliant blue behind her and the dress a ribbon of liquid satin. The sense of imminent movement, of flight, was so strong that the viewer yearned for the next frame, where this woman and this dress might take off to anywhere.

She passed it to Adam, but he shook his head. "That one's yours. To remind you who you are." He stood up. "I've taken up your morning and it sounds like my mom could use some help to dilute the Molly-effect. C'mon," he said to his sister, whose eyes were moving slowly back and forth between Remy and her brother.

* * *

The next day, Adam came over as promised to finish the shoot. He joked with Antoinette, made them his signature eggs for brunch and was both businesslike and collaborative, proposing ideas, listening to Remy's suggestions and always checking that she was happy.

"He's like a different person," Antoinette said to Remy when they were touching up her makeup. "He must have got laid."

It took all of Remy's strength not to burst out laughing. She was still trying to hide her grin when Adam called her over to see if she'd decided what she wanted to do for the next shot.

"What?" he asked, seeing her unsuccessful attempt to hide her smile.

"Antoinette thinks you got laid," she said. "I didn't want to shatter all her dreams by telling her I yelled at you and pushed you away after we kissed."

"Hey, I might have gone into Nice last night and met up with someone."

Remy felt her smile fall off her face. "Right," she spluttered.

Now Adam was laughing. "Of course I didn't! I'm kidding. I thought you decided it wasn't too soon to laugh about it."

"Ha ha," she said weakly.

"Thanks, though," he said.

"What for?"

"For saying, when *we* kissed, rather than when *I* kissed *you*."

Remy shook her head. "I said it like that because that's how it was. Now," she said, needing to turn her mind away from all discussions about kissing Adam, "what's next?"

"The last shot," he said. "You weren't sure which one you wanted to try."

Remy studied the images he'd printed off the internet. One was another Dahl-Wolfe photograph, *Nude on Beach*. The model wore a Claire McCardell bathing suit and a scarf over her face. She wasn't nude but her swimming costume was so closely matched to her skin, and to the sand—even the slight wrinkles on the bathing suit mimicked the ripples on the shore—that she might look that way to the uncareful viewer. Or *California Desert*, in which the camera was tilted so that, while the model lay on the sand, back to the camera, she appeared to be lying semi-vertically, wearing only a towel around her hips.

Antoinette was desperate for Remy to replace the towel with a bikini bottom, to have her back shiny and bare, be the mirage in the midst of a majestic landscape.

"I'm not sure," Remy said. It felt vulnerable for some reason. She didn't care about the nudity—and all that was on view was her back—but…

"It's such a beautiful pic," Antoinette exhorted.

"Even if you want me to set up for it," Adam said, "and then you decide at the last minute that you don't want to do it, that's okay. Although we have the perfect hard light for it today."

It was him giving her the out—saying he didn't mind the hour's work involved in setting up for a shot that she might choose not to have taken—that made Remy trust him to work with the vulnerability she felt. "Let's give it a try."

She and Antoinette waited inside so her makeup wouldn't melt while he got everything ready at the cove. After he texted to say he was ready, they made their way downstairs, where Adam was busy and bare-chested, having thrown off his T-shirt. Antoinette almost drooled and Remy had to bite back another smile at her friend's reaction because Adam really was quite splendid: tanned and muscled chest, black shorts sitting low enough to see the toned expanse of his stomach. Then Remy snapped her head away, afraid that some part of her mind had imagined touching a finger to his hip bone and tracing its curve.

Antoinette laid out a towel and Remy lay upon it in her bikini while Adam looked through the viewfinder. He had her move just a little to take best advantage of what was, indeed, the perfect hard light: unfiltered sun that would give the shot the sharp edges and contrasting textures it needed. When he said he was ready, Remy slipped off her top, back to Adam, and Antoinette rubbed a shimmering lotion over her skin.

"Let me take a test shot," Adam said. A moment later he called out, "Do you want to see, Remy?"

"I'm good," she said, knowing that on a shoot like this twenty years ago she would have just stood up and not cared that she was half-naked but she was somehow bashful of doing that now in front of Adam.

She could hear him behind her, moving over the beach, taking shot after shot, could feel something disarranging the air between them or perhaps it was just that she couldn't quite relax, felt like a rucked-up silk gown that needed smoothing out.

"Imagine you're on the terrace in the sun lounger," Adam said and Remy jumped; she hadn't realized he was quite so near. "Reading. Drift off to anywhere. Don't be on this beach, right now."

She closed her eyes. If she could drift off to anywhere, where would she go?

She would go up into the sky and bring back her daughter.

It was a wish so hopeless that Remy knew she would never be able to let it go. The impossible was the most difficult of all things to relinquish.

She couldn't hear Adam moving behind her now, knew it meant he was fixed in place taking the picture that would have within it everything she'd just thought. He would take her sorrow and suspend it in black and white. But she knew he would also find something else she hadn't known was there: the possibility beside the grief.

He didn't speak and nor did she. They didn't have to.

After several minutes of that poignant silence, voices and a child's protestations rattled the air. The Henry-Joneses had come down to the beach.

There was a whistle and then Lauren's voice: "You look hot, Remy!"

Remy couldn't help laughing.

She heard the camera click.

"Looks like Adam's up to his old tricks again." Matt's voice.

Judy, with only the merest shred of patience in her voice, said, "Give it a rest, Matt."

"I'm done." In those two words, Remy heard that reserved-Adam was back, no longer the Adam-who-made-eggs-for-lunch.

She sat up, facing away from everyone, and slipped on her top. Adam packed up his things and Antoinette packed up hers too, carrying the lotions and potions back up the stairs. As Remy watched Adam dismantle the last light, she felt her feet walk over to him and her mouth say, "Can I see?"

"Sure." He must have heard the uncertainty in her voice because he said, "It's a different Remy to the other one." He passed her the camera.

He was right. The picture was somehow sensual—how did he do that with every shot?—the downward curve of her hip into her waist and the upward curve out of her waist mimicking the contours of the shore. Head propped up on a languid hand as if she were dreaming. And in the image was the question he'd caught: *Do I want this?* This expanse of life spread out before her, limitless, its contours ready for her to run her hands over whenever she chose to stand up and turn around and let herself be seen.

He swiped to the last shot where he'd photographed her laughing, head tipped back as if someone had just whispered in her ear and the sound was rapture.

"I think these are some of the best shots I've taken in a very long time," he said to her.

"Then why don't you show us?" It was Matt, who'd come up behind them.

Remy felt both herself and Adam stiffen at the same time.

"Hi Matt," she said. She saw—but Matt didn't—Adam slide his thumb over the screen on the back of the camera to bring up the shots from earlier, the ones they'd taken at the house.

Adam gave the camera to Matt. "I don't know how interesting you'll find them."

"You seem interested enough."

"It's my job."

"What about the ones you were just taking?" Matt asked.

"Didn't work out. Too much light."

Remy felt peculiarly as if she wanted to slip her arms around Adam and hug him for his perceptiveness. But that would mean feeling his bare skin beneath her hands, against her body, and the thought made her shiver, but she wasn't sure that, this time, it was a shiver of revulsion.

Adam began to take his gear back to his house and Remy stepped into the water to cool off. She drifted lazily for a while, and there was only the satisfying burn of sun and its quenching with water as she turned over, the rocking sound of idle waves, the murmur of voices from the Henry-Jones side of the cove, and the high-pitched shriek of Molly, who was playing in the water with Adam.

It was nice to hear a happy child.

The thought startled Remy and she stopped floating on her back and stood up in time to see Adam chase Molly through the water. The girl stumbled, fell, took in a mouthful of water and came up coughing.

"You're all right," Adam said, scooping her up, taking her out a little further and tossing her in, an arm's length away, as Remy had seen him do before.

The quiver of fright on Molly's face and the tremble of tears quickly turned into a smile and a laugh, and then back to tears when Matt came racing over to say, "She can't swim."

"I know she can't," Adam said patiently. "She's fine. She got some water in her mouth. Happens to all of us."

"Not if you're watching her properly."

Rather than reply, Adam carried Molly to the shore, deposited her on the pebbles and continued to walk, away from his brother and toward Remy's side of the cove, clearly not wanting to enter into any kind of argument.

Matt followed him. "You need to be careful with her."

"She won't break, Matt."

"You don't know that," Matt said and Remy could hear what Matt wasn't saying: *My wife did.*

She felt suddenly sorry for him, for all of them, trying to get on with life when life wasn't always so easy to get along with.

"You're right, I don't," Adam agreed, perhaps having heard the pain beneath the anger in his brother's voice. "I'm going for a walk."

"You always have to do the wild things, the crazy things, the zany things, don't you? It's easy when you're not a father to do that stuff. But when you are a father, all you can see is her slipping out of someone's arms and falling too far down into the water and drowning. I've told you not to…" Matt's voice grew louder, carrying over to where Molly sat, her creased face about to spill into tears as she watched.

"I'm going for a walk," Adam repeated, his back to his brother, and Remy could see the stiff set of his shoulders, the screw-you stance he'd adopted the minute Matt had said, *when you're not a father.*

"Go on, walk away. Avoid it as always," Matt said now.

Judy stepped worriedly in the direction of her sons, while her husband placed a restraining hand on her.

While the altercation between the two brothers needed to end, someone stepping in to stop it would only make it worse. And Remy was sure that, while Adam might want to punch his brother right now, he wouldn't. If only Matt would let him walk away, would talk about it later when tempers were cooler and Molly wasn't there. But she recognized too well the "Anger" stage of grief, that it was an overwhelming and uncontrollable and selfish thing and she could understand why Matt wasn't able to let it go. It made her cringe to see it, to understand that she had probably done something similar over the past year and a half.

"I'm not doing this in front of Molly," Adam said, still walking resolutely onwards, as if he would walk to the end of the earth to avoid this particular scene.

"So you get to be the good guy," Matt said. "The one who can keep his shit together in front of the kid while I'm the jerk who doesn't know how to pretend that nothing's the matter. Trust you, right now, to be the good guy for once."

"Yes, Matt." Adam turned to face his brother at last. His face was furious, voice low and very cold. "In this instance I am, for once and only once, the good guy. Now fuck off."

The effect of those last two words on Matt was like a slap.

"See, I'm back to being the dick already," Adam said.

This time, when Adam walked away, Matt let him go.

Remy knew, from being the one who'd wanted to tell everyone over the last two years to go to hell, that letting Adam storm off to be by himself wasn't the best thing. She said to Antoinette, "There's something I need to do. Can you distract Matt for a bit?"

"You're going to help Adam, aren't you?" Antoinette said.

Remy nodded.

"Look at you, thinking about someone other than yourself. Maybe you're on to the fifth stage already."

"He's been taking photographs of me for two days. I owe him something."

"You do," Antoinette said. "Right, I'll parade in front of Matt in my skimpy bikini"—typical of Antoinette, she wore a Brazilian bikini—"and off you go."

Remy hurried to catch up with Adam. "If you follow the shore, you'll come to another set of steps up to my house," she said when she reached him. "They'll take you to the very end of the gardens. It's a bit of a hike back to the house, so I'll see you there in about twenty minutes."

"I don't..." he began, voice flat, face closed but Remy was too familiar with that expression to listen.

"You can stride around Cap-Ferrat being furious with your brother and the world, which doesn't sound particularly fun, or you can come for a drive with me. I don't expect conversation. I just think my option will be better."

"Did Lauren tell you to do this? It's the kind of thing she'd do—"

Remy cut him off. "I haven't spoken to Lauren. I'm here because..." How to finish that sentence. Because she owed him for all his work? But she knew that wasn't it. "I don't know, okay?" she said. "I'm here because I'm here."

His face softened, just a little. "Fine," he said, and then he continued on toward the other set of steps.

Which he might well ignore. Remy wasn't absolutely sure he was coming. But she would act as if he were.

She marched back to the Henry-Joneses. Antoinette was doing a very good job of listening to Matt's grievances, Judy and Alistair were playing with Molly, who seemed fully recovered, and Lauren was talking to her husband, who was shaking his head as if he thought all the grown-ups should just get their shit together and behave themselves.

Remy didn't particularly want to ask Lauren her question in front of her husband. Luckily, Lauren saw her and, with uncanny intuition, asked Tom to go up to the house and bring back some drinks. He kissed Lauren as he stood up, squeezing her bottom, and Remy saw in that gesture the kind of easy love she couldn't imagine ever having again.

Her words tumbled out. "Can you get me some of Adam's clothes? And shoes? Please?"

"Sure," Lauren said, asking nothing, just running up the stairs.

She returned in a few minutes with a bag. "Shoes, shorts, shirt," she said crisply. "If he complains they don't match, tell him I'm not his fashion adviser." Then she softened. "He is not only once the good guy, you know."

"I know."

Remy took the bag up to the house and waited on the terrace for a few minutes before Adam appeared.

"Clothes," she said, holding them out to him. "There's a shower over there." She pointed to the side of the house. "I'll see you out front when you're ready."

NINETEEN

Inside, Remy showered quickly and threw on a one-shouldered Tina Leser jumpsuit in the most beautiful shade of duck-egg blue, cinched a tan belt around her waist, and shoved a couple of gold bangles on her arms. When she looked in the mirror to do her hair, she saw that she looked different to the Remy of just two weeks before: skin tanned, hair blonder than ever, eyes reflecting the blue of the jumpsuit, her face less tightly drawn.

Everything changed. Except Emily and Toby. They were frozen forever just as they had been on that fateful day almost two years ago, smiling maybe, as Emily recounted what she'd done at school and Toby asked, as he always did, *What was the one thing you liked best of all?* To which the answer was supposed to be—*Seeing you.*

Another ordinary moment whose preciousness was only apparent now that the possibility of it ever happening again had vanished.

Don't, she told herself. *Don't remember any of it.*

She turned away from the mirror and went out to meet Adam before her memories made her crawl back into bed.

"Where are we going?" was all he asked.

"Èze."

In the car, she turned up the radio and French songs swirled around them as they crawled through the chaos that was Saint-Jean-Cap-Ferrat in summer, then headed a little inland, away from the coast, before driving east, in the direction of Monaco. Finally, the car wound upward until they could see it in the distance: the town perched on top of a hill.

Adam finally spoke, a note of interest in his voice. "Are we going there?"

"Yep."

By some miracle, she arrived in the carpark as someone was leaving and snagged a spot. "It's pedestrian-only up there," she said to Adam. "And it'll be busy. But it's stunning. Worth the crowds."

They strolled up the hill. All that was visible atop the sheer rock was the church towering above them. The cliff face was marked with shutters, concealing windows that lived like troglodytes in the walls. Then they reached the *poterne*, the archway cut through the medieval fortifications, and passed through.

All at once they were in fairy-tale France, surrounded by blue shutters, ivy-covered walls, doors hiding like secrets in unexpected places, jasmine and bougainvillea sprawling immoderately everywhere, narrow cobblestone streets: everything small and secret and beckoning explorers into dead-end lanes and alleyways that might take you somewhere magical.

Adam stared at the mazelike passages, at the trompe l'oeil shutters and doorways that tried to surprise the ingenuous, and she knew he'd forgotten everything that had happened on the beach that morning.

"When I came to France after the funeral," she told him, "I used to go out driving every day, with no destination. I'd just follow signs to any place. One day, I came here and I stood in this very spot and decided on a whim if I would go right, left, or straight ahead, and then every time I reached a turning or an ending, I'd do the same thing; just choose a direction before I could see what lay ahead."

"Right. Up those stairs," Adam said decisively.

Remy smiled and he almost did too.

When they reached the top of the stairs, Remy chose to turn right again and they found themselves beside the towering nave of the Église Notre-Dame-de-l'Assomption. Inside the church, it was quiet and cool. They were alone. Remy could almost see Adam's jaw unclench—the Adam she'd started to get to know when it was just the two of them together returning bit by bit.

They walked down the aisle toward the marbled blue-gray pillars near the altar. A chandelier sparkled gemlike above them. On the walls hung paintings and crucifixes and objects designed to bring comfort, but the only comfort either of them needed right then, Remy thought, was that of solitude—together.

While Adam contemplated—perhaps unseeing, perhaps seeing something else entirely—the abundance of art that waited without pomp or explanatory plaques to give to the viewer whatever it was that they needed, Remy turned into one of the side chapels and lit one candle. She hesitated, knowing she should light one for Toby too. Toby, who was speeding.

Her mind went straight to its usual jumping-off point, a point that let her forget sadness in the face of blame and anger. It hurt less to be angry than to be sad. But, suddenly and for the first time, she felt so sad that she'd let anger damage her memories of Toby. The accident was just that—an accident; it wasn't his fault. He was the one who'd always made sure Emily was strapped into the car properly, always giving the buckle an extra tug, just to be sure. She'd loved, quietly and never saying anything, the way he did that, the way that small gesture showed how much he cared for his daughter.

So she lit a second candle. As she put it down beside the one for Emily, she felt the tears come but she didn't hate herself for it this time. It was, in Èze that afternoon, all right to be sad.

"You okay?" Adam asked, having come up beside her.

"I am," she said. "I've been sad about Emily but mixed in with the sadness, I've been so mad at Toby, my husband. So mad," she repeated, watching the shimmer of heat from the candle blur everything behind it. "I think I just let some of that go. So even if today doesn't work out for you"—she gave him a small smile—"it's worked out for me already."

"Me too. I can't remember the last time I was in a church—too scared the doors might slam shut if they saw me coming—but this feels...I don't know." He cast around for the word. "Serene. Maybe it's what they put in the incense."

Remy laughed, then wiped her eyes. "Serene is exactly it," she said. "Ready to face the less serene outside?"

They stepped into the crowds outside but it didn't feel oppressive; it felt light, as if the breeze carried joy and was intent on spreading it around.

"I know this won't come as a surprise," Adam said. "But I'm starving."

"There are a few Italian restaurants in the center of town. Let's go there and then we can wind our way out afterward."

They found a table on the edge of a terrace in the shade of tendrils of bougainvillea and ordered pasta and wine. They talked about nothing at all really, until the conversation turned back to Remy's house and the gardens Adam had walked through that morning. "They're amazing," he said. "There's a Japanese garden and then one full of sculptures, then roses like I couldn't believe..."

"I know," Remy said. "I couldn't believe it either the first time I saw the house. Apparently the fountains in the pools even dance in time to music—or so one of the gardeners told me. Thankfully the house came with gardeners—they're paid out of some kind of trust fund."

"Tell me to mind my own business, but do you know anything about your birth parents?"

Remy sipped her wine. "A little," she said, hesitating, unsure how much he really wanted to hear. "I was put up for adoption soon after I was born because my parents were dead. My adoptive mother was given some information about them. Apparently my father was German and my mother English."

She stopped but Adam said, "And?"

"Well, they were both brilliant scientists—a talent that clearly skipped a generation," she said wryly. "They met at a conference in Poland. My father was from East Germany and he wasn't normally allowed to travel but he'd been given special permission to go to the conference. After only a week, he'd fallen in love with my mother and she followed him to East Germany."

"Behind the Berlin Wall?" Adam asked, attention completely caught.

"Behind the Berlin Wall," Remy agreed.

"Wow."

"I always wondered why she did that," Remy said, moving her fork idly through her pasta.

"I guess if he was from East Germany, and they were in love, she had no choice. Otherwise she'd never have seen him again."

"I sometimes wonder if their love was worth everything that came after," Remy mused. "My adoptive mother was told that when my birth parents were at the conference in Poland, my father gave my mother a scientific paper he'd written. She passed it on to some colleagues in London and it was published. East German scientists weren't allowed to publish in Western journals; it marked him out as a traitor. The Stasi put him under surveillance and tried to force him to join the Communist Party, which he didn't want to do. They restricted his work, and wouldn't let my mother work at all; it was a way to starve them into submission. So my parents decided to escape."

"They tried to escape from East Berlin?" Adam had even stopped eating, so engrossed was he in Remy's story. "They must have been desperate if they thought trying to get across the wall was the better option."

Remy nodded. "A friend of theirs lived in Berlin-Mitte, an area where apartments abutted the wall. They climbed out of a window and down a rope, taking with them the deeds to the house in Cap-Ferrat, my painting and some clothes. But the border guards saw them. My father was shot in the death strip. My mother, who was pregnant with me, was shot too, but she didn't die. She made it to West Germany, and to the British Embassy. Then she traveled back to England. But she was still weak from infection and blood loss when I decided I wanted to be born early. She died too."

"Jesus, Remy," Adam said, staring at her.

"My birth mother's parents were elderly and unwell and couldn't care for a newborn, so I was put up for adoption in England," Remy said, ignoring the empathy Adam had offered her. "My adoptive parents moved to Australia a year later to find a better place to raise a child. Hence my blonde hair and blue eyes. I'm the model Aryan citizen."

She put down her fork and studied her plate. She could feel that Adam wanted to say something.

Eventually he said, "One of Lauren's friends works at the Louvre. I called her up yesterday to ask about the painting you own that's in Göring's Catalogue. She said you should pay her a visit."

Remy looked up at him, frowning. "Why would I do that?"

"Don't you want to know?" Adam asked. "You have an incredible house, given to you by some anonymous person, with gardeners and maintenance all paid for. A house that's literally been waiting for you all your life. And you have a painting—Lauren's friend said the paintings in the catalog were all really valuable pieces, mostly stolen from wealthy private collectors in Paris during the war. You have blank sheets of paper where most people have a history and you need to, I don't know, develop them into something before the paper is too old and there's no one left who can tell you what should be there. Sometimes I can't bear to be in the same room as my family but I know who they are and I know all of their stories and they're my stories too; it's how I was made into me. All you have is a figure posed on an empty backdrop."

"Something not worth looking at," Remy said sharply.

"I didn't mean it like that."

"Past and future are things I can't bear, not anymore. The present is hard enough." She stood, opened her purse and threw some euros on the table. "I'll meet you out front."

She strode away to the bathroom and stared at herself in the mirror. The woman without a story, because why would anyone want a story like hers?

Get it together, Remy. She'd brought Adam here to take him away from it all, not to be rude and dwell on her own problematic past.

She left the sanctuary of the bathroom and found Adam outside, leaning against a wall, hands shoved in pockets, frowning.

"I thought you might do a runner," he said. "I was interfering and, like Lauren said, I hate being interfered with. I'm sorry."

"It's okay," Remy said. "And stop frowning. If I return you to your family looking like that, they'll think I took you to soulless Saint-Tropez instead of beautiful Èze. Let's walk until we can both smile."

At which point they both started laughing.

"We're going right," Remy said, mouth twitching, and they walked companionably together through street after street, each taking turns to choose the direction, sometimes circling aimlessly, other times finding streets so unbelievably charming that Adam took out his camera, snapping pictures of Remy beside an excess of the picturesque.

"Lauren and Mom are going to be so jealous when they see these pics," he said after they'd wound their way down to the Château de la Chèvre d'Or.

"I'll bring them back another day," Remy said.

"There's a bit of future right there," Adam said with a sideways smile at her.

She couldn't help smiling back. "You got me," she said. "Remind me not to do it again, will you?"

"Nope. I'm not promising that. Even if it means I have to walk home."

"Walk? You'd call an Uber the minute I left."

"I would. Because I'm unafraid enough of the future to foresee the blisters I'd get from walking. See, the future's not always a bad thing to think about."

They turned another corner and came upon the view that had stolen all of Remy's breath the first time she'd visited the town: the promenade at the front of the château that looked across to the Mediterranean.

"Let's have a drink," Adam said, indicating the crowded terrace on which there were a couple of spare seats.

They ordered champagne and talked about photography and Remy's business, just as they'd done on her terrace the other night, and occasionally they lapsed into a contented silence, the ribbons of clouds threaded over the sun above them subduing the light and coloring everything pastel.

Remy heard the click of Adam's camera and realized he'd taken another picture of her, looking out toward the sea. She reached out her hand for it and scrolled through the images from that afternoon: one of Remy laughing as she pretended to open one of the trompe l'oeil doors; one of her taken from the back as she walked a little ahead of Adam, then another taken seconds later when she'd turned around to smile at him; the one he'd just taken of her in profile, the hint of a smile not just on her lips but over her whole face. Remy, contented.

And she realized that she felt, right then, just as she looked: at ease. She glanced up at Adam, who was watching her. The ease retreated a little, forming into a strange mixture of gratitude and sadness, which she needed to explain because now she was frowning, and that had made Adam frown worriedly in response.

"In all your photos of me…" she began haltingly, "you keep giving me back parts of myself that I'd lost, or forgotten—I don't know. And the logical half of my brain understands it's a gift; that I'm lucky to have someone show me I'm more than the grieving mess I thought

I was. But…" She swallowed champagne, hoping it might help her to articulate the rest. "But it's a gift I'd give back in a heartbeat, for Emily. This last fortnight there've been so many new things and every new thing feels like a bargaining chip that I don't want to accept in case it's a currency I can offer in exchange for my daughter. If I accept it, it's like saying I don't want her back…"

Her voice trailed off, swallowed by the hubbub of laughter and conversation around them. She stared at the ocean, a pale Cinderella-blue glittering like promises she didn't believe in.

"There's nothing you wouldn't give, is there," Adam said quietly, eyes fixed to the water too and she knew he was talking about Molly. "It's like every valuable thing in the world is suddenly worthless in comparison because none of it's enough to give you what you most want."

"Yes."

A minute passed, then two, until a loud eruption of laughter at the next table brought Remy back to the present, to the gift of what she did have right then, which was someone who listened and maybe even understood. "You know," she said, trying to lighten the mood that she had made heavy, "you're surprisingly deep for an asshole."

This time, the eruption of laughter came from the two of them. Remy's head tipped back with it, letting the sunlight onto her face. She turned to Adam and smiled and something visceral passed between them, like the lingering warmth of the late-afternoon sun.

Adam swore.

"What is it?" she asked warily.

"I have to say something. I'm about to really piss you off though."

He finished his champagne and met her eyes, his so much like the ocean: an arcane and depthless blue. "I said that I didn't know why I'd kissed you. I do, actually. I kissed you because I have fun with you. I like spending time with you, and working with you. And also because…" He hesitated. "Because I think you're a gorgeous and incredibly sexy woman. There's no chance at all that I'm not going to dream about the way you looked on the beach this morning: your back, your skin."

He strangled the stem of his champagne glass with his hand. "I needed to tell you. If I didn't, I'd be lying by omission. I'm not going to do anything about it. I have more than enough self-control that I can go out with you like this and never kiss you again. Unless you wanted to, of course," he amended and then swore again. "I know you don't want to. Not now, maybe not ever..." He sighed. "I'm going to shut up now."

Remy remembered how, on the beach that morning, her mind had most definitely given consideration to how it might feel to run a finger over Adam's hipbone. And while he'd been speaking just now, she'd been unable to stop herself imagining a different version of that morning: Adam coming up behind her on the beach, her turning to face him. The way he would look at her...

She shivered and knew that was where everything had to stop. But also that she couldn't get mad at him for what he'd said.

"It's okay," she said, finding she couldn't look at him while she spoke. "How could anyone be mad about being told—by someone who spends his life working with often barely dressed models—that they're gorgeous." She felt herself blush scarlet.

"You are, Remy," he said softly. "And you know what? You spend as much time looking at apparently beautiful women in various states of undress as I do and you become almost immune to the naked female body. You realize it's all about who that body belongs to, not the body itself."

It was her turn to fidget uncomfortably. "I like spending time with you too," she said, daring to look back up at him. "But you're right. Kissing, even holding someone's hand; those are intimacies I can't face. I don't know when I'll ever be able to face them. So I understand if you don't come and visit me anymore."

"Even if there wasn't the incentive of escaping my family, I'd still want to visit you." He smiled gently but also, because he couldn't help it—it was just who Adam was—charismatically and definitely sexily.

At his smile, she felt something and she knew what it was: that primal, bodily, necessary urge to touch one's lips to another's, to feel their mouth open in response, to fit body to body, to articulate need without words.

Instead, she finished her champagne. "We should head back. Your mum will be wondering what's happened to you."

* * *

Once in the car and without the distraction of champagne, Adam's earlier questions about Remy's painting and her house—*Don't you want to know?*—sat uncomfortably on her shoulders like a fur stole in summer. Every time she told Adam something burdensome, whatever weight she was feeling pressed down less forcefully. So she said, without any kind of easy segue, "What if I do find out something about the painting, or the house, and it's bad? I feel like I've reached my limit of bad things. Like insanity is just one awful experience away and rather than succumbing to it, I just want to build my tower at Cap-Ferrat and hide at the top and only let the good things in." She shook her head. "Now I sound like a crazy woman."

She reached out to turn the radio on, intending to finish the discussion she'd meant to conduct more rationally.

Adam turned the radio off. "If I was going to build myself a tower, Cap-Ferrat would be the place to do it." He smiled at her.

She couldn't help but smile back. "Why are you not leaping out of the car and running away from all of my strangeness?"

"Because you're driving so fast I'd break my legs."

He always made her laugh and she laughed now. He leaned one elbow on the rim of the window, which was down, the scent of sea and summer tumbling in. "It's not going to go away if you ignore it," he said. "It'll just be a different kind of bad thing that will drive you nuts: not knowing, but worrying over it anyway."

"You're right," she said. "Tell me about Lauren's friend from the Louvre. I have to go to Paris at some stage anyway. I always go picking at the Puces in Paris—the markets—when I'm in France and August is a good time as it's quieter then. I could pay her a visit when I'm there."

"Do you…" He paused and Remy could hear something in his voice: a hesitancy that made her want to squeeze his hand. "I could go with you if you wanted company," he finished. "I have no idea what you'll find at the Louvre but, in case you need a friend, I could come along."

Remy took the biggest leap she'd taken in almost two years. "What the hell would we say to your family?"

"That we're having a debaucherous weekend in Paris?" he said wryly. "They'd believe that of me, at least."

Remy smiled. "Your mum and Lauren wouldn't. How about we all go? Your whole family."

"No fucking way."

She laughed. "Jeez, tell me how you really feel."

"I'm not going to troop through Paris with my family."

"If I tell Lauren I'm going shopping at the Puces, there's no way she won't want to come."

He shook his head and smiled at her, a genuine smile behind which she could see all of him: the hurt and the anger over Molly, the artist trying to forget art, the confident man he fell back to being because it was simpler than being anything else, the vast complexity that was Adam.

"All right," he said. "Let's do it. The Henry-Jones expedition to Paris. I can hardly wait."

TWENTY

The Marché aux Puces de Saint-Ouen were massive, a collection of fifteen different markets, each with its own personality and treasures, requiring a map or a guide or an inexhaustible sense of adventure for first-time visitors. Even Adam was impressed.

"We'll start at Marché Paul Bert Serpette," Remy said decisively. "It's expensive, but has something for everyone. We can search for bargains at the other markets later."

Antoinette and the Henry-Joneses followed Remy along Rue des Rosiers and into the *marché couvert* and she watched with a grin as everyone's mouths dropped open and they stared at the cornucopia of strangeness: armor and chandeliers and marble mantelpieces and real stuffed animals and bewitching diamonds and even a staircase for sale.

"I've got to say, I thought this would be a drag, but it's…" Adam halted in front of a gallery selling art and photographs. "Unbelievable. Look," he said to Remy. "There's one of the Dahl-Wolfe's we used. And," he peered closer. "It's numbered and signed. It's the real deal."

And there, on the wall was the picture of the women waiting for someone in front of a fireplace. Adam took out his wallet and bought it.

They all had immense fun for the next few hours. Even Matt seemed affable enough, not saying anything when Adam snapped a picture of Molly, mouth open in astonishment as she patted a stuffed lion in one of the stalls. Not saying anything either when Adam took Molly's hand

and led her over to see a daguerreotype camera, picking her up so he could explain to her how it worked.

As Remy watched them, she felt the all too familiar corset of emotion tighten around her heart but, this time, she couldn't have said for sure if it was from yearning for what she'd lost or if it was from the ache of seeing what someone else wanted but would never have.

Antoinette slipped her arm through Remy's and she whispered, just as she'd done on the beach a few days ago, "Look at you. Thinking of someone else again."

Remy managed a half-smile. Pain was not, it seemed, limited to wanting what could never be recovered; it also came from fleeting moments of beauty, moments you would give anything to preserve—not for yourself, but for someone else. Remy took out her phone and snapped Molly in Adam's arms, his hand pointing out something, the little girl tipping forward to get a clearer view, one hand holding trustingly on to Adam's shoulder.

Then they wandered down to Chez Sarah at the Marché Jules Vallès, where Lauren splurged on a beautiful Chanel gown, and finally into Marché Vernaison.

"I think this is our chance to make a run for it," she whispered to Adam as Alistair turned to look at antique maps, Judy's hand joined with his, listening to her husband not as if she particularly cared, but as if she knew he did. Antoinette and Molly goggled at expensive jewelry while Matt laughed good-naturedly at them, and Lauren was whispering besottedly to her husband.

"I think you're right," Adam said, surveying his happy family.

They navigated through the crowds, which were thick now. At one point, Adam touched a hand to Remy's back to steer her out of the way of a tourist overladen with bags and she almost instinctively relaxed back into it, but then her thinking mind screamed at her, *How dare you, Remy?*, so she didn't react to his touch and it was quickly gone.

An hour later, they reached the Louvre, where Lauren's friend Chloe, a tall and elegant redhead, greeted them.

"Your painting is a bit of a mystery," Chloe said to Remy, leading her and Adam into one of the galleries where, unbelievably, on the far wall was a painting very similar to Remy's own. It depicted a couple embracing in a window embrasure, the night sky an oceanic blue above them, punctuated by a white circle of moon, unlike Remy's painting, which had no sky and no moon—just the same couple.

"Wow," Remy said. "There's another one just like mine."

"Yes. This one is signed; the painter's name was Luc Dufort," Chloe went on. "He was something of a Resistance hero, which has made this painting a popular piece. We've always wondered what happened to the other: the one called *Le Traître* in Göring's Catalogue, which we assume, based on the similarities, Luc Dufort painted too. I can't believe it's been in your bedroom all these years."

"A hero?" Remy asked, intrigued.

"He was involved in saving stolen paintings during the war," Chloe explained. "Hermann Göring used a museum not far from here as a warehouse for artwork that his German cronies stole for him and Adolf Hitler. Luc Dufort worked with a Frenchwoman called Rose Valland who spied on the Germans."

"I had no real idea, until I saw *The Göring Catalogue*, that so much art was stolen," Remy admitted.

"Most people don't know about that part of the war." Chloe smoothed a hand over her hair and smiled at Remy, as if to reassure her that her lack of knowledge didn't mean she was ignorant. "But the part of Luc Dufort's tale that's always captured everyone's attention and made this painting a little famous, is the story of what happened soon before the liberation of Paris in 1944."

Remy and Adam leaned in like children eager to hear what happened next.

"An entire trainload of artworks was being evacuated by the Nazis from the museum. The Resistance were told about it, and they helped to stop the train and keep the artworks here in France. Luc Dufort was on the train. Apparently he held up this painting to shield himself from a German bullet. Some say the bullet hit the painting but, as you can see, the painting is undamaged. Regardless, Luc Dufort died from that bullet. He died for art," Chloe said a little reverently. "Can you imagine anyone doing something like that today?"

"My painting," Remy said slowly, "has a weird hole in the top right corner. I never knew what it was from…"

"You're kidding." Chloe's eyes were like moons, staring unblinking at Remy.

"I guess it could be a bullet hole. Do you think that means my painting is…"

The one in your story? Remy's voice trailed away at the preposterousness of what she was saying.

"I don't know," Chloe said excitedly. "Maybe. Do you know if it has anything on the back of it? Like this." She pulled on gloves, turned off a security device and lifted the painting off the wall.

Stamped in a corner on the back was a swastika. Remy shivered as she recalled a smudged mark on the back of her painting that could have been, once upon a time before age had smeared it almost beyond recognition, a swastika too. "There are some markings on the back of my painting," Remy said. "Letters, or numbers maybe. I'll get my mum to take a photo and send it to me."

"This one has letters on it too," Chloe said, pointing to lines of faded black ink in one corner. "I'm not sure why. I used to wonder if they were codes, like they used in the war to identify the real *Mona Lisa*, but this painting wasn't in the Louvre during the war."

Remy squinted at the markings, which seemed to be the letters *XL/ED.*

"I'd love to see your photos when you get them," Chloe continued. "I'd actually love to see your painting."

"It's an incredible story," Adam said, moving closer to the painting. "It's also an incredible work. You feel like you're actually looking at love and it's somehow real..."

"As if the painter has captured a fairy and is holding out the bottle to say, see: this is what it is. And you finally believe in it," Chloe finished.

Adam glanced at Chloe and Remy realized that Chloe was very intent on Adam, which was understandable given how Adam looked: casual in navy shorts and a dark blue T-shirt, tattoo peeking suggestively out from his sleeve, tanned from all the time spent outside over the last couple of weeks, unshaven in a way Antoinette had described only that morning as "beddable." And Chloe was stylishly Parisienne and most likely emotionally available and Remy felt both a certainty that Adam would quickly get over his interest in Remy and also a sharp ache at the prospect of a future time when she wouldn't be able to jump into a car with him and go for a drive knowing that, no matter what happened, the outcome would be that she felt better.

That was why it didn't do to think of the future; here she was, mourning it before it had even arrived. There was enough to mourn in the present.

"My painting makes you feel the same," Remy said, stepping in next to Adam. "Sometimes that made it hard to look at."

She pressed her lips together. She was such a moaner. She couldn't just say that she liked the painting and be done with it; she had to find something wrong, some fault, some flaw. The dark side of everything was Remy's métier.

"It's called *Les Amoureux—The Lovers*, naturally," Chloe continued brightly, a glowing example of lightness.

"Göring's Catalogue says Remy's painting is called *The Traitor*,"

Adam said. "Which is kind of a weird name for a painting that looks very intimate."

"Maybe one of them wasn't faithful to the other?" Chloe suggested.

"But you'd hardly paint a picture like this of someone you hated. Technically it should be in the Musée d'Orsay as it's their period. But the benefactor was most insistent it be kept here."

"Benefactor?" Remy asked.

"A woman donated the painting to us many years ago. Elke König was her name. She might know something about your painting. I'll call her and ask if I can give you her details. In the meantime, I have a few other ideas. The best place to look for information is actually Washington DC. Most of the papers to do with the Monuments, Fine Arts and Archives section of the Allied Armed Forces, who were charged with finding and recovering looted artworks at the end of the war, are kept at the National Archives there. They have the index cards for each painting—its title and artist—that entered the Jeu de Paume museum during the war."

Remy had stopped listening after the first two sentences. She didn't want to say it in front of Chloe but it was impossible not to say it. *König.* "My birth father's surname," she began falteringly, "was König."

Chloe's eyebrows shot up to the ceiling. "Well, that's a beautiful coincidence. Did he have a relation by the name of Elke König?"

Remy wasn't about to tell Chloe that she couldn't ask her father because she'd never met him. "I'm not sure..."

"Well, there's a researcher in New York who did a fellowship here last year," Chloe said. "She knows a lot more about the Jeu de Paume museum and Luc Dufort than I do. I can give you her details and maybe you could visit her if you go to Washington. And I'll get in touch with Elke König too, if you like?"

Would she like that? Remy didn't know. Still, she said, "Thank you. You've been really helpful."

"Lauren and I went to school together so I'm happy to help any friend of hers. In fact, I'm glad you called." Chloe turned to Adam now. "It's been ages since I've seen you. We should catch up properly while you're here. Go for a drink?"

Remy wanted to slink away. Then she saw the look on Adam's face and grinned. Complete surprise. He had no idea that Chloe had been ogling him the entire time. In that moment, she almost felt sorry for Chloe.

"Ummm, I'm only here for a couple of days," Adam said. "I have a family dinner tonight. And I'm helping Remy with some stuff…"

He caught Remy's eye and Remy didn't quite hide her grin in time, which in turn made Adam actually flush a little.

They left an only slightly disappointed Chloe, who was good-natured enough not to mind Adam's evasive reply, and as they were walking through the galleries toward the exit, Adam glanced sideways at her and said, self-consciously, "Don't."

Remy exploded with laughter. "That was the worst excuse ever! *I'm helping Remy with some stuff.*" She mimicked his vague tone. "Surely you're more practiced at deflecting offers than that? Or you're so used to accepting them that you've forgotten how to deflect?" she teased.

"Given how often my offers to a certain woman have been deflected lately, I'd say I've had some solid training in that," he replied, teasing her now. "And at least I didn't deflect by telling her she was repulsive."

Even though she knew he was making light of their situation, she still felt herself blush a very obvious red. "You're not repulsive," she said quietly. "Not at all. I'm just the crazy lady who finds kissing repulsive. I don't want you to think it has anything to do with you."

"Hey." He stopped in the middle of the Cour Napoléon, forcing the crowds to step around them. "I understand. In fact," he shoved his hands in his pockets. "At the risk of sounding like an asshole again, my crazy thing was that I hated kids for the longest time after Matt told me to stay away from Molly. What kind of person hates kids? I couldn't look at them, couldn't even go jogging in daylight in Central Park in case I saw them out playing."

"That wasn't hate you were feeling," Remy said quietly. She'd seen him with Molly and it was clear he loved that girl. What he'd felt, she knew, was fear.

Which also meant—her train of thought continued on to something like self-awareness—that maybe it wasn't revulsion she felt when she thought about kissing Adam. She cut off the thought right there.

"Maybe not," he said, sighing.

On the way to the hotel, Remy's mind turned over the fact that in her possession was a painting possibly stolen by the Nazis, a painting that had been so important to her parents—both of them? Or just one of them?—that they'd chosen to take it with them when they tried to escape East Germany, and had then written specific instructions that the painting stay with the baby.

Remy had seen that letter, written in her birth mother's hand from her hospital bed as she lay dying. And then there was the letter her adoptive mother had shown her nearly two years ago granting Remy ownership of the house on the Riviera. It had been written in a different hand: her birth father's, whose surname was König. Was he Elke König's brother? Father? Son?

"Washington," she mused aloud as they approached the hotel. "There's not really any point going to Washington." But now that she'd started this odd quest, could she just give it up? Especially if a man—the Luc Dufort whom Chloe had mentioned—had lost his life for artworks like the one she had hanging on her bedroom wall in her house in Sydney.

"I'll come to Washington with you if you want me to," Adam said as the elevator stopped on his floor. Then the doors opened, and he was gone before Remy could think what to say.

* * *

Antoinette pounced on Remy the minute she stepped into their room. "Where did you two disappear to?" she asked, grinning.

"We went to the Louvre," Remy said, sitting on the bed and taking off her shoes.

"The Louvre?" Antoinette said incredulously. "You spent the entire afternoon with Adam looking at fusty old paintings."

"I did."

Antoinette flopped on the bed. "You know he's interested? He can't stop looking at you."

"I know he's interested," Remy said flatly.

Antoinette sat up, open-mouthed. "You know? How? I don't believe anything other than the absolutely obvious would have made you see that."

Remy stood up and pushed open the bathroom door. "I need a shower," she said. "Otherwise we'll be late."

Which didn't deter Antoinette. She followed Remy into the bathroom, perched on the edge of the bath and waited expectantly.

Remy groaned, dumped her clothes on the floor, stepped into the shower, turned on the water and turned her back on her friend. "He kissed me," she said. "Actually, we both kissed each other. I stopped it. He told me that he thinks…" Remy put her hands to her ears, knowing Antoinette was about to squeal. "He told me he thinks I'm gorgeous."

Covered ears were no match for Antoinette's shriek. "What?!"

Remy winced. "None of it matters, okay?" She turned to face her friend at last, scrubbing herself vigorously with soap.

"You don't like him?"

"It's not that."

Antoinette stood, hands on hips, eyes fixed on Remy. "Then there shouldn't be anything stopping you. Becoming a nun won't change anything. Emily and Toby will still be dead. It's coming up for two years now. It's time, well and truly."

Remy dropped the soap, not sure she could withstand Antoinette's excessively brutal brand of tough love just now.

"Do you really think," Antoinette continued, "that they'd want you to spend the rest of your life lonely and unloved and unhappy? Is that what you'd want for them, if you had died? For Emily to erect a mausoleum to you in her mind and worship only that, to never love? Is that what you'd want for Toby?"

If you had died. And that was the thing. How Remy wished that it had been her and not them. How much easier it would have been to die and to not always feel this loss, this hurt, this sadness. But if she had died, then her husband and daughter would feel those same things— how could she wish that they suffer the pain instead?

"I wouldn't want that," she said haltingly. "But...but..." She looked at Antoinette through tears and water. "What if I fell in love again, with Adam, which I think maybe I could do"—and there it was, that same sharp and terrible fear she'd felt the night he'd kissed her—"and something happened to him? I couldn't go through this again. I couldn't."

Antoinette's face transformed into the kind of exquisite tenderness only the oldest and dearest friends were capable of. "Come here, you goose."

She held out a towel and her arms and Remy stepped into the towel, wrapping it around herself, and then into the arms of her friend and she wept for possibly the millionth time since everything had happened. But it felt different, as if something was letting go, the guilt and some of the fear easing.

* * *

They were meeting the Henry-Joneses at Café Marly, a place she and Adam and Antoinette all knew from fashion parties. Set under the vaulted stone arches of the exterior of the Richelieu wing of the Louvre, it was a hard-to-find, long and narrow space with the most incredible view of the Pyramide du Louvre. Remy and Antoinette had decided to dress in a way that did justice to the stunning building whose *terrasse* was sheltered by spectacular carved ceilings, a work of art in themselves, and columned with immense pillars of ancient ivory-colored stone.

Antoinette wore a stunning crimson 1940s silk-crepe gown that looked demure from the front. But when she turned around, the deep V of the back was revealed and the combination of innocence and daring made many heads turn Antoinette's way. She accepted the stares with insouciance, as if the attention were an uninteresting trifle, and Remy smiled; this was why her friend would remain perpetually and happily single.

Remy had chosen a gown from the 1930s in black silk with a V neckline and the kind of angled deco seams that embraced the curves of a body. It too had a low back, and a faux draped bustle adorned with black and red silk flowers. It was the kind of dress that made anyone feel they could be a starlet, celestial rather than earthbound.

As a waiter led them over to the Henry-Joneses' table, the first thing Remy did, unconsciously, was to look for Adam. He wasn't there yet. It was only as disappointment set in that she realized what she'd done, but the disappointment was momentary: Lauren and Adam appeared just behind them and Remy felt her lips lift into a smile. Antoinette was at her most forbearing and limited herself to elbowing Remy's ribs.

Adam wore a navy suit with a navy shirt, the top button undone, and he could have been on the model side of the camera he looked so good. Remy felt a sharp shock of what could only be called desire burn through her.

Lauren took the side of the booth next to Antoinette and Adam slid in next to Remy. It was cramped, intimacy being very much the venue's vibe, and Adam's leg pressed against Remy's as he sat down, which didn't help dampen the sensation of heat.

"Sorry," he said, trying to shift away.

"It's okay," she said, feigning nonchalance. "You'll end up on the floor if you move that way."

"We need to order food now that everyone's here," Matt piped up, eyeing Adam. "Molly's hungry."

Matt summoned the waiter, who started with Adam. He ordered in perfect French, which made Molly jump out of her seat and scuttle around to sit on Adam's lap, whispering what she wanted into his ear so he could order her meal in French too. Then Molly tried endearingly to copy him until even the waiter was laughing.

As soon as he'd finished, Adam said to Molly, "You'd better go sit back next to your dad."

Molly shook her head. "Tell me more French," she ordered.

"*Tu es la plus belle fille dans la salle—à part de Remy,*" he said.

"You said her name." Molly pointed at Remy, who was laughing.

"He did," Remy agreed.

"What did Uncle Adam say?" Molly asked.

"That you're beautiful," Remy said.

"You are too," Molly said wistfully. "I want this." She touched Remy's necklace, a deco, jet-black, carved glass pendant on a long chain that sat just above Remy's breastbone.

"You've got excellent taste for a five-year-old," Adam said, "but you can't have another one of Remy's necklaces."

Instead of pouting and protesting, the little girl nestled her head into Adam's shoulder and rested contentedly there, clearly tired after a long day of traipsing around Paris and, probably, at almost half past eight at night, needing sleep. Adam's hand lifted to stroke her hair and she sighed, like a kitten. Remy met Adam's eyes over the top of Molly's head and there were so many very painful and also very lovely things held there.

His expression changed and Remy realized that Matt was watching. And Judy was watching Matt. Lauren was chatting brightly about her misadventures at the Puces, obviously willing everyone to join in and forget about why Adam looked suddenly guilty, as if he'd done something wrong, and all the lovely things fell out of his eyes like tears.

Thankfully Matt let them be until the food arrived. "You'd better go sit with your dad now," Adam whispered and Molly blinked sleepily and scampered to her seat. Over the meal, everyone chatted and Remy felt herself relax, and Adam too.

Near the end, when the group began to speak less generally and more specifically to the person beside them, Adam said to Remy, "When I got here, you looked like you'd been crying."

"Something I do way too often," Remy said ruefully. "But I'm okay. And I think…" She sipped her champagne for courage. "I think I'll go to Washington."

"I'll miss you."

The buzz and blast around them fell away. It was just Remy sitting right beside Adam, so close that she could see the blue of his eyes darken, could feel the warmth of his leg against hers and, if she had the courage or was able to give herself the permission, she could reach out and touch his hand, or even his jawline, run her thumb close to his lips.

The Remy of a week ago would have leapt up and run to the bathroom to escape her thoughts. The Remy of today stayed where she was, through all the mixed feelings in that small moment of intimacy.

He must have seen the strength it took for her to stay because he leaned in and whispered, "Thanks," so softly that nobody else would hear.

Opposite Remy, Antoinette was saying to Matt, "I'm leaving in a couple of days. Remy's finished shooting, so I can stop being a hair and makeup artist and go back to being a marketing director—although staying with Remy in a spectacular house on the French Riviera wasn't exactly a hardship. Are you sure you don't want to take any more pics?" she said pleadingly to Remy.

Remy shook her head. "No. I'm going to Washington." She almost stopped there. But then she added, at the exact same moment that the music fell away and the conversation at their table dimmed, "Adam's coming with me."

She froze, aware that she had just invited Adam to DC in front of his entire family. Antoinette's mouth fell open, Lauren's too. The eyes of every single person—Judy, Alistair, Matt, Lauren's husband—turned to Remy and Adam.

Adam's hand was resting on the seat of the banquette next to Remy and she slid her own hand into it, under the table, where no one could see.

She felt his fingers tighten over hers as if to say, *Screw them. It's our business.*

TWENTY-ONE

Thankfully Adam was still capable of speech. "It's only a couple of days," he said to his mother. "I'm not skipping out on the family holiday. Remy has to do some research in Washington. She's never been before, so I'm going to show her around."

"Sounds marvelous," Judy said, obviously feeling Remy's desperate need to move the conversation on to something else. "Let's order dessert."

Remy let go of Adam's hand, took up the dessert menu and forced herself to remain at the table for five long minutes, pretending to decide what she wanted to eat. Finally, she said to Adam, "Excuse me."

He slid out of the banquette and she marched to the bathroom, sat down on a lounge and just about hyperventilated. She wanted him to come with her. She did. But she also knew that holding his hand for thirty seconds had been such a colossal and frightening step that she wasn't sure she'd be capable of speaking to him for their entire sojourn in Washington.

She walked over to the mirror and made sure her face had a degree of composure about it before she left the bathroom, almost shocked that Antoinette hadn't followed her, whooping. When she stepped back out into the dark hall, a man was waiting for her.

"I told them we're going for a walk," Adam said quietly.

How did he know? How could he tell that all she wanted was to run away into the Paris night?

He led the way out and they began to wander through the Louvre gardens and into the Jardins des Tuileries.

"Are you sure?" he asked as they strolled, not hand in hand but side by side, both lost in labyrinthine thoughts.

"I want you to come. Not just to show me around. But because... I'd miss you too. But it was really selfish of me to announce it to the whole table without asking you first. And it's selfish of me to want you to come when holding your hand tonight felt about as draining for me emotionally as anything I've done in nearly two years. Not because it wasn't exactly what I needed but because there are so many things to leave behind in doing that. It's hard to let some of those things go."

One bleak tear rolled down Remy's cheek. "It's like I have to acknowledge that they won't ever come back. Like I'd somehow, stupidly, been expecting them to. And tied up in all of that is the knowledge that I miss Emily more. That if I could choose one of them to come back, it would be her and not Toby. Which makes me a horrible person. But those are the things I think of at night, the things that stop me from sleeping."

They had reached the Place de la Concorde when Adam stopped and said, "Jesus, Remy, it's so hard to see you so sad. All I want to do is hold you and I know I can't. But what can I do? Tell me."

Remy swiped at her eyes. "Putting up with me is more than anyone should do. It's all I need right now. But I understand..." She paused. "I understand if it isn't enough for you."

"It's plenty," he said, which almost made her cry again.

Instead she blinked and offered him a small smile. "I think I should go back to my room. It's been a teary day and I'm ready for it to be over. But there was good stuff too," she added, lest he think that she didn't count holding his hand as one of the loveliest things that had happened to her for a long, long time.

* * *

Washington was eye-straining work, sitting side by side with Adam and scrolling through rolls of microfilm—the inventory lists created by the ERR staff at the Jeu de Paume museum during the war—some of it in French or German, but thankfully most of it translated into English.

"Remy?" Adam said after a time.

She looked across to his screen and there it was. Her painting. And the one from the Louvre. Side by side.

"It says in the notes on this reel that this photo was taken in the Salle des Martyrs at the Jeu de Paume," Adam said.

"What's the Salle des Martyrs?"

"I don't know." Adam rubbed his eyes.

"Well, it's a much-needed reward. My eyes feel like they're about to fall out."

Not long after, Remy found something too. Two cards from the index of paintings taken to the Jeu de Paume; one showed her painting, the other the painting at the Louvre. *Les Amoureux*, the latter was called, just as Chloe had said: *The Lovers*. But the card showing Remy's painting called it: *L'Amour*, or *Love*. Not *Le Traître*.

"Look at this," she said to Adam.

He studied the card. "It's definitely a more fitting title."

"Does that mean there's a third painting? Or that . . . I don't know . . ." It was Remy's turn to rub her eyes. She checked her watch. "It's about half an hour until we're meeting the researcher Chloe told us about. Why don't we grab some lunch, talk to her, and then we can come back and search with functioning eyeballs."

"Great idea."

They went downstairs, ate lunch, and soon Taylor Edwards, a brunette with shampoo-commercial hair and a dimpled smile joined them.

"Thank you for meeting us," Remy said. "I'll try not to take up too much of your time."

"It's my peculiar pleasure to meet you," Taylor said. "I'm obsessed with art theft and forgery in a way that other people are obsessed with puppies and yoga. I'd be fitter and better at small talk if I was the latter."

Remy laughed. She'd been worried a researcher might look down upon Remy and her one tiny painting.

"I'm also obsessed with your painting—well, with its painter really," Taylor went on.

"Luc something," Remy said.

"Luc Dufort is recorded as the artist, yes. But I think it's someone else's work."

"Whose work?" Adam asked. "And are you talking about just Remy's painting, or the one at the Louvre too?"

"Both," Taylor replied. "But let's start at the beginning. How much do you know about the art thefts from the Jeu de Paume during the war?"

"I've flicked through Göring's Catalogue and that's about it," Remy said.

Taylor proceeded to give Remy and Adam a brief account of the Nazi theft of Jewish paintings during the war, and the role of the Jeu de Paume museum as prison and sorting facility.

Then she smiled wryly. "Poor Chloe. She had to put up with a whole lot of my crazy theories when I was at the Louvre on my fellowship. And one of my crazy theories is... Well, to cut a very long story short, my mom owns a gallery in Manhattan. Her mom bought the business in the late 1940s off the man who started it. As well as the Manhattan gallery, this man had a gallery in London and one in the Rue La Boétie in Paris which, back in the day, was the place to be. He wanted to walk out and leave both the mess and the treasure for someone else to deal with. Lots of his personal stuff was there, including a group of paintings by his son, Xavier Laurent. My grandmother liked them so she hung them in her house, then my mom hung them in her house and now I have them hanging in my house. I think Xavier Laurent painted the work at the

Louvre signed by Luc Dufort. I grew up with his style all around me so I could identify it even if I was standing on top of Mount Everest and you put the painting at the foot of the mountain. Ever since I saw the index card here with your painting on it, I've been dying to know what happened to it. I had no idea it was in Australia, of all places."

Taylor spoke passionately, knowledgeably and Remy found herself believing her. "Why would he let someone else sign his work though?" Remy asked.

"And that's where my theory falls apart," Taylor said. "I have no idea. And, when you're dealing with a work that's supposed to have been painted by a Resistance hero, nobody wants to know about vague theories."

"Does any of that mean the painting is technically yours?" was Remy's next question. "I don't really know how it came into my family's possession."

"*The Göring Catalogue* indicates it was stolen from Édouard de Rothschild," Taylor replied. "And the Rothschilds' records show that he bought the painting now in the Louvre in 1939, and your painting in 1940, not long before he fled Paris."

"You're saying my painting belongs to the Rothschild family?" Remy's eyeballs, having just recovered from microfilming, were about to fall out of her head again.

"How certain are you about all this?" Adam asked, placing three coffees on the table, coffees Remy hadn't even realized he'd left the table to order.

She sipped hers gratefully and was thankful again that he'd come. Her mind was leaping all over the place—what if the Rothschilds wanted reparations from her for having kept their painting for so long?—and he was being calm and rational and not jumping to any strange conclusions.

"You obviously know a lot about it," he said, "and I'm not doubting you. It's just that, for Remy, the painting might be tied into her background." He briefly filled Taylor in on the painting having come with Remy's mother from Germany.

"And that's something I really want to find out more about," Taylor said, dimples deepening as something like anticipation swept over her face. "I'm hoping what you know might help me solve another mystery I tried to tackle in my research. My PhD was focused on the Salle des Martyrs at the Jeu de Paume," she explained. "It was supposed to be about what happens socially, financially, culturally, and artistically when you declare an entire group of artworks to be transgressive—I had to couch it in academic terms of course. But all I really wanted was to write about that group of paintings shut up in a room and watched over by one or maybe two women. Rose Valland, and possibly Éliane Dufort, although she and her story seem to have been lost somewhere in history and nobody's entirely sure if she was really there or not. Resistance heroines."

Resistance heroines. The story was becoming more preposterous and elaborate. "What do you mean by 'lost'?" Remy asked, trying to fit this piece into a puzzle that was growing so large it almost spilled out of her head. "And do either of the women have a link to my painting?"

Taylor stirred sugar into her coffee and sipped. "Éliane Dufort is the sister of Luc Dufort—the man who's supposedly the artist of your painting. And I say 'lost' because Rose Valland wrote an extensive memoir about how she risked her life for the paintings in the museum, recording what artworks were stolen and where they were sent, which made finding them again after the war a much easier task than it would otherwise have been—she basically saved tens of thousands of artworks from being lost forever. But her memoir, despite being so detailed, never mentions Éliane, not once.

"It's a mystery," Taylor finished with a raised eyebrow, "because here at the archives, kept as part of the evidence gathered by the Monuments,

Fine Arts, and Archives section of the Allied Armed Forces when they were investigating the people who stole the artworks, is the diary of a German man called Ernst König. He was one of the art historians working for Göring at the Jeu de Paume and he mentions Éliane Dufort all the time. He says that she worked there with Rose and that he was in love with her."

König. That surname again. And, she thought now with a sharp shock, the timing . . . No. She didn't want to ask.

She looked across at Adam and could see he knew what she was struggling with. She drew in a breath and then said, in a very low voice, "Do you know . . . Do you know if Ernst König was married? If he had a baby during the war?"

"He did!" Taylor said brightly. "In 1944. A little boy called Alexandre. And this is the part I really don't get. Even though he mentions he had a wife called Elke—he doesn't waste many words on her—he says he had a child with Éliane Dufort. But if she was working with Rose to protect the art, why would she have had a baby with a man who was helping to steal the art? I'm guessing, if you look at what so many Frenchwomen did during the war to keep themselves and their loved ones safe, or to cover up their Resistance work, that she maybe felt like she had no choice. Either that or," Taylor shook her head sadly, "he forced her, which was horribly common at the time. So many half-German, half-French babies born and then their mothers ostracized after the war for their so-called acts of collaboration."

Remy hardly heard the latter part of Taylor's explanation. Taylor had just said that Ernst König's son was named Alexandre. Remy's biological father, the brilliant scientist who'd died trying to flee East Berlin, had been called Alexandre König too. And he'd been born in 1944. Which made Remy the granddaughter of a Nazi art thief.

Why had she come to Washington? Why hadn't she stayed at Cap-Ferrat? Why hadn't she, in fact, just stayed at her home in Sydney with

Toby and Emily and never gone anywhere and then they would be alive and she would be with them and everything would be perfect.

* * *

Remy and Adam drove straight to the airport after their meeting with Taylor, Remy unspeaking and Adam leaving her alone with her tornado of thoughts, which was what she wanted.

She had come to Washington looking for the pedigree of a painting and had perhaps found a pedigree for herself that she wanted to tear to pieces. What did it mean for the house at Cap-Ferrat? That it had been bought with the profits made by stealing paintings from French Jews who'd suffered in every possible and unimaginable way throughout the Second World War?

She jammed her earbuds in at the airport and tried to fill her head with every kind of music—relaxing, angry, upbeat, and cacophonic—but none of it helped.

The only time Adam spoke to her was after they'd found their seats on the plane. "I still think you should talk to Elke König if Chloe can reach her," he said. "Assuming she's the wife of the Ernst König who Taylor mentioned, she might tell you that everything you're worrying about isn't true—or that it is. I don't know. And I'm not going to say you shouldn't worry or that you are who you are no matter your heritage because we both know that, given Molly's messed-up heritage, I'm not in a position to make any kind of argument. I'm just going to say that you're one of the best people I know, Remy. That'll never change."

Remy was one blink away from crying. "Thank you," she said. "For the sake of my eyes though, can we not talk about it for a while? I'm going to try to get some sleep."

She reclined her seat and arranged herself in her airline blanket, not really expecting she would sleep, but she did, not waking until morning when the flight attendant announced they would soon be arriving in Paris. She blearily rubbed her eyes and sat up, wondering where she was, not remembering what had happened the day before, remembering only that, while she slept, she'd heard something like her conscience talking to her. If tracking paintings like the one she possessed had been important enough for one or perhaps two women to spy on the Germans in order to do it, and if her own painting had perhaps been used as a failed shield by a Resistance hero who lost his life, then shouldn't Remy, at the very least, try to return the painting to the person it truly belonged to? Shouldn't she stop thinking about herself and be grateful that she was alive and in a country without war and most likely would never have to hold a painting up to her head to try to save herself from a gunshot?

Yes. She should.

She pushed her hair out of her face, sipped water, and tried to let resolution rather than fear guide her now.

Adam, in the next seat, was watching her, looking as if he hadn't been sleeping on an airplane seat all night—or perhaps it was just that he could carry off every guise, even the slightly unkempt, with the same finesse as if he were wearing a dinner suit.

"Morning," he said, smiling at her. He rubbed the back of his neck and stretched, his T-shirt lifting an inch or so, affording Remy a glimpse of the body she'd admired on the beach a week ago. It was impossible to stop her eyes from roving over that glorious terrain.

He caught her. His cheeks flushed and he lowered his arms.

Rather than being embarrassed or running away and locking herself in the bathroom, Remy actually found herself laughing, enjoying knowing that even Adam Henry-Jones could get a little flustered sometimes. "I confess. I was checking you out," she said, still laughing because he was still blushing very endearingly.

And instead of making a big deal out of it, he mock-stretched again. "I can do this all the way to Paris if that's what it takes," which made

Remy laugh all the more, and him too, until the flight attendant told them sternly to put on their seatbelts and prepare for landing.

Maybe it was the lightness, or that she'd somehow relaxed, or maybe it was everything that had happened over the last couple of weeks but Remy could feel now, dazzling the air between them, the shiver of attraction requited, which was different to one-way admiration. This was visceral; it warmed her skin and beckoned her closer, made her hold one of her hands inside the other so it wouldn't stray into that charged space.

She feigned fascination with a magazine while Adam scrolled haphazardly through music on his phone until the plane landed.

As they stood up, Adam asked, "Do you want to drive straight back to Cap-Ferrat? Or stop somewhere?"

Remy's phone buzzed before she could reply. It was a message from Chloe. Elke König would be happy to meet her at ten o'clock that morning. Yesterday's aching jaw returned but Remy took a deep breath and forced it away. She showed Adam the message.

"You're already worried and you haven't even seen her," he said. "So maybe speaking to her isn't actually going to make you feel any worse."

"You're right. Let's get some breakfast—I know you'll be dying of starvation by now—and then we can go see her."

"If breakfast is involved, I'm in," he said.

They found a brasserie at the end of the Parisian *passage*—Galerie Véro-Dodat—in which Elke König's apartment was located.

"I don't suppose they have your eggs on the menu," Remy said. "I could really do with some right now."

"I think a Parisian chef can probably make something a hell of a lot better than my eggs but, if they don't, I'll make you some when we get home."

When we get home. As if a future lay shimmering, just beyond them, with Adam and Remy in it together, in a place called home. For the hour or so as they sat in the brasserie, eating eggs that would never be as good as Adam's because he hadn't made them, Remy let that vision hover just an arm's length away.

At just before ten o'clock, they stepped onto the *passage*'s black and white marble floor. Beautiful mahogany shop façades, porticos of Parisian antiquity, softened the contemporary dazzle of Christian Louboutin and other high-end boutiques. Marble columns with gleeful cherubs flying atop added to the sense of elegance. The scent of fresh bread and coffee followed Éliane and Adam up the whirling spiral of stairs to the third floor.

Remy knocked on the door.

An elderly woman, backlit by sunlight so it was impossible to make out her features, opened the door. Her voice was soft velvet and almost hypnotic as she said, "I've been waiting for you to come."

Remy reached blindly for Adam's hand.

PART FIVE
FRANCE, 1943

TWENTY-TWO

The train to Saint-Jean-Cap-Ferrat could have been derailed seven times, could have detoured to Italy, could have been blown up and Éliane wouldn't have noticed. All she could think about was that, three years ago, she'd destroyed a love she knew she would never find again. Nowhere in the world was there another man such as Xavier.

Slow, hot tears rolled down her cheeks, not even ceasing when the Germans checked her travel pass and tried to jolly her out of her misery by telling her that such a beautiful fräulein had nothing to cry about. She stared at them mutely.

At the station, she knew she had to pull herself together. She must be the Éliane whom König and von Behr thought she was—decorative, dumb and awed by the Nazis. She must find out whether the Schloss collection had been found and who, out of the competing factions of French and German art thieves, had found it. She must find out what they planned to do with it.

She opened her valise and concentrated on her toilette, wiping away the tears, powdering her face, scraping out the last of her mascara to divert attention from the redness of her eyes, and applying lipstick. Once finished, she saw that the mascara had made her eyes more green, the lipstick lent her complexion the color it needed, and that she would pass as Éliane, the German sympathizer.

She stepped off the train.

König's face lit up and his joy at seeing her was almost childlike. How was it possible that she inspired such devotion in this man when the one man she most wanted to inspire something in could barely stand to speak to her, given the way she had treated him? She pulled a smile onto her face.

As they drove onto the boulevard along the shore, Éliane fixed her eyes to the view, trying to behave as she ought. "I've never seen the sea before," she remarked and heard how toneless her voice was, knew she would have to do better.

"You'll see so much of it at the house that you might grow bored of it," König said, still beaming.

When she saw the house, pink and perfect and perched atop a cliff that fell dramatically away to the sea below she wondered how König could ever imagine she might grow tired of this. The car swept into the driveway and the sea was momentarily hidden but once she stepped out, there it was again: vast, stretching on forever—as if it would never end. Like the love she still held inside her, the pentimento ghost beneath a layer of paint she must be sure never became thin enough for anyone to see through.

Water cascaded down a series of steps that led up to a white rotunda. Xavier had once told her it was called the Temple of Love, that it had been built as an exact copy of the temple at Versailles. He'd also told her about the gardens: a Japanese garden, a Spanish one, the lapidary garden full of sculptures, one for exotics, and one for roses. And the French garden she stood in front of now, with parterres and hedges extending out from the house and toward the sea like the deck of a ship. She wished it would sail away with her aboard, and Xavier too.

"Mademoiselle Dufort." An older woman wearing black approached. "I'm Madame Mercier, the housekeeper. Please follow me." The woman's smile was warm and, for the first time since the revelations of the night before, Éliane relaxed, but only slightly.

König followed behind as Madame Mercier led Éliane up the stairs to the second floor—too far away for anyone to hear her screams. But also far enough away that she might be able to use the vial and no one would know.

Madame Mercier opened the door to a room dominated so entirely by a bed that König blushed, predictably. "Perhaps if you leave Mademoiselle to get ready," Madame Mercier said to him, indicating that he should return to the stairs.

"But..." König began, looking from the woman's now rather stern face to Éliane. He nodded meekly. "We're to gather downstairs at eight," he said. "It's important to be on time."

Then he disappeared and the relief at not having to bathe and dress in front of König made Éliane exhale audibly.

She stepped into the room to find that Madame Mercier was running her a bath. "Please take everything with you when you leave," Madame said, indicating the luxurious creams and lotions. "And there is a bell here," she pointed to a switch on the wall in the bedroom, "in case you need me." Then she was gone too and Éliane realized she hadn't even said thank you, and also that she was so grateful for the bell that she almost cried again.

Instead she put down her valise, undressed slowly and lay in the bath, tension easing still more.

After too much time had passed, she forced herself to climb out. She investigated the toiletries, intending to use everything at her disposal to give her the strength to appear downstairs looking like a woman ready to be seduced. There was even a powder compact, mascara, lipstick: everything she was running out of. Surely Xavier hadn't equipped every bathroom in the house like this?

Then a small square bottle caught her eye. *Joy de Jean Patou.*

She picked it up, took off the lid and time contracted, forcing her back to the night Xavier had given her a bottle of the same perfume and told her that only fifty bottles were made each year, meaning she wouldn't smell like anyone else and he would always be able to find her.

No matter what happens, he'd said and she hadn't understood at the time.

Now she did.

She rubbed it on her neck and on her wrists and between her breasts. She had to close her eyes against the memories it painted in sharp pointillist strokes against her senses. A knock sounded at the door and she jumped, eyes flying open.

"Are you ready, Fräulein?" König's voice called.

"Almost."

She stepped out of the bathroom to find a dress lying on the bed. Black silk jersey cut so closely against her body that she couldn't believe it hadn't been sewn onto her one night while she slept. The skirt skimmed her hips, falling down to her calves in an ever-narrowing column, then flared out gently into a train. Draped over her shoulders, and also the scooped-out back of the dress, was a sheer lace caplet. It dipped down to the small of her back, obscuring her skin just enough that it looked even more sensual than had it been left completely bare.

Only one man knew her body well enough to have ordered a dress that fit her as precisely as this one did. She held on to the bedpost.

She had to gather herself. Thinking of the way in which Xavier had once known her body was disastrous. It made her unable to see anything other than the way his face had looked when he'd undone her buttons and slowly kissed every inch of her skin.

König called her name again.

She opened the door.

* * *

König actually spluttered when he saw her and his whole face suffused in a red so intense that Éliane had to bite her lip to stop herself from laughing. Thank goodness for König, who always allowed her to find the comedy in every decidedly unfunny situation.

It was only as she placed her foot on the third to last step that she realized she would soon see Xavier, and that she wanted to see him. But she also knew that she mustn't search him out, mustn't even glance around the room for him because, as he had said, no one should know that they once believed they loved the other. But also because she loved him still and she thought her eyes might betray that fact.

Luckily the *grand salon* was busy and noisy. König put a hand on her back to allow her to step in front of him, and then recoiled instantly, giving his hand a shake and his trousers a hitch and she wondered if she might not need the vial after all; perhaps he'd be too overcome to ever touch her.

At the same moment, Xavier appeared in her periphery. She flinched, and almost thought she saw him start, but he had a woman at his side, his arm casually draped around her waist. The woman spoke to him and then he was no longer looking at Éliane, had probably never been looking at Éliane.

"*Mon Dieu*, Fräulein." Von Behr stood before them now. "You should exchange your waitressing uniform for that dress." He smirked and Éliane felt König's hand slide around her waist, his uncle giving him the strength to do what his body had wanted to and his dumbfoundedness had made too difficult.

"We are in the *petit salon*," von Behr continued smoothly. "This way."

He led them to a curved banquette in an alcove meant for the whispers and caresses of lovers. Göring was sitting in it now.

Von Behr was the first to think of offering Éliane a cigarette, which she declined, extracting her Gauloises from her purse. "I still prefer these," she said.

"It's time to develop a taste for the Teutonic," von Behr said coolly. "Especially tonight."

And even though she knew she shouldn't, Éliane couldn't help goading von Behr. "I already have," she said, bestowing a heavy-lidded gaze on König that almost had him squeaking.

"Already?" von Behr said delightedly to his nephew. "But she must only have been here for an hour." He clapped König on the back and laughed. "Good boy."

"Had we only one minute, it would have been long enough," Éliane said languidly. "Excuse me." She stood up and walked to the bar. Von Behr was the one rearranging his trousers now and König looked bewildered, as if he thankfully hadn't understood the implication at all.

The bar was crowded with Germans wanting champagne and it took Éliane some time to make her way to the front. She was almost there when she heard a voice in her ear. "Don't provoke von Behr." Then the sound of a long breath, as if the person behind her had inhaled deeply, like someone tasting a favorite wine. Or smelling a favorite perfume. She turned and saw Xavier's back departing.

He was right. Von Behr would be far more difficult to handle than König. And unlikely to be stopped by a vial of noxious medicament. She needed to sit by König and listen, take what she could from these men and give it to Xavier so he could, in turn, use it to destroy everyone there.

She collected her champagne and her wits, returned to the men and slipped her hand into König's. He gazed at her with adoration.

"Nobody should find the Schloss collection before we do," Göring was saying. "I want to be the first to select from it, when it's discovered. You said it would be found soon."

Von Behr began to bluster but Göring cut him off. "The Vichy government knows the Führer covets the Schloss artworks and the Vichy government needs the Führer to reduce France's Occupation tax before they go broke. I'm worried about who Laval wishes to endear himself to."

Éliane lit a cigarette while her mind worked furiously to translate the conversation. Laval, Vichy France's traitorous leader, was indeed struggling to pay the crippling tax levied against France by Germany and he would certainly wish to endear himself to the Führer with a set of paintings Hitler would be happy to pay vast sums for. Hence the French police arresting the Schloss family, although it appeared that, for now, Hitler was unaware the collection was close to being discovered and Göring wished to keep it that way—and keep the collection for himself. Von Behr would be desperate to help him.

"Shall we…would you…" König's face was saturated with every shade from the white of faintness, to the gray of terror, to the pink of pleasure as he indicated the dance floor.

"I think my nephew wishes you to dance with him," von Behr said mockingly. "Good God boy, do you need me to do everything for you?"

Éliane could see that Xavier was dancing just nearby. His charming smile hid the fatigue that must be like lead on his eyelids if he had indeed left her apartment at two in the morning and driven for hours to reach his house to ready it for the arrivals. He looked impeccable—bow tie precisely tied, black jacket fitting his body perfectly, his shirt a true titanium white: velvety, radiant—although he hadn't shaved, as if he'd run out of time. She remembered the tickle of his stubble against her neck.

She ripped her eyes away from him and nodded at König, who led her into the crowd. As they danced, she stared at the paintings on the walls. One was of the house they were in now, done in a style she thought was Xavier's, the exuberance of color and the movement of the oils suggested a spontaneity and a joy that could only come from painting *au premier coup*, in one sitting, as one was struck by inspiration. The heavy impasto of color in the ocean made it come alive and Éliane wished she could stand out on the clifftop and see the water in the early morning light, as it was in the painting.

Von Behr sailed past, sending a goad König's way. König responded by sliding his hand clammily down Éliane's back to her sacrum. Then he pressed an openmouthed kiss onto her lips, lingering for so long she thought she mightn't be able to stop herself from being sick.

She let several excruciating minutes pass and then excused herself, hurrying through the noise and the laughter and the German language and the couples outside on the lawn, as depraved as von Behr, indulging in innumerable pleasures. She kept going, following the terrace toward the sea, ascending a set of white steps flanked by two blue and white urns. There, she spied an opening between the green hedges and abundance of soft pink roses and she slipped through.

A path led her down the cliff to a shore of water-smoothed pebbles: gray, brown streaked with white, whipped cream, eggshell, and a brilliant reddish-brown. She felt the pressure in her head ease, the creeping revulsion in her body from the taste and touch of König vanish. She picked up a handful of pebbles and let them drop back to the ground.

Then a sound made her jump, and a voice spoke her name.

"You shouldn't be down here," Xavier said, stepping onto the shore, jacket gone, sleeves rolled up, bow tie draped around his neck as if he'd been suffocating too. "What if von Behr had followed you, rather than me?"

She shivered. What if von Behr had? Nobody would hear her scream. "I couldn't breathe," she said, staring out over the water at the ripple of gold where the moon had cast its light.

Xavier stepped in beside her, facing the water too, inches from her. If her hand moved even slightly, she would touch him.

A wave crashed against the shore as powerfully as the heat burning in the space between her body and his.

But it was a heat that Xavier seemed unmoved by and she realized, shockingly, that she knew nothing about him now. Perhaps he was married and had a wife in England. Or a fiancée. Why would a man as beautiful as Xavier be single still?

He had bought her perfume, the perfume of a potent and aching memory. But it was for her costume tonight, to give her the strength she needed. Everything was for that far-off and distant hope that, one day, his house might not be filled with Germans, that France would not be on German time, that nobody would ever see a Nazi salute again.

"Close your eyes," he said suddenly.

Her stomach clenched.

"The painting of the couple, Luc's painting, the one in the Salle des Martyrs," he said. "Always have that in your mind. Whenever you need to breathe, slide into the painting and be the woman with nothing at all around her, with none of this"—his words were fierce with the hatred of everything that was around them now. "Happy."

The woman with nothing around her. Except love, and the arms of her lover.

Éliane felt the sting of tears against her closed eyelids. So often she had sent herself into the safety of oil on canvas and become the woman who knew only the love that was inside that frame. But the reason she and Xavier were standing on a beach now was because there was a much larger context, frameless, infinite it seemed. The only way to bring it back down to a size small enough that it could finally be destroyed was to swallow, to wait for the tears to pass, to open her eyes and to speak.

"You might know this already but Göring is desperate for the Schloss collection," she said. "And von Behr is desperate to find it for him. Laval is chasing it too, perhaps for Hitler. Göring would prefer Hitler to know nothing of it so that he can skim the cream for once."

Xavier looked at her for the first time. "The Bonny-Lafont gang was here this afternoon with von Behr," he said and she could feel the alertness sparking from him in a way she hadn't felt his matching response to her yearning.

The Bonny-Lafont gang, otherwise known as the French Gestapo, was a group of criminals rumored to do the work even the Gestapo didn't want its name attached to. As Frenchmen, the gang would certainly be able to move an entire collection of stolen paintings out of Vichy France without anyone thinking it a German heist—if they found it. But of course they would. The Schlosses and their friends would be unable to withstand both imprisonment and the Bonny-Lafont gang.

"If von Behr discovers the collection, can we…" Éliane began, trying hard to stay afloat, to not sink into the sea of liquid despair. There must be something they could do. "Can we somehow make use of it anyway, rather than simply recording its theft and hoping to keep track of it? From what Göring said inside, it sounds as if he wants to keep the collection from Hitler. What if Hitler were to find out it's been located…"

Her voice trailed away. She had no idea how the world of men and war and espionage and politics worked.

Xavier was silent. There was only the breaking of a wave into submission on the rocks, the brush of wind past the cliff face. And the thud of her heart, saying things she wished she had the courage to say to Xavier. *I want you. I love you. I was such a fool.*

Then he spoke. "If von Behr gets his hands on the Schloss artworks, I can make sure Hitler knows about it by tomorrow evening. Göring's star is descending. The losses in North Africa have made certain of that. Maybe if the Führer knows about Göring's double-dealing, his star will descend further and the art thefts will stop."

Maybe. There were so many maybes.

Then Xavier said quietly, "Von Behr's goads are making König more determined."

"Earlier in the evening I was wondering if the vial would even be necessary," Éliane said lightly, unwilling to let Xavier shoulder any more burdens. "He couldn't even touch my back without suffering a paroxysm. I thought maybe just sliding off my dress would finish him off. Death by *déshabille*." She smiled a little at the ridiculous image. Then her smile fell away. "I'll use the vial when I return to the house."

"Madame Mercier is keeping an eye out for you too. You can trust her. But..." He sighed. "We've been gone too long." His reluctance to return to the party was as obvious as the crescent moon, a golden curve of bone piercing through the skin of the sky.

So she said something she should have said the other night. "I'm sorry I called you a coward."

He smiled and it was almost too much: a Xavier smile was like a van Gogh sky, alight and alive, the richest saturation of every color sparkling all at once before your eyes. "You didn't just call me a coward."

Éliane laughed, a real laugh, and the long-forgotten sensation almost made her dizzy. "Don't," she said, blushing like König. "I can't believe I said that to you."

Xavier's smile fell from his face and the night turned to flat black, all richness of color gone. "I *was* a coward. And a bastard. I should never have gone to the hotel with you that night, knowing I was leaving Paris."

"Yes, you should have." She made herself look at him while she spoke and he didn't turn away from whatever emotion or disclosure was painted onto her face with her words. "You should have," she repeated. "I've needed the memory of it...I've used the memory of it...often..."

Too many things tumbled into her mind just then, everything she'd lost since 1939: her honor, her reputation, her mother, her sisters, her art, her lover. Her future with Xavier. She closed her eyes against it all.

"I'm sorry about your sisters. And your mother."

She opened her eyes to find him watching her still and she asked, suddenly, "Where do you go when you need to breathe?"

He shrugged and she understood. He had nowhere. He was always the Xavier the Germans knew.

She touched his arm. "You should have come here last night, rather than coming to see me," she said gently. "Here, you would have been able to breathe."

He picked up her hand and returned it gently to her. "If I hadn't given you that vial, it wouldn't have mattered where I'd gone; I would never have been able to breathe."

He gave her another smile, one that held a spark of the Xavier she had once known. Then he was gone.

* * *

Back at the house, she walked purposefully to the bar. She ordered two champagnes and, amid the bustle, tipped the contents of the vial into one. Then she found von Behr and König and she handed König his drink.

"For you," she said, sliding her arm around him.

König goggled at her as if it had just struck him that he was to spend the night with her. She felt her eyes flash steel for a moment as she thought—*No, you will not.* She blinked away both the thought and the steel so there was only a silly girl in a sultry dress that she couldn't wait for König to slide her out of.

He gulped his champagne and, emboldened by the knowledge that she had nothing to fear, she whispered into his ear, loud enough for von Behr to hear, "Come upstairs."

Von Behr smirked at his nephew. "Enjoy yourself, Fräulein. You can always come back downstairs if you don't find satisfaction."

König clattered his glass onto the table, took Éliane's hand and marched from the room. Éliane followed but, before she did, she sent a subtle nod to Xavier so he would know she was fine.

They reached the staircase. Éliane didn't know how long she had until the potion would work. König needed to be in their room when it did so that, the following morning, she could pretend that everything von Behr and König imagined would happen, had happened. She hoped, above all, that this party would be a rare event; the vial was a stopgap and couldn't be used more than once.

Madame Mercier materialized from nowhere just as König stumbled on the top stair. The women each put a supportive arm around him. They needed to hurry.

They made it inside and to the bed before he fell, in a stupor, onto his stomach, head turned to the side, mouth open, looking, she suddenly thought, young and actually innocent. But he wasn't; he was in Paris helping Nazis steal artworks. He despised Jews. He continued to do what he was told despite the busloads of French people taken from their homes in the middle of the night, despite the shootings, the guillotinings, the deaths. He might have occasionally shown humanity toward Éliane, but not toward her country.

"Let's get to work," Madame Mercier said, rousing Éliane.

Éliane started with his shoes while Madame tackled his shirt and tie. Then Éliane forced herself to remove König's trousers and, finally and grimly, his underwear.

He was thin, and Éliane's mind returned unwittingly to the body of another man who had once lain in a bed naked with her. Xavier's body had been muscular, his chest ridged, legs strong; she hadn't been able to stop touching him, had been aroused just by looking at him.

König's body made her gag.

She swallowed, breathed deeply and both women pushed with all their might so that König's legs were properly on the bed, the sheets rucked up around him, and the scene looked like a debauch.

"Thank you," Éliane said to Madame Mercier. "I'll be fine now."

"Ring the bell if you need me. I'll be up on this floor all night." The woman gave Éliane a reassuring smile.

Éliane crossed to the door, slid down it and sat on the floor, trying to escape into a painting where she was held in the arms of a man she loved.

Some time later, the faintest of footsteps sounded in the hallway. A shadow blocked the slit of light at the bottom of the door.

"Éliane," she heard Xavier say, softly. "Are you all right?"

"I am," she whispered.

Then the light reappeared at the bottom of her door and she wept.

* * *

When König woke in the morning, Éliane was dressed and waiting with her valise in hand. She had sprayed her perfume onto the pillows, pulled strands from her brush and tossed them onto the sheets, molded a dent into her pillow, done everything she could to make it appear as if she had slept beside him the whole night long, rather than sitting awake on the floor.

"I think I tired you out, Monsieur," she said shyly and König blinked at her, once, twice, three times, then sat up with a start, which made him groan and fall back onto the pillows.

"There is something for your headache," Éliane said, indicating the glass of water and the aspirin on the bedside table. "I have to leave. I'm working tonight. Thank you for a lovely evening."

König tried once more to sit and was, once more, defeated. "I should drive you to the station," he said groggily. "But the champagne…"

"You enjoyed it a little too much," Éliane agreed. "Go back to sleep. I can get myself to the station."

She opened the door, wishing she could run. But she made herself walk at a sedate pace through and out of the house, not really having any idea how she would get to the station, other than she hoped a car might pass by and offer her a ride. It was a good hour's walk and she wasn't sure she had the strength for it after no sleep and too much fear and champagne.

She'd only walked for about ten minutes when she heard a car behind her. She turned to see Xavier drawing over.

"You really are all right?" he said as he climbed out and she smiled all of a sudden as the relief of having survived the night without having had to bed König suffused her, joyfully at first, and then so intensely that she had to put a hand on the car to steady herself.

Xavier was around to her side in a moment. "You're not all right."

She shook her head. "I am. I think it just hit me though. That it worked. I'm not sure I thought it would."

Brilliantly and blindingly, Xavier smiled too.

Éliane's hand lifted up. But instead of letting it touch his face, his beloved face, she smoothed her hair and whatever could have been had gone, frightened off by her uncertainty about what he felt.

Xavier turned away and opened the car door. She stepped in and they drove onwards, a Picasso-blue sea unrolling alongside them.

"Won't they notice you've gone?" she asked to fill the too-full silence.

"No one will stir before midday. I saw you leave; I was in the gardens."

"The gardens are beautiful," Éliane said, truthfully. "And the house. You must miss it."

"I do," he said, eyes fixed to the road.

"Will you," she asked, wanting to know something that had been worrying her since she'd found out what Xavier was doing, "will you ever be able to live in France again after all of this is over? Will you ever be able to say that you were helping the French people, not working for the Germans?"

The silence went on for so long she didn't think he would answer.

"Even if, after this is over, I could tell anyone what I'd been doing, they'd still be suspicious," he said at last. "It's not easy to believe someone who appeared to be serving a Reichsmarschall for years."

"Perhaps," she said, searching desperately for a solution for him, because he deserved at least that, "you could come back to Cap-Ferrat? Not many people there will know what you've been doing."

"The house might not even be here in a year's time," he said soberly. "Göring is uneasy about the Allies' successes in North Africa and they're soon to mine and evacuate the whole area. It could well be blown to pieces."

"I hope not. It's worth preserving."

"So many things worth preserving have been ruined," he said as he pulled into the train station, watching the traffic, not Éliane. "It's too much to hope that this will be different."

We were worth preserving, she wanted to say. *Don't you think?*

Surely, if Xavier cared nothing for her, he would not have been so concerned about her. If Xavier cared nothing for her, he wouldn't have remembered her body so well that the black dress fitted her to perfection. Was it possible? Or was she, in this small space carved out of the horror of her life, just creating an artwork to carry in her mind: a picture in burning red in which Xavier cared something for her too?

She couldn't survive another night of serving the Nazis their meals at the brasserie and of spying on Nazis at the gallery without images of Xavier to buoy her up. If she said nothing to him now, she could pretend that he still loved her and she could keep dreaming about him. If she said something and he told her he didn't feel the same way, then she wouldn't be able to hope—and it would be so much harder to survive. Better to let the car draw to a stop, open the door and climb out.

Except.

At the very last moment she leaned in and kissed Xavier's cheek, so quickly that her lips barely met his skin. But she heard his shocked and desperate gasp of breath all the same.

TWENTY-THREE

After the nine-hour train ride from the Riviera and another four hours on her feet waitressing, Éliane locked the door of the brasserie, thankful to have been spared the onslaught of König and von Behr that night. Luc, whom she hadn't been able to speak to properly while they were working, came upstairs with her and told her there was to be a meeting at their apartment. Then he added, "Xavier told me you know."

"You should have told me." She let nothing of what she felt show on her face because Luc was watching her closely.

"I thought you still held a candle for him."

"Not for a long time." She lied so convincingly that she surprised herself. What had she become? A liar, a cheat, a drugger. She'd become what the Germans had made her.

"How was your Nazi last night?" Luc asked. "Did you rouse the good soldier?"

For the first time in her life she wanted to swear at her brother. Instead, she pushed open the door to the apartment with all the force she wanted to expend on Luc and made herself a mug of the awful, sandcolored, ground-chicory pretense at coffee, stirring the liquid as if it were the source of her fury. Not long after, Rose arrived and told Éliane she needed to get some sleep and Éliane knew how terrible she must look. She poured Rose a glass of wine.

A sequence of four knocks interrupted them. The door opened, admitting Monsieur Jaujard.

And Angélique.

"What's happened?" Éliane cried as she ran across the room to her sister, wrapped her arms around her and stared, horrified, at Monsieur Jaujard. There was no reason at all for Angélique to be back in Paris unless there had been some catastrophe.

"I know what you're doing." Angélique's voice was not that of the impetuous child who'd had difficulty managing Yolande's tempests. It was the voice of a woman who knew her own mind.

Éliane let go of her sister, eyes still on Monsieur Jaujard. He wouldn't have told Angélique what Éliane was involved in. How then did she know?

She was suddenly aware that Luc was kissing Angélique's cheeks and that he didn't look all that surprised to see her.

"What did you do?" she asked him, very slowly and very, very quietly.

"He didn't do anything," Angélique said and Éliane didn't believe her sister for one moment. "I asked to do this."

"To do what, exactly?" Éliane demanded.

She felt a hand on her arm, Rose's gentle hand, guiding her over to the table. "Come," Rose said. "Let's not talk about these things so near the door. It will do everyone good to sit down."

Éliane let herself be led to the table where she sat with Rose on one side of her, still holding her hand, and Angélique on the other. Luc sat across from her, a sardonic smile on his face and she wished she *had* sworn at him earlier. Or worse.

"I'm a courier for the Resistance," Angélique said, which preposterous.

Now Éliane did swear at Luc knowing that, despite her sister's protestations, he had drawn Angélique into this. This danger. Couriers cycled around France, taking messages—and sometimes equipment:

guns, pamphlets, money and cigarettes—between Resistance cells, and from radio operators to Resistance leaders. Éliane knew that most of the Louvre staff in the depots in the countryside were working with the Resistance; that, when she'd sent Angélique to a château used by the Louvre, she was sending her to a place where risk of a different kind to von Behr existed. This was especially true since the theft of Belgium's altarpiece—which indicated the Nazis might have nefarious plans for the Musées Nationaux artworks stored in the depots also.

But Éliane hadn't, for one minute, thought that Angélique would get herself involved.

Luc, however, was often at the depots. Which was why Éliane stared at him now.

"Look at me, not at Luc," Angélique said and Éliane felt her head turn to take in her sister's nineteen-year-old face. She was so young.

"I was worried you might actually kill me," Angélique said. "The only thing I wasn't sure about was whether you'd kill him"—she gave Luc a wry smile—"or me first. But you know as well as I do that messages about art and resistance can't be sent via post and that someone has to get them from Luc and take them to the Maquis. I have the perfect cover; I'm at the depots as a Louvre secretary. A woman has to do it because all the men are meant to be in Germany for the Service du Travail Obligatoire. They can't cycle around the countryside."

"But—" Éliane began to see not a younger sister who needed protection, but a brave woman who would not be dissuaded from her cause.

"When I arrived at the château," Angélique continued, "I asked Monsieur Jaujard to show me the *Mona Lisa*. You'd always said she was a queen among paintings and I wanted to see; to know why you and Luc were taking so many risks for a painted woman. It was almost evening and when Monsieur lifted the lid off her crate, I saw it: the sfumato, those edgeless shadows you'd often talked about. They were…" She paused, groping for words. "Depthless," she settled on. "As if they went on and on through time and into forever. Then I looked up at Monsieur Jaujard and even though he's seen the *Mona Lisa* a thousand times—but maybe never before in the darkness of France's broken heart—he was crying too. So I had to do something—and I won't stop until the Nazis are gone forever."

How could Éliane do anything other than hug her sister as hard as she could? "I love you," she said to Angélique. Then she smiled. "And I promise not to kill you. Not yet."

There must have been a knock on the door but, amid everything going on, Éliane didn't hear it. She realized only from the sudden scent of his cologne that Xavier was in the room. She watched him take in Angélique's presence and a look of horrified comprehension crossed his face. He swore and his gaze jumped straight to meet Éliane's.

"I—" he said, and then cut himself off.

Éliane understood that he'd had no idea what Angélique was doing, but nor was he going to admit that in case it got Monsieur or someone else into trouble.

Angélique hurried across the room to him, flinging herself into his arms like a child.

"I knew you weren't a Nazi-lover," she said, kissing his cheeks. "Monsieur Jaujard told me as much as he could about what you've been doing. And he also told me that for everything you're all working on together to be most effective, you need someone to pass messages on for you, too. That's me."

Xavier looked across at Éliane again and she shrugged helplessly in acknowledgment that her sister was now part of their small band too.

"I'm disappointed." Luc spoke in a voice that hovered somewhere between teasing and mocking. "I thought there'd at least be a screaming match. And I suppose you're old enough to drink wine now," he added, filling a glass for Angélique and indicating that she should come and get it.

Angélique led Xavier over to the table the same way Rose had led Éliane. "You look like you need it," Angélique said to Xavier, passing him the wine.

It was true. Xavier's face was dark-shadowed. He still hadn't shaved and it almost covered up the tiredness but it was there in his eyes, which were ivory black tonight, the secrets hidden there like the ashes of the burnt bones that gave the color its name. He sipped the wine and Éliane hoped to see his irises return to umber but they remained impenetrable.

"Hitler has been made aware of the capture of the Schloss collection," Xavier said to Monsieur Jaujard. "I'm sorry, but the Bonny-Lafont gang found it. Better we use the loss for some purpose."

Monsieur Jaujard nodded, a gesture that conveyed both pain and understanding.

"Now that Hitler is almost certain to interfere with the Schloss collection, I think the Jeu de Paume will be a very unpleasant place over the next few weeks," Xavier went on quietly. "Will you be all right?" He spoke to Rose, who nodded the same way Monsieur had done.

"While we're dealing with problems," Angélique said to Xavier, "I have a British pilot, whose plane crashed nearby, hiding in the cellar with the *Mona Lisa*. I need a contact on an escape line. My Maquis are expert saboteurs and can blow up anything that will infuriate the Nazis but they don't know how to get a man out of France."

Éliane only just checked herself. As if couriering messages to the Resistance wasn't risky enough, smuggling Allied pilots was deadly.

"He had nowhere else to go," Angélique said simply, as if she'd noticed Éliane's attempt to swallow her remonstrances. "I couldn't turn him away."

"Of course not," Éliane said, managing another smile. "I'm proud of you. And you can help her, can't you?" she asked Xavier, unable to keep the pleading note out of her voice, willing him to know how to move an Allied pilot away from the same château that housed her sister.

"I can," Xavier said briefly. Then he checked his watch. "And there might be some good news, which we all need." He walked over to the oven, where Éliane had hidden the forbidden radio tuned in to the BBC's broadcasts. "I'm hoping the Allies will have received the message about the *Mona Lisa*."

Éliane knew he was referring to the recent relocation of the *Mona Lisa* and many other paintings from Montauban to Montal after the ceilings had begun to crack above the irreplaceable treasures. They had been trying to arrange for one of the Resistance circuits to send a coded message—which Éliane now suspected Angélique had most likely couriered—informing the Allies of the paintings' new hiding place so air strikes in the area could be avoided.

Over the airwaves came the words: "*La Joconde a le sourire.*"

The Mona Lisa is smiling.

Xavier smiled too, just a little. "It means the Allies have received the message. She should be safe."

Angélique's hand flew to her mouth as if she were suppressing an excited whoop. Monsieur Jaujard beamed. Rose squeezed Éliane's hand.

The flicker of elation didn't last long though. After they'd drunk a quiet toast, Xavier moved to the window and leaned on the sill, where Éliane could only see him in shadow, the edges of light picking out the things that most caught her breath: the outline of his body, the jaw she wanted to dance her fingers along, the lips that she wished might kiss her fingertips.

Xavier's head turned.

Their eyes met and it was as if the walls had opened up, the ceiling too, and she was in a space that didn't exist: just her and Xavier and it was impossible to see anything other than longing in his gaze, a longing that matched her own. It was only for a moment and then, as if the scene had been doused with turpentine, the apartment returned and the walls too and Xavier was merely standing in the window embrasure with his head turned to the blackout curtain and Éliane was frozen by her chair, unable to tell if what had just happened was real or if her fatigue had created a seductive hallucination.

Chairs scraped back and Monsieur and Madame said their goodbyes. Angélique hugged her sister. "Monsieur Jaujard says it's safer for me to stay at his apartment, rather than here with you and Luc. That we shouldn't have the three of us under one roof."

"Thank you," Éliane said to Monsieur because he was right.

"I'll walk with you," Luc said to Angélique "I have some messages of my own to pass on."

"And you can go home at last," Rose said to Xavier, mothering him the same way she mothered Éliane.

Xavier pushed himself away from the window. "I need sleep."

It was the first time Éliane had heard him admit, aloud, that he needed something. How tired he must be.

She busied herself with clearing the table and threw a general goodbye in the direction of the group. Then, instead of going to bed, she stood where Xavier had stood. His lingering scent filled her like absinthe with its illicit thrill.

For it didn't matter if Xavier did feel something for her; they could never do anything about it. The risk was too great. Better to stick to their roles and pray that not many more years would pass before they were rescued—God, how she hated to admit that—by the Allies.

She tore herself away, went into her room and exchanged her dress for her nightgown. The rose silk was almost transparent with wear; she'd been terrified at the thought of having to put it on in front of König as it revealed much more of her than she wished him to see. The ribbon straps attached to a lace bustier, both of which were beginning to fray and she felt, at that moment, as threadbare and as poor and as bereft as she actually was: unable to find a new nightgown in this rationed city, working two jobs, both of which she hated, with men she hated, the only good thing in her life was these irregular meetings with like-minded people, meetings she hoped took place across France in apartments and farmhouses and cottages.

If enough meetings were held, enough plans made, then surely France would be returned to her people soon. And then Éliane could ask Xavier two questions: *How much of this have I imagined? And how much is real?*

TWENTY-FOUR

Thoughts of sleep tantalized Éliane but her mind wouldn't allow her to rest. Eventually, she rolled out of bed to fetch a glass of water and stopped still when she heard a faint sound outside the door. She placed her hand upon it.

How could she tell that it was him? How did she know it wasn't König or von Behr or someone she would never let into her apartment? "Xavier," she whispered.

"Yes."

She opened the door.

One of Xavier's hands was braced against the doorframe. There was hardly any light to see him by, except the lines that broke in through the gaps at the edges of the blackout curtain, transforming black night to grisaille, and Xavier from stranger to beloved.

"This would be the most dangerous thing of all," Xavier said, voice low, not stepping into the apartment but standing on the threshold, a line that, once crossed, brought with it a peril so enormous it seemed neither was sure they could do it to the other.

"I know," Éliane said. What she saw in his face shocked her. This was ruining him. What would be left of him if the Occupation continued on for years more, unrelenting? "You're so tired," she said.

"Sleep is the cure for that, Éliane." He smiled.

She knew there was no stopping them, not now.

"If you come in here," she said, smiling too, "you won't be sleeping."

He laughed and Éliane's entire body contracted at the sound.

"If Luc knew I was here..." Xavier began.

"He would kill us." Éliane finished the sentence for him. Then she lifted her hand to the doorframe, stood on her tiptoes and leaned across the demarcation line.

She kissed his jawline so softly that she almost didn't feel the tickle of his stubble on her lips. "Just once," she said, her mouth near his ear, their bodies still separated, her in the apartment and him just outside. "We both need this."

He turned his head a little, not too much, but enough for her to know that all he wanted was to kiss her properly. His hand tightened on the doorframe.

"I will put you in so much jeopardy, Ellie."

"I'm already in jeopardy. I need to remember what it's like to..." She hesitated, not yet sure what this was for him, if perhaps it was only bodily. She trailed her lips along his jawline, closer to his mouth. "To love. I need you."

Her lips landed the softest blow right beside his.

His inhale was sharp and unsteady.

"Éliane." He drew back his head so she could see his face when he spoke. "I love you," he said, hand relinquishing its hold on the doorframe at last and moving up to her cheek, stroking her skin with his fingertips. He leaned his forehead against hers.

"We can't do this ever again—" he began.

"Until..."

"I dream of untils. And of this." He shifted his head so quickly that the shock of their lips finally touching was like a single drop of red spilled into water, spreading out instantly, everywhere.

The last time they'd made love, years ago now in 1939, it had been fervent and spellbinding but so innocent she'd thought it was all they needed: their love and that naked and heartfelt expression of it. The fervor was still there but the innocence was gone, replaced by a sadness that shadowed every kiss, every caress, so that as much as Xavier's lips roaming all over her body made her cry out from hunger, it also made her cry: real tears. This was love in wartime, an urgency that almost outpaced their bodies' ability to express their need for one another in the touch of hand or mouth or skin against skin.

When Xavier's hand, threading into her hair, discovered that her cheek was wet with tears, he whispered, "I'm sorry."

"I am too," she said, and she saw the glint of his own damp eyes before he closed them and lifted his body over hers, sliding into her, one hand gripped tightly in hers, the thumb of his other hand stroking her cheek as if he wanted to take the sadness away. But nothing could.

When the final moment came, Éliane did not just cry out, but she cried too, and so did he. No love had ever hurt so much, nor been so perfect.

* * *

"Don't cry, Éliane," Xavier whispered when they both lay exhausted in one another's arms. He drew her in as if she could somehow be closer still—which wasn't really possible—but she felt, somehow, that she did shift into him even more.

He pulled the blankets around them and there, in the darkness of their blacked-out city, they held on to one another until they both fell asleep, wrapped tightly together.

Éliane slept dreamlessly for the next hour or so until the heat of Xavier against her body woke her. She smiled and knew what she would do: that she wanted this time to be without tears, to be only pleasure and so much love. She untangled herself from him and found the black silk dress he must have had made for her. She slipped it on, daubed *Joy* onto her neck and wrists and between her breasts and then she stood beside the bed waiting for his dreams to understand that the perfume was real.

It took only a few moments before he opened his eyes and cast out a worried arm for her. When she said his name, he was out of bed and at her side in an instant, mouth finding hers, telling her that no matter what they'd done, no matter what they did, he would never have enough of her, would want her always and forever. If they had a forever.

Éliane pushed that last thought away as Xavier's hands slid over the dress, down her sides and to her hips.

"I've been wanting to do that since I first saw you in this dress at Cap-Ferrat," he murmured.

"Only that?" she asked, smiling. "Surely you imagined more than that."

It was his turn to smile.

He bent his head down toward her and whispered in her ear. "I imagined doing this too." His thumb brushed over her nipple, again and again, the friction of the silk and the pressure of his thumb as heady as freedom. "With both hands," he added, untangling his fingers from hers.

"What else?" she asked, words almost strangled in her throat.

"I imagined..." He reached up and undid a hook and eye closure that Éliane hadn't even realized was there. The lace cape slid off so that her back was bare. "I imagined dancing with you."

He slipped one hand into hers, the other stroking her back. They began to move, swaying to music only they could hear.

"Just dancing?" she asked, the ache in her body obvious in her voice.

He shook his head. "When we were standing on the shore, I imagined doing this."

His hand on her back began to tiptoe over each of her vertebrae, making her shiver, even though everything he was doing was scorching. "I imagined, so much it hurt, doing this." His hands slid inside her dress, over her sacrum and caressed the bare skin he found there.

"Xavier." She almost couldn't say his name, felt the irresistible pull of her leg lifting and wrapping around him, pressing her body into his.

"I wished so much that you would do that," he said, voice hoarse as he stepped her backward, against the wall, nothing except the thin black silk of her gown between them.

"I didn't dare imagine this, though. It would have been too much." He unfastened her dress, eyes on her body as the silk slipped to the floor. "It's still too much," he murmured, lifting one finger to trace a line from her collarbone, down the middle of her chest to her navel.

How was it possible to feel so much, to be so close to the edge already when they hadn't even kissed, had used only words and touch, the sound of their longing echoing in everything they said.

"In my imaginings," Éliane managed to say, "your hand didn't stop there."

"Ellie."

Her name was a choked whisper, and then they were on the bed, one of Xavier's exquisite fingers traveling to her hip bone, following its curve to her thigh, coloring over the darkness and the sadness and the shadows with light and love and all the colors of flame. He traced his way down and then back up the length of her leg, not kissing her, watching her face, watching her lips as they opened and said his name.

His hand returned to her thigh and her eyes closed for a moment, her head tipping back as heat and hunger tore through her. But she made herself open her eyes because they wouldn't be together like this for the longest time and she wanted to remember every moment of it.

"I don't think I've found the right place yet," he whispered in her ear, the raw need in his voice almost too much. "I need to use my mouth."

He kissed her navel then, lips retracing the path his finger had traveled. It was impossible not to tilt her hips toward him, impossible not to gasp when she felt the exquisitely concentrated, breath-stealing sensation of his mouth exactly where she wanted it, doing exactly as she had dreamed.

She called out his name, felt his hands grip her hips as she fell out of this world and into another where nothing existed except her and Xavier.

When she could breathe again, she smiled down at him. "Now we need to put into practice all of my imaginings."

Xavier laughed, and then they both fell heedlessly once more into what was, as Xavier had said, the most dangerous thing of all.

* * *

They had only just drawn apart, Éliane resting her head on Xavier's chest, when they heard the front door open and close, footsteps cross the floor and then the door to Luc's bedroom shut.

"I'd meant to be gone by the time he returned," Xavier whispered, kissing her forehead. "You've been very distracting."

Éliane smiled, then frowned. "Where's he been? He left here hours ago."

Xavier frowned too. "He shouldn't be out after curfew. It's too dangerous."

"Yet you're planning to leave here after curfew."

"I have German protection. Luc doesn't."

Éliane touched a finger to his lips. "Let's not talk about that, not now." She drew herself up onto her forearms and stared down into the eyes in which she could now read everything. "I love you, Xavier. More than anything on this earth. Which means you cannot, ever, do anything as reckless as this again."

"I know," he said. "Kiss me. Go back to hating me tomorrow but at least I'll know it's an act. I can get through anything if I know you don't hate me."

They kissed again, for so long and with mouths locked so tightly together that Éliane could feel his stubble tearing at her skin.

"Wait a moment." He rolled over and reached for his trousers. "I went back to my apartment after the meeting to get this for you." He held up a sapphire shot with a white star. "Your engagement ring. Keep it. Sell it if you have to—the paperwork is all there so you can get a good price for it. Don't hold on to it for remembrance. It's not me. I'm in there," he pointed to her heart, "not here."

He gave her the ring, his damp eyes betraying the fact that he hoped she would never again want to give it away.

"One day, I'll always wear this," Éliane said, not slipping the ring onto her finger because, if she did, she wouldn't be able to bear taking it off. "For now…"

She climbed out of bed, moved aside the mirror on the wall and placed the ring into the cavity gouged behind. She stood with her hand on the wall and found the strength to say, "I know you should go. It's all right. I'll be all right."

She waited with her back to him while he dressed, not wanting to witness his departure. But he turned her around before he left, stroked her face and whispered, "I love you."

She drew the sensation into her body, tucking it away like a portrait miniature into the locket of her heart, which would never open for anyone besides Xavier.

TWENTY-FIVE

It wasn't until she reached the Jeu de Paume the next day, having not noticed the German uniforms or the queues or the weather or anything else as she walked, so absorbed was she in memories of the night she'd just spent with Xavier, that she remembered König. The guard checking her papers reminded her when he stepped in very close to her and said, "You had a nice weekend."

It was a statement rather than a question. Her night with König was obviously knowledge as common as von Behr's tryst with his secretary. She'd been cast in the role of French whore.

But that wasn't the worst of it. As the guard glanced slowly from the papers to Éliane, standing right in front of her, the fabric of his jacket against the thin cotton of her shirt, she wondered what König would expect from her now. Would one false night together be enough? Or would he want more? And: what would Parisians do to French whores when the Occupation ended?

A truck grumbled past, drawing up along the side of the museum, loaded with crates. One of the waiting historians said the words, "Schloss collection." It had arrived at last, in purgatory.

"A pleasure, Mademoiselle." The guard handed Éliane's papers back to her.

She gave him a cool smile and stepped into the museum where König was waiting for her.

She forced herself to forget Xavier, his lips all over her body.

König shifted from one foot to the other. "Mademoiselle," he said. "I..."

He was back to speaking in half-sentences. Éliane took charge. "Thank you for a splendid evening," she said, looking over her shoulder as if this conversation were private, meant only for König. Then she slipped past him while he was recovering.

She didn't get very far before she heard a man screaming and she knew it was Göring: that his fat face would be red and spittle would be flying. Hitler must know that Göring had the Schloss collection. And they were all in trouble.

* * *

Éliane and Rose stayed in their office until the screaming abated. No piece of information was worth collecting while Göring was raging and von Behr the likely recipient of that rage. Midmorning, König came in to see Éliane and to show her, proudly, a handwritten list.

"I'm making an inventory of the Schloss collection," he said. "It will be bound up into a catalog for our Führer so he can enjoy the works he's acquired." He beamed at Éliane, standing tall.

Suddenly, she could see the resemblance between König and his uncle.

"How wonderful," she murmured, trying to look as if she meant it.

"You'll accompany me to the exhibition of the Schloss works," he continued. "The Führer has been generous enough to allow the exhibition to go ahead. Afterward, there is a hotel..." The diffidence returned. "We'll go there..."

"König!" *Thank God for von Behr*, Éliane thought for the first time ever.

König spun around.

Éliane felt Rose looking at her but she didn't meet her gaze. She pretended to work for the next half hour, but in that time the only plan she came up with to avoid going to a hotel with König after the exhibition of the Schloss works was to drink too much herself so that *she* was incapable. But it was a temporary and worrisome plan. If she didn't have control of herself…

The background silence that had varnished the air since Göring's paroxysm of shouting faded suddenly became a boot-clattering noise that spilled out onto the Tuileries terrace.

Rose and Éliane crept over to the window to see what was happening.

The first thing Éliane noticed was the smell of smoke. Then a cloud of white rose up from the terrace. She had to put a hand on the glass to brace herself.

The smoke billowed from reds and blues and yellow and blacks. From the blood and bones and soul of art. Stacked in a blazing pyramid in the courtyard were hundreds of paintings, aflame.

"From the Salle des Martyrs," Rose whispered, pointing at what was once a Picasso, a Miró, a Klee.

The sense of the words struck Éliane. *From the Salle des Martyrs*.

She tore herself away from the window and ran outside. For the first time ever in this place of thievery and pretense her heart was outside her body for all to see. She ran straight to the fire and was about to thrust her hand in because she could not lose that one painting—*L'Amour*: the painting of love.

König pulled her back, shouting. She felt tears all over her face. Heard von Behr's whiplash tongue and the detonation of his hand against her cheek as he slapped her, hard. She fell to the ground.

She checked herself, grasping hold of a lie. "I saw a painting that didn't belong in the fire. A van Dyck, I think."

There was no evidence to support or deny her claim. The fire had seen to that.

The Reichsmarschall spoke in sharp German to von Behr. "If I discover that one of the Schloss paintings our Führer expects has been destroyed..."

"The girl is young and emotional and has mistaken herself. Get up!" Von Behr shoved Éliane with his foot.

She didn't move. She didn't understand German.

"Mark off each painting against the inventory," Göring snapped at von Behr.

Von Behr smiled thinly and said to König, "She can help." He pointed to Éliane, who nodded submissively.

She stopped briefly at the office to collect paper and pen, where Rose whispered to her, "Don't worry. Your painting is still in the *salle*. I checked."

"Thank you," Éliane said. "I shouldn't have..." She blinked, trying so hard not to cry in front of this woman who endured as much as Éliane but who never cried.

"Yes, you should have," Rose said firmly. "We need to keep alive the things that keep us alive." She paused, looking suddenly un-Rose-like, her face bleak and empty and hopeless. "Perhaps you should stop. I don't like what's happening. With König. And here." Rose gestured to the museum. "And now your sister too. Someone else for you to worry about."

Unbelievably, Éliane found herself smiling. Here was Rose worrying over Éliane and one of her worries was that Éliane had too many people to consider. She kissed Rose's cheek. "I'm here until the end. Just like you."

But Rose was right. In the main gallery, the historians' grumblings spread like match to wooden frames. The two men involved in a tryst with the same secretary accused each other of carelessness. Von Behr's secretary, who had no doubt borne the brunt of von Behr's temper that morning, told Rose that her glasses must be the most ineffectual in all of France given how slow she was. Éliane knew why Rose was slow; she was making her own careful mental inventory. Von Behr entered every now and again, lashing out with his tongue.

The atmosphere was a stew set to boil.

The inventory list wasn't checked off until almost ten o'clock that night. Three paintings were missing. One was a van Dyck. Éliane looked across at Rose and knew that, in the chaos, Rose must have slipped them upstairs to the Salle des Martyrs so Éliane was proved right about the painting in the fire. So that more mistrust and jealousy was fomented.

"Where are they?" von Behr screamed, unfortunately catching sight of Rose at the same moment, the woman who always took the blame. "Get out! Do not come back. Every time something goes wrong, you are there."

König stepped in front of Éliane, hiding her from his uncle.

Rose was marched out of the Jeu de Paume by Luftwaffe guards.

Éliane would have to flatter König—or worse—once more.

On the way home from the museum, Éliane saw a man and a woman, about her age, standing with their hands splayed against a wall. Nazis held guns at their backs. Another Nazi emerged from a building with a pile of papers in hand and she heard him mutter that the couple had been assisting Parisian men evading the compulsory work program in Germany. It was lucky, the Nazi continued, that he'd had the building's concierge on his payroll to inform him about Resistance scum.

The Nazi lifted the man's head and rammed it into the wall. He kicked the woman's legs out from under her so she fell. The couple were dragged away, bleeding, almost insensible.

Éliane was almost sick, right there in front of the Nazis. What she had just witnessed, if some traitorous Parisian ever suspected Éliane was a *résistant*, could be her own fate, and that of Xavier and Rose and Luc and Angélique and Monsieur Jaujard.

It didn't matter how repulsive König's advances were. She would accept them with smiles so that no one would inform on her, so that she could keep her family and friends alive.

* * *

She made sure to serve König an extra helping of smiles with his meal at the brasserie even though she really didn't have time to linger; the restaurant was so popular now, given its obvious connection to powerful Nazis. In fact, she was so busy that she almost didn't realize she knew a sleek Parisienne in a beautiful gown until she'd passed the menus to her and the Nazi official she was dining with. Even then it took Éliane a moment to make the connection between the docile well-groomed creature and the rather more wild artists' model Luc had brought to the apartment on several occasions before the war. She had scandalized Éliane's mother with her inability to survive for more than five minutes without kissing Luc.

The woman's eyes flickered over Éliane and her stained apron and returned to the menu without a word. Still, Éliane hurried into the kitchen, thinking her brother would be pleased to take on the challenge of making his former *amour* turn her eyes to him and away from the Nazi.

"Louise is out there," she said to him.

He stepped over to the doorway and looked across to the table where Louise had her head tilted charmingly up at the Nazi.

"Make some mischief," Éliane said. "We both need the distraction of something to laugh about."

Luc said not a word. He looked down at his rumpled and grease-spattered clothes, then over at the clean and polished and freshly pressed German who was sipping one of the most expensive wines they had. Louise lifted her eyes at the same moment and they passed over Luc in the same way they had passed over Éliane. The distinction was clear: a powerful man who moved in the best society or a cook who served that same society.

Luc returned to the stove and shouted at his kitchen hand, an unreadable expression on his face.

Éliane wanted to hug her brother. Instead, she poured five times the amount of salt she should have into Louise's dinner and smiled mirthlessly at Louise's puckered mouth.

* * *

After a hideously prolonged farewell from König, Éliane returned to her apartment, arriving later than the others, knowing that her face was strained, her eyes most likely dead.

"Did your German enjoy his digestif of kisses?" Luc asked her. "We'll have to charge him extra for all the time he takes."

Éliane flushed, and then saw Xavier's eyes blaze at Luc. She needed to mollify her brother before Xavier's fury gave them both away. "Don't be hurtful," she said to Luc, more shortly than she'd meant to.

"You can't always help the hurts that come from human interactions," Luc said sardonically. "Surely if you've learned one thing in the last three years, it's that."

She should have tipped the entire saltcellar into Louise's dinner, Éliane reflected. But Luc was right, and his meaning stretched beyond Louise's cruelty. Now, anything and everything they did could hurt the other. One facial expression that revealed too much. One secret passed on in a place where ears heard more than they should. Their lives were in each other's hands and, looking around the table, Éliane saw what a motley collection of hands they had. Luc's were wine-stained, Rose's small and feeble, Xavier's well-manicured, Monsieur Jaujard's clasped together, and Éliane's had been almost burned that day.

She explained about the fire to everyone and Rose finished the story by saying contemplatively, "I only hid one painting in the Salle des Martyrs. A van Dyck, to match what Éliane had told von Behr. But when the inventory of the Schloss paintings was finished, three were missing."

"Do you think someone is stealing them?" Éliane asked, frowning. "Who?"

Rose shook her head. "We should look for anyone who suddenly seems to have more money or power than they ought."

"And be careful," Xavier said, face turned to Rose, eyes flicking to Éliane.

No sooner had he spoken than the door of the apartment burst open, less quietly than it should have, and a wild-eyed Angélique appeared—Angélique, who should have been at Montal with the *Mona Lisa*, not here in Paris again. She shut the door behind her, leaned against it, and gasped, "The Das Reich were at the Louvre depot at Valençay today. And then they came to Montal."

"What?" Éliane's and Xavier's voices rang out at the same time. The Das Reich, a division of the SS, were known as killers. Brutal killers.

"The art is safe," Angélique added quickly. "But one of our guards is dead." She sank into a chair.

A Louvre guard was dead. A man who looked after paintings. How could he be a threat to the conquering German army?

"They marched us out and made us lie on the lawn," Angélique continued flatly. "They shot at the windows. Then they told us to stand up and they shot at us too."

"Are you hurt?" Xavier asked her urgently.

Angélique shook her head.

"What were they looking for?" Monsieur Jaujard asked somberly.

"The pilot," she said.

Xavier stood up too quickly, knocking his chair over. It clattered against the floor, echoing like gunfire.

The pilot. Éliane's fist curled tight, a rock of tension.

"How many people knew about the pilot?" Xavier asked, whirling around.

"Hardly anyone," Angélique said slowly, as if she were piecing something together, something Éliane had not quite grasped but that Xavier must have, given his gaze, intent and very serious, on Angélique.

"Only the two maquisards who brought him to Montal," Angélique went on. "And the woman who runs the safe house I took him to this morning. She wouldn't have said anything that would bring the Das Reich to her own doorstep. And the Maquis wouldn't let anything slip. They don't want the Das Reich on their doorstep either."

"The other people who knew are all right here," Xavier added, eyes on the five of them as he spoke.

A colossal silence met his words. Then Luc stood up, his chair clattering to the floor too. "You include yourself in your conjectures?" he asked, voice low.

"Yes." Xavier's voice was equally low. "This happened either because someone was careless or someone was calculated. Both are unforgivable. Neither should happen again."

"I'll talk to the Maquis," Luc said. "It must have been one of them. Let's go." He summoned Angélique, who followed her brother to the door.

Éliane couldn't speak, couldn't even say goodbye. And nor could she think. It was impossible to imagine Rose betraying them all by forgetting herself and speaking of the pilot to Monsieur Jaujard in too public a place. Or Xavier. Or Angélique. Or Luc. Or even Éliane herself. Had she somehow given away what she knew? No. Luc was right. It could only have been one of the maquisards.

TWENTY-SIX

For the exhibition of the Schloss collection the following week, von Behr told Éliane to wear the black dress from Cap-Ferrat. She changed into it in the bathroom at the museum, painted her face with the rouge and mascara mask that would make her into the Éliane the Nazis wanted to see. The Éliane whom König was planning to take to a hotel at the night's end, something she'd forgotten about in the tension of the preceding days, something she could no longer forget about as the evening was now upon her.

Nausea pressed into her throat. She closed her eyes, made herself breathe, waited until it had passed. When she opened her eyes and saw her face in the mirror, she knew she had never been more scared in all her life.

"Mademoiselle!" König's voice sounded, calling her name.

She had to leave the sanctuary of the bathroom. She had to convince König to let Rose return to the museum. She had to, somehow, get through tonight without giving anything away.

She had no idea how she would do any of it.

"Mademoiselle!" His voice was right outside.

Think about the one good thing from the week, she told herself. Luc had found the maquisard who'd betrayed them, and had dealt with him. Éliane hadn't asked how. It was enough to know there would be no more betrayals.

She opened the door.

König took her straight into his arms.

She slapped him away, trying to make it seem playful. "Monsieur," she scolded. "I am at work."

He frowned a little and Éliane hoped he hadn't noticed that she tried to dissuade his kisses and embraces as much as she could. He would notice soon, she knew. Possibly in a matter of hours.

"Where's our waitress!" von Behr bellowed and, for the second time in her life, Éliane thought: *Thank God for von Behr.*

She hurried into the main gallery, picked up a bottle of champagne and readied herself to pour.

Xavier arrived with the very first guests. Éliane tried not to look at him, keeping her attention on filling glasses. The doors to the museum opened again and a short and generously curved woman entered. Her appearance caused König to stop dead in the midst of his beeline to Éliane.

Von Behr's displeased voice rang out. "Elke, what are you doing here?"

"I arrived this afternoon," the woman said in German. "I grew tired of waiting in Berlin. I hear that Paris is enchanting. Ernst," she said nervously to König, who still hadn't moved. "Aren't you pleased to see me?"

Xavier stepped forward and König had no choice but to introduce the woman to him. "This is my wife," König said to Xavier. "Elke."

König had a wife? Éliane almost choked on air. Who would have thought that the König of the unfinished sentence would have lied so spectacularly? And, following on immediately and deliriously from that thought: she was safe. If König's wife was in Paris, Éliane would not have to go to a hotel with König.

Von Behr switched to French. "Paris has proven to be most enchanting." He looked at Éliane as he spoke, a lazy grin on his face and Éliane realized that her complete surprise was going to work for her right now in what would need to be the performance of her life.

"You have a wife?" she said to König.

"I'm...I'm sorry," he spluttered. "I didn't know she was coming."

"That's not really an apology," Éliane hissed.

König winced, studying the shuffle of his feet on the floor. Then his head snapped up. "I liked not being König-from-Berlin who is married to Elke. I liked being König-in-Paris who might somehow convince a beautiful woman to dance with him."

Éliane saw Elke's face crumple with hurt. But she had to keep going.

"We did more than dance," she said and because of tiredness and pity and over-excitation a tear leaked from her eye. They were all playing games. "How long have you been married?" she asked, voice low as if she cared.

"Four years."

"And how many other women have you seduced at grand parties?"

"None. I would never—"

"But you did."

"Don't you see," König cried. Heads turned their way. "She's nothing compared to you. She's plump and plain like a potato dumpling. You are..."

"Ernst," Elke pleaded but was ignored by all.

"A rapidly deflating soufflé!" Éliane snapped. "Your metaphorical skills are as bad as your *competences de la chambre.*"

A round of titters and guffaws greeted Éliane's outburst. She left the gallery, taking herself to the bathroom, where she locked herself in a cubicle and wrapped her arms around her sides, uncertain whether she was going to laugh or cry.

* * *

The bathroom door flew open after only a few minutes and she knew from the scent that it was Xavier. She unlocked the stall and, when she saw his face, she asked, her whole body tensed, "What now?"

His words came in a rush. "They're going upstairs to the Salle des Martyrs to look for the van Dyck painting from the Schloss collection. The one Rose hid there. König received a tip-off from the SD telling him to search the Salle."

Éliane didn't know exactly what the SD—the Sicherheitsdienst— did but she knew it had to do with hunting down people who were working against the Nazis. And if König found the van Dyck painting hiding in the Salle des Martyrs it would cause a cascade of suspicion and searching that could only result in the arrest of everyone she cared about.

She raced up to the first floor, thanking God for the party below. There were so many people to maneuver past. She could see von Behr trying to force his way through the crowds, König resolute at his side, but the crowd of Nazis, and now Xavier, slowed their progress. She made it to the Salle des Martyrs before anyone else and removed the van Dyck from its hiding place. It was too big to stuff under her dress. But if they were coming now, they would catch her with it.

She had no time to be truly careful. The broom closet would have to do. She hurried in, tucked the painting behind the mops and gathered up some wine Rose had thought to keep there.

Sweat washed the back of her neck. The wine bottles trembled.

"Mademoiselle!" von Behr barked. "Why are you up here?"

Éliane appended her giddy smile onto her face and held up the Bordeaux. "The best of the red wine has been kept in here since the incident with Herr Schmidt." Thank goodness for Herr Schmidt, an art historian who had secretly tippled his way through much of von Behr's wine cabinet.

"Hurry up," he said curtly and Éliane needed no prompting. She scurried down the stairs and hoped to God they wouldn't search each room. But at least what she had done would prove their informant didn't know everything.

How hard it was to pour wine while von Behr and König were upstairs. How hard it was not to look at Xavier. How hard it was to see König and von Behr return almost twenty minutes later, empty-handed, König's cheeks red with mortification.

She watched as von Behr took up a glass in one hand, and a woman in the other, as Elke claimed her position at König's side, as Xavier slipped in beside them, flattering Elke, then turning to König and drawing him away for a private conversation.

Éliane made herself wait for ten minutes after their conversation had finished, then she returned to the bathroom, hoping Xavier would notice. Before she reached it, Elke appeared in front of her.

"You're very beautiful," Elke said, not accusingly, but wistfully.

Éliane wondered how it must feel to be called a dumpling by your husband in front of a crowd of laughing men. It forced her to offer the truth, although it would be no consolation. "I didn't know he was married," she said.

"I believe you," Elke said, her clear gaze not moving from Éliane's face. "You didn't want to save yourself for a husband?"

"You say that as if you think refusal is a choice open to me," Éliane said incredulously.

Elke blinked. "But Ernst wouldn't..." The hesitation was momentary. "He would not force you."

"Even if he didn't use physical force, there are so many ways to make someone do what they don't want to. I hope you never discover that for yourself."

Thankfully Elke didn't follow her to the bathroom. Thankfully Xavier did. He was there within thirty seconds, again speaking fast.

"Only the people at our meeting knew what you and Rose had done with that van Dyck painting," he said. "Unless somebody saw Rose hide it up there."

Éliane shook her head. Rose was too careful to have let that happen. Her mind raced.

This time, the exposure of secret information could not be blamed on the Maquis. It could only have found its way to the SD via one of the six people in their group. How? An impossible accident? Or something more deliberate?

Her eyes locked with Xavier's, as if they shared the same thought.

"Von Behr has dispatched Rose from the museum," Xavier said in a low and desperate voice. "And today in a meeting with Göring, Monsieur Jaujard was told he'd be put in the ground if he continued to obstruct the Nazis' attempts to help themselves to the state-owned artworks, which they're no longer content to leave safely in the depots. Now this. This could all fall down on top of everyone very soon. And you'll be caught in the middle of it." Worry colored Xavier's eyes a fierce and unrelenting black. "Especially if there's—"

He cut himself off but Éliane knew what he'd been about to say: *Especially if there's a traitor in our midst.*

PART SIX
SAINT-JEAN-CAP-FERRAT, 2015

TWENTY-SEVEN

Y ou've been waiting for me," Remy repeated dazedly, hand held tight in Adam's. She tried to make out more of the woman but, against the backlighting of sunshine, all Remy could see—like an over-exposed photograph—were patches of white: white hair, white hands, white shirt.

Then the sun shifted and there stood an unthreatening elderly woman. The lines on her face masked her true expression but her eyes were pale blue and sympathetic, as if she were about to say something that would hurt.

Remy took a step backward.

"Please come in and sit down," Elke König said in a voice that held within it, only slightly softened by life in Paris, a guttural German accent.

Remy followed her into the apartment, toward two armchairs by the window, unable to recall how to sit, so disconcerting had the woman's greeting been.

"Are you sure you won't sit down?" Elke asked, almost wistfully, as if she hoped Remy might make herself comfortable, might stay. Her hand gripped her cane as she shuffled across to one of the chairs.

"Where's your husband?" Remy asked. "Ernst König." He was the connecting puzzle piece, the one Remy needed to find.

"You don't know?" Elke asked, before lowering herself to sit. "My dear, he's been dead for seventy years."

Remy felt her hand clasp Adam's even harder.

"Ernst and his uncle, Colonel von Behr, took the coward's way out." Elke's voice was quiet, and her hands on her cane shook. "They drank champagne laced with poison in early 1945 when they knew it was all over. He took his life rather than face what he had done."

The man with her father's surname, the man who might be her father's father, had taken his own life. Only the guilty did that.

Remy didn't want to hear any more. She didn't want these people. They were not hers.

She withdrew her hand from Adam's and left the apartment.

* * *

Adam caught up to her at the bottom of the staircase. There was so much compassion in his eyes that she tucked her head into his shoulder, wrapped her arms around him and held on, not even realizing what she was doing. After a long moment, he placed a gentle kiss on the top of her head. Then he slowly disentangled himself.

Only when he drew back did she understand that she'd just embraced him. She looked up at him and his expression was that of the Adam she'd first met: rigid, reserved. Unreadable.

"I'm guessing you don't want to go back up there," he said quietly.

Remy shook her head.

Neither spoke much as they drove to Cap-Ferrat, other than polite requests to stop for coffee or to check directions when the GPS malfunctioned. Remy could put the lack of conversation down to the strange meeting with Elke. Or she could reason that she and Adam had always been able to be together without needing to speak. But this silence filled all the space in the car with its thunderous absence of sound.

Remy tried to turn her mind to work, anything but what Elke König had said. But she couldn't concentrate on lookbooks or clothes. And the longer the drive went on, the more she couldn't ignore the suspicion that embracing Adam had been too much for him, stirring feelings he'd told her he would keep hidden for her sake. She was making it so hard for him. Why? What purpose did it serve to ignore what both her body and her mind knew: that Adam was someone she felt something for. A physical pull. An emotional attraction. An unmistakable attachment.

She let herself sit with that, glancing across at him while he took his turn to drive, unable to see his eyes as they were hidden by sunglasses. She could see one side of his face, his cheekbone and jawline, the dark stubble shadowing it. The line of his shoulders, his arms—toned and tanned—the T-shirt covering his torso, which she knew was muscled and tanned too because she'd seen it on the beach so many times.

Her hands clenched at her sides and her stomach clenched too. She coughed.

"Okay?" Adam asked.

"Just thinking," she said.

"Me too."

Neither of them asked the next question: about what?

Her mind filled with snapshots of the last couple of weeks: Adam going to Paris for her, and then Washington; Adam staring at microfilm until his eyes were dry; Adam holding her hand while she had that awful conversation with Elke König; Adam never telling her to embark on this quest by herself.

When had anyone ever given her so much? The thought struck her like cold water.

"I need to stop," she said, even though there wasn't an *Aire* sign in sight.

Adam pulled off the road to the sound of blaring horns and watched her step out. He didn't follow her. She walked over to a tree and stood with one hand resting against it.

When had anyone ever given her so much?

The question asked itself again. She shook her head but it wouldn't be dislodged. A ream of loyal and disloyal thoughts wound through her: Toby waking up on a Saturday morning and saying, *Let's go someplace*, throwing their things in a bag and driving them to Thredbo or Jervis Bay or even Byron Bay for a weekend of fun. Toby wanting her to go to corporate dinners with him but always begging out of hers because they were "fashion things." Toby reading a book to Emily at night if he was home. Toby telling Remy in the morning that he had a meeting late that night and never looking in his diary to see if she was out too. Toby never booking the babysitter, even on one of those mornings he'd forgotten to tell her about a meeting. Toby always saying, before he left in the morning, *You look beautiful*. Toby never asking her a single question about the vintage fashion she collected.

She and Toby had shared one kind of love. She hadn't realized other kinds existed. Adam had shown her a compassion so tender, so deep, she hadn't been able to see it for what it was because she'd never experienced anything like it.

She'd put up a wall and told him not to breach it. And he hadn't, ever. That wall had been a test, she understood now. A way to see whether he would stay, despite every obstacle and no matter what. Or if he would leave, like Toby had.

Except Toby had had no choice. Adam had a choice. He hadn't exercised it. Until, perhaps, now, when she'd made him exercise it for self-preservation.

She managed to breathe despite the tightness of her throat, and then returned to the car where he was waiting for her.

"I'm okay," she said as she sat in the car and before he could ask, which she knew he would.

But what was she going to do about it?

* * *

When they pulled into Remy's driveway, Adam climbed out, opened the trunk took out his bag and Remy knew he was going to go straight to his parents' house, have a long shower and brood until one of his siblings provoked him.

"My parents are having a dinner party, as you can probably hear," he told her. "They texted me to invite us both to come over when we arrived. I told them you'd probably be too tired. Like I am."

Remy understood. "Thanks for coming with me," she said quietly. "I'm glad you were there."

He gave her a brief smile before he shouldered his bag and walked away.

Inside, Remy found a note from Antoinette letting her know she'd left behind some things that didn't fit in her suitcase but that Remy might find useful. Remy rifled absently through the bag, discovering— amongst lipstick and hair curlers—an enormous box of condoms. She winced.

She texted Antoinette to thank her for coming to France and added a raised eyebrows emoji about the bag of "useful" items.

Antoinette replied immediately. *Is Adam with you? If not, why not?*

Adam is at a party at his parents' house, Remy replied. She almost pressed send but then added, *I'm scared of the way I feel about him.*

It was at least ten minutes before Antoinette replied. *I was going to tell you off*, Antoinette said. *But then I realized that scared is part of any relationship. You should be scared if you really feel something for him. Scared is actually normal.*

Scared is actually normal. Remy went outside and sat on the lounger, the place where she'd first seen Adam.

Normal. She was behaving normally. Like any person who'd met someone they cared for. Because life, even if you hadn't lost a husband and a child, was never without hurt or fear or disappointment. She'd forgotten that. She'd equated normal with the kind of emotional sterility that probably didn't exist. Had thought she needed to stop grieving before she could truly move on. But would she ever stop grieving?

She would *never* forget Emily, or Toby. But perhaps grief could coexist with life. Perhaps living didn't mean she had to stop missing them. Surely if there was one thing she'd learned lately it was that hearts were vast treasuries, able to hold an abundance of feelings for so many people.

She looked at her watch. It was almost midnight. The noise from next door had quieted somewhat, meaning the dinner party was winding down. She walked down to the beach and stared at the water. Then she took out her phone, found Adam's number and texted him. *If you're not asleep or exhausted, would you meet me on the beach? I'll be here for half an hour or so. Remy x*

She'd never put that little *x* next to any message she'd sent Adam. Whether he'd notice, she didn't know. And whether she'd pushed him too far and he'd completely withdrawn and everything was over before it had even begun was something she was about to find out.

She slipped off her dress, placed it onto the stones, lay her bra and underwear atop it and walked into the water, diving under and holding her breath for as long as she could, kicking out. She swam away from the Henry-Joneses' house, then turned to look at the shore, treading water. She could see nothing on the beach. He wasn't coming.

She dove back under the water.

When she surfaced she saw, in the gentle glow cast by the light at the bottom of her steps, Adam. He had his hands shoved in his pockets and he was looking out at her.

She swam in a little way, everything except her blonde hair and the ivory of her face hidden by jet black water.

He walked closer too, stopping by her cast-off clothes, glancing down to where her bra and underwear sat in plain sight because she'd wanted him to see and to understand, so that he could then decide.

He said, voice unsteady, "I think I should probably go back up."

"I messaged you because I was hoping you'd stay. I was hoping you'd..." She paused. Courage. She could do this. "I was hoping you'd come into the water." The last words came out in a rush.

He ran a quick hand through his hair. "I don't think I should."

"I understand if you don't want to," Remy said quietly, realizing she had most likely ruined everything. "But I really want you to."

He didn't move, didn't speak and Remy braced herself for him to turn around and walk back up to his house. But in one quick and impatient movement, he pulled his shirt over his head and walked into the water, swimming out until he was an arm's length from Remy.

"What now?" he asked and she could hear in his voice the same kind of uncertainty she felt—a wariness that came from wanting to protect oneself from hurt. She knew then that he wanted to be there too; if they both didn't want it so damned much then they both wouldn't be so damned scared.

So she told the truth. "I'm scared of kissing you. But I also really want to."

The look on his face was almost enough to take away the fear. Tender and fierce and so gentle, as if he heard everything she was saying in those words. He leaned over and kissed her forehead softly, then asked, "How was that?"

"It was fine," she said, smiling a little because it had been, not just fine, but heady—as if she'd leapt and wasn't falling down, but up into something better. Also a headiness from being this close to him, her naked and him almost, a shiver at what might happen.

"Only fine?" He feigned disappointment. "I'll have to try harder."

Her smile grew—he always made her smile—as he stepped in closer still. Two kisses this time, one at her temple, the other on her right cheek.

"How was that?"

She pretended to consider. "Not bad."

Three more kisses on her other cheek, the third one falling beside her lips. Her mouth opened.

"And that?" he murmured.

"It was quite good," she whispered as the current shifted her body right up against his.

He froze, the self-control slipping back over him and she knew he was about to leave the water. So she slid her arms around his neck and brushed her lips achingly slowly across his.

"Remy." Adam's voice was low and husky. He leaned down toward her.

Then a wave knocked her sideways and she spoke without thinking. "This isn't such a good idea."

Adam's body tensed. "I'll go," he said.

"I didn't mean it like that," she hurried to explain. "In the water, kissing is a lot trickier. I can hardly stand. And I'm out of practice anyway so this is beyond my current skill set. Maybe we could try this over there." She pointed to the shore.

Adam exhaled a long and shaky breath. "Are you sure?"

"I think so. Is that okay?"

He nodded. "Just kissing though. I won't do anything else."

She led the way out of the water and, just before she stepped onto the pebbles, she turned to look over her shoulder at Adam. The expression on his face, eyes running over her body, made her stop, and, over the too-fast beat of her heart, say, "I really need to kiss you again."

This time their mouths did not meet quickly or lightly.

"God, Remy," he whispered, moving his mouth away to kiss her neck, "I thought this would feel good but I had no idea..."

True to his word, he was only kissing her, hands not straying anywhere other than her back. But she could feel, because they were standing so close together, how aroused he was and there, in the moonlight by the water, he had never looked more beautiful, the night highlighting the contours of his chest, the tattoo on his arm as sexy as hell.

"We need the sun lounger," she murmured into his ear.

His eyes darkened to the deepest possible blue and neither let go of the other for even a second as they stepped across the pebbles.

Then they were lying on the lounger together, just kissing still, but for so long that both heat and an ache built inside Remy, stronger and stronger, especially when Adam began to kiss her neck again. She could hear her breath coming so fast, knew that Adam must be able to hear it too. His lips found their way to her collarbone then he looked up to make sure everything was still okay. She nodded.

His mouth moved lower, traveling ever so slowly down the side of her breast. Remy arched toward him.

He glanced up at her again and whatever he saw on her face made him finally slide his lips over her nipple.

She gasped his name. "You need to do that again," she whispered and he laughed softly, breath hot on her skin.

Then it was her stomach's turn to writhe beneath the attentions of Adam's mouth, then the tops of her hip bones. She was breathing so fast she almost couldn't take in any air, felt like she might actually die right there on the beach because Adam just kissing her was like nothing she'd ever experienced in the whole of her life.

He looked up at her again and, this time, rather than nod, she said a very husky but very definite yes. He smiled at her and that was almost all she needed. Then his mouth moved lower, kissing again, and it took almost no time at all before she couldn't remember anything, didn't even know where she was, knew only the touch of this man on her skin and the way he made her feel and that she would do this every single minute for the rest of her life if she could.

* * *

It took so long for her breath to settle, for her body to relax, for her to even be capable of opening her eyes. Adam held her against him, covering her face with kisses until at last she was able to kiss him back.

"That went further than I meant it to," he said.

Remy's heart squeezed. "Adam." She made herself move, rolling him onto his back, eyes fixed to his. "If you think that was something you need to apologize for, then you seriously misunderstood everything that just happened. I want you. That was nowhere near enough—"

She didn't get to finish her sentence because his hand threaded into her hair, drawing her mouth onto his, him as desperate as she had been moments ago.

He pulled back with a groan. "We can't. I don't have…" He paused. "I didn't bring anything down here with me because I didn't think you wanted this. And if I go back up to my house now and then try to disappear again it'll be like the Spanish Inquisition—it was bad enough trying to leave after you texted me—and I'm sure you don't have a stash of condoms at your place."

Remy grinned. "Actually, I do. Luckily Antoinette has more foresight than either of us."

"You're kidding? Please tell me you're not though," he added, suddenly serious.

"I would not kid about that. Let's go." She jumped up.

Adam shook his head and picked up her clothes. "You have to put something on. We won't make it up the steps if you go like that."

Remy's grin grew wider. "We'll see."

She walked over to the stairs, naked, Adam following her. They'd made it halfway up when she felt him tug on her hand. He kissed her again, his hands not restrained now, but impatient, hungry, everything she wanted them to be.

"I couldn't see you properly down there but now, in the light, I can and you're killing me, Remy."

She smiled against his lips. "Stop kissing me otherwise we'll never make it to the house."

"I did warn you," he said, eyes darkening.

The minute the door closed behind them, his mouth was back on hers, hands too, until he stepped backward, eyes wandering over her body. She wanted to squirm away but she couldn't move because everything in his gaze made her breath catch, trapped in his admiration and the sheer, unmistakable want.

She managed to say, voice as shaky as her knees, "If you keep looking at me like that, we're in big trouble."

"We're definitely in big trouble. Where are Antoinette's supplies?"

"In here."

On the way to the kitchen, she slid off the rest of his clothes. The feel of all of him next to her was so powerful—for both of them, she thought—that they forgot to move, just stood, kissing, hands everywhere but never in enough places, nor for long enough. Aware that they were both nearing the limits of restraint, Remy found what she needed and took his hand.

They made it as far as the *petit salon* where he sat on the curved sofa and pulled her down onto his lap. For a minute she just held on—there were too many sensations, so much to feel and she didn't want to miss any of it—until he kissed her, mouth telling her of this need that was greater than anything she'd ever imagined. One of his hands was entwined in her hair, the other held on to her back, and it wasn't long before it happened again: a vanishing of the world, a reduction of everything to just her and Adam, their bodies and minds joined in a passion so fierce Remy wondered, for just a moment, if it could possibly last.

* * *

They eventually found their way to her bed and collapsed into it, lying on their sides so they could see each other's face.

"Are you okay?" Adam asked and Remy felt her heart ache—that he would ask her that, now. That he would be so unselfish as to let her complicated feelings and her husband into the bed with them, because he cared.

"I am," she said. "I don't know if I'll feel horribly guilty about it tomorrow. I hope not, but I know grief isn't predictable and I suddenly do crazy things. Right now, I'm just thinking about you and," she grinned, "about when we can do that again—and there's another bit of future right there."

He laughed. "You need to give me five minutes."

It was her turn to laugh. "If we did all of that again in just five minutes, I don't think either of us would survive."

"Okay, make it ten."

She laughed again and while she was laughing, he said, "I love you, Remy. I know you don't love me and that you don't want to think about loving someone else. I don't expect any declarations. But I hope it's all right with you, how I feel."

Tears—why were there always tears?—sprang into her eyes and she nestled into him and kissed his chest, his neck, his cheek. "Thank you," she said and she felt his arms tighten around her.

TWENTY-EIGHT

Remy woke to light more brilliant than it should be. She glanced at the clock and realized it was ten in the morning. She stretched her arms over her head and felt Adam's fingers trailing across her skin and she smiled. "We are so lazy."

"Lazy?" He arched an eyebrow at her. "I'd say we've both earned our sleep."

She laughed. "You're right. Which probably means you're starving and you've been lying here desperate for me to wake up so you can eat."

He grinned. "But I can't decide whether to have you or eggs first."

"Good to know I've reached the illustrious status of being equal to eggs. How about I have a shower, you cook and then we'll eat... something."

She slid out of the bed with a backward glance at Adam that had him shaking his head and then she shut herself in the bathroom, turned on the tap and stood still, enjoying the sensation of the water on her skin. For the first time in so long, simple things that had once felt good—but that had become devoid of any sensation—now felt good again. Shower water. The smell of food. Laughter.

She braced one hand on the wall, waiting for the wave of guilt and shame to hit her. But it didn't. She was still enjoying the shower. She had adored the last few hours with Adam. None of it made her a bad person.

Finally she stepped out, threw on a 1930s nightgown very similar to the one Adam had photographed her in and sat on the bed, phone in hand, flicking back to photos of her daughter. One of Emily asleep in that fathomless way only young children are capable of. One of Emily frowning with concentration as if trying to understand the entire world. One of Emily running toward Remy, arms outstretched, ready to cuddle. An Emily hug was like no other.

Remy squeezed her eyes shut and remembered how good those little arms had felt. She knew she was crying, but that was okay. Far better to remember Emily's hugs than to banish them from her thoughts forever.

She wiped her eyes, stood, and went out to the kitchen where Adam was piling plates with fruit, yogurt, eggs, toast.

"Can I show you something?" she said.

"Sure."

She held out her phone. "This is my daughter, Emily."

"She looks like a dark-haired version of you," he said, taking the phone from her and scrolling through more pictures, smiling when he saw the one of Emily asleep. "Molly sleeps like that." Then he asked, "What about your husband?"

Remy swiped through until she found one of Toby, a silly selfie she'd taken of them in the car while driving to the Blue Mountains for a weekend. Emily was waving her arms wildly in the background.

"That's Toby," she said quietly, slipping an arm around Adam's waist. "Is it weird, seeing that?"

Adam shook his head. "No. I know you don't un-love somebody just because they died. It's good to see them. And you with them."

Remy hesitated. "You're very different to Toby. I don't know whether I should say that. I'm not comparing you. It's just..." She paused. "I'm different too. And I kind of like that. If the accident hadn't happened, I wouldn't be different; I wouldn't be the way I am now. I can't quite get my head around it—that some good things have come out of that terrible day. Like you. I would never have met you otherwise. And I'm so glad that I have."

"Thank you," he said, kissing her gently.

They ate breakfast on the terrace, enjoying the ease of being with one another, of Adam helping himself to food from Remy's plate, of Remy making coffee and him reaching up to kiss her, of chatting about everything: photography, Remy's business, what work he had lined up after summer was over. But not Elke or the painting or Ernst König. Neither of them was letting that intrude just yet.

Eventually, Remy told Adam she'd clean up while he had a shower. As she was clearing plates from the table, she heard a knock on the front door.

She opened it to find Lauren there, looking worried. "Have you seen Adam? He was weird last night and then he went out and didn't come home and—"

A voice called, "Remy, where can I find…" and Adam appeared, thankfully with a towel around his waist, stopping when he saw his sister.

Lauren's grin was gigantic. "Looks like I found you, big brother. I'll report back that you're safe and well and that we mightn't see you for a while."

With that she was off down the driveway, laughing.

Adam looked sheepishly at Remy. "I guess that cat's out of the bag. Not that I was planning to keep it a secret. I think the way I feel about you is written all over my face."

Remy shut the door and touched his cheek, watched his eyes trace over her lips, saw that yes, in his face and in his eyes, was everything he felt for her. Her hands flew down to dislodge the towel. "If you're going to walk around looking like that, then you know what will happen."

Before she could even kiss him, he had her nightgown over her head and on the floor. "Is that the one I photographed you in? I've been wanting to take it off you since then," he murmured, stepping her backward against the wall so they could be as close as possible, mouths locked together.

The way he made her feel when he spoke like that.

She drew back only enough to shake her head in answer to his question and to whisper, "I want you."

Adam's eyes darkened still more. "We are always going to be like this," he said. "Two people who can never wait until they find a bed." He lifted her up and wrapped both her legs around his waist. "Two people who drive each other completely crazy. God, Remy," he said and she knew just what he felt because she felt it too.

* * *

The day passed lazily and sensually, and the night too. The next morning after breakfast, Remy heard, rising up from the beach, the sound of people swimming. A child's voice.

"We should go down there," she said.

Adam looked askance at her.

"We should," she repeated. "You're meant to be spending time with your family, but you've been over here for—I don't even know how long. We have to leave the house some time, not least because you'll eat all the food. Let's go to the beach."

He put down his book. "All right. I kinda hoped we could stay here forever but I guess that's wishful thinking. And Remy?"

She knew what he was going to say. "We need to talk about Elke König," she said slowly. "I know. I just..."

"Want another day of this." He stood up from the lounger and kissed her forehead. "I get it. But let's talk about it tomorrow."

They threw on their bathing suits, and when Adam saw Remy in hers—a 1950s Catalina leopard print, two-piece halter-neck—she had to bat him away. "Later," she said. "Otherwise we'll never get to the beach."

They walked hand in hand down the steps. When they reached the pebbles, Remy felt Adam tighten his grip on her hand and she felt a rush of something inside her at the knowledge that this man, this tough, tattooed guy turned to her when he needed shelter. Thank goodness for his mother, whom Lauren must have reported back to; she simply walked over to her son, kissed his cheek and said, "Hello, darling." Then she kissed Remy's cheek too. "It's good to see you both."

Adam relaxed by Remy's side. But then she saw his eyes lock with Matt's, who was staring in confusion at their joined hands, and Remy realized Lauren had chickened out from telling her other brother.

Remy led Adam over to the water, dived in and swam out a little way, before stopping and surfacing to find Adam beside her, drawing her in, wrapping his arms around her. She grinned. "Maybe you were right. The beach is a little too tempting." Then, "Are you okay?" He'd asked it of her so many times and now it was her turn to ask it of him.

"I am. Until Matt opens his mouth."

They swam for a while and then headed back to the shore, where everyone lay lazily in the sun. Molly ran over to hug Adam but she tripped and fell, hard. After the shock had passed, she began to cry. She was closest to Adam when it happened, but she went straight to her father. It was what children did: in moments of pain, they ran to their parents. Nobody else would do. Not even an uncle who was really a biological father.

Remy didn't say anything, knowing it must have hurt Adam, but that he wouldn't want to talk about it now. He picked up the ball and threw it into the water, whistling for the dog, who leapt up and swam out gleefully to retrieve its prize. She let him do that for half an hour until the dog flopped exhausted on the shore. Then she said, "Let's go for another swim."

As he stood up Molly, recovered now, extricated herself from her father's arms and raced over.

"Uncle Adam," she called. "I want to swim too."

"Okay." He picked her up, resting her on his hip and carrying her out until the water was at his waist. "How's this?" he asked.

She shook her head. "Not far enough. Up to my head."

"Maybe not that far," Adam said, looking back to where his brother sat on the shore, and Remy ached at the way he tried to do what his brother wanted while at the same time pushing the limits with Molly a little so she could emerge from her cocooned existence.

"How about just to here." He walked one more step, so the water covered her knees.

"Good," she cried. "Now I want to swim."

"Why don't we go back in and find some rocks," Adam said.

"I don't want rocks. I want to swim."

Adam glanced over at his brother again and, for a minute, Remy thought he really would risk Matt's wrath and throw Molly into the air, let her splash down and then scoop her up. Matt must have thought the same thing because he jumped up.

Adam kissed Molly's forehead and said, "Let's paddle in the shallows instead."

But Matt didn't hear and he shouted at his brother. "How many times do I have to say I don't want you doing that? A million? Can't you just listen for once?"

He reached out for Molly, trying to take her from Adam, who was in the process of handing her over anyway. Once Molly was safely in Matt's arms, Adam tried to turn away and ignore it all. But Remy couldn't, not anymore.

"I know this is none of my business," she said to Matt, "but you're being unfair. Molly enjoys being in the water with Adam. You and I both know that anything that gives joy after you lose someone should be treasured, not prevented. She will always run to you first when she's hurt. That's the most precious thing of all and it's yours. Nobody else's. All Adam wants to do is make her laugh. You should let him."

Matt stared at Remy and Molly stared too. Then Molly said chirpily, "See, Daddy, laughing is good for us. Remy said so."

But Matt took his daughter back to the shore anyway. Remy saw the look on Judy's face and she wanted to cry at all the pain that sat between these people, to cry for what couldn't be undone, to cry for what would never happen.

Then she felt Adam grab her hand. He walked them determinedly back to her steps.

Shit. He would have hated her doing that. She felt a strange churning in her stomach, a pain at having hurt him, a pain that was nothing to do with her own suffering but that had everything to do with watching somebody else suffer at her hands. It hurt worse than anything had hurt in a while.

They were halfway up the steps and out of sight of everyone when he turned to her and kissed her with even more passion, if it were at all possible, than ever before. Then he said, eyes blazing, "Nobody has ever defended me like that."

Remy felt herself wilt against him with relief. "I thought you were mad."

And she realized that the tumult of emotion inside her was familiar; it was the same fierceness she'd felt whenever she'd seen Emily threatened in a playground. It was a wildness that came out of a feeling so primal and so formidable that she suddenly saw it for what it was. She smiled. "I had to say something to Matt because I love you."

"What?" he said, head jerking back as if she'd hit him, and she supposed she had—hit him right in the heart because that was where she felt it now: this love that was both everything she wanted and everything she didn't want, everything that would hurt and that would also bring her exuberant, rapturous joy.

"I love you," she said again and at last he smiled.

"You need to take your swimsuit off now because I'm going to die," he said and she felt his hands undo the ties around her neck.

"Adam, we're outside. Anyone could come up these steps," she whispered, laughing. "We should actually try and make it to a bed."

"We are always never going to make it to a bed, remember," he said, taking her hand and running with her up the stairs, where they made it to the sun lounger before they couldn't wait anymore.

* * *

They made the concession of dragging the lounger in out of the sun but that was all. Afterward, as they lay in one another's arms, Adam was very quiet and Remy knew he was thinking about Molly.

"What will you do?" she asked, holding him close.

Adam sighed and rolled onto his back, cradling her head on his shoulder. "Withdraw," he said. "I don't have any choice. Otherwise she'll just see me and Matt fighting all the time. So I'll be the distant uncle who sends her presents twice a year. A guy who's just a name. It's killing Mom, watching me and Matt. And it's bad for Molly. If I'm around, Matt feels threatened. So the only thing to do is to not be around."

She pictured what might happen tomorrow, Molly toddling along the shore, begging Adam to take her into the water and him refusing, him not picking her up anymore. She saw how hurt the little girl would be for a time but then, as the summer ended and the memory faded, how Matt might settle down as Molly forgot Adam altogether. She felt how sad, how very sad, it would be for Adam.

"Are you sure?" she asked.

"No," he said. "I hate it and I'm going to be pissed for a long time so if you don't want to stick around..." He stopped and held on to her and Remy felt herself holding on to him just as tightly, tears in her eyes because he had just said with his embrace: *You make me feel better and I need you.*

"I want to stick around," she whispered. But she also knew she had to tell him something. It wasn't fair not to be upfront.

"I want to stick around," she said again, lifting her head up and looking down at him. "And I don't know where this is going or anything at all about futures but one thing I know is that I can't bear to have children ever again. Ever," she repeated in case there was even a chance that she hadn't sounded serious the first time. "And you probably want them. You're not too old. I've seen how you are with Molly. You'd be an amazing dad. But I can't be a mother again."

He stared at her for a long moment and she saw a lot of things pass behind his eyes. He rubbed his hand over his face and reached up to touch her cheek.

"Life is such a bastard, isn't it?" he said. "It's been so tempting over the last couple of days to think that this is all there is: this house and this lounger—and various other places"—he managed a wry smile—"and us. And you know what's crazy?" he mused. "If I could go back and undo everything that happened to you, I would. Even though it means you wouldn't be lying here. I'd give anything for you never to have been—not to still be—so hurt. But I can't undo things. I can only do whatever I can to make you happy. And if that's not having kids…" He shrugged. "Like you said, I don't know what's going to happen with us either. But I don't want to give you up for the promise of children who don't even exist. You exist. I want you, however you come."

Tears were pouring down her cheeks as she lay her head back down on his chest and wrapped her arms around him. She couldn't say a single thing. Could only cry. And she thought there was a good chance that, were she to look up, his eyes might be damp too, mourning Molly and the sacrifice he would make for his family, the sacrifice he would make for Remy.

Lying there with him, Remy knew only that Adam was the best man in the world and that neither she nor Matt probably deserved him.

PART SEVEN
PARIS, 1943–1944

TWENTY-NINE

Éliane stood at the window of her apartment, one hand pressed to the glass, shawl wrapped over her shoulders, shivering with cold and with fear. Autumn had arrived and she watched leaves tumble onto the pavement and dance with the wind—away from what had once been a city of light and was now a city of shadows—as she worried over what she should do.

She should be thinking hard about traitors. Who it could be. Someone connected to the six of them, because it was impossible to imagine it might *be* one of the six of them. Would they act again? When? Why had they done nothing since the Schloss exhibition?

But there was something even more pressing than a traitor to be dealt with right now.

An errant leaf fluttered up, rather than down, caught by a sudden gust, almost escaping until, from nowhere, a branch cracked, crushing the leaf against the pavement where it lay, trapped and fluttering. The Allied landings in Italy, the almost nightly air raids over every part of France and the clamorous rumor that the Allies would invade France within the next month or two had lately driven the Nazis to mania. Everyone looked over their shoulders now, Jew or gentile, collaborator or *résistant*. But everyone kept their eyes fixed to the sky too, waiting for the invasion that was so confidently predicted, wishing it would come that very day.

But Éliane couldn't wait any longer.

* * *

She stopped at her desk at the museum just long enough to leave her purse and her coat and to say to Rose, "I need to visit the Salle des Martyrs. I'll be back in a minute."

Rose took one look at Éliane's face and frowned. "What is it?" she asked.

"Soon," Éliane promised. "I'll tell you soon."

She left a note in the Room of the Martyrs for Xavier, stuck to the back of Luc's painting of the lovers embracing beneath the moon; she'd hidden the other one deep inside the *salle* as it was too precious to have out on view. Notes were the only way she and Xavier had to communicate between monthly meetings—they couldn't risk bathroom trysts at the Jeu de Paume unless it was urgent.

I have to do something, she wrote. *It will be surprising.*

She hoped Xavier would come to the museum that day, would see the note and somehow find a moment alone with her so she could tell him what she meant to do. But another week passed and Xavier didn't come. She hadn't seen him at the museum for weeks. They hadn't been able to speak any further about whether someone was actually betraying them to the Nazis. They hadn't been able to speak about anything at all.

She assumed he was in London; she knew he had to go back there from time to time—which he passed off to Göring and von Behr as trips to Switzerland to deal in artworks—to receive new orders and pass on information too sensitive for radio transmissions. She wondered if he was searching for evidence of further information leaks, other breaches of trust. How long would he be away for?

Regardless, she had run out of time. The more weeks that passed between the night at the Riviera and her telling König, the more he might be inclined to disbelieve her.

So she went to find König.

"I must speak with you, Monsieur," she said, and then she began to cry. Crying was easy; there was so much to cry about. That she would tell König about this before she told Xavier.

"What is it?" König asked, flailing a handkerchief at her. "What can I do?"

"You've put me in a very difficult situation, Monsieur."

"I know," König cried. "I'm trying to convince Elke to return to Berlin. But—"

"It's not only your wife," Éliane interrupted, touching her stomach. "I'm going to have a baby. Your baby."

Nausea curdled in her stomach and whether it was from the lie, the pregnancy, or the hunger, she didn't know. Her monthly cycles had been so sporadic for more than a year, given she really only ate one meal a day from the brasserie, that she hadn't imagined she would still be able to fall pregnant. Nor had she realized for quite some time that she actually was. She made herself breathe as König caught her in his arms and embraced her.

"Is anyone working today?" von Behr interrupted them.

König took hold of Éliane's hand. "We have some news, Uncle," he said, face aglow, so obviously happy.

Suddenly, Éliane hated herself. That König had equally deceived her was not justification. But desperation and a greater good were surely reason enough? Or was she as bad as the Nazis? Would the future forgive her, or condemn her? Her stomach turned again.

"We're having a baby," König said.

"A baby," von Behr repeated coolly. "But how do you know it's yours?"

Éliane blanched.

König stepped forward, the news obviously giving him some spine. "I will thank you not to talk to the mother of my child that way, especially as your own affairs are so dishonorable and bring the wrong kind of attention to the ERR."

I'm sorry, Éliane whispered silently to her child, and to Xavier. It was the only thing she could do. König would protect her now, would perhaps share with her more than he ought to.

"What will your wife think?" von Behr asked, lighting a cigarette.

"You know how much Elke wants a child," König said.

This is my child, Éliane wanted to shout. "Excuse me," she said. "I'm not always well." She pressed her hand to her mouth and stepped away.

"This evening," König called to her. "We'll drink a toast to our child at the brasserie."

* * *

Éliane just had time to tell Luc before the evening shift at the brasserie began. She told him—her brother to whom she'd once told everything—that the child was König's. Everyone must believe it. She couldn't risk telling anyone the truth, except Xavier. But where was he?

"A German child," Luc said disgustedly. "How can you bear it?"

His words were a blow. Would she say the same to him if he told her he was having a baby with a German woman? She didn't know. She didn't know anything anymore.

Then Luc added, in a manner reminiscent of von Behr, "Don't you have work to do?"

Just as she obeyed von Behr, she obeyed her brother. She gathered the cutlery to set the tables, left the kitchen and began to fold napkins without knowing what she was doing.

Soon the smell of meat—meat!—drifted into the restaurant. Even with Luc's restaurant permit, he hadn't been able to find meat for at least a week. Her stomach growled, both her body and the baby telling her she needed to eat, now. She hurried into the kitchen.

On the benchtop, laid out like a feast, was a bowl of steaming *boeuf bourguignon* full of tender, delicious beef. It sat atop a white cloth and beside a large glass of white liquid that Éliane almost didn't recognize. Then she realized it was milk—something she hadn't seen for months. She stared at the food, stunned, and then at Luc, who was grinning.

"For you, Mademoiselle," he said with a flourish.

"I want to hug you, but I want to eat that more," she said, grabbing the fork and closing her eyes as she tasted the first mouthful. "Heaven," she said, opening her eyes, chewing, then smiling at her brother, who was laughing at her.

"I've been a bear," he said. "And you need food."

"You mean you're sorry?" she said teasingly.

He kissed her cheek. "Hurry up and eat that before the Nazis get here."

She didn't need to be told twice.

* * *

"Champagne!" came the boisterous cry as von Behr and König and the usual crowd entered the brasserie. Xavier was not, thankfully, among them.

One bottle was not enough for von Behr though and she was busy searching for more in the rapidly dwindling cellar, not paying any attention to the door, and didn't see Xavier enter, only realized he had arrived when she turned back to the table and saw him slip into a chair beside von Behr.

Nom de Dieu. There was no possible way Xavier would have read her note—the museum was closed up for the night. There was no possible way he was prepared.

Éliane watched in horror as von Behr opened his mouth.

"My nephew is to be a father," von Behr said to Xavier.

Éliane's hands worked desperately at the champagne cork.

"Congratulations," Xavier said, slapping König on the back. "Perhaps your wife will return to Germany to nest?"

"But it is not the wife who's baking the bun," von Behr smirked. "It's our dear fräulein here."

Crash! The bottle fell, as Éliane intended it to, onto the floor. An explosion of glass and liquid flew up into the air, all over the trouser legs of the men.

Thank God she'd dropped the bottle. Thank God she'd given Xavier a few seconds to recover himself as everyone around him swore and swiped champagne. He looked as if he might be ill and she saw the moment the terrible understanding passed through him as his gaze locked with hers in a kind of anguished, silent howl. But it was only for a moment. Then he began to wipe his trousers and curse Éliane too.

"I don't expect to find that bottle on my bill tonight," von Behr snapped.

"Of course not, Monsieur," she said, hands trembling as if she were scared—and she was, not of von Behr but of what she had done and what Xavier would say. *I did it for you*, she tried to tell him with her mind but there was so much noise and so much mess she knew he would never hear, or understand.

König tugged at her with his cold hands and drew her down onto his lap, kissing her fully on the mouth in front of everyone. He raised his glass. "To my son!"

Von Behr shouted, "To my great-nephew."

Everyone at the table toasted, the broken bottle and the spilled liquid forgotten. The door of the brasserie opened, admitting more customers, and Éliane was able to say, "Excuse me," to König, before she led the newly arrived couple to a table, then hurried to the bathroom, and threw up in the toilet.

When there was nothing left inside her, she wiped her mouth and sat on the floor and told herself to stand up and go back out and continue the charade. It didn't matter whether she was sick from the pregnancy, from disgust, or from worry over Xavier. She must walk into the restaurant and smile and allow König to call Xavier's child his son. She must serve champagne and pretend not to understand German. She must not, even once, wonder if she had the reserves of energy to get through another year like this, and then perhaps another, and another, until the very end of time.

* * *

Éliane knew Xavier would come to see her that night. So she locked the door to the apartment. The risk was too great, especially now. It was why they'd sworn to have only that one night. He would understand, she hoped, that there was no other explanation she could give to König for her being pregnant that wouldn't expose Xavier and Luc and Angélique and Rose and Monsieur Jaujard. Either Éliane lied to everyone about her baby or she gave everyone up to the Germans.

She slept, exhausted, one hand on her child.

She woke with a start some time later. Xavier was sitting on her bed.

"You shouldn't have come," she whispered. "I locked the door."

"One of the many unsavory skills I've acquired over the last couple of years is that of picking locks," he said wryly. Then a smile as fragile as gold leaf bloomed over his face and Éliane would have given her heart to have that smile trapped forever in paint, unalterable: Xavier, happy.

"We're having a baby," he said.

And she smiled for the first time since she'd discovered she was pregnant, the sudden delight catching her off guard. Of course it was a joyful moment. How could she have forgotten?

She didn't think she had ever loved him more than in that moment when, by leaning down and kissing her stomach—the carapace that shielded their child from this terrible world—he made her forget she'd told another man that he was the baby's father.

Then gently, so gently, he kissed her lips. "I love you so much, Ellie."

All she wanted to do right then was to kiss him too. But, more importantly, all she wanted was for him to stay alive so that one day they could all be a family. "You should go. What if someone comes up here?"

He ignored her, saying instead, "I hate that you've had to do this. But I know that if König and von Behr found out…"

She touched a finger to his lips not wanting to talk about consequences. "König might share even more with me now," she said, trying to find the lining of silver amid so much that was black.

Xavier's hand caressed her stomach. "When is the baby due?"

"In six months. And they say the Allies will come soon, so perhaps before the baby is born we'll all be free."

"They won't come this year." His voice was barely audible, as if he couldn't bear to say it. "Maybe not until next summer."

Éliane closed her eyes. Summer was eight months away. She had to get through another winter. Months more of König and von Behr. A baby born into Occupation rather than liberation, into a city without food, a city where electricity could be relied upon for perhaps two hours a day, and gas only a little more as the Allied planes had begun to bomb crucial supply lines and utility plants, and as coal supplies vanished into Nazi fires.

"I should get you and the child out," Xavier said, kissing her forehead. "To England."

For just a moment, she imagined boarding a plane and taking her child away to a country where it would be safe. But if she were to suddenly disappear, there was no chance at all that König and von Behr wouldn't investigate everyone who knew her. She opened her eyes, returning to her apartment in Paris, and her two true loves.

"I can't," she said. "Perhaps that makes me selfish: that I can't put this child above everything. But one child for a nation seems a poor trade." If everyone creating a little piece of light in the chiaroscuro of Nazi-occupied

Paris were to stop, then there would only be darkness—so much that none of them would ever escape from it. "Do you understand?"

This time, he closed his eyes. "I didn't really think you'd agree."

She finally made herself say the thing that had sat within her like a disease for the past week. "It's even more dangerous for you now that I'm carrying your child. If König even suspects how I feel for you..." She withdrew her hand from his. "You should forget about me—"

He wouldn't let her finish. "I can never un-love you, Éliane." He kissed her softly, a feather stroke of pearl on an ivory canvas. "There's one thing I want you to agree to though."

He drew back a little, gaze locked with hers, eyes the color of oxblood, pain a deep red behind the browns. "If I ever get caught," he said resolutely, "don't give yourself up trying to save me. Love is watching me go and saying nothing, doing nothing because, if you do, they'll take you too. If you're left behind, you can't sacrifice yourself for a love that will end right then anyway because they *will* kill me."

She sobbed then, too loud; what if Luc heard? She pressed her hand to her mouth, struggled for air and composure. "I don't know if I can do that."

"You have to. For the baby."

"Then you have to promise too. That if anything happens to me, you'll let them take me. And you'll take the baby."

He looked stricken. "I can't do that—"

She interrupted, finding the self-command she needed, making her voice firm too. "I'll only promise if you will. We have to. Our child deserves it."

He swore, feelingly. Then he bent his head and kissed her stomach again, making the promise she knew he didn't want to make but that he would make for the sake of the innocent life they hoped to give a new world to.

* * *

They woke to the sound of the air-raid sirens screaming.

"Where's your bomb shelter?" Xavier asked, sitting up, alert.

"I don't go," she said. "Nobody does around here. We sit in the window and watch the sky instead."

It was true. With more and more Métro stations closed and thus unable to serve as bomb shelters, and the planes coming in every night, Parisians had become fatalistic. Éliane took Xavier's hand, led him to the window, rolled up the blackout curtain and hardly flinched at the sound of the bombs detonating somewhere in the north of the city. The sky flamed orange-red, then mahogany, a little like Xavier's eyes earlier, as if the city were expressing its hurts too.

Xavier drew her in front of him, wrapping his arms around her and kissing the top of her head. "You're too thin, Ellie. A baby will take everything from you. And the food will only get less and less."

"Yesterday I wondered what grass would taste like," she admitted. "I've always been able to manage on the one meal a day at the brasserie. But now, even Luc's gray market is short of food. The baby needs greens; I give it rutabagas."

Xavier's arms tightened around her. "I hid a bag of food under the bed when I came in. Some things from England. Make sure Luc doesn't find them. And I have something else for you." He reached down for his trousers, took an envelope out of the pocket and gave it to her.

She opened it slowly. Inside was money, a key, a title deed for Xavier's house in Cap-Ferrat and a letter granting Éliane and her child ownership of the house and detailing a trust fund that had been set up to maintain the house in perpetuity.

"There's also a note that tells you how to get in touch with Madame Mercier at Cap-Ferrat if you need to," Xavier said. "You can go there and hide if things get too much. You can send her these papers to keep them safe. You need a fallback, especially now."

Éliane nodded.

Another bomb blast, closer, the sound of a city burning. What would be left of it, of any of them, when rescue finally came?

She buried her head in Xavier's shoulder and then said something she knew she had to say, for everyone's sake. Something that would make her lie about the baby's father easier to bear, that would give her strength of purpose. "I'm going to try to find out from König who's been giving the SD information," she whispered. "The baby gives me a new way of getting closer to him and if I don't use it—"

"Don't," Xavier said sharply and she heard black fear shadowing his words.

"He might tell me. I'm the only one who has a chance of finding out."

"I'm trying to get the name from von Behr. I *will* get it from von Behr." Xavier's voice was fierce.

"Which is just as dangerous—or more so—than what I'm proposing." She rested her forehead against his. "Whoever it is, they haven't done anything further. We all know to be even more careful with what we say and where we say it. Perhaps that will be enough to make it stop."

Xavier said nothing and she knew it was because he didn't want to take the risk of "perhaps." That he would keep looking until he discovered who it was. So, then, would she.

"I love you so much," she told him.

"I know," he said, tears on his own cheeks now.

"You need to go." She made herself step away from him. "You've been here too long."

"There's chocolate in the bag," he said, smiling a little. "Have it for breakfast."

Her laugh was half-sob. "If I do that, then soon I'll be so plump you won't recognize me."

"I can't wait to see that because then I'll know it's true. That the baby is real." He hesitated, and looked so vulnerable she could feel her heart crack. "It's so hard to believe in good things right now when you can't see them..."

Good things. Like the Allies invading France. Like the paintings being somehow, miraculously, returned to their owners. Like art, everywhere. Like their baby, invisible now but growing, she hoped. Please God, let it—despite rations and cold and evil—let it grow.

THIRTY

É liane didn't see König for some time and thus had no opportunity to introduce the subject of his informant into a conversation. He and Göring's Catalogue disappeared for several weeks. Rose, who had simply turned up at work a week or so after the Schloss exhibition, wearing her drab disguise that made her oblivious to most, had discovered the catalog's absence.

She and Éliane had held a whispered conference.

"Do you think they've changed its hiding place?" Éliane asked.

Rose shook her head. "Perhaps König has it with him. One of the drivers told me he'd gone to Carinhall."

Carinhall. Göring's country home in Germany. It made sense that he might take the catalog there.

"I hope he brings it back," Éliane said.

"And I hope you're well," Rose said, studying Éliane. She hadn't treated Éliane any differently since the announcement of her pregnancy. She hadn't said, *a German child*, as if the life in Éliane's belly were the most appalling thing in the whole appalling city of Paris.

"The baby has started to move," Éliane said, letting herself smile just like she had the previous night when she'd felt a wave of motion beneath her skin. How she had wanted to tell someone, but Luc had been in a drunken stupor. And she wasn't sure she would have told him anyway, because she didn't want to hear him say again: *How can you bear it?*

Rose smiled too and Éliane wondered how the Nazis could be so blind as to not see her, to not see how extraordinary she was. Day after meticulous day, recording detail after detail, serving art with the diligence that few granted their masters.

"I'm knitting the baby a bonnet," Rose said. "And booties. It will still be so cold when it's born."

"But…" Éliane tried to protest. The only way to get wool was to unravel a garment you already owned. Rose was giving up her own sweater, her own knitted scarf, in order that the baby be warm.

Rose was already walking away, scolding Éliane. "Take out the rubbish. It's a mess in here."

Éliane hid her own smile in the pile of papers she carried out to the garbage.

A fortnight or so later, Éliane heard that König was returning. So, the following day, she wore the navy dress with the long sleeves that had once been her finest dress and was now almost worn out. But it showed off the slight curve of her stomach. Once at the Jeu de Paume, she saw König's eyes flicker over her as she took his hand and placed it on her belly, pretending it was Xavier's hand.

"The baby has started to move," she told him too, summoning up a smile.

His hand stroked her stomach.

"You've been so busy." She drew away as if she were concerned about taking up his time rather than wanting his hand off her.

"I'm never too busy for you."

"Have you been doing more important things for the Reichsmarschall?" she asked, eyes wide, feigning awe at his power.

König put his head through the door, turning it from side to side, and Éliane said, "I saw your uncle leave to take a walk with Mademoiselle Putz. They won't return for some time."

"Then I can show you my masterpiece." König walked over to the chiffonier, slid out the cornice and withdrew the catalog, which he must have returned to its hiding place.

And even though she had already seen the catalog and knew what was written inside it, she still had difficulty containing her excitement at the fact that König was now trusting her so much that he would voluntarily show her something so secret. She'd been right to tell him the baby was his. Now she would find out what she needed to know, what Xavier had told her not to pursue. How could she not take advantage of an opportunity like this, an opportunity to save them from further betrayals? If Xavier had been given such an opportunity, he would use it.

She'd told König that sex would harm the baby and, being unschooled in all things to do with women, he'd believed her, so she wasn't concerned about where caresses or kisses might lead. But she only had that protection for a few months. If she didn't use it, she was a coward.

König turned the first page of the catalog and she saw the familiar names of artists and artworks, and the photographs of each painting, and a new column: one detailing which room in Göring's manor the work was destined for. "I've been helping the Reichsmarschall plan how to display his collection so we're ready when we retrieve everything from storage. You should see his house. Everything fine and rare and valuable is gathered there. He even has two lions."

Two lions. Who had Göring stolen those from? He must have to feed them the same pills he swallowed himself to keep them from savaging him; surely lions could smell evil? Éliane kept those thoughts hidden as she ran a finger over König's precise handwriting. "This is all your work?" she asked.

"It is."

The pride in his voice was almost too much for her. She made herself turn the page, jaw throbbing from the effort it took to keep the smile on her face. "It's a masterpiece," she said, leaning in closer to him. "It's been so nice this past month. No exhibitions. Rose is back. I like it when everything is calm. I hope nothing will happen to upset the peace."

"I don't know of anything that will," he whispered into her ear and she held on to him because she needed still more.

"I'm so glad. And happy you have people who tell you things like that. Important men always seem to know how to get information."

"Well," he admitted, pride creeping back into his voice, "my uncle used to take care of that. But now I do."

Éliane turned over more pages of the catalog, letting her eyes record details from entries she knew were not in the notebooks she and Rose kept. "How do you even find people like that?"

"They usually find us," König said. "They want money, of course. They think that gives them the power they've lost or have never had. It's often the people you'd least expect. Although some of them are quieter now they think the Allies—" He stopped himself, unwilling, like all Germans, to admit that the tide was turning.

Von Behr's laugh echoed down the hall. "I should go," Éliane said. "I enjoyed talking to you. With Elke here, we don't have the chance to do this enough."

She kissed his cheek and left the office, turning over what he'd said.

* * *

She was still turning it over the following week as the year turned too, into 1944, and she had just three months more of keeping her child safely inside her.

"I have something for you." König's voice interrupted Éliane's thoughts as she entered her office. "I need to give it to you in private."

Éliane froze. Private meetings with König were not what she wanted. She thought quickly. "There's a bench in the Jardins that is private."

He looked as though he were about to insist on another location but she could see his mind considering and discarding options: the brasserie was far from private; his home likewise; the museum was a zoo of people. "Tonight. After work," he said, smiling as if he were excited at the prospect of both this meeting and this gift.

What would it be? Not a key to an apartment for trysts after the baby was born. Éliane shuddered.

At the end of the day, she dragged herself through the cold to the park bench where she often met Rose. König was there already, bundled up in Nazi-issue long wool coat, scarf, leather gloves, cap, and thick, new boots. Éliane wore the fur coat, grateful now for the fact that rations meant her entire body was smaller than it ought to be and thus, even with the pregnancy, she could still tug the coat—or what was left of it—over her belly. Her stocking-less legs felt as if the cold had frozen her blood and she wished she could stop her teeth from chattering. König noticed none of it or, if he did, he chose not to lavish her with clothes and food and other items that would make her grow strong; he preferred to keep her weak and powerless, she thought now with a frown.

She sat down beside him and he wrapped an arm around her shoulders, drawing her in. Rose walked past, not looking at them but Éliane knew she would take up a position nearby in case Éliane needed her afterward.

König placed a large wrapped package on her lap. It couldn't possibly be a key. It felt like Pandora's box and Éliane didn't want to let out whatever lay enfolded within the pink tissue paper.

She untied the ribbon slowly.

The paper fell away and there, in Éliane's hands, were two people wrapped together forever. It was one of Luc's paintings from the Salle des Martyrs, the first one she'd seen at the museum. *Les Amoureux*: the painting with moon and sky. The couple in the world, not the couple without world.

"I was told you like the painting," König said, almost making Éliane stiffen but she caught herself in time.

Who had told König she liked the painting?

She stared at the oils swirled into colors beneath her hands and saw only questions. Who? Whoever it was had confused the paintings. Or didn't know that the other, the one Éliane preferred, was in the Salle des Martyrs too.

"I cannot accept this, Monsieur. If von Behr finds out I have it, he will kill me. He'll think I stole it."

"You cannot refuse a gift," König said. "If you don't tell my uncle, then he won't know. I can give you anything."

To anyone listening, König's tone might have sounded self-congratulatory. But all of Éliane's blood froze now. Perhaps he meant bouquets of edelweiss, paintings, protection. But if he could give her those, he could also give her a jail cell, an interrogation, a death sentence for having a stolen painting in her possession.

There was more to this painting than simply a gift.

It was König's insurance. Or his blackmail.

But what did he want from her?

She stood up. "Thank you," she said, knowing she had to accept it. "I'm so lucky. You've always done so much for me. I won't forget it."

A useless threat when set against his. He kissed her goodbye the way a man kissed a woman he wanted. She let him.

Finally, she was allowed to walk home, one hand resting on her child, the most innocent thing in a wicked world. Under her arm she carried the painting, the most dangerous thing in a dangerous world.

* * *

Not long after, in the early morning before work and with Luc at Les Halles searching for food for the brasserie, Éliane waited in her apartment, eyes fixed on the door and on the clock. If her sister didn't come soon, Éliane would have to leave for the museum. But there wouldn't be time to do this later and still make it to the brasserie for the evening service.

At last her focus on the door was rewarded by the appearance of Angélique, who ran to her. Éliane took her into her arms the way she'd always done—as if she were Angélique's mother.

"It's König's child," Éliane said quickly, as Angélique's hand circled delightedly over her stomach.

"Hello, little baby," Angélique said. The baby replied with a decided kick. "You're a feisty thing!" She looked up at Éliane, whose eyes were as full as Angélique's own. "I can't believe Luc didn't tell me."

"He doesn't wish to be uncle to a Nazi-child."

"But it isn't—"

Éliane shook her head. "Hush. I'll be late for work if we talk about the baby. I need you to take these to Montal. A woman called Madame Mercier will come to collect them from you. She's going to hide them in Xavier's house in Saint-Jean-Cap-Ferrat."

Éliane handed Angélique Luc's painting, the envelope filled with the money Xavier had given her, her engagement ring, and the title deed and key to the house in Saint-Jean-Cap-Ferrat.

"Of course. But..." Angélique stared at the picture. "Where did you get that? If König or von Behr found you with it..."

"König gave it to me."

"König gave it to you," Angélique repeated slowly. "He means to use it then."

"I'm sure he does. Perhaps as some kind of insurance to do with the child."

Éliane saw her sister's eyes rest on the artist's name in the bottom right corner. "Luc painted it?" Angélique asked, her disbelief as obvious as Éliane's rounded stomach.

"His name is on it. And he told us he sold a painting to the Rothschilds."

Éliane could see doubt in her sister's eyes.

Angélique sat down, gaze fixed on the painting, but it was as if she were looking at something else entirely. A frown marked her brow, a pucker tightened her mouth.

Éliane stared too and, as she did, she recalled something that she should have noticed at the time—but she had been too distracted by the tumult of her feelings for Xavier. On the beach at Saint-Jean-Cap-Ferrat, Xavier had said to her, *The painting of the couple, Luc's painting, the one in the Salle des Martyrs. Always have that in your mind. Whenever you need to breathe, slide into the painting and be the woman* with nothing at all around her...

The woman with nothing at all around her.

Xavier had seen Éliane back in 1941 with the other painting, the one of the couple backdropped by sky and moon—the one they used to pass notes to one another. He had never seen her looking at the painting of the couple with nothing at all around them. So how did he know it existed? She supposed he could have seen it in the Salle des Martyrs too, but she had hidden it in a dark corner of the room to keep it safe...

Then Angélique spoke, interrupting Éliane's train of thought before it could reach a destination. "I tried to find out which maquisard Luc had discovered to be the traitor—the one who'd told the Nazis about the pilot hiding at Montal. I wanted to know if I should have seen their deceit for myself; if I'd somehow been guilty of betrayal by ignorance. But none of my Maquis knew who it was—nobody had disappeared."

Éliane could sense the minutes ticking past on the clock, knew she would never be on time for work, had no idea what her sister was driving at but she also knew that she could not leave now; that whatever it was, Angélique wanted her to hear it.

Angélique's pause went on and on. Then she said, in a strange segue,

"You know I see Luc from time to time when he's in the countryside passing on messages to the Resistance. The Maquis all think he's a hero. They call him d'Artagnan. I'm sure it strokes his already good-sized ego. They call him that because he brings them money, coffee, meat, guns, wine. I wish he gave you some of that money for food."

Éliane was now so still she could be a painting, a Madonna, no, a *Mona Lisa*: one thing on the surface but something else entirely beneath her skin.

"Last time I saw Monsieur Jaujard," Angélique added, as carefully as if the words were tiptoeing from her mouth, "I said how lucky we were that the Allies were sending him so much money for Luc to pass on to the Resistance. It boosts their morale no end. But Monsieur Jaujard said he hadn't given Luc any money from the Allies."

Angélique met Éliane's eyes for the first time since she'd sat down. "I asked Luc about it and he said he'd done a special deal on coffee and meat for the brasserie and he had too much even for the *Boche*. That coffee was the least he could give to a group of men who'd been waiting and hoping and preparing to fight since 1940. I told him his need to be adored would get us all into trouble—why risk stealing coffee meant for the Germans in the brasserie? Because that's what I thought it must be; that his love of being idolized was behind it all."

And what do you think now? The question, mute though it was, must have been expressed in Éliane's eyes because Angélique said, "I don't know."

THIRTY-ONE

Éliane waited, with an impatience that was almost impossible to disguise, for the Germans to leave the museum for their two-hour lunch. Then she hurried up to the Salle des Martyrs and stretched her arm into the dark corner where she had hidden *L'Amour*: the painting of Love. She took a step back and studied each element of the picture, her eyes always returning to the expressions on the faces of the couple and the woman's hair, which was especially fine work. Then she moved closer, examining the brushwork, the layering of the paint.

How had she not realized it sooner?

When she had first seen the other painting in this pair, she had been heartbroken and furious at Xavier. She'd had no wish to recall his style as an artist. Besides, Luc's name was on the first and the second was so similar, there had been no reason to think they weren't his.

But now...

All she knew for certain was that she'd once told Luc she liked the painting König had given her. And she'd said that to Luc before she knew that the one in front of her now—the one she preferred—existed. She hadn't mentioned the second painting to Luc because he'd responded so coldly to her praise of the first. But he had never mentioned a second painting to her either.

She needed to speak to her brother.

It was a long day at the Jeu de Paume and an even longer shift at the brasserie and she wasn't able to say anything until she and Luc were cleaning up at the end of the night. "The painting you sold to the Rothschilds, the one in the Jeu de Paume," she began, making her words sound conversational rather than urgent.

She waited to see if he would say, *Which one? I sold him two almost the same.*

He only yawned exaggeratedly.

"I was trying to remember which of your many *amours* was the subject of the painting," she tried again. "Was it Louise?"

"God knows." Luc pulled the cork out of a bottle of wine and poured himself a glass, his usual means of avoiding conversations.

"I can't remember all of them by name." He drank deeply, then moved to turn off the lights.

"Will I see you upstairs?" Éliane said, smiling the same way she smiled at König and praying that her brother would say no.

Luc shook his head and left. "I have more work to do."

And the only thing Éliane knew for sure was that her brother was a liar. But what exactly was he lying about? And what work was he doing that night?

We should look for anyone who suddenly seems to have more money or power than they ought, Rose had said. Luc had no money. How then had he afforded guns and cash for the Maquis?

They want money, of course, König had said. *They think that gives them the power they've lost or have never had.*

Like money, power was something Luc had rarely had. Except with his artists' models and for that one brief moment when he'd sold a painting to Rothschild and their father had called him maestro, garlanding the word with pride.

She had always thought that, in trying to save art, Luc had had art taken from him. But what if he had never really had art? What if he had had only the life of an artist: the fringe benefits of artists' models and artistic society?

No. She was wrong. Luc would never...

She cut off the thought, hurried upstairs to the apartment and took out the painting König had given her—the one she'd meant to give to Angélique that morning and had instead told her sister she'd bring to Monsieur Jaujard's later that night.

For there was something more that bothered her. She'd seen, in the records at the Jeu de Paume, that this one, *Les Amoureux*, had been bought, as she knew, by Rothschild in September 1939. The second, *L'Amour*—Éliane's favorite, the one still in the museum—had been purchased in June 1940, not long before the Rothschild family had fled France.

Why hadn't Luc simply sold Rothschild both paintings at the same time?

She lay down on her bed, closed her eyes and placed her hands on her stomach. "Perhaps it doesn't matter," she whispered to her baby, talking to it as she often did alone in her room at night. It rippled in response and she stroked the place where it had moved.

And perhaps it *didn't* matter. There had been no more betrayals. Even if one of the six had let slip some small pieces of information to the Germans in exchange for money—money for guns for the Maquis? Maybe that made it all right?—they had done nothing further. She had imagined that, with the Allied victories in North Africa and the landings in Italy, the traitor thought the Allies were coming and there wasn't anything more to gain by selling information to the Germans. That perhaps the consequences of his or her actions—one dead Louvre guard at Montal—had been more than they had reckoned on and they had rediscovered their conscience.

She should forget all about it. The baby kicked her again.

Had the money been, not just for guns, but for power and adulation too?

Her hands pushed her up off the bed. She took out the bottle of solvent she'd stolen from the Jeu de Paume, tore a scrap of fabric from her bedsheets, doused it, then daubed it onto the paint in the top left corner of the painting. As the paint dissolved, a layer of titanium white was revealed. That wasn't unusual: canvases were expensive and most artists painted over old ones, using the white to obscure a work they knew they couldn't sell or didn't want.

She rubbed harder and what she saw made her want to cry. Under the titanium white was a word beginning with the letters *Xa*—and it was written in the same place where Xavier had always signed his paintings.

This canvas had been Xavier's. And while there was a small chance he had given it to Luc to paint over and reuse, knowing his financial straits, there was also another possibility.

Luc had never painted anything on this canvas. The work was Xavier's. As must be the other painting still in the Salle des Martyrs.

Xavier had given Luc the painting, made the introduction to the Rothschilds and pretended it wasn't his own work. He had done that for Luc, and thus for Éliane.

Luc had been nothing and Xavier had been everything, always.

She sat down on the bed, her legs no longer steady.

If anyone had told her a year ago that she would not be able to cry when she found out her brother was a traitor, she would not have believed them. But her eyes could summon up only a dry-eyed emptiness born of shock.

She wanted to close them against everything she had just learned. But pretense was the domain of cowards and she would leave that to Luc. For the more she thought about it, the more the appalling questions presented themselves, demanding she consider the answers.

For instance: how had Luc come by the second painting, the

masterpiece of the entwined couple that was still in custody at the museum? In June 1940 when Rothschild had bought it, Xavier had already left Paris.

The gallery on the Rue La Boétie had not been packed up. Xavier's paintings were still at the gallery. Luc had known that.

It could only mean that her brother had broken in and stolen his friend's work, sold, it and kept the money for himself.

How can you bear it? Luc had said.

Now, if he said that to her, she would ask him: *How can you?*

* * *

It was half an hour before curfew. Éliane turned the painting over and wrote some letters on the back—her own code, just like the *Mona Lisa*'s back in 1939. She wasn't entirely sure why she felt the need to do this, except that it was important to record who the painting truly belonged to, in case—

She didn't let herself finish the thought.

She covered the painting in a shawl and took it to Angélique not mentioning her suspicions. If she did, then who knew what Angélique would do—and what Luc would then do to her. Éliane would only give voice to her fears if Luc did something else to hurt them. It was better and safer for everyone to simply rejoice that the traitor had stopped, better to do nothing to give him cause to start up again.

Luc had the adoration and devotion of the Maquis to make up for women like Louise no longer idolizing him. It should be enough to get them through.

So she let her sister kiss her stomach and ask, "Do you think the baby will be like Yolande?" and Éliane nodded and said only, "Yes, I do," because Angélique's whole family had been taken from her and Éliane was all she had left.

* * *

In mid-February, Éliane's pregnancy began to offend von Behr and she was forced to take leave from the Jeu de Paume. It meant she couldn't work at the brasserie either, and thus she didn't see Xavier at all. Then in late March, two weeks before she was due to give birth, Rose appeared on Éliane's doorstep with a valise.

"I'm staying until the baby's born," Rose said. "You can't be here alone."

At that, Éliane sat at the table and wept. She was alone most of the time now. Luc went out after the brasserie had closed and often didn't come home. She couldn't go to meetings at Monsieur Jaujard's as she couldn't move quickly through the streets. She knew Xavier had insisted they not meet at her apartment so that no one put the baby in jeopardy. So Éliane was usually by herself in the two rooms of the apartment that she hadn't closed off to keep the scant heat in. But now she had Rose.

Rose sat beside her, took a book out of her purse, opened it, and began to read aloud in a soft and gentle voice, the kind one would use with a child. *Il était une fois un gentilhomme qui épousa, en secondes noces, une femme, la plus hautaine et la plus fière qu'on eût jamais vue.*

Cendrillon, the story of a young woman who married her prince. The baby squirmed in response.

Éliane wiped her face. She had given too many tears to this war already. The baby needed more than sadness. A story of love fulfilled, of sacrifice rewarded, of evil vanquished was the right kind of nourishment. "Thank you," she said to Rose.

"You're interrupting the story," Rose scolded, but then she smiled and Éliane did too.

A week later, a terrible pain gripped Éliane's belly. It took all night and the following day too, so many hours and so much pain. Éliane's body shook and shivered with the force of it. She was unable to cry tears now, able only to cry out again and again before subsiding for too short a time into a curled-up ball on the bed as she tried to save the energy she didn't possess. She looked down at her arms wrapped around her belly and saw that they were almost as thin as twelve-year-old Jacqueline's had once been.

The apartment blurred to blackness and she thought the candles had gone out. She tried to say Rose's name but her mouth wouldn't work. Nausea was the only thing that roused her, that and Rose pressing a damp cloth to her forehead, frowning. There was no point trying to find a doctor in Paris in 1944.

"I will do everything I can to make sure you stay awake," Rose said. "Even if it means singing '*La Marseillaise*' to you."

Éliane reached out for Rose's hand and held on as the pain crested once more.

Finally, after an almost endless twenty-four hours, the last moments of which she couldn't recall at all, she found a bundle in her arms. The bundle nuzzled its head against her chest and she understood that both she and the baby had somehow survived. And that the baby was hungry. She managed a tiny laugh.

"You're not like Yolande," she whispered, for it was a little boy. "Hopefully Angélique won't be too disappointed."

She kissed his cheek, then her son fixed his eyes on her and the shock of love was devastating, a heart-stopping blow she knew she would never recover from. That something so strong and so magnificent could emerge from war. And she understood for the first time that whatever was most truly part of a person's soul was the thing that took them over at the darkest of moments. Xavier had sculpted her soul, and now her son would too.

She sank back against the pillows and gave her son her breast. He fed as if he were starving. Firelight and warmth leapt up all around as

Rose piled wooden crates into the grate, crates she had asked König for, explaining to him that Éliane needed heat.

Éliane watched the baby feed, his dear face, his tiny hand on her skin, his closed eyes and concentrated expression. The wash of dark hair on his head. It was impossible not to cry.

"I'm going to call him Alexandre," she told Rose.

"Do you think that's wise?" Rose asked quietly, and Éliane understood that she, like Angélique had guessed.

"König will never connect the two names." She wanted so desperately to ask and she had made herself not ask anything for the two months she'd been shut up in the apartment. "Is…" She faltered. "Is Xavier…"

"The story is that he's in Switzerland buying art. That he'll be gone for at least a month. He's in London, though. He says it's getting closer."

Éliane's eyes squeezed shut. It was getting closer—but would it be liberation or conflagration? Xavier would be busier than ever. When would he see his child? And who would win? If the Germans did, they would finally take everything from the *Mona Lisa* to the tiniest amulet—victory would enable them in ways that a mere armistice had not.

Rose leaned over and stroked Alexandre's hair. "He's beautiful, of course. I could sit here all day and watch you with him. But," she frowned, "I have to go to the museum. Will you be all right? And shall I tell König?"

"I suppose you'd better. But tell him I'm not up to visitors."

Two hours later, the most extravagant bouquet of edelweiss arrived. Éliane left it on the table to die.

Luc came upstairs briefly, bringing her food and kissing his nephew, before he left to open the brasserie. Éliane stayed in bed with her baby, watching him sleep, watching him snuffle and snort and sigh. She studied his delicate eyelids fringed with Xavier's dark lashes, his little round mouth making shapes as he slept, the impossible delicacy of his painterly fingers. She learned her baby by heart that first night, almost as if some premonition told her she should.

Later, she bathed him, running her hand over his kicking legs, his miniature toes and she wept again because he was so small and precious and defenseless. He had only her and she didn't know if she would be enough.

THIRTY-TWO

É liane spent two days inside with the baby and then she knew she
had to go back out into the world, to buy food, to find more cloths
for nappies—she hadn't comprehended how many one small being
could use and they didn't dry quickly enough in the apartment without heat—she'd burned all the crates König had supplied. She hadn't a
perambulator of course, but over the last few months she'd seen many a
baby carried in slings fashioned from old sheets and that was what she
did now, tucking Alexandre securely and warmly against her chest. His
eyes flickered at her, then he sucked his lip and fell fast and pleasantly
asleep.

She walked with him around the corner to the Rue Saint-Honoré
and joined the queue of women at the boulangerie. Hours passed. She
fed Alexandre while she waited, but it wasn't as easy as it was at home
and he didn't seem to get enough; he awoke an hour later crying for
more.

She needed to change him but she couldn't lose her place in the queue.
So she lay one of the cloths she'd brought with her on the pavement and
placed him on top, outside in the early April cold. He howled the whole
time and she could see his skin turning blue from the wind that was as
brutal as any Nazi.

"Fräulein!"

Éliane's head whipped around, as did the heads of the other women in the queue. All of them, even though they'd simply been lining up for food, looked suddenly guilty and Éliane knew then, really knew, that she wasn't the only one doing something for Paris. Whether it be accidentally humming the "Marseillaise" in the food queue, or ironing a hole in a Nazi's jacket as König's laundress had once done, there were so many small acts of resistance in Paris that, one day, they must surely add up to something larger.

Then she realized that the person calling out was König and that he was heading straight for her.

"Is this my son?" he called delightedly, kissing her cheek.

The women in the queue hissed at her and one of them spat at Éliane's feet.

Shame made Éliane stagger. Would anyone ever believe, when—if—this was all over, that she'd been trying to do the right thing?

"We need to go," Éliane said to König. "I won't be able to queue for bread tomorrow."

He looked around at the hostile faces of the women as if he suddenly understood and allowed her to lead him away.

"I can bring you food. Here is some chocolate." He passed her a useless package—she needed meat. "Surely you take food from the restaurant?"

"There's nothing left to take," Éliane said. "You and your friends eat it all. There's been no meat in Paris at all this month."

König waved a hand in the air and she knew he had no idea how a Parisienne lived. "I came to see the child."

She had no choice but to take him to her apartment. If she let him coo over her child in the street, she would likely have stones thrown at her.

He followed her up the winding stairs and, as she opened the door, she saw the apartment as he must. Tiny. The doors to the bedrooms closed, all life happening in two rooms that were furnished with only a sofa, her mattress on the floor as she couldn't heat the bedroom, and a table and four chairs—Éliane had burned all the furniture for heat over the last winter. The window fitted with its compulsory blackout curtain, no other adornments as she'd had to take down the drapes and use them for rags for herself. Those rags hung from the line beside Alexandre's nappies. That morning, they had seemed like fluttering white angels' wings. Now she saw that they were all still faintly and rankly stained, despite the washing. The smell of baby, that beautiful milky smell, was strong and close after the fresh air outside.

König wrinkled his nose. "You can't live here," he said, dropping into a chair.

"I need to feed the baby," Éliane said.

König's eyes were suddenly everywhere, not knowing what to fix on. "I'll wait over there."

He walked to the window, to Xavier's place, and Éliane tried not to think that König had seen Alexandre before Xavier had. She sat down, unbuttoned her blouse and let her son have his fill.

It didn't take long for König to drift back to the table, watching until Alexandre collapsed into sleep and let go of her nipple, leaving her breast bare for König to see. His eyes widened, his skin flushed and Éliane tried so quickly to cover herself that she accidentally knocked Alexandre, who mewled. That König still saw her as desirable was a blow. She'd hoped his affection would wane, that his wife, who was available for his attentions, would seem easier to love.

"You must return to work tomorrow," König said, eyes on her fingers closing each of her buttons.

"I have the baby to look after," Éliane said dismissively.

"The baby will stay with my wife while you're at work," König said without hesitation, as if it were something he'd thought much about. "There's too much work for Madame Valland and there's no time to train someone new."

Éliane clutched Alexandre so tightly she had to remind herself how delicate he was. "But I have to feed him."

"You'll feed the baby at my apartment before you leave him in the morning. Elke will bring him to you at lunchtime. My apartment is warm. My son should be kept warm," König said, in the manner of von Behr. "You will have the baby each evening, and on the weekends. And I will be able to see you each day."

What had she done? She should never have said that the baby was König's.

It was two months until summer—surely the Allies were coming. And surely Xavier would be back soon.

* * *

Every morning Éliane walked to König's apartment. She sat on a padded green armchair and fed Alexandre while König looked on and his wife watched König watching Éliane. Then Elke would take Alexandre from her and he would start to mewl at first, as if he expected to be rescued by his mother, and then to cry and Éliane would steel herself not to seize her child from Elke and run out the door.

The days went on like that until one morning in May, as the sun began to take precedence in the sky, König said, "I've spoken to Elke. She's agreed that you should live with us as the baby's nursemaid. Your apartment is…" His face twisted with distaste. "Intolerable. You will much prefer a large room of your own adjoining the child's, at our apartment. Elke understands my needs and is prepared to accommodate them."

His needs. How the cracking and crumbling of the Nazi landscape over these last few months had altered people. Von Behr raged more; it strengthened in him all the vices he'd always possessed. But in König, it had fostered qualities he'd never known how to use. Even last year, he would never have spoken to her so boldly of his needs.

Éliane studied the pavement as if she were embarrassed. "But I'm not…available now for your needs…I'm still bleeding from the birth."

Her last words were a tiny whisper. They had reached the museum and Éliane dragged her hungry, bleeding body up the steps. Her breasts ached for her son.

König looked half-embarrassed, and half-revolted. "I will give you time, of course," he said curtly to cover his ignorance. "Surely that doesn't last forever?" He sounded so stricken now that Éliane, had she been in any other circumstance, might have laughed.

"No," she said. "Nothing lasts forever. But for some time yet." It was a lie, but still. She doubted König would ask anyone for particulars.

"You must still come to live with us," he said. "We can commence... the other when you're ready."

* * *

König was not at the apartment when Éliane arrived the following day. Elke didn't speak, other than to say good morning. She sat and watched the ritual feeding with troubled eyes, her fixed gaze tightening every muscle in Éliane's body so that her milk did not let down easily and Alexandre fidgeted and fussed. She tried to calm the tension, otherwise Alexandre would be hungry again before Elke came to the museum at lunchtime, but the fear only wound around her like a noose.

Alexandre had begun, over the last few days, to complain less when Éliane handed him to Elke and it was the same that morning. When the baby was safely in her arms, Elke smiled and she looked almost beautiful. That a child could do that. Make a woman Éliane hated become, suddenly, a woman in love with a baby, just as Éliane was.

Elke looked up and Éliane didn't have time to shift her eyes away.

"He is happy when you're not here," Elke said.

Éliane flinched but Elke held on to Éliane's eyes. "I love him," Elke said. "You think I'm not capable, and that my husband isn't capable. We are humans too."

Of the worst kind. Éliane only just stopped herself from saying it.

"I'm trying to take away one of your worries," Elke said, voice low. "Alexandre cries very little—only as much as any baby would—when you're at the museum. Nothing happens here that is bad for him."

Alexandre did not spend the day fretting. Perhaps Éliane was not damaging her child. Perhaps it was just like her own mother leaving Éliane and her siblings with the woman in the next apartment until Éliane was old enough to care for them.

If only Éliane could think of Elke as a woman caring for a child, rather than a Nazi's wife. But she would never think of Elke like that. Ernst König's wife was not capable of loving anything the way a mother should.

Elke touched her arm. "I know you don't feel for Ernst what he feels for you."

Éliane froze, staring at her son, the only thing in the room that gave her any strength. She had eaten a bowl of soup yesterday from the brasserie, the last of the broth left in the pot, most of the vegetables gone, a piece of fat the only meat remaining. Rose had found a carrot in the vegetable gardens of the Louvre and made her eat it for lunch, and a potato to take home. Luc had put it into the soup for the Nazis.

"Your husband is…" Éliane searched blindly for words. The room darkened at the edges; her skin was damp, clammy with sweat. Hunger crawled like ants inside her belly. She would not faint in front of Elke. She'd do it outside on the pavement instead and hope nobody from the neighborhood recognized her as a Nazi's mistress and spat on her.

"I understand, now, how things work," Elke said. "You don't want my advice but I'll give it to you anyway. It's the only thing you can't throw away the minute you leave the apartment. You won't break Ernst's heart. The one with all the power never has their heart broken."

Something like water glimmered in Elke's eyes. She nuzzled her face onto the top of Alexandre's head. When she looked back up at Éliane, the shine had gone. "It will take me at least a fortnight to furnish a room for you. It's so hard to find things in Paris now. I've told Ernst it won't be ready until June sixth. That should give you some time to decide what to do."

What to do. Elke still thought Éliane had a choice.

Éliane stepped out into a street where sun shone so brightly it was almost offensive, a showgirl's costume clothing a vagrant. She let herself sit on the step for a moment, head resting on her knees until the darkness at the edges of her vision cleared and her skin cooled and the hunger curled into a fist that sat unmoving in her belly. Then she dragged herself to her feet and walked to the Jeu de Paume, Elke's words—*The one with all the power never has their heart broken*—making her own eyes glimmer now.

Elke had no power either. And it broke her heart too.

"Don't let me pity her," Éliane whispered. Hate was single-minded and of the head; pity a splinter in an already injured heart.

* * *

The last week of May dragged its muddied hem along the sidewalks of a city that had forgotten spring. Winter seemed to lurk everywhere still, in the gray and hungry faces, in the unswept paths, in the absence of birds, all scorched by fire and bombs. She received one note from Xavier, who was still in London, smuggled to her by Angélique. It was brief and impersonal as it needed to be, but her soul needed the forever and the intimate.

On June sixth, Éliane walked despairingly to König's apartment. In a stroke of fortune, he wasn't there to accompany her to work. Elke took Alexandre from Éliane, saying not a word; in fact Elke was the one who looked like winter now and Éliane assumed it was because Elke thought she would lose her husband to his lover that night.

At the museum, the Luftwaffe guard stood with guns in hand rather than shouldered. They not only checked her Ausweis and her purse but patted her down, hands lingering on her body—not one guard but two. Éliane closed her eyes and imagined herself in the painting with Xavier, without backdrop, nothing at all in the world besides the two of them. And Alexandre. She drew him into the painting too.

"Straight to your desk, Mademoiselle," the guard snapped, finishing his inspection by prodding her with a gun.

When she stepped inside and saw the faces of the historians, faces just like Elke's, she realized something had happened. Then König came to find her, and she finally understood.

"It is a terrible day," he said, voice low. "The British and the Americans have landed on a beach in Normandy."

He said the words Éliane had been waiting to hear for four long years. The room whirled, the faintness almost overtook her and she only just managed to collapse into a chair rather than the floor. "Landed," she whispered.

"I'm a clod!" König cried. "To tell you that without warning. Here." He handed her a glass of water.

Only then did she realize she'd almost given herself away and that she was very lucky König had thought her reaction was fear and disbelief rather than a joy so shocking she almost couldn't endure it.

She made herself touch his arm, made herself say, "Will you be all right, Monsieur? And your uncle?"

König leaned his forehead against hers, placed his hands on her shoulders and sobbed. He cried like Alexandre: helplessly, unstoppably.

She let the tears of his horror fall onto her face.

The sound of movement at last made him stand up and pull away. "I'm sorry," he said.

"I understand," Éliane said, because she did. He should cry. He should weep. He should howl and snivel and bawl. He should be afraid.

* * *

A fortnight later, with verifiable news of what was happening in Normandy almost impossible to come by, and with the plan for Éliane to move into König's apartment thankfully on hold due to the invasion, Éliane pushed open the door of her apartment to find someone waiting for her. Angélique!

Angélique scooped her nephew up in her arms and covered his face with kisses. He wriggled about, screwing up his face at first and then submitting to the barrage of love.

Angélique looked at Éliane and they both smiled in a way they hadn't smiled since they were children. Freely, ecstatically.

"Invasion," Éliane whispered.

Angélique nodded. "The Maquis are armed and ready for when the Allies make their way off the beaches and start to move through France. Liberation is coming, I promise." She stroked Alexandre's cheek. "In the meantime, I don't know if I can give him back."

"Looking after Yolande didn't cure you forever of taking care of children?"

"Yolande was never this good."

Angélique laughed, and Éliane did too, holding on to her sister, who held on to the baby. Alexandre smiled at them both as if he wished he could laugh too.

But of course the joy was short-lived.

Rose and Monsieur Jaujard stole into the apartment with somber faces. Éliane steeled herself as she tucked Alexandre into a dresser drawer she'd fashioned into a makeshift crib. Then she asked, "What's happened?"

"We've been asked to provide an estimate of the cubic footage of the Musées Nationaux artworks stored at the depots," Monsieur Jaujard said starkly.

"But why…" Éliane stopped before she finished the question. The only reason for wanting to know how much space the country's collection of artworks occupied was so it could be moved somewhere.

"They want to take everything," Monsieur Jaujard finished.

Mona Lisa. Winged Victory of Samothrace. The entirety of French culture and thus the French people's heart so they had no spirit with which to fight back.

"We had planned to work very slowly on the calculations," Angélique explained, "hoping liberation would come first. But one of my messages to Monsieur was picked up from one of our mail drops. Luckily I'd made it sound as if I were simply too stupid to calculate such things and it wasn't very incriminating. But if they know where one of our mail drops is located…" *Then they were only one step away from discovering everything.*

"How?" Éliane met her sister's eyes. The sound of footsteps ascending the staircase had them both turning toward the door.

"Perhaps the Allied invasion has made the Germans put pressure on their old informant," Monsieur Jaujard said. "The Nazis need information more than ever now and they're likely to lean on anyone they think might bend…"

But Éliane wasn't listening. She was watching her brother walk into the room, hardly hearing Rose add, "Actions like this mean the Nazis are worried. The Allies must be winning at Normandy. They're coming, surely."

"When?" Luc's tone was savage. "We've been saying for months that they're coming. And do you really believe Hitler will give up now, just because a few English and American soldiers are fighting his armies on a little beach in Normandy?"

Right then and there, almost four years of wrath, everything Éliane had swallowed, erupted from her. "Where is the man who told me he was going to fight? Where is the man who said he wasn't a painter anymore? Now you're neither painter nor fighter. What are you?"

What are you? The question hung in the air for many long seconds as Luc and Éliane stood facing one another across the table.

She felt her hands shaking with fury, knew she had to somehow take hold of herself, that she had to be very careful not to push Luc too far. It couldn't all fall apart now.

Luc spoke dully. "What am I? I'm a man who can hardly tell right from wrong anymore. Not in this city of people who bow to the Germans one day but who now pull out their tricolor flags in readiness for the English. I'm a man whose sister has a German baby, something that was supposed to have been done for the right reasons but I've almost forgotten what those reasons were."

Éliane almost sank into a chair. It *was* falling apart. Right here and right now in the apartment of her childhood with her brother on one side of a scratched and worn-out table and her sister on the other.

He's not as strong as you. Angélique's words from a long time ago sounded in her head. Éliane hadn't believed it then but now she did. Éliane had Xavier and Alexandre to make her strong. Luc had no one. Except Éliane. She had to give him the strength he needed.

Find his heart, she told herself. *It's in there somewhere.* Otherwise, she could hear in his voice that whatever adulation the Maquis had given him, it wouldn't be enough this time.

"Do you remember," Éliane said quietly, "when we stood at the bottom of the staircase at the Louvre and watched the *Winged Victory of Samothrace* carried downstairs?"

Luc didn't respond at first, and then he nodded.

She pressed on, seizing the small advantage. "Do you remember that everyone held their breath in case she fell? Why did we do that? What does it matter if we lose a hunk of stone, or chip a piece of marble? What would Paris be without her *Winged Victory*, Luc? Think what Paris is now with only the gray of the Nazi uniforms, the brown of their boots, the never-ending shout of their Heil Hitlers. When *Victory* descended the staircase, we were scared but we were hopeful too—hopeful that she would make it unscathed. If she'd broken, every one of us there would have cried."

Angélique began to sob. Rose's cheeks were wet too and Monsieur Jaujard's eyes bloomed with tears.

Luc slid his back down the wall and sat on the floor.

"Art reminds us that there's a world opposite to this one we live in," Éliane continued resolutely, speaking as much for herself as anyone else, speaking to forget about Xavier and the son that he hadn't seen, as well as to Luc, the traitor in their midst. "Didn't Schiller say that Art is the daughter of freedom? When we stood together watching the *Winged Victory* we were all connected by something beyond ourselves. Art is all we have when words fail us, when mankind fails us, and when we each fail each other. If we don't save these works, we can't save ourselves."

"Hear, hear." It was Xavier's voice.

Éliane spun around.

THIRTY-THREE

Éliane was not aware of the others around the table repeating Xavier's words: *Hear, hear.* She simply stared at her love, her heart, her soul. Her Art.

Xavier stood frozen too, his eyes on the child sleeping in the dresser drawer by the window. Then he smiled at Éliane, a brilliant, beautiful smile and she couldn't stop the sudden press of her hand to her heart.

She knew why she hadn't seen him smile like that for so many years, knew why he hid it. Because Xavier in love was an artwork that had yet to be painted, an artwork that perhaps this cruel world did not deserve. If the Germans ever saw what she had just seen…

For the first time ever, she was truly frightened.

She stumbled across the room, landed in his arms and he held her there while she cried. She hardly saw Luc's flash of surprise, nor did she notice Angélique Monsieur and Madame's happiness. There was only Xavier.

After a long, long time, she lifted her head and realized the others had gone. She took Xavier's hand and led him across the room. He reached down, lifted up his son and held him against his chest, and Éliane started to cry all over again. Xavier stretched out his other arm and drew her in, leading her over to her bed. "I just want to lie beside you and our child," he said.

He lay the baby down so gently. Éliane lay down too, on one side of

Alexandre, Xavier on the other. His hand reached up to stroke his son's cheek. "What did you call him?"

"Alexandre."

Xavier's eyes glittered and he swallowed. "I love him already," he said, astonishment in his voice. "How must you feel?"

Éliane reached out to touch Xavier's hand, still resting on their son's cheek. "It's almost overwhelming," she confessed. "It's like a wildness, a savage instinct to do whatever I can for him. Except that," her voice dropped to the merest breath, "I don't. Instead I give him to König's wife every morning."

"Ellie," Xavier lifted his finger from Alexandre's cheek and stroked hers. "If you didn't..." He shuddered and, for the first time ever, he looked scared too. "What have I got us all into?"

Éliane wiped away the tear that had made its slow and desolate way down his cheek.

"It's not your fault," she said. "I was doing this before I knew you were too."

"Let me get you out," he said. "You and Alexandre."

Éliane shook her head. "Not now. If they've asked Monsieur to estimate the cubic feet of the artworks, then they'll also be planning something for all the pieces left in the Jeu de Paume. I have to help Rose. I've..." She faltered. "I've almost convinced myself that, later, Alexandre will understand why I didn't leave. Do you think he will?"

"Understand that his mother is the bravest woman in the world? He'll understand that," Xavier whispered.

It was his turn to stroke away a tear from her cheek.

Neither spoke. They watched one another, and they watched their baby sleep. If only they had one whole night. If only that precious, love-soaked silence could linger. But she knew Xavier had already stayed too long. She had to tell him, now. "König gave me one of the paintings from the Salle des Martyrs. The first of your paintings that Luc sold to the Rothschilds. I've had Madame Mercier hide it at Cap-Ferrat."

Xavier winced. "Are you angry that I gave it to Luc?"

She smiled. "How could I be angry with you for painting something so breathtaking? I could never be angry with you."

She threaded her fingers into his, resting their joined hands on their son's sleeping body. And, for all their sakes, she asked the next question. "How did Luc get the other painting? The one of just the couple? Did you give it to him to sell?"

He shook his head. "I left it in the gallery here in Paris when I returned to England. It hurt too much, back then, to look at it. Now I wish, more than anything, that I'd taken it with me."

Which meant Luc *had* stolen it from Xavier's gallery.

Éliane shut her eyes, not wanting to talk about that yet, wanting to stay in the moment of Xavier and his extraordinary paintings. "When did you paint them?"

Xavier shifted in closer to Alexandre and tightened his grip on Éliane's hand. "I painted the first one the day after we moved the art out of the Louvre. The day after we kissed for the first time. I painted the second one the night after you walked out of the hotel. I painted it as a promise to myself that what we had could survive anything. That I would one day be able to give the painting to you. In fact…" He paused and reached down, pulling an envelope from his trousers and passing it to her. "I wired Rothschild in America and asked if I could buy the paintings back from him. He said I could. Here's the bill of sale. Put it with the other papers. The paintings are both yours if…" He shook his head. "Not if. They're yours *when* we get the other one out of the Jeu de Paume."

"When this is all over and you and I and Alexandre live together at Cap-Ferrat." Éliane put the dream into words as if it were fact.

Then Xavier frowned, as if he had just understood the most important thing. "Why did König give you the painting?"

"I think he wants something to hold over me." She paused, then said it aloud for the first time. "The only person who could have told him I liked it is Luc."

Xavier closed his eyes as if it hurt too much to see the world. "You know it's him?"

Éliane nodded.

Xavier opened his eyes and fixed them on her. "I've had people watching him for months. A maquisard I trust. Lately, Angélique too. I'm watching him. I think he knows he's under suspicion. Which means I should get you out. And Angélique as well."

"I think that"—was she a fool to think this or was she right?—"if I go to London, there'll be nothing stopping him. Perhaps I'm stupid to believe this of someone who's deceived all of us but I hope that, if I stay, he'll only make small betrayals; he won't do anything to hurt me. Which means he won't hurt Angélique or Rose or Monsieur Jaujard. Or you. So I can't leave." Her voice cracked. "I'm the best insurance policy we have. He's always been closer to me than to anyone."

"No," Xavier said fiercely. "I can't let you take that on."

"But nor can you stop me," she said resolutely. "Just like I can't stop you from doing what you need to." She spoke over his protests. "Besides, it can't go on much longer now the Allies have landed," she added hopefully.

"It could still take months, Ellie. Months more of everything you're suffering now."

Months. It wasn't the news she'd hoped for. She touched a finger to his lips. "You need to leave soon. Let's talk about something else for these last five minutes."

"I love you," he said, stroking her face, fingertips painting love and beauty and hope over her skin and she drew it all inside her, needing it more than ever. "Tell me about our son."

"He's a hearty feeder," she said. "And he loves to be bathed so I do it every night and he smiles so much that I feel like I might shatter into a thousand pieces because I can't hold in me all the love. I have so much love for him..." Her voice trailed off.

"He has dark hair." Xavier pointed to the soft shadow on Alexandre's scalp.

"Like you," Éliane said. "And the bluest eyes. When he wakes, you can see them."

When he wakes, you'll be gone, Éliane thought but didn't say. *Let the fantasy continue. Let it never stop.*

"His eyelashes are so long," Xavier said, running a finger lightly across them.

"Like yours too," Éliane said, doing to Xavier what he had done to their son. "I've always loved your eyelashes. After the first time I saw you again in 1939 I dreamed about your eyes. How dark they were. And how your lashes half hid them. I thought you were the most handsome man I'd ever seen."

Xavier smiled a little, then leaned across their son and kissed her so deeply, one hand caressing her cheek, the other slipping into her hair. The kiss went on for so long, and Éliane knew why.

"It'll be a long time before I see you again, won't it?" she asked when he drew back.

He nodded. "I'll pass what messages I can through Angélique."

"Let's lie here for five more minutes," she whispered.

Alexandre slept peacefully between them, their hands on him, their eyes raveled together. In Xavier's, Éliane saw everything she didn't want to see, but everything she knew she must face.

"Goodbye," she said softly. "In case something happens to either of us and I…" *Never see you again.* She couldn't make herself say the words. "I have loved you so much, Xavier. I will always love you. No matter what happens. No one can take that away from us."

Xavier's sharp sob unleashed Éliane's tears. "There is nothing in this world," he said fiercely, "better or more beautiful than what we've made together. If Art is the daughter of freedom then our love is the antecedent of it all. Love like this is why freedom matters, and what art celebrates and I'm so lucky to have had this, Éliane." He stopped, eyes a brilliant black, a starry night, a constellation that was hers alone. "I adore you," he said hoarsely. "And Alexandre. It will take more than Nazis to destroy that."

He pressed his lips onto Alexandre's forehand, and then onto Éliane's mouth. And then he was gone.

* * *

Half an hour after Xavier had left her apartment, Éliane woke to someone shaking her. Her eyes flew open and landed on Luc's face.

"What is it?" she asked, gathering Alexandre to her.

"König is suspicious of Xavier. I was seen talking to him."

"What?" Éliane's sleep-blurred mind fumbled through the implications of Luc's words.

König had seen Luc, his informant, talking to Xavier. Her hold on Alexandre tightened.

König would want to know why his informant was talking to Xavier, a man König had always considered to be a kind of rival. At best, it made Luc appear to be someone who sold his secrets to the highest bidder. Someone not to be trusted. But also…

Her thoughts whirled faster and her mouth opened into a silent scream as Luc began to move toward the doorway.

Luc knew that König had seen him with Xavier. Therefore, König must have already spoken to Luc about it. But Luc was here in Éliane's bedroom. Why would König let someone who wasn't to be trusted go free?

Her heart seemed to simultaneously speed up and stop. Her breath the same. Her grip on Alexandre was desperate now.

Luc would have had two options when confronted by König: first, to tell König that he was selling information to Xavier too. But if König checked whether Xavier had ever passed on any information from Luc to the SD, it would expose Xavier as someone who gathered intelligence too—but not for the Nazis. *No*.

She tried to call out to her brother but her mouth wouldn't form any words. Because Luc's second option was more terrible still: that he had told König something so valuable it had paid for his freedom.

Luc's hand was on the front door now.

"Luc!" she screamed at last. "Luc!"

He turned back to her. She couldn't see his face, couldn't see anything at all in the blackout. But she heard what he said, "I'm sorry," heard the hitch in his voice on that last word.

Then he was gone.

What had he done?

She heard the sound of boots pounding up the stairs toward her.

PART EIGHT
SAINT-JEAN-CAP-FERRAT, 2015

THIRTY-FOUR

The day after Adam told her what he planned to do about Molly—that he would withdraw and become a distant uncle in order to protect the little girl—he and Remy walked through the gardens, talking about everything they could do: get the fountains operating again, explore all of the grounds properly, make a darkroom in the house for Adam, set up a studio for Remy. Plans—plans involving both of them. They discussed them tentatively at first, but soon each idea billowed into the next and suddenly they were surrounded by so much future.

Two weeks passed by like that, blissful and almost perfect. Adam stayed every night at Remy's house. Sometimes they'd have dinner with his family, sometimes they'd have dinner alone and sometimes they would drive into civilization to eat. They'd wake up together and she would work on her lookbook and he would help her, or he'd take photographs of the garden. Afterward, they would go swimming or explore the little towns on the Riviera.

Two things stopped those weeks from being perfect. Molly, and Elke.

Molly pestered Adam every day to take her into the water. Each time, Adam found a different excuse: he had to walk the dog, he had a sore leg and couldn't swim, he'd promised her grandma that she could take Molly for a swim. Molly would stare at him, confused, the hurt she didn't know how to express making her pout and whine. Remy watched as Adam tried to sit as far from Molly as possible at family meals, as he took the dog for punishing runs to let off steam, as Judy's eyes became sadder than ever.

He didn't say much, just that he wanted not to think about it and not to talk about it. So she let him try to forget Molly and she tried to just love him and hoped it would be enough.

They had one conversation about Elke. "I don't need to know anything else," Remy said. "It was so long ago. Like you said, I'm me, not a duplicate of anyone in my past. Some things are best not to think about or talk about."

When she put it like that, she knew Adam wouldn't be able to object. He let her have her silence too.

Throughout that time, they were never out of sight of the other for more than a couple of minutes, which drove Lauren mad and made Judy smile.

Until one day when there was an unexpected knock on the door. Remy opened it to find Elke, the woman she had tried to forget, standing there.

Remy stared. So did Elke.

"You are your father's daughter," Elke said. "Alexandre König might have had dark hair but he had your eyes."

Despite herself, Remy whispered, "Was he your son?"

Elke gave Remy a wistful smile. "That's not an easy question to answer. Would you let me come in? I don't... I don't wish to hurt you."

"Who is it, Remy?" she heard Adam call. He strolled over as if he were expecting Lauren or his mother and stopped when he saw Elke.

Remy knew she couldn't leave a woman aged in her nineties standing on her doorstep. So she led the way into the *petit salon* and over to the curved banquette.

"It was in here," Elke said. "She wore a black dress that he told me was like an invitation. How could he refuse an invitation? That was his excuse."

"I don't know what you mean," Remy said.

"A woman named Éliane Dufort and my husband came to this house for a party in 1943. Then they went upstairs to bed. It was the first and only time they slept together." Elke stared at her cramped, curled fingers. "In 1943 I could still tell when Ernst was lying. So I know he told me the truth. It was only in 1944, when everything fell apart, that I could no longer tell." She met Remy's eyes. "Éliane found out not long after that night that she was pregnant."

"She was unlucky," Remy said slowly, not at all sure where this was going, "to fall pregnant after just one time."

Elke nodded as if Remy had said the right thing. "A little too unlucky. I always wondered about it, but Éliane could never have told me the truth. And probably Ernst didn't understand that he ought to have been curious. At any rate, I didn't ask because it made no difference to me. But it might to you."

"I still don't know what you mean," Remy said, shifting closer to Adam, who took hold of her hand.

Elke smiled. It was a kind smile, no trace of evil or malicious intent in its curves. "I mean that your grandfather was possibly not my husband," she said. "And that you're definitely not related to me. I have never given birth to a child. I raised Éliane's child, not my own. She's your grandmother, and she was a true hero, in the old sense of the word, not the way it's used today to describe someone who wins a sporting trophy. I told Alexandre all I knew the night before he and your mother tried to flee East Berlin for the safety of the West. I still can't believe he's gone..." Elke's voice died and her eyes shone with tears of genuine pain, and of genuine love.

Remy's hand let go of Adam's and held on to Elke's now. She couldn't yet process the news about who her grandmother really was, not when Elke so obviously needed comfort. Elke gripped Remy's fingers tightly as she continued to speak.

"Alexandre knew he couldn't bring you up in East Germany. He didn't want his daughter to be limited by the regime in the way he and his scientific brilliance had been. He was so like his mother Éliane in single-mindedly doing whatever he could for his child. When I told him about Éliane, I gave him the painting—your painting—and the deed to this house. I told him to find out about Éliane when he made it to England. I couldn't give him the other painting, the one that's now in the Louvre, because I'd left it here." Elke sighed. "I'm not explaining things well."

"I'll get you some water," Adam said.

"While you're up, could you go to the drawer of the little gaming table in the next room. There should be some things inside it."

Adam nodded and Remy could hear him in the kitchen, and then in the *grand salon*. When he came back, he had a glass of water in one hand and some papers in the other.

"Thank you," Elke said. Then she turned to Remy. "In late 1944 and into 1945, I lived here with Alexandre for a time. I waited here because it was where Éliane would have come, if she could have. After the Allies landed in France, when Paris was in chaos and the Germans were running away, she left me a note with the address of this house. She told me to look after both her son and his inheritance. So I did. I waited here until fall of 1945, but because so much time had passed, I knew something must have happened to her. So I returned to Germany, where I discovered that my home was in the Russian zone of what became East Berlin. I only took one painting with me, the one that was left to you because... Well, a German woman after the war did not want to travel through France and be found to have something so expensive in her possession. I could only hide one painting in the lining of my suitcase."

Remy's mind swirled. Her grandmother was Éliane Dufort, the French *femme de la Résistance* who Taylor thought had risked her life to save artworks during the war. And her grandfather... might not have been a Nazi. But who was he?

"I came to France in the nineties after the wall was pulled down," Elke said. "I hated Germany by then. It was the place where Alexandre had died, where I'd lost my family. I moved into the apartment in Paris where he'd been born so I could feel closer to him. I came here briefly and collected the other painting by Luc Dufort, Éliane's brother, and donated it to the Louvre. Did you know Luc was a hero too? That he saved your father's life?"

"How?" Remy asked, unable to believe that, a couple of weeks ago, she had thought she was related to evil when the truth seemed to be that she was related to warriors.

"Ernst and I were on a train in 1944, along with a great deal of stolen artwork, trying to flee Paris. Shots were fired and Luc picked up your painting—my husband had it with him—stepped in front of Alexandre and used the canvas as a shield. He saved the baby. But he lost his own life. I have a lot to thank the Duforts for. Alexandre's life. Alexandre's love."

Elke paused, pressing a white folded handkerchief to her mouth, then her eyes. "Alexandre," she repeated, smiling. "I was so surprised— and so glad—when I saw, through the window of my apartment, Éliane leaving the note in my letterbox that asked me to care for her son. I thought she hated me. I was never able to thank her or Luc for any of it. Regret is a burdensome thing, you know," she said, eyes fixed on Remy. "I don't recommend it as a strategy for living one's life."

Remy flinched. Was her own terrible life story written somewhere on her face? But was her story really so dreadful if she set it against tales of people suffering and fighting against Nazis for years and then losing their own lives?

Elke passed Remy the papers Adam had fetched from the salon and Remy opened them wordlessly. The first was a bill of purchase documenting a transfer of funds made from a London bank by Xavier Laurent to a bank in New York, which was receiving the funds on behalf of Édouard de Rothschild. Xavier Laurent had purchased two paintings from Rothschild: *Les Amoureux*, the one now in the Louvre, and *L'Amour*—the one hanging in Remy's bedroom in Sydney.

Next was a beautiful ring. Its centerpiece was a stone that looked like the sea with a star drowned within it. Accompanying the ring was more paperwork, this time showing Xavier Laurent had purchased the ring in 1940.

"What does Xavier Laurent have to do with any of it?" Remy mused aloud as she opened the next paper to find a letter written by Xavier to Éliane Dufort, transferring ownership of the house Remy was now in to Éliane. She frowned as she stared at the initials *XL* at the bottom of the page. She had seen those initials before. But Elke pushed something into her hand before Remy could recall where.

"There's this one too," Elke said in a very thin voice. "I never opened or read this one. It's not addressed to me, so…" She paused. "And I was too afraid."

Remy glanced down at the envelope in her hand. It was addressed to Éliane Dufort. "Afraid of what?" Remy's own voice was tremulous.

"That…" Another hesitation, a shake of the shoulders, a mouth set in a determined line as if it must speak. "Afraid it might be a denunciation; that it would tell me everything Ernst had done. Afraid he'd done worse things than I knew of. Afraid he might have been as bad as his uncle. Afraid that I could have stopped him if I'd spoken up. Afraid that this letter was evidence of my guilt."

Remy stared at it, not sure she wanted to read it either.

"Remy," Adam said and she met his eyes, letting herself take the strength he was offering her. "No matter what's in there, you'll be all right."

She touched her hand to the name *Éliane* looped on the front of the envelope. "Where did it come from?" she asked Elke, stalling still.

"Éliane left it for me that night in Paris when she put the note in my letterbox about the house here and about Alexandre."

"She left you a letter addressed to herself?" Remy shook her head. "That's a very strange thing to do."

"That's why I thought it must be..." Elke's eyes fell away from Remy's face. "A denunciation. Something she intended to hand to the authorities."

"And it's been sitting unopened in the *petit salon* since 1944?"

"Yes."

Remy slipped a finger under the seal and withdrew an aged and yellowed sheet of paper.

PART NINE
PARIS, 1944

THIRTY-FIVE

Éliane had no time to move from the bed before the door of her apartment was kicked in and a swarm of soldiers with guns drawn flooded inside. She held one useless arm up to her face and one arm over Alexandre.

"Where is the man?" one of the soldiers barked. His uniform was Gestapo.

They were there for Xavier.

Terror gave way to rage, pushing her out of the bed, so furious that Alexandre could feel it too. It made him cry pitifully—tears for his mother who could not afford to cry right now.

"A boy is here," Éliane spat. "A boy who was asleep."

Alexandre wailed as the soldiers tramped around her apartment, searching.

Then Éliane saw König standing by the door. "What is the meaning of this?" she demanded.

"A reliable source informed us you were providing succor to a traitor," he said stiffly.

Éliane laughed wildly, crazily. "Succor? How am I to provide succor to anyone when I need all the strength I have to care for my child?"

Alexandre howled. She opened her nightgown and let him feed. "Tell me," she said, savagely, "who would want succor from the body of a woman given over to meeting the needs of her baby?"

Although she looked only at König, Éliane was aware of the movements of the soldiers around her. They were looking for something else, not just a man. A man wouldn't hide in her kitchen drawers, nor in the oven, which no longer contained the radio as she'd got rid of it the day after König gave her the painting.

They pushed aside the mirror on the wall and found the empty cavity.

It was lucky she was smarter than König thought. There was no painting hiding in the apartment. No ring. No money. No title deeds. Everything had been sent to Cap-Ferrat, where it was in the care of Madame Mercier. Everything except the papers Xavier had just given her regarding the purchase of the paintings from Rothschild; they were tucked into Alexandre's clothes and she knew König wouldn't look there.

The soldiers gathered by the door, looking accusingly at König for bringing them out on this wildest of goose chases.

"Tell me who," she asked, keeping her voice at the pitch of anger and not letting any of her terror show, "was I supposed to be succoring?"

"It has come to our attention that Monsieur Göring's art adviser is not what he seems," König said thinly. "We will leave you now."

Éliane did not sleep that night. Nor did Alexandre. His big, serious eyes, fringed with his father's lashes, watched her as she cried and she hoped. Had Xavier got away? How far? And how long until they hunted him down?

Luc didn't return to the apartment. She had been wrong in thinking he wouldn't do anything to hurt her.

He had given Xavier up to save himself.

* * *

The next morning, Éliane ripped her blouse while feeding Alexandre and she had to take one of Luc's as she had nothing else to wear. Then she walked to König's apartment in her wood-soled shoes, wondering if König still expected her, if he had believed her protests last night.

Elke greeted her, wearing a Chanel suit and stockings, manner the same as always. "My dear, your shirt is adorned with the remnants of last night's dinner."

Éliane almost shrugged as if she didn't care. But she needed to find out whatever she could about Xavier from König so she let her lip tremble—which wasn't hard to do—and said in a small voice, "I have no other."

Elke led Éliane upstairs to a lovely room with no diaper rags hanging from a line and a fire stacked with wood even though it was summer. She took a cream silk blouse out of the wardrobe and an almost-new black skirt and lay them on the bed. "They will be too big," Elke said. "I will help you pin the skirt once you're dressed."

Elke turned away as Éliane dressed herself in Elke's clothes. When she saw herself in the mirror, Éliane drew in a breath. Her stocking-less legs were like skewers poking into what was more a plank than a shoe. Her face was pale and her cheekbones were etched too hard onto her face. *This is what war does to people*, she wanted to say to Elke.

König came into the room then and Elke withdrew, mumbling about fetching some pins.

Éliane thought of Alexandre and Xavier, of lying in a bed beside them both. She made herself take strength from the picture, soaking in all its blues and golds and pinks and reds. "Did you really think…" she whispered to König, "that I would share my bed with Göring's art adviser?"

"I hoped not," he replied softly, and Éliane caught the shiver of fear in his voice and she knew the boy-König still lived in him: the pianist, the one who blushed, the diffident young man. But she knew the boy-König would die soon, that invasion and panic would mean the man emerging from him, the man like his uncle, would be who König became.

She took what might be her last chance to ask. "Have you captured him?"

"Not yet," König answered. "But today might bring more success."

Not yet. But the way König had spoken his last sentence betrayed a certain confidence, as if he had a reason to hope.

Where was Luc? What had he told König? Enough to blow Xavier's cover and get himself out of trouble—or enough to also lead the Gestapo straight to wherever Xavier was hiding? Eliane's head pounded with worry and hunger and fear.

"Where was the painting I gave you?" König asked her then, unable to help himself from exposing his hand.

"I sold it," she lied. "I needed the money. I'm sorry."

"I must pin Éliane's skirt." Elke bustled in, shooing her husband away.

Éliane waited for König's wife to adjust her clothing but instead Elke opened the door of the wardrobe, reached in and pulled out two paintings. "My husband brought these home some months ago," Elke said conversationally. "They are such beautiful paintings; I'm sure we should hang them somewhere prominent so others can view them rather than hiding them in here."

Éliane was about to say she wasn't interested in König's art but then she saw the heavy, illuminating impasto used to paint the skin of the man in the painting, the particular shade of brown—Egyptian brown, or mummy, a pigment made from the flesh and bones and wrappings of those no longer resting in peace, exhumed from the mummy pits of Egypt. It was the color of betrayal.

The two paintings in Elke's hands were the ones that had gone missing from the Schloss collection at the Jeu de Paume. They would fetch extravagant sums in the present art market.

The pain in Éliane's head twisted into nausea. König was thieving, not just for Germany, but also for himself. He was far more ambitious, and thus far more dangerous, than Éliane had realized. And he was also the man who thought he was her son's father. God, *what* had she done?

* * *

What to do? What could she do? Xavier was smarter than Luc, she told herself as she waited to hear something from him, and as she waited for König to let something slip about where his informant might be.

She drew strength from the planes bearing Union Jacks and Stars and Stripes that flew overhead. The nightly show of fire and flame that had once been a distant, dun-colored lightening of the night sky was now a brilliant, incendiary amber. The only discernible smell was that of burning. Explosions and gunfire rattled constantly in the background. There was no silence.

It was two long weeks before Éliane's questions about her brother's absence were answered. Believing König had left for the night, she had just collected several pages from Göring's Catalogue and stuffed them inside her bra, and was readying herself to go home when the sound of her name rapped out made her gasp.

"*Mon Dieu*," she said to König, who had materialized in her office. "I didn't see you there."

"My uncle and I would like to speak with you." König's face was hard-set.

Please let them not have found Xavier, Éliane prayed helplessly as she followed König. *Anything but that*.

In von Behr's office stood Rose, face drawn.

"Your brother has been taken into custody," von Behr said to Éliane, lighting a cigar. "He disappeared just when we most wanted to speak to him. Which makes us feel he isn't to be trusted. And that means neither are you two, perhaps."

"Hands in the air," König said sharply.

Éliane lifted hers and heard the rustle of notepaper.

"What was that?" König asked.

Éliane didn't lower her hands. She behaved like the bewildered innocent she had once been. "Cabbage leaves, Monsieur," she said. "For inflammation from feeding the baby."

Von Behr's nose wrinkled in disgust. "I don't think our fräulein has any state secrets in her cabbage leaves. Desks and purses."

They were marched into the office and their desks emptied onto the floor, their purses too. Von Behr's nose wrinkled again as the diaper rags she'd stored in there fell out, along with the nursing compresses, and she thanked God for her leaking body. She prayed that von Behr would not kick the wall on which hung the painting of the Führer with the master notebook behind it.

"Nothing," König said, studying Éliane's face with dispassion, rather than lust or even interest.

Von Behr turned to Rose. "If I have to, I will take you to the German border and liquidate you."

Éliane cried in her apartment again that night. Was Xavier safe? Had Luc really been arrested or was that a pretense to see what Éliane would do? And if they had arrested Luc, it meant the Nazis were tired of him: he hadn't given them enough. What might he say now in order to save himself?

* * *

It was still possible to break even after already being broken, Éliane discovered a few days later when König called her into his office.

"I've thought of a way to secure your brother's release. Sit," König said, just like his uncle.

Éliane sat, hands clasped, hoping the price would not be beyond her.

"In exchange for your son, you may have your brother. My scruples do not allow me to steal a baby from its mother. It must be given willingly."

It was almost impossible not to fall to her knees and beg for König to take something else from her, anything else. But she knew that if König discovered her most vulnerable point was Alexandre, he would exploit it. So she ground down inside her the red of her shock, the black of her horror, and the blue of her tears and spoke in a tone colored an unthreatening beige.

"He," Éliane said. "Alexandre is a baby boy."

"He," König said dismissively. "We are willing to overlook your brother's transgressions—he has been giving restaurant supplies to the Resistance—if you give me the baby. You have ten days to decide. At the end of that time, all the artworks remaining here will have been packed up, the building closed, and I will supervise the removal of the paintings by train to Germany. Your brother will be dead."

Éliane had been so wrong. She had been afraid of von Behr when all along she should have been afraid of König. He had orchestrated all of this.

But it seemed that Luc had given up no more secrets and no more names. It must stay that way. So, with all the sincerity she could summon from the bones of her dread she said, "Of course I will save my brother. Please tell him that. And you and your wife will have a baby."

Now she had ten days to come up with a plan to save her child from König.

* * *

Two days later, as Éliane walked to the Jeu de Paume in a fog of unworkable and impossible ideas, she saw Angélique waiting on the bench in the Jardins des Tuileries. She hurried over and sat beside her sister, holding her hand while tanks and guns roamed around them.

"I got your note about the evacuation of the Jeu de Paume," Angélique said quickly, the way they all spoke to one another now, not knowing how much time they had. "The Resistance will stop the train not long after it leaves Paris. So you won't have to record everything that the Nazis pack onto it. Both the Germans and the art will be taken into custody by the Resistance."

"Thank you," Éliane said, trying to smile at what should have been wonderful news. And then she did smile, just a little, because Angélique words had given her an idea. It was an idea she needed to think through before she involved her sister. But it was an idea that just might work.

Then Angélique dropped her gaze to the ground, hiding something. Éliane almost couldn't ask what it was. How much more could she bear before her heart split in two? But she never wanted to be a coward like König and his uncle. "What?" she said, voice low.

"I haven't had any transmissions from him." Angélique voice was tiny. "I should have, by now."

Éliane wrapped her arms around Alexandre's sling. "I could have forgiven Luc for everything, perhaps," she said quietly. "But not for Xavier." She stared dry-eyed at the city she had given almost everything to. Everything except Alexandre.

She tried to push out of her mind what she'd heard only that morning: that the Nazis had shot thirty-five young men in the middle of the night in the Bois de Boulogne, before throwing a grenade onto the pile of bodies, dismembering them. The gruesome arrangement of flesh and bone had been discovered yesterday, some men still warm, suggesting that death had taken a long time to come.

Éliane could not even vomit at the news as she had nothing left inside her. She was no longer living in Paris but inside van Dyck's *The Last Judgement*, a hell vaulted by a diabolic skeleton. Underneath, the screaming people were gnawed and gnashed and broken.

What would the Nazis do to Xavier? She wanted to howl like Alexandre did when he was frightened.

"I love you, Éliane," Angélique said, breaking through the terrible image, reminding Éliane that a present, and that love, still existed.

* * *

At the Jeu de Paume, everything was packed into crates, ready to be taken to the station and loaded onto trains bound for Germany. The Nazis were running.

Éliane had always thought those last four words would be the most beautiful she had heard since May 1940. But nothing was beautiful anymore.

Xavier was at best silent, at worst missing.

Luc had been arrested.

König wanted Alexandre.

To save her brother, she had to give up her baby.

She made sure to tell Rose, weeping, of König's proposition. That she had no choice. Rose stared solemnly at her and that nearly broke Éliane's heart too.

Then Éliane ascended the staircase and walked into the Salle des Martyrs. She picked up the painting of the couple without moon and sky. The couple without a world. *L'Amour*. She took a pen out of her pocket and, on the back, she wrote another code. König's name was on Alexandre's birth certificate. There was no record anywhere of who her son really belonged to. Except, now, on the paintings.

She took the painting to König's office where he paced, sweat glistening on his upper lip. His power was crumbling. But he could still have her brother killed. Could still take her baby. The Allies weren't in Paris yet.

She indicated the painting. "I want this to go with Alexandre. For it to be his."

"I will allow that," he said, as if he were being magnanimous.

"I'll bring Alexandre to the train station for you before you leave," she finished. "And you will bring Luc there."

There was silence as they eyed one another. König was the first to look away. He stared at the window, not through it, and said, "Things could have been different."

"No, they couldn't."

He recoiled, so used to deference that truth was a slap. But he let her go.

"You're a fool," Rose said to Éliane when she returned to the office. "Somebody else will wish to have a say in what you plan to do."

"Find him for me and then he can," Éliane said bleakly.

Rose grasped Éliane's hand. "Perhaps he's in hiding."

What a lovely story. Xavier was alive and in hiding. Éliane placed both hands on the desk, bracing herself.

"You love Luc," Rose said, "but he isn't worth saving."

"He is my brother."

"And Alexandre is your son. The son of the man your brother gave up to the Germans."

Éliane closed her eyes. It was so hard to keep up the pretense. But Rose had to believe, everyone had to believe, that Éliane was doing what König wanted. Luc had to believe that she was going to save him. Because, if he didn't, how many more of them would he give up before the Nazis fled? It was the only way Éliane could ensure Luc's silence and keep the rest of them safe until the Allies arrived.

"They are both my flesh and blood," Éliane said, opening her eyes. "How am I to choose between one or the other? Between a man I've known for twenty-five years and a child I've known for five months. If I don't give König the baby, Luc dies. If I do give König the baby, they both live. Two lives saved, rather than one. Elke will be good to the child."

Tomorrow. It would all be done tomorrow. König and von Behr and Elke would board the train with Alexandre. Luc and Éliane would walk away free. Which meant Rose and Monsieur Jaujard and Angélique would walk away too. Alexandre would never see his mother again.

It was what she wished for everyone to believe. Because, *If I ever get caught, don't give yourself up trying to save me*, Xavier had said. *Love is watching me go and saying nothing, doing nothing.*

It was so hard to appear to be doing nothing. But if she didn't, they would arrest her, she knew. Then Alexandre would have no one. If she didn't appear to be doing nothing, they might find out that Alexandre was not König's child. Then Alexandre would be dead, and Xavier too. She could not let that happen.

So she played along, as if she were doing nothing other than what they asked of her.

THIRTY-SIX

Éliane had no idea if Angélique would, in the confusion that was Paris right now, receive her note or whether her sister would be able to make it back to the city in time. She waited anxiously on the park bench at the Tuileries two days before König's deadline but Angélique did not appear. Then, on the last possible day, there was Angélique. Neither sister could hide her smile of relief at seeing the other.

"They say liberation should only be days away," Angélique whispered.

How lovely those words sounded. But Éliane's smile wouldn't return.

"What is it?" Angélique asked, obviously having expected some sign of joy from her sister.

Éliane told her what König wanted. "I'm giving him Alexandre," she finished.

"No." A small, futile word.

"I need König to believe it's real," Éliane explained, praying for no Nazis to hurry past, needing Angélique to understand it all, and the part she would play. "That he's getting what he wants. Only then will he bring Luc to the station. No matter what our brother has done, I can't leave him to the Nazis. He can face the Allies' justice instead, which will be harsh, I hope, but not inhuman. When the Resistance stops the train," Éliane spoke more slowly now, as this was the most important point of all, "I need you to be there too, with the Maquis. Then you can take Alexandre from König."

"Of course." Angélique eyes shone with tears as if the idea that Éliane would trust her with the most precious thing of all was almost too much.

"Then you can bring him back to me—" Éliane's voice caught on a sob. "Then we can find the Allies and we can tell them that Xavier is…" Her voice failed her now and the tears on her face were a torrent. Two more weeping women backdropped by the macabre canvas of war.

"The people Xavier works for will find him," Angélique said resolutely. "Then you and he and Alexandre can be a family."

"And you'll be part of our family too. We'll all go and live in Cap-Ferrat."

It was Angélique who sobbed now.

Neither spoke for some time; words were impossible to form. But there was another outcome that had to be considered. Éliane wasn't sure she had the courage to voice it, but her adoration for Alexandre made her as strong as she needed to be.

"If König doesn't keep his word and I'm not allowed to leave the station after I've given him Alexandre," Éliane said starkly, "then you'll have to look after my baby for me until you can find Xavier."

Angélique grasped her sister's hands. "I will love him like my own son," she said fiercely. "But I pray it won't happen, that you'll always be his mother."

"I pray for that too." Éliane's words were the softest whisper.

But she had to press on, to explain to Angélique that Alexandre would have a painting with him. On the back of the painting were the letters AD; for Alexandre Dufort. "Take the painting and Alexandre to Cap-Ferrat," Éliane said. "Madame Mercier, the housekeeper, has money and papers. She won't give them to anyone other than the person who arrives with the coded painting. It's the only way I could be sure that König wouldn't somehow get his hands on everything."

A Nazi approached.

It was time to stand up and walk away.

PART TEN
PARIS AND
NEW YORK, 2015

THIRTY-SEVEN

R emy withdrew the letter addressed to Éliane from its envelope.

To my darling sister, Éliane,

I promised you I would be with the Maquis when they stop the train and also that, if you are not able to leave the station because König double-crosses you, I will love Alexandre as if he is my own son.

But…

There is another possible outcome you haven't planned for. So I have. I've written this letter to explain.

After we met in the Jardins des Tuileries, I went to Elke König's house. There is no one else who Alexandre knows, and perhaps loves, who is certain to survive this. Luc might well give the Nazis Rose's name, so I can't take the risk of entrusting Alexandre's birthright to her.

I left a note for Elke with the address of the house at Saint-Jean-Cap-Ferrat. I told her that if she loved Alexandre at all, she would take him and the painting he will have with him to the house at Cap-Ferrat.

I left this letter in Elke's mailbox also, sealed and addressed to you.

If everything goes well at the station, you will be free and I will have Alexandre and I will meet you as arranged at Cap-Ferrat. Then we will find Xavier. And Elke will never need to give you this letter.

But I had to create an extra safeguard. Because everywhere now I can see shadows in the dark beneath the tiny spotlights of blackout-blue. I don't know who those shadows are watching, who they're waiting for, but I can't fail you, Éliane.

So you might arrive at Cap-Ferrat to find not me and Alexandre, but Elke and Alexandre, waiting for you with this letter. Because perhaps I will not be able to make it to the train to rescue your son.

Perhaps neither of us will.

But Alexandre will still have someone to love him.

All my love,

Your sister, Angélique

* * *

It was impossible to read a letter making selfless plans for a child, a letter in which every word was underlined with both love and terror, and not cry. Remy passed it to Elke to read while she wiped her eyes. Elke's face turned a shocked and ghastly white.

"Are you all right?" Remy asked.

"It wasn't Éliane…" was all Elke could say before she bowed her head and pressed her hands over her eyes.

There was something about the pain Remy saw Elke trying to hide behind her closed eyes, doubly shielded by the hand covering her face—like the attempts Remy had made to shut out the world, to retreat into the nothing-space where her husband and child had vanished to—that made her draw the older woman into her arms. Elke began to cry as if the letter had destroyed her.

Remy held on, not letting go.

"I thought…" Elke whispered bleakly, face still buried in her hands. "I thought, that if anything happened to her, she wanted *me* to have him…"

The words gave way to a raw and laid-bare weeping resonant with a particular kind of heartache Remy recognized: that of a mother for a child.

Remy's eyes fell onto the letter, trying to make sense of what Elke had said: *I thought she wanted* me *to have him.* And then she remembered: Elke had said she'd seen Éliane leave her a note in her letterbox with instructions about Alexandre. But this letter suggested it wasn't Éliane who'd left those instructions; it was her sister Angélique.

And now Elke was saying, over and over, "What have I done? What have I done?"

Remy gently drew Elke's hands away from her face. "All you did was to love a child."

Elke spoke in an anguished whisper. "A child Éliane never wanted me to have. A child she wanted her sister to have. A child I should never have taken. Dear God...I thought she'd forgiven me. That she didn't hate me. That this was the one right thing that I did. But..." Elke's eyes shuttered over. "It seems my entire history is a succession of the most unforgivable wrongs."

My entire history is a succession of the most unforgivable wrongs. Oh, Remy knew how that felt. To have still not, not really, forgiven herself for not being there when her daughter had died. To have pretended, in the balm of Adam's love, that she had. Now Remy wanted to sob too, from the hideous, sharp sorrow she'd believed was a scar on her heart but was still actually an open wound.

But Elke was an old woman, so old and so tired and so sad and she needed help more than Remy did. "Tell me," Remy asked, "did Alexandre, did my father ever tell you that he loved you?"

The words came too quickly for untruth; they were impulsive and real and accompanied by a smile. "All the time," Elke said.

Remy smiled too. "You can't force a child's love. They give it, and they give it utterly and completely. There's nothing wrong or unforgivable about that."

* * *

Later, when she had tucked Elke into a bed in a spare room to rest, Remy called Taylor, knowing she would be interested to hear that the name Xavier Laurent had come up again, this time on painting and jewelry receipts, and on title deeds. "You said you thought Xavier Laurent painted the work at the Louvre signed by Luc Dufort," Remy began, "but maybe there's more to it."

Remy told Taylor what she thought: that if Xavier had given Éliane title deeds to a house he owned, as well as the two paintings Taylor thought he had painted, plus a ring, then...

"Then Éliane and Xavier were close at the very least," Taylor mused.

"Also," Remy added, "Elke said that, after the war, Éliane didn't come back. Do you know what happened to her, or to Xavier? If his father sold your grandmother the gallery rather than giving it to his son..."

"It doesn't sound good, does it? I'll do some digging and I'll call you as soon as I find out anything."

Adam found Remy staring at her phone not long after she'd hung up from Taylor. "You look very deep in thought," he said, coming up behind her and wrapping his arms around her.

She swiveled around to face him, to tuck her head into the shelter of his shoulder. "It's been an emotional morning," she admitted. "Finding out Elke is my sort-of grandmother. And that Éliane Dufort is my real grandmother. But I still don't really know who my grandfather is."

Adam stroked her back and she closed her eyes, curling into him, thinking over everything they'd discovered that morning. The letters XL forced their way to the surface of all the revelations, as if they were the most important puzzle piece.

Remy's eyes flew open and she stepped back. "Except maybe I do. Do you have Chloe's number at the Louvre? Do you think she'd mind if I called her? And can we use your phone because I need to look at mine while we talk to her."

"She won't mind," Adam said. "But put her on speaker so I know what's going on."

As soon as she'd been put through to Chloe, Remy asked, "Can you tell me more about the codes you mentioned on the back of the painting?"

Chloe told Remy that the Louvre's treasures were all marked with letters when they were moved out of the museum to safety. "The codes were in two parts. Firstly MN, for Musées Nationaux, designating that the Musées Nationaux owned the painting. The second part of the code identified the particular artwork," Chloe explained. "So, putting it together: the first part stood for who owned it, and the second part stood for what work it was; what they owned, if you like. The *Mona Lisa* was the only artwork incompletely coded when it left the Louvre; it had the letters MN on its crate but the rest of the code was added when it arrived to safety to show that it was genuine."

"And yours has the initials XL/ED on the back," Remy said excitedly, "because Xavier Laurent and Éliane Dufort owned the painting. And mine has"—she flicked through to the photo her mother had sent over to her—"AD. The second part of the code."

Remy beamed. Because now she knew. She thanked Chloe and hung up the phone.

"AD: Alexandre Dufort," she said to Adam, still smiling. "He was Xavier and Éliane's artwork. Xavier Laurent and Éliane Dufort are my grandparents, and my father's parents."

She felt her heart stretch out inside her, expanding with both the pain and the beauty she'd experienced over the past year, the past month, and the past day. Her grandparents: Resistance fighters who'd battled to save artworks during the war. She'd never had a chance to know them. Where were they now? Was there any chance at all that they might be alive?

Now it was more important than ever that she find out.

* * *

Early the next morning, Remy's phone rang, waking her from her nest in Adam's arms.

"You wouldn't believe what I found," Taylor said without preamble. "This might sound macabre but I spent yesterday looking through the Heinrich Himmler Collection at the National Archives. It includes SD and Gestapo records. I cross-referenced the names König, Dufort, and Xavier Laurent and I found something."

"Gestapo records?" Remy repeated.

Adam, who had half-opened his eyes when he heard the phone, frowned at her words.

"What do you know about the Gestapo?" Taylor asked.

"Besides the fact they were evil, not much," Remy said, wriggling closer to Adam and putting her phone on speaker so he could hear too.

"One of the Nazi intelligence organizations was the Sicherheitsdienst or SD. They gathered information about anyone working against them—spies and the like. When they wanted someone arrested and interrogated—or gotten rid of—they called in the Gestapo."

"I'm not going to like where this is going, am I?"

"Probably not," Taylor conceded. "To cut a long story short, in the SD records, there's a list of their Most Wanted. Xavier Laurent was put on that list in 1944. Apparently, he'd been posing as an art adviser to Hermann Göring but they received information from an informant that he was actually a spy, working for the British government. And in the records, there's also a list of SD informants. Luc Dufort's name is on that list. He was the person who, via Ernst König, gave the SD Xavier Laurent's name."

"I thought Luc Dufort was a Resistance hero?"

"Legends have a way of not always being true."

Remy turned this over in her mind for a moment before asking, "What about Éliane? Is she mentioned?"

"Yes," Taylor said soberly. "Luc Dufort gave the SD their sister Angélique's name, which led the SD to Éliane. Luc was unquestionably a traitor." Taylor hesitated before adding in a strange voice, "Now that you know all this, take another look at the last page of Göring's Catalogue."

Adam climbed out of bed to fetch it.

He passed it to her and she ran her finger down the page, remembering that strange entry—*bébé*—in the column entitled "Name of Painting." Something else caught her eye, letters that had been meaningless to her when she'd first seen the catalogue. The notation *XL/ED* was written in the column entitled "Artist," beside the word *bébé*, thus confirming everything she'd started to believe yesterday.

"Can you see it?" Taylor's voice broke in.

Remy moved her finger further down the page. There was her painting, *Le Traître*. The artist's name was recorded as Luc Dufort. *Le Traître*. Luc Dufort.

It was all there, if you knew what you were looking for.

"It's not the name of the artwork at all," she said aloud. "It's a record of what he did."

"I think you're right," Taylor replied.

Remy knew that her breath was held and that the least painful thing to do would be to hang up, to end the conversation without asking anything more. It's what she would have done just last month, perhaps even last week. But now she said, "Tell me what happened to them."

"I've sent you a link via email," Taylor said. "I'm really sorry, Remy. Call me back when you've read it if you need to."

Remy made herself open Taylor's email. The subject was Buchenwald Concentration Camp. *They sent some political prisoners there*, Taylor had written. *Political prisoners included spies and* résistants.

Remy clicked on the link and a terrible list appeared: those killed at Buchenwald.

A search field. Remy typed. First Xavier Laurent. Then Éliane Dufort.

"Are they...?" Adam started to ask.

Remy dropped the phone onto the bed and said only, "I need to go for a walk. By myself."

* * *

She walked for hours, going nowhere. Everyone died. Everyone. Was that all life was? An endless succession of deaths and colossal hurts?

Why had her grandparents given up their lives for bits of wood and stone and canvas and oil? Why had her parents given up their lives trying to take her to the safety of the West? Why had her husband and daughter given up their lives to careless driving? Why? Why? *Why?*

She sat on the pebbles on a different stretch of beach to the one near her house and closed her eyes. She didn't open them again until she heard two voices very nearby, one a man's saying, "I think it'll be a girl," and the other a woman's saying, "I hope so."

Her eyes flew open and landed on a couple a few feet away. They were standing facing the sea, smiling, the man's hands on the woman's stomach.

And a queasy little piece of fear Remy had not looked directly at made her jump to her feet and hurry into town, to a pharmacy and then back to the house.

THIRTY-EIGHT

Give me a minute," Remy said to Adam, before disappearing into the bathroom.

She opened the box from the pharmacy, took out the tester and did what was required. She was three days late. She was never late. Not even through all the loss and grief. She stared at the faint line on the stick.

She remembered the night when Adam had said he thought maybe the condom might have leaked or torn but it was hard to tell and probably not—that he was most likely being paranoid but did she want to do something about it? They could see the doctor the next day. He'd said *probably* and *maybe* and that it was *hard to tell* so she'd thought nothing of it. And then she'd forgotten all about it. But now...

No. *No.* A thousand times no.

She could feel the hard beat of her heart in her chest, the too-fast speed of her breath, the unsteadiness of her legs, the nausea, and knew she was having a panic attack, which she'd had in the weeks after Toby and Emily had died. She slid down the wall and sat on the floor, trying to catch her breath, trying to make time turn backward, trying to think of a way to undo this because this was *impossible.*

She could *never* have a child again. How could she when she had so monstrously let Emily down? Her daughter had been calling out for Remy in the back of an ambulance and Remy hadn't been there. Her daughter had been more frightened than she'd ever been in her life and

Remy hadn't been there. Her daughter had slipped away with nobody beside her. *Nobody*.

Oh *God*.

She was back there again, more than eighteen months ago, in the hospital with Emily's hand in hers, crying, begging the doctors not to take Emily away. But they had. And Remy had sat on the floor just as she was sitting now and she hadn't been able to breathe, had had to be taken away too and sedated. But there was no one there now to take her away and sedate her from the news that she was going to have another child whose hand she would inevitably have to let go of.

Because everyone she knew died.

Breathe, she told herself. *Breathe*. She was going to pass out. Maybe that would be okay. She could just lie down and pass out and go wherever Emily was.

Adam knocked on the door. "Are you all right?"

She reached up one shaky hand to press the flush button so that he wouldn't come in, not yet. Then she hauled herself up to the basin and splashed water on her face. She had to get out of there. That was all she knew. She had to get away from this news.

If she could stand, then she could walk. If she could walk, then she could get away. She made it to the door. She opened it and almost walked into Adam, who had his arms outstretched as if he wanted to hold her.

In a desolate voice she said, "The condom did leak. Or tear. I'm pregnant."

"What?" Adam said as Remy picked up her handbag and walked toward the door.

"I have to go. I need to..." Remy shook her head. "I don't know what I need but it's not this."

"Remy, for fuck's sake. You can't just go. Let's just..."

Let's just what? she wanted to scream. Let's just be a bit more serious about a leaking condom? Let's just say it like you actually mean it, like it's something I should worry about? Let's just get married and have a baby and watch it die? *No.*

"It was the only thing—" Remy stopped, unable to finish. She closed the door against Adam calling her name.

* * *

Somehow, Remy's drive took her to the airport at Nice. Her passport was in her handbag so she stepped onto a plane, away from Adam's texts saying, *Where the hell are you?* and *We have to talk about this.*

Antoinette picked her up from JFK. "What are you doing, Remy?"

"I'm pregnant."

Antoinette stiffened beside her, then said more gently, "You can't run away from this. Adam's already grieving Molly. You're being unfair, Remy."

Unfair. What was fair? Losing a husband and a child?

Fury blazed red and violent and almost unbearable inside Remy. "All I know is that I can't have a child," she shouted at Antoinette. "And yet, apparently, I am. Let me just digest that for a day or so before I figure out the rest. I can't talk to Adam right now because I don't even know what to say to myself."

Antoinette's face softened. "You're right. I'll give you some time."

And Antoinette didn't ask anything more, not for months.

But over those months, Remy still didn't know what to say about any of it so it was impossible to speak to Adam. She worked relentlessly, every hour of every day, publishing her lookbook with the photographs Adam had taken of her. The collection sold out and then Scarlett Johansson borrowed one of Remy's archive pieces—a black, late-1939 Vionnet gown—to wear to the Oscars and Meghan Markle borrowed one to wear to the Emmys and Remy was busier than she'd ever been, sourcing vintage dresses for celebrities, selling her stock and supplying pieces for magazine fashion editorials. She always asked who the photographer would be on the shoot and had to decline two because the photographer was Adam.

She saw his work in different magazines and Antoinette inexplicably hired him for the marketing campaign for fashion week. The images were beautiful, the best work he'd ever done. She almost called him then. But on her way to find her phone she looked down at her stomach and saw the bump and knew what it meant: that, if her past was anything to go on—a grandmother and grandfather brutally killed, a mother and father too, and then a husband and child—she would have to watch on as this child died too.

The inevitability of it was like a bodysuit of nails that she couldn't peel off, pricking her always with the question: when would it happen? When the child was one month old? One year old? Ten years old?

Remy woke most nights sweating, gasping, dreaming of its death, never recalling the circumstances but knowing only that it had happened and that she was lying curled up on her bed again, unable even to sob because her body had ceased to function, falling into a coma of agony.

There was no question now that she could see Adam again. Her mind could not turn that awful extrapolation of death toward him. If she stayed away from him, at least he wouldn't die too.

She texted him to tell him she'd returned to New York, that she didn't wish to speak to him, but that she understood he had rights. Antoinette would keep him appraised of the details of the pregnancy. Once the child was born, they would work out visitation through their lawyers; he would be able to see it as much as he wanted to. She asked him to let Lauren and Judy know that Remy wouldn't be able to reply to their texts; that they should speak to Adam rather than Remy.

He replied, telling her he loved her, that he wanted to talk to her, but also that he wouldn't push her. In his message, she could hear the echo of what he'd said to her about Molly—*I'll withdraw. The only thing to do is to not be around.* The only way not to hurt is to not be around, is what she knew he meant now.

He finished by saying he'd look forward to Antoinette's updates. Antoinette made a point of telling Remy every time she texted Adam— or he texted her—asking Remy if she had any messages to pass on, but Remy always shook her head.

She did what she had to do. She ate properly and went to her medical appointments and provided a physical shelter for the life growing inside her. Antoinette spoke to the child all the time and so did Remy's mother, through the telephone, but Remy didn't. She couldn't talk to it or rub her hand over her stomach or allow herself to feel. The longer she was unable to feel, the more protected she would be when the child was born.

Her mother and Antoinette both ordered her to see someone she could talk to but she refused.

Then Elke König died and left Remy the apartment in Paris. Remy cried a little for Elke, but knew she would never visit the apartment again.

One night, her stomach cramped. She winced and Antoinette saw her.

"It's time," Antoinette said.

Remy paced around the apartment for a couple of hours until the pains were stronger. Antoinette stayed with her, leaving the room only to call her boss to tell him she wouldn't be at work the next day. Then she drove Remy to the hospital where the pain intensified and Antoinette gripped her hand, leaving her side only a couple of times until, after several more hours, a baby entered the world and was placed in Remy's arms. Remy let it suckle at her breast until it fell asleep. Then she wrapped it in a blanket, tucked it into the crib and got up to have a shower while Antoinette stared dotingly at her godson.

In the shower, with the water rushing down over her, Remy felt her heart speed up, racing, felt herself shiver with cold even though the water was hot, felt the world spin, her skin sweat and knew she was having another panic attack. She didn't call the midwife or Antoinette; if she breathed in and out and thought of nice things, it would stop. Except it didn't.

She put a hand on the wall, dropped her head down so she wouldn't faint and saw that the shower floor was covered in blood. Far more blood than was normal. She felt herself falling down onto the tiles. Then nothing at all.

* * *

Sometimes, Remy could hear fragments amid the nothing. Antoinette's scream. A baby's cry. Her baby. The baby she'd had with Adam.

Her baby was crying. She tried to lift her arms, to pick up her son. Her breasts squeezed and the ache of need, a primal thing, coursed through her body.

You can't force a child's love. They give it, and they give it utterly and completely, she had said to Elke. And so too did a mother give that kind of love to her child.

Remy suddenly understood that what she'd been scared of this whole time wasn't that she wouldn't be able to love her child—but that she would love it so very much.

But now she couldn't open her eyes and she understood one more thing: she'd been wrong. It wasn't the baby who would die, but Remy.

And now that it was happening to her, she didn't want it. She didn't care if she lived forever with the threat of her child dying hanging over her; she only wanted to live, to be with her child and to love it. To show Adam what they had made.

But all of her thoughts vanished—and then there was nothing.

PART ELEVEN
PARIS, 1944

THIRTY-NINE

On the day the train with all of the art was due to leave—one hundred and forty-eight crates no less—the Allies were known to be on the outskirts of the city. A threatening rainbow of incendiaries colored the sky an impenetrable black. All around were frightened faces and outstretched arms, the sharp points of teeth and guns, *Guernica* come to life on the streets of Paris.

Éliane tried not to see any of it as she walked to the station with her son in her arms and Rose at her side. Gathered there on the platform were two people she never wanted to see again: Elke and König. He had with him the painting of the lovers she had requested to go with Alexandre.

"I want to have every moment with him," Éliane said to Elke. "Let me hold him for as long as I can."

König, willing to be benevolent now that he had what he wanted, agreed. But that moment on the train station platform was subject to the laws of time and it could not last forever. Éliane kissed her son. "I'll see you soon," she whispered, so quietly that nobody could hear.

The Gestapo arrived with Luc. The exchange was ready to be effected.

"What's going on?" Luc demanded.

König and Elke stepped up to the train. Éliane followed them with the baby.

"They're running away," Éliane said tiredly. "The Allies are nearly here."

"I didn't know they were so close," Luc said, his face a stark and sludgy gray, the same wretched shade produced when all the colors—brilliant blues and passionate reds and hopeful yellows and adoring pinks and the golden color of dreams—were mixed and, rather than a hue more spectacular than each individual shade, what appeared was something ignoble.

"They locked me up," he continued, desperately. "They told me the Allies were fleeing rather than winning. And they did things to me... I had to..."

Éliane passed the baby to Elke.

"What are you doing?" Luc asked, eyes shifting rapidly between his sister and her child now in Elke's arms.

"Paying your ransom," Éliane said coldly. "Now you can leave. Angélique and I will tell the British what you did. You can atone for it with them instead of with the Nazis."

The wheels screeched and turned. The train with König, Elke, and Alexandre aboard began to move away.

Rose, beside her, cried.

Éliane slipped her hand into Rose's. "Angélique will be with the Resistance when they stop the train," she told Rose as the train departed. "She's waiting for Alexandre."

Luc's face whitened now. "Angélique's been arrested."

"No." The word was the tiniest whisper Éliane had ever spoken. Angélique could *not* have been arrested.

"I had to... I had to tell them something, enough that they'd let me go." Luc's words were frantic. "I didn't say anything about you, I swear it. But Angélique—" He rubbed his face with his hands. "I thought I could get to her and fix it before anything happened... I really did... I'm sorry," Luc whispered now and perhaps he was crying too.

Éliane sagged onto the platform. She felt her heart actually break, split into three pieces: one on the train in Elke's Nazi arms, one fixed inside Xavier's heart, wherever that was, and one here on the platform, crushed in her brother's fist.

Luc started to run, like the coward he was. He ran toward the train, jumping aboard at the last minute.

He pushed past König. Stopped in front of Elke. Reached for Alexandre.

Shots cracked into the air, tearing open the awful silence.

"No," Éliane wailed, her eyes on her baby. "No!"

Another shot. She saw Luc seize the painting, holding it up and putting himself and the board in front of the baby.

Then he fell.

"No." The word was an even tinier whisper than before.

Then a guard took hold of her arms and hauled her to her feet. She forgot to struggle as she was dragged away, shoes scraping along the platform, her whole body insentient. Her last thought before her mind shut itself down was that it didn't matter whether Luc had given König or the SD her name. He'd given them Angélique's name and that was enough for them to come after her too.

König had won.

PART TWELVE
NEW YORK, 2015

FORTY

It was such a surprise when Remy suddenly saw light. She didn't feel her eyelids flicker open, just felt them burning. Then blinking. Shapes, colors appeared. A room with white walls. Pink flowers. A violently beeping machine. Antoinette's tear-soaked eyes.

"Remy! Thank God. Nurse!" Antoinette shouted.

Remy wanted to put her hands up to her ears but she couldn't move. Perhaps this was the moment of lucidity that she'd heard people had before death: the chance to say their goodbyes.

"Goodbye," she whispered.

Antoinette glared. "Don't you dare say that."

Two nurses hurried in, shooing Antoinette away, doing things to Remy and asking her questions, which exhausted her. She fell asleep and this time she knew it was sleep because she dreamed—of Adam standing beside her bed, face wet with tears. He was holding the baby, who didn't cry because he was happy in his father's arms.

The next time she woke, Antoinette was there again and Remy felt a little less like loose thread, a little more in control of her limbs and her mind.

"What happened?" she managed to ask.

"You had a bloody hemorrhage four days ago and you went into shock and they couldn't stop the bleeding. You had a laparotomy to try to stop it and when that didn't work, they said you might actually die.

So they performed a hysterectomy, but even that was…" Antoinette was sobbing, eyes red, as if she'd been doing a lot of weeping for a long time.

"Where's the baby?" Remy asked.

"I'll bring him here."

Remy nodded and fell straight back to sleep.

* * *

There was something different about the room the next time she woke. She moved her head a little and saw, right beside her, the transparent crib and the tiny bundle wrapped up inside it. She tried to lift herself up, but couldn't.

Antoinette, who was asleep in the chair, woke with a start.

"Every time I go to sleep, I keep thinking you'll leave, no matter that the doctors say the biggest danger has passed," Antoinette wept. "I feel like you were slipping away all of last year and this year too and I still don't know if you'll stay."

Remy managed to say, "Come here," and Antoinette perched on the edge of the bed and bawled.

"I'm not going anywhere," Remy said. "I promise. In fact, I'd really like to see him. Do you think they'll tell us off if we slip him in here with me?"

Antoinette shook her head. "They wouldn't dare."

She lifted the baby out of the crib and tucked him in beside Remy, who was crying herself now at her small, beautiful, and perfect son. Yes, she was still scared, but she also knew she could live with the fear because her love for her child was greater than everything else.

As was her love for Adam. Adam. What had she done to him?

She fixed her eyes on Antoinette. "I have to speak to Adam. Can you call him? Please. Tell him he can come and see the baby. If he wants to." God, what if he didn't want to now?

Antoinette's mouth twitched strangely. "Sure thing. Give me a minute." She hopped off the bed and slipped out of the room, leaving Remy to stare into the sleeping face of her son and marvel at his very existence.

She heard a movement by the door and tried to turn her head but it was still so hard to move. "What did he say?" she asked quietly, fearfully. "He hates me, doesn't he?"

"Never." The answering voice was male.

Then a man came into view. Adam. Somehow, he was here already, even though Antoinette had only just called him. Remy stared at him in confusion.

"You scared the shit out of me, Remy."

And Remy could see that his face looked more tired than anyone could possibly be and that his eyes were red from something other than fatigue.

He lifted his hand and she thought he was going to stroke her hair but then he stopped himself.

"How did you get here so fast?" she asked, wishing her head would work properly.

He shifted uncomfortably. "When Antoinette called to say you were in labor, I came to the hospital. I've been here since then."

"You've been here since then?" Remy repeated in disbelief. "Adam... How long ago was that?"

"Five days. I know I'm not supposed to be here. But I couldn't leave. I'm so glad you're going to be okay."

He blinked, and Remy knew he was trying not to cry.

"Also..." He hesitated as if he thought he probably shouldn't say the next thing. "Mom and Lauren are here too. I'm sorry. I know you didn't want..." He rubbed his palm over his forehead and then his eye, trying to remove the tear before she saw it. "But I couldn't stop them from coming in every day. And if that's not bad enough, Molly's here now too."

"Molly?" She must have started to hallucinate again because that couldn't be real.

But Adam nodded. "Yeah. After you left…" He exhaled and shook his head, running a hand through his hair. "Things somehow changed with Matt. I get to spend time with Molly now. She stays with me one night every week. It was supposed to be my night last night and she had a tantrum when Matt told her she couldn't come to my apartment, so he ended up bringing her here. And now she won't go home until she's met the baby. She slept on my lap in the lounge last night. I'm sorry," he repeated, looking guilty even though he had nothing to be guilty for.

Lauren and Judy were there. Molly was there. Antoinette was there. Adam was there. Her son was there. A whole family of people.

"Could you," she asked, trying to shift over, "could you come here and lie down so I can see you properly. Lie next to him," she said, feeling herself grow a little stronger as she said it, as if truth and honesty and Adam fortified her.

"Really?"

Remy watched a terrible tear trickle down his cheek. She would have given anything to have had the strength to brush it away, to hold him. "Please," she said. "I can't bear seeing you like that and not at least holding your hand."

He let himself down slowly onto the bed, head on the pillow across from hers, their child in between their bodies, sleeping peacefully. Remy lifted her hand and threaded it into Adam's, their arms reaching across their son.

"I love you," she said. "I'm so sorry. I messed everything up. I didn't know what I was doing. I don't deserve for you to be here, but I'm so glad you are. I love you so much," she repeated. "And him too." She smiled at their son and then at Adam, whose eyes were soaked with tears now.

He swallowed hard and his voice was hoarse when he spoke. "I get it," he said. "When Antoinette came out of the delivery suite and told me you'd hemorrhaged and gone into shock and they were giving you trans-fusions...I was wild. I freaked out—I really thought you were going to die and then Antoinette had me to deal with too. But sitting out there on those shitty plastic chairs and thinking I might never see you alive again..."

Adam closed his eyes and tightened his hold on her hand, before wriggling in even closer to his son and to her. "It made me understand how you felt about Emily and Toby and about having another child," he said, eyes fixed to her now. "It made me realize that I should have said to you, back in France, 'I'm staying with you no matter what.' I'd told myself that letting you go was, I don't know, respecting your grief. But, back then, I didn't really get why you were so set against having a baby. I was pissed off and thinking only about myself, not about you. I didn't want things to end up like they were with Molly: me loving a child I couldn't spend any time with. So I didn't try hard enough to understand what you were going through or to make you believe that we could get through this, together. That we can do anything, together."

"Adam," she whispered, crying openly now. "I dreamed about you. I knew you were here in the room. We *were* together through all of this last week. And I'm not planning on dying. I have too much..." She looked down at their son and then up at Adam. "Too much to live for."

He leaned across to touch a kiss to her forehead. "You need to get bet-ter soon so that," he stroked the baby's cheek, "we can take this little guy home and spoil him with love and give him a name."

"Xavier," Remy said decidedly. "I want to call him Xavier. Is that okay?"

Adam smiled at her, then nodded. "It's perfect."

"And we'll make sure he's as brave as both his great-grandfather and his great-grandmother, but that he has a longer and better life."

Adam kissed her again and said in a voice still husky with tears, "We will."

Then Remy felt herself drifting back into sleep, warm and cozy with the baby beside her and Adam too, her hand in his. She knew that, the minute she woke up, no matter how much the nurses protested, he would still be there, lying on the bed, waiting for her to open her eyes. He would be smiling at her, would be reaching over to kiss her, to stroke their son's cheek, to tell her he loved her.

Like the way Éliane had loved Xavier. Like the way Éliane and Xavier had loved their son, Alexandre. Like the way Alexandre had been loved by Elke. And while none of those people, who might have loved her too, had they ever had the chance to know her, were alive now, their legacy was.

"I love you," she whispered to both Adam and her son before she fell asleep. And she felt Adam's grip on her fingers tighten, and the heartbeat of her son beneath their joined hands thrum with the words he couldn't yet say, telling them he loved them too.

PART THIRTEEN

EPILOGUE

At neither of these next moments do the heavens weep. They pass by unremarked amid the shadow of so much cruelty. Was it all, then, for nothing?

Wait. There is König and von Behr drinking champagne laced with poison. The world will know what they did and condemn them for it. And there is Hermann Göring, swallowing cyanide. The world will condemn him too.

The actions of these men will be recorded because it cannot ever happen again. This is what Rose Valland thinks as she works tirelessly for years after the war, finding many of the stolen paintings, rejoicing as they are returned to their owners. There are so many that get away, even from her careful recording. She remembers them all.

Not long before she dies, Rose takes out Göring's Catalogue. She has kept it all these years, a secret, because within its pages is so much pain. She should never have let Éliane help her. But then Éliane and Xavier would not have given one another their hearts, nor would they have given their shared heart to Alexandre. Such hearts they each had, beautiful, the color of the truest enteral love: incarnadine, tempered by moonlight.

At the end of the catalogue Rose adds two new entries. One for the traitor and one for the child and his parents. Perhaps it is time for their stories to be told, but only by others whose hearts can endure it. She places the catalog into a box and sends it to the National Archives to be found by someone in some later decade.

Then she closes her eyes and remembers when, with Monsieur Jaujard by her side, she watched the *Winged Victory of Samothrace* ascend the staircase at the Louvre and retake her rightful place at the top. She remembers too when the *Mona Lisa* left her refuge so she could continue to smile for decades into the future and for millions of people. She remembers when Édouard de Rothschild donated Vermeer's *Astronomer* to the Louvre so that, later, a woman might stand before it and let it stir something in her heart that she'd forgotten was there.

The world still has its masterpieces. But how many people know what it cost to save them?

Neither Angélique, nor Xavier, nor Éliane see any of these things.

* * *

The first moment.

Angélique is taken to Fresnes prison. There, things are done to people like Angélique—*résistants*—that are too terrible to write down. There is no humanity, no art in Fresnes. Angélique learns this within the first minute of her arrival as her toenails are removed.

That is the best thing that happens to Angélique at Fresnes.

No, that is wrong. The best thing is that she does not give up Rose or Monsieur Jaujard or Xavier or Éliane. She is not to know that Xavier and Éliane's fates are already decided, no matter what she says.

She only cries when she realizes she will never see her sister again, and that there will be no one there beside her when she dies.

* * *

The second moment.

Éliane limps along the Largerstrasse at Buchenwald concentration camp. Her toes are broken. She can feel the angry purple of her bruises trying to force her eyes closed. But none of it matters. Not now that she is alone, without Xavier and Alexandre.

What has happened to them? To her son? He should be in Angélique's arms now.

She turns a corner leading toward a set of barracks and rests a hand against a wall. A rifle jabs her in the back, pushing her forwards. Why doesn't she just turn around, hold up her hands, and ask the soldier to shoot her? Because she still, despite everything, has hope. Hope that she might hear something of Xavier, hope that they will survive long enough to be rescued by the Allies. Hope that they will find their son and live together, happily ever after, as if in a fairy tale.

But these are not the times for such stories.

The stories of 1944 are darker, crosshatched with despair.

And then Éliane sees, exiting a compound a little way ahead, a man with a shadow of dark hair. He is so terribly thin. One of his arms hangs at an impossible angle as if it has been broken over and over and never repaired. He treads slowly, the shuffle of someone for whom just breathing is painful.

Look at me, she wills him.

He turns his head in her direction.

Now she can see his eyes. They are a particular shade of brown and they still hold within them the light of a man with love inside him. Love for her.

Thank God, she thinks as she ignores the guards and steps over to him. Thank God, she thinks as he takes her in his arms and kisses her as if there were no war and no pain. Thank God, she thinks as she sinks into him and he into her, oils blended together on canvas to form a new color: the shade of their locked-together hearts, shimmering with the white light of eternity.

The guards behind them shout in German and she knows she should let go and shuffle away. But she will not.

Xavier tightens his embrace until they are, suddenly, the couple in the painting. The couple without backdrop, without context, without time. The couple without past or present, and most certainly without future.

Thank God, she thinks. We will die together.

But she is wrong.

Xavier and Éliane live forever in a painting suspended first above Remy and Adam's bed, and then above their son Xavier's bed, and then above his daughter's bed, and so on through time. They never die because a love like theirs exists out of place and out of time. Neverendingly. Forever after.

AUTHOR'S NOTE

If I'd known how hard this book would be to write, I don't think I would ever have started it. I first heard of Rose Valland in Anne Sebba's book, *Les Parisiennes: How the Women of Paris Lived, Loved and Died in the 1940s*, which has been a source for at least two of my book ideas. The story of a woman risking her life for art intrigued me and I wanted to know more. Not long after, I read an article about *The Göring Catalogue*—a terrible record of avarice and thievery—and thus I began to work on *The Riviera House*.

But writing about the theft of artworks—many of which are still missing—from two hundred and three Jewish families during World War II is a subject that must be dealt with sensitively. I have tried so hard to treat it with the respect and consideration it deserves and I hope I have succeeded.

Understanding the sensitivities meant I had an obligation to research the topic thoroughly, which I also tried to do. The papers relating to the Nazis' art pillaging during World War II are spread over thirty-five archives in ten different countries. Thankfully, the internet helped make that search a little easier, although at many times during the writing of *The Riviera House* I felt weighed down by how much there was to know, how much there was to say, the obligation I had to the people who suffered, and how on earth I would compress everything into a readable and compassionate story of fewer than one hundred and thirty thousand words.

The starting point for writing about Rose Valland is to read her memoir, *Le Front de l'Art*, which is only available in French. Because it was so important to my book, I sat down and read it, one chapter a day, slowly and carefully, understanding the majority, but not necessarily every word.

Rose was a true hero who spied on the Germans in the Jeu de Paume and meticulously recorded the details of many stolen paintings and their destinations, all the while passing information on to Jacques Jaujard. Colonel von Behr did threaten Rose exactly as I have described in this book: to take her to Germany and liquidate her. She was fired from the museum four times during her tenure but managed to return each time to continue her work, slipping back, almost unnoticed. She was nearly caught recording details in her notebooks on at least a couple of occasions and was able to get away with it by telling the Germans that nobody would be stupid enough to spy on them. After the war, Rose worked tirelessly to track down the missing paintings so they could be returned to their owners.

Rose came by *The Göring Catalogue* sometime after 1945—no one knows where or how—and she held on to it, showing nobody, telling nobody. She put it into a box with all her papers when she was dying and sent it to the French Ministry of Culture in 1980. It languished there until the boxes were sent to the Ministry of Foreign Affairs in the 1990s, when an inventory of the contents was made and the catalog discovered. Why Rose chose not to reveal its existence to anyone during her lifetime is a mystery and I have invented a reason for her secrecy.

Rose had other secrets that she needed to protect. She was a lesbian who, according to Corinne Bouchoux in *Rose Valland: Resistance at the Museum*, did not officially acknowledge her relationship with her partner, Dr. Joyce Helen Heer, until after Heer's death.

Rose's secrecy is understandable, as many lesbians ended up in concentration camps like Ravensbrück. It would have been far too risky for Rose to draw attention to herself. If questioned about her sexual orientation, persecution and torture might have caused her to reveal her knowledge of what the Nazis were up to at the museum. And discussing it with Éliane would have been one more secret for Éliane to protect, one more burden that, given the political climate, I felt Rose would have been reluctant to place upon her friend. This is why Rose remains something of a mystery and we find out nothing about her personal life, not even where she lived or how she spent her leisure time.

I felt it was important to explain this here; my intention was not to hide or dismiss Rose's sexual orientation but to write the book in a way that I thought reflected what would have been most likely to have occurred at the time of the events.

Many of the events in the book are based on fact; if you've read any of my previous novels, you'll know this is important to me. The Louvre was emptied of most of its artworks in late August 1939 when the museum was closed for several days. The *Mona Lisa* did travel to the locations I've mentioned in the book, in a red velvet-lined crate, coded in the manner I've referred to. The *Winged Victory of Samothrace* was also removed from the Louvre in the way I've described, but this happened a month later than the timeframe in my book.

There were various edicts from different personages and departments within the German government concerning the "safeguarding" of artworks, particularly those owned by Jews and Freemasons, beginning with Adolf Hitler's own order of June 30, 1940. The Einsatzstab Reichsleiter Rosenberg, or the ERR, was the primary taskforce established to carry out this "safeguarding" of cultural property in Germany's conquered territories.

I have had my invented character Ernst König use the disgraceful rationale put forward on August 18, 1942 by Hermann Bunjes, an art historian officer and part of Göring's retinue, to explain the way the Nazis viewed the appropriation of Jewish artworks and the Jewish people themselves. This awful reasoning can be found in full in translation in the *Consolidated Interrogation Report No. 1 Activity of The Einsatzstab Rosenberg in France* compiled by the Office of Strategic Services Art Looting Investigation Unit, which is held at the National Archives in Maryland. I have used this report and *CIR No. 2 The Goering Collection* compiled by the same military organization and held in the same location extensively throughout my research.

Éliane, Xavier, and Angélique are figments of my possibly overactive imagination. Jacques Jaujard did work closely with the French *résistants*, in particular a woman by the name of Jeanne Boitel, whom he later married. The Louvre depots in the French countryside liaised frequently with the Maquis, and Jacques Jaujard's apartment was a meeting place for the Resistance.

Baron von Behr (his title of Colonel was an honorific from the Red Cross) was the ERR's chief in France. He was difficult to write about as all reports concur that he had no humanity whatsoever. The abovementioned CIR describes him as an "unscrupulous maniac," a man of "excessive vanity and selfish ambition" who used "gangster-like methods" and relied on "criminal and near-criminal types" to assist him with his many and various "depredations." He had an affair with his secretary Ilse Putz, and the Jeu de Paume is described in many sources as a hotbed of intrigue and affairs.

Göring visited the Jeu de Paume twenty-one times to view exhibitions of the stolen artworks and to make selections for his collection. I have had to compress many of these visits, including shifting the date of his first visit from November 1940 to February 1941 so as not to have the novel become too unwieldy. The signed order regarding the distribution of artworks to Hitler, to himself, and to three further groups of beneficiaries is fact, as are the exchanges that were orchestrated by him using so-called degenerate paintings kept in the Salle des Martyrs at the Jeu de Paume.

Ernst König is an invention of mine, loosely based around Bruno Lohse, who was an art historian and Göring's special assistant at the ERR. In Valland's memoir, she states that she believes Lohse took paintings from the Jeu de Paume and, indeed, some were recently discovered in a Zurich bank in a deposit associated with Lohse. It was from this history that I had König steal paintings in my book.

I have altered other minor factual details, mainly to do with time and personage, in order to ease confusion for the reader. For example, von Behr's headquarters were at the Hôtel Commodore, but he spent much time at the Jeu de Paume. The Schloss collection was taken to the GCJA headquarters on Rue de la Banque in October 1943 rather than the Jeu de Paume museum. The rivalry between Göring and Hitler is mentioned in many sources but there is no evidence to suggest it was stoked by external forces. However, on more than one occasion, Göring was found to have paintings that had been earmarked for his Führer, including one that I have used in my book: Fragonard's *Girl with a Chinese Sculpture*.

I purchased and read a copy of *Le Catalogue Goering*, again in French—if there's one thing *The Riviera House* has done, it's to vastly improve my ability to read French! As well as the above-mentioned sources, my reading included some of the very earliest reports on the art looting such as Janet Flanner's series of articles in *The New Yorker* from 1947, "Annals of Crime: The Beautiful Spoils" and James S. Plaut's 1946 piece in *The Atlantic*, "Loot for the Master Race."

Other important sources were Nancy Yeide's *Beyond the Dreams of Avarice: The Hermann Göring Collection*; *Art of the Defeat: France 1940–1944* by Bertrand Dorléac; Lynn Nicholas's excellent *The Rape of*

Europa; *The Lost Museum* by Hector Feliciano; *The Battle of the Louvre* by Matila Simon; *Rose Valland: Resistance at the Museum* by Corinne Bouchoux; *Saving Mona Lisa* by Gerri Chanel.

Other archival sources include the ERR Inventory Card Files at the National Archives in Maryland, and I also found Patricia Kennedy Grimstead's archival surveys in the *IISH Research Papers* "Reconstructing the Record of Nazi Cultural Plunder" to be very useful.

ACKNOWLEDGMENTS

I am so lucky to have the most tenacious, brilliant, and generous agent. Thank you, Kevan Lyon—you are the kind of woman every author needs by her side. You were the first person to tell me that you loved this book and your belief in me and my novels is an incredible gift.

Enormous thanks also to Rebecca Saunders at Hachette Australia. You have been with me through every book since 2016 and I could not ask for a better publisher. As usual, you helped me make this book better than I could have on my own.

I want to thank the rest of my amazing team at Hachette Australia: to Alex Craig for your always perceptive copyediting; to Sophie Mayfield for making everything seamless and easy; to Fiona Hazard and Louise Sherwin-Stark for virtual celebrations and champagne; to Dan Pilkington and the sales team for your unfailing enthusiasm for my books; and to my marketing and publicity team of Emma Rusher, Eve Le Gall, and Jemma Rowe—thank you for your energy and ideas.

I also have a wonderful team at Grand Central Publishing in the U.S. and I'm very grateful for the boundless enthusiasm of Leah Hultenschmidt and Jodi Rosoff. You've both made quite a few of my dreams come true!

Sara Foster is always my first reader outside my agent and publisher and she was, as usual, insightful and wise. I don't know how I'd get along without our frequent chats, text messages, and laughs!

To the Lyonesses—I can't quite believe that I've found such an incredible group of supportive writers. Thank you for admitting me to the pride!

To Megan O'Shea, physiotherapist extraordinaire, for taking away the aches and pains so that I can continue to sit down at my desk and write.

My readers are the very best. I love every message, every email, and every comment you send to me. Never stop getting in touch—please know that your love of my books inspires me to keep writing and if I could say a personal thanks to each and every one of you, I would.

Booksellers are also pretty special people. Your commitment to spreading the word about my stories is very much appreciated.

Finally, the last word goes to the most important people of all. To Darcy, Audrey, Ruby, and Russell: I love you.

READING GROUP GUIDE

DISCUSSION QUESTIONS

1. Before reading the book, did you know about the theft of artworks from Jewish families in Paris by the Nazis during WWII? Had you heard of Rose Valland and her role as art savior? Why do you think the story of these paintings, and that of their protector Rose Valland, is a less well-known aspect of wartime history? Did reading *The Riviera House* make you want to find out more about Rose?

2. Éliane asks her brother if, after the war, they will be judged by others and whether "instead of saving paintings, we should be saving people." What do you think? Were the paintings worth the danger of spying on the Germans? Should her efforts and Rose's efforts have been focused on rescuing people rather than rescuing artworks? What is the value of a piece of art?

3. In the Author's Note at the end of the book, Natasha Lester explains that Rose Valland came by Göring's Catalogue sometime after 1944, kept it a secret, and that the catalogue was only discovered after her death. Why do you think Rose didn't share the catalogue more widely? Should she have? What might have impelled her to keep it a secret?

4. Like Natasha Lester's other books, *The Riviera House* mixes real people and real events with fictitious people and fictional events.

What do you think of this approach to writing historical fiction? Is it wrong to create a narrative around Rose Valland and then change some of the events and insert people into those events who didn't exist? Or can this way of telling a story bring the events of the past to life and ensure these events and people reach a wider audience so that more people can learn from and about history?

5. One of the themes of the book is about what makes a culture—is it the people, the language, the artworks, the buildings, the collective spirit—and whether war can destroy a culture or make it stronger. "So many things worth preserving have been ruined," Xavier says to Éliane at one point. Why does war ruin some people and bring out the best in others? What parts of your culture are worth preserving and would you fight to protect them?

6. In the contemporary narrative, did you enjoy visiting the towns of Saint-Jean-Cap-Ferrat and Èze? Which elements of this narrative were your favorite? Being introduced to the photography of Lousie Dahl-Wolfe? Remy and Adam's love story? Remy's journey through grief and to a new way of understanding both herself and her past? Something else?

7. Remy's home on the French Riviera is based on the Villa Ephrussi de Rothschild in Saint-Jean-Cap-Ferrat. Google some pictures of the house and discuss how the two houses are similar and different. Did reading about the house bring it to life in the same way as the pictures do? Does it look how you imagined it might?

8. Matt and Adam have a complicated relationship. Is Adam always understanding of his brother's pain or does Adam inflame the situation? Or is Matt solely to blame for their conflict? When could

both of the brothers have behaved differently towards one another and thus improved their relationship?

9. Should Elke have done more to help Éliane and to actively work against her husband—or was Elke in an impossible situation? Most especially, do you think Elke could have done something towards the end of the book to ensure the baby stayed with Élaine? Or would that have placed the baby in too much danger?

A LOOK INSIDE *THE RIVIERA HOUSE* BY NATASHA LESTER

Those of you who've read my previous books know how important the historical research is to me, and that I always visit the places where my books are set—and not just because I like to travel to France! *The Riviera House* was no exception and I hope this brief look behind the scenes at the research and travel I undertook gives you lots to discuss with your book club.

Getting Started—A Riviera House and Rose Valland

Back in early 2018, I read a book called *The Riviera Set* by Mary S. Lovell. It was a narrative about American actress Maxine Elliott and her famous Château de l'Horizon near Antibes in France. I knew immediately that I wanted to write a book about a wonderful house on the French Riviera, a house with a complicated history, a mansion that might be resurrected and redeemed sometime in the future. But I didn't yet know what story I would weave around this house nor who might occupy it.

Not long after, I heard of Rose Valland and was intrigued by the idea of a woman risking her life to save artworks during the war. I love art, I love French history, and I love tales of daring women from the past. So I decided that Rose's story, and the story of what happened at the Jeu de Paume Museum in Paris during the war, might be worth looking into further. The more I looked, the more I knew I wanted to base my next book around this chapter in history.

Paris: Art, Archives, Galleries, and Markets

This decision meant I had several different strands to research: the titular house, Rose Valland herself, the Jeu de Paume museum, the theft of artworks from Jewish families and Hermann Göring's involvement in those thefts. So I jumped onto a plane to France and spent most of December 2018 and January 2019 there.

I started in Paris at the Louvre, searching out some of the key paintings that were stolen by Hitler and Göring during the war, including Vermeer's *Astronomer*. Knowing its complicated history and how it had suffered during the war gave me a quite different appreciation for the work. I also spent quite some time admiring the *Winged Victory of Samothrace*, imagining her being winched down the Daru staircase and thinking about what it might feel like to witness such a strange spectacle on the brink of another world war.

I visited the Jeu de Paume museum next. The exterior is exactly the same as in Rose's time although the interior is quite different. But my online research had turned up a floor plan from the Second World War period so, armed with this, I was able to get my bearings in the museum and see precisely where the Salle des Martrys was located. That area of the museum still feels haunted, I must say.

The National Archives in Paris holds numerous papers about the evacuation of the Louvre and Jacques Jaujard's mission to manage the artworks in all the different depots around France and the role of the Jeu de Paume as triage, storage, and transit facility for thousands of stolen art treasures. Most fascinating to see was some of the correspondence between Rose Valland and Monsieur Jaujard from that time.

I discovered the petite and lovely Galerie Véro-Dodat shopping arcade when I was in Paris in 2016 and I was captivated by a spiral staircase that could be glimpsed from the archway of a portal bearing the words 33 Escalier. As soon as I sat down to write *The Riviera House*, I knew Élaine would live at the apartment at the top of those stairs. If you're ever in Paris, make sure you visit the Galerie and search out that staircase!

My final stop, all in the name of research, was the Marché aux Puces de Saint-Ouen that Remy and the Henry-Jones family visit in the book. I'd spent some time at the Marché many years before, but you always see a place with different eyes when you visit for research, so off I went. And yes, the Marché Paul Bert Serpette really does sell everything from stuffed lions to staircases!

Onto the French Riviera

If you've read my previous book *The Paris Secret*, you might recall that in the book club notes I mentioned driving all over Cornwall searching for the perfect seaside village. Well, I did much the same for *The Riviera House*, except this time I drove from one side of the French Riviera to the other!

I started around Juan Les Pins and Antibes where Maxine Elliott's house was located. I even stayed in a hotel that had once been the villa where Zelda and F. Scott Fitzgerald lived, and where he wrote *Tender Is the Night*. I'll do anything to get myself into the right mood for research!

But those towns didn't have the right feel. It might sound odd that even though I didn't know exactly where on the Riviera I wanted to set part of the story, I knew exactly how that place would feel, what kind of mood it would have, what type of ambience it would possess. And as soon as I drove to Saint-Jean-Cap-Ferrat I knew that I'd found my setting.

I had mainly gone to the town to visit the Villa Ephrussi de Rothschild, as I'd hoped it might inspire the house in my story and boy, did it ever! You can safely say that Remy's house in the book is an exact replica of the Villa Ephrussi de Rothschild. What a magnificent house it is! And the gardens are simply superb.

But I made one important change. The villa is located quite a distance from the water, whereas I wanted my house to be right on the water. And when I went for a walk around the Promenade des Fossettes, a craggy coastal path that encircles a small peninsula near the Cap, I knew I would place my house there. It's such a beautiful part of the world, sea all around, secluded beaches, sweeping views of the coastline, and incredibly private houses occupying large tracts of land. When I'm a billionaire, I'll be buying myself one! If you're ever in the area, walk around to Paloma Plage (Paloma Beach). I imagined the house in the book to be situated just to the east.

From there, I began to explore all the nearby towns and simply fell in love with Èze, which is just as I describe it in the book: the perfect place to get lost in, especially if accompanied by someone like Adam! It is one of the few ancient perched villages on the Riviera, so called because they are quite literally perched on top of hills, affording them an excellent view over the water and the advantage of remaining small and picturesque.

AND THE LESS GLAMOROUS RESEARCH

As well as the traveling, there is the far less glamorous but equally important task of sifting through historical records, including much documentation from the war, now held at the National Archives in Maryland.

Many of the characters in the book are based on real people, including Colonel von Behr and, of course, Hermann Göring. Archives are the best places to learn more about such people as the records they hold are primary sources, not colored by the passing of years or one author's interpretation. So I based my development of these characters around the consolidated interrogation reports I found in the National Archives. A consolidated interrogation report is much what it sounds like: a collection of the many different interviews (or interrogations) conducted by the specialist Art Looting Unit of the US Armed Forces with people connected to the wartime art thefts and also the Jeu de Paume. It was quite shocking to see what some of the guilty parties said to try to get themselves out of trouble or to shift the blame onto others.

To conclude, I hope that gives you some more background to the book, and to my research. Most of all I hope you enjoy reading *The Riviera House* and that you enjoy discussing it with your book club. Can I also recommend that you, like Remy and Adam, indulge in some champagne when you meet and perhaps enjoy some food from the Provence-Alpes-Côtes-d'Azur region of France, where Saint-Jean-Cap-Ferrat is located. It's a region heavily influenced by its proximity to Italy and you might want to try *socca*, a street-food staple, much like a flatbread, or *pissaladière*, very similar to what we call pizza. *Bon appétit!*

ABOUT THE AUTHOR

NATASHA LESTER is the *New York Times* bestselling author of *The Paris Seamstress*, *The Paris Orphan*, and *The Paris Secret*, and a former marketing executive for L'Oréal. When she's not writing, she loves collecting vintage fashion (Dior is a favorite!), practicing the art of fashion illustration, learning about fashion history, and traveling to Paris. Natasha lives with her husband and three children in Perth, Western Australia.

For all the latest news from Natasha visit:
NatashaLester.com.au
Instagram @NatashaLesterAuthor
Facebook.com/NatashaLesterAuthor